THE RESURRECTION

UNLAWFUL MEN BOOK 3

JODI ELLEN MALPAS

Editing by - Marion Archer

Proofing by - Karen Lawson

Cover design by – Hang Le

PRAISE FOR JODI ELLEN MALPAS

"Malpas's sexy love scenes scorch the page, and her sensitive, multilayered hero and heroine will easily capture readers' hearts. A taut plot and a first-rate lineup of supporting characters make this a keeper." —*Publishers Weekly* on *Gentleman Sinner*

"This book is JEM at her best, the secrets, lies, enemies... and tongue it cheek humour. It's all there on every single page! I had no idea where this book was going or how the book would end. The journey was as captivating as it was enigmatic." - *Kindle and Koffee Book Blog on Wicked Truths*

"It's just twist after dark and delicious twist; a completely, unquestionably unpredictable ride from start to finish. This is the kind of book where every page is important, because there is just SO MUCH going on, and it's an intricate dance from loathe to love for this couple." - *Jeeves Reads Romance on The Brit*

"So it's safe to say, Jodi has once again completely smashed it with another sensation making it the best read of 2021! Hold on tight your about to be enthralled." - *Booksobsessive on The Enigma*

"A magnetic mutual attraction, a superalpha, and long-buried scars that are healed by love. Theo is irresistible." —*Booklist* on *Gentleman Sinner*

"Filled with raw emotions that ranged from the deepest rage to utter elation, Jodi Ellen Malpas wove together an incredible must-read tale that fans will certainly embrace." —Harlequin Junkie on *Gentleman Sinner*

"The characters are realistic and relatable and the tension ratchets up to an explosive conclusion. For anyone who enjoys *Sleeping with the Enemy*-style stories, this is a perfect choice."—Library Journal on *Leave Me Breathless*

"*The Controversial Princess*, told from Adeline's POV, is thick on plot, rich in character development with Kindle-melting sex and the perfect blend of twists and turns, shockers and villains!" —SueBee, Goodreads Reviewer

"*The Controversial Princess* is an all-consuming, scorching hot, modern royal romance with twists, turns and a jaw-dropping cliff-hanger that will leave you begging for more." —Mary Dube, *USA Today HEA*

"*The Controversial Princess* provided us with the romance our hearts needed, the passion our hearts craved, with jaw dropping twists and turns that kept us guessing and eagerly flipping the pages." —TotallyBooked Blog

*To every alpha I have created
and to those I am yet to dream up.*

THE
RESURRECTION

JODI ELLEN MALPAS

1

DANNY

St Lucia – Present Day

I don't know why I'm smiling. I've not long found out that someone wants to kill me, and that's a fucking achievement, since I'm supposed to be dead already. But it's this place. The sound of the sea. The salty air. The turquoise waters that can be seen for miles.

And the fact that my beautiful, savage wife is waiting for me to get home from my trip to Miami. The trip she refused to allow. The one that, if I went, would result in her filing for divorce. She knows what'll happen if she so much as *dares*. The divorce papers will be stuffed up the arse of the lawyer who delivers them, right before I ram a shotgun up behind and blow them to smithereens.

I shut the Escalade door and stare at our villa, pulling out a cigarette and lighting it. I've smoked more in the past three days than I have in three years. Finding out you've been resurrected will do that. I pull a long drag and exhale slowly and thoughtfully. "Time to face the consequences, Danny," I say quietly, throwing my bag over my shoulder and trudging up the path.

I don't use the front door, diverting around the back, leaving my bag on the terrace. I kick off my shoes and head down the path to the beach, coming to a stop at the top of a dune when I see her standing on the shore, staring out at the sea. I can hear her thoughts, hear her worry, even from here. Her arms are wrapped around her midriff protectively, her long hair billowing in the breeze, her willowy, tan body shimmering under the blazing sun. I groan under my breath, rolling my shoulders back, the urge to do what we do best—fuck—overcoming me. And we will fuck. Right after I've appeased her.

One of our staff appears, rounding the pool with a hose pipe coiled around his arm. "Mr. Black," he says, nodding his respect. "Welcome home."

"Thanks, Keith." I look back to Rose on the shore, bracing myself for our reunion. It'll be both electric and dangerous. "How's she been?"

"Quiet, Mr. Black."

I nod, not hearing anything I didn't already know. Quiet, yes. I know that because she's ignored my fucking calls. Refused to reply to my texts. I've resorted to checking in with the head housekeeper to make sure my wife is alive *and* hasn't left me. I understand she's pissed off with me, but she's made her point. I'm about to make mine.

I force my feet to move, taking one last drag of my cigarette and flicking it away, my eyes never moving from Rose. I know the moment she senses my presence, her shoulders lifting, her back straightening. But she doesn't swing around and welcome me home with open arms. She doesn't dive at me, ravage me, tell me she's so thankful to have me back in one piece. *Alive*. The silent treatment. Bring it on. I'll soon get some noise out of her.

"You remind me of someone I used to know," I whisper, reaching forward and pulling the tie of her bikini top. It unravels, the ends falling under her arms.

"Don't," she says to the water, her arms unmoving, holding the material to her body.

I move in, resting my mouth on her shoulder, tasting salt mixed with her familiar fragrance. She's been swimming in the ocean. Up and down, killing time. But I'm back, and I could do with some appreciation and distraction from the shitstorm that's brewing in Miami.

Circling my arms around her front, I take her wrists, pulling them away from her body, feeling her defiant resistance. I put my mouth at her ear. "I don't want to fight."

"Then you shouldn't have gone."

"You want me dead?"

"No, that's the fucking point." She jerks, wrenching herself out of my grip. "You shouldn't have gone."

"So you *do* want to fight?" I ask, looking at the clear blue sky. "Come on then, baby. Let's get this over with so I can fuck my wife brutally." That was the hardest thing about being away. Not the death threats. Not the appearance of an assassin, The Enigma. Or James Kelly, as I now know him. Not even the few fucking murders that went down. I simply missed Rose. But now she's playing hard to get. There's only so much rejection a man can take. She's deliberately pushing me. She knows the outcome of this situation.

She turns, unfolding her arms, and as a result, her bikini top falls to the sand. I quirk an eyebrow, my eyes falling to her breasts and imagining all the things I plan on doing with them. "No," she breathes.

I dart my eyes up. "What?"

"I said no," she grates, reiterating her low blow. "No, Danny. No, no, no, no—"

I see red, moving forward and grabbing her jaw, getting my threatening face up close to hers. Of course, she's not fazed in the least. My warrior. Still as gritty as ever. "You agreed the day before I married you that you would *never* brandish that word in situations like this."

Pushing her forehead hard to mine, her eyes angry lasers, she takes my hand on her face and yanks it away. "And you promised never to leave me." She turns and stomps away, and like the idiot I am, I grab her wrist, giving her the perfect anchor to swing. And boy does she swing.

Her fist smashes into my face with force, knocking me back a few paces, actual stars springing into my vision. "Fuck," I splutter, feeling at my nose, which is far from straight since I met this woman. Jesus.

I wipe the blood away and pin her in place with an incensed glare. "That fucking hurt."

"Good," she hisses, but I can see she's shocked herself. And now bracing for my retaliation.

Game on.

I charge her and throw her to the sand, pining her down. "Fucking kiss me, woman."

"No."

"Do it, Rose," I warn. "Do it now, or so help me God."

"What are you going to do?" she asks, thrusting her chest up, pushing her naked breasts into my pecs. "Kill me?"

Kill her? Oh, I'll kill her. With fucking pleasure. I heave and puff above her, hating the goading in her stare, but also loving it. Like I said, electric and dangerous. I snarl at her, rubbing my face across her breasts, spreading the blood dripping from my nose. Her back arches.

"No," she reiterates.

I growl and push my way to my feet, reaching down and hauling her up. "Move," I order, spinning her and seizing the back of her neck, pushing her toward the villa. What's about to go down is not something that should happen outside the walls of our villa.

"Get the fuck off me, Danny," she hisses, wriggling, her hands reaching behind her to try and pry my fingers away.

"Shut up, Rose." I wipe at my throbbing nose. "You wanted a fight, you've got one." I manhandle her back into the villa, passing Keith on our way. He doesn't bat an eyelid. "Get in there." I shove her inside, slam the door with force, and brace myself for what I know is coming. I have always let her take her frustration out on me. It's how it's been from day one, and it will always be like this. I've persistently told her that the only person in this world who should be able to hurt her is me. And I will *always* let her fight back. Give me her all, because she's long past being controlled, and I'd be a fucking dickhead if I thought I could bring her to heel. She'll never have her back against a wall again.

Unless I'm putting her there in preparation to fuck her.

She swings around, her blue eyes dark and threatening. It's dick-twitching stuff.

"Say it again, Rose," I order, prowling forward, my scar tingling. "Refuse me again."

She answers with another swing, her frustration getting the better of her, and I catch her fist, wrapping my palm around it, forcing it down. "I fucking hate you," she hisses, and then she's on me, making the first move, lunging up and smashing our mouths together. I move her wrists to one of my hands, using the other to rip her bikini bottoms off, and then she's up against the wall, her body colliding with it hard. Our kiss is manic. Our teeth clash, our tongues spar. *Yes.* I've missed this. *Us.* I shove her arms above her head and drop my spare hand to the apex of her thighs, driving three fingers into her ruthlessly. She's mad and turned on. Also standard. "So fucking wet for me." I move my mouth across her face, homing in on her neck, sucking her flesh hard, marking her. She cries out, part pleasure, part frustration as I go to her chest, biting at her nipples, then sweep my fingers wide within her. "Say no to me now, baby," I order. "I dare you."

She whimpers dejectedly, and I smile ruefully, withdrawing my fingers and plunging hard. She knows a *no* now will have me halting this. So she won't say no. I return to her face, pushing my forehead to hers with a force she returns. My eyes on hers. My fingers massaging her. My grip of her wrists flexing. "Did you miss me?" I ask, slipping gently around her clit.

Her body subtly bows, her exhale shaky. "Fuck me, Danny," she demands, and I smile. She wants to expel her anger. I'm here for it.

I withdraw and spin her, pushing her face into the plaster, taking her neck, getting my face close to hers as I yank my trousers open. Her cheek squished into the wall, she pants, her eyes pouring with want. I take hold of my dick, guiding it to her, and with the first dash of contact, I choke, Rose blinks slowly, and then her tongue leaves her mouth, licking away some of the blood on my face.

I groan, sinking into her, and she takes each inch with ease until she's full to the hilt. I breath in, twitching, my legs fucking shaking. "Move your head away from the wall," I order, giving her space to brace her palms against the paint. I take her hips, grind, and then watch my cock slip out of her, glistening, coated in her pleasure. "Fuck," I breathe, my head falling back, my feet spreading. I snarl as I power forward, smashing into her callously. But she takes it like a pro. Always does, moaning and forcing her arse back, egging me on.

"Yes," she says, and that's all I want. The key word. I launch my attack and bang into her repeatedly, over and over, smash after smash, and she screams her satisfaction, meeting my drives. "Harder," she yells.

She gets what she wants. My hips are out of control, the pleasure ransacking every inch of me, my gruff barks loud, my vision foggy. "You like that?" I yell, pounding on. "You like that, baby?"

"Yes!" She smashes her fist into the wall repeatedly, her head tossed back. "Danny!"

Her internal walls greedily squeeze, and blood surges to my head. We're going to come. Urgency takes over as I thrust, dripping wet, pushing us to the edge. I bellow her name, crashing forward erratically, shooting my load on a choke. "Holy shit," I cough, shaking the stars from my vision, falling forward. Her gasps are breathy, her body heaving, and I'm right there with her.

"Don't say you're going back to Miami," she pants.

I close my eyes, turning my face into hers and kissing her damp cheek. "I'm going back," I whisper, telling her what she already knows.

She's silent for a few moments, and I brace myself, preparing for what comes next. She eventually breathes in deeply and wriggles from beneath me, and I hiss when my dick is unexpectedly pulled from the warmth of her pussy.

She walks away, and I sigh, putting my forearm on the wall and resting my head there, closing my eyes. "I don't have a choice, Rose," I call into my darkness.

"No, Danny, you have a choice," she says, her voice getting quieter the closer she gets to the bathroom. "You've just made the wrong one." The door slams, and I sag on a sigh.

"For fuck's sake," I mutter, pushing myself up with some effort, not only physically spent, but mentally too. I fasten my trousers, turning to face the closed door. "Baby, I really don't."

The door flies open, and she appears, still bollock naked, but now wearing a face of fury. "Don't talk to me about choices," she yells. "I didn't have any for years, so I damn well know the difference between being backed into a corner or going there yourself. You've put yourself in the fucking corner, Danny."

She really does know how to say the right things to get my back up. "We don't talk about that."

"Today we do," she hisses, her hands bracing on each side of the doorframe, getting comfortable, her stance threatening. "I spent years with no choices. Being beaten. Doing what I was told or paying the price."

"Rose," I warn lowly, my veins beginning to burn. She knows it kills me hearing this.

"Being raped."

My nostrils flare. *The vicious bitch.* "Stop it." Nothing quite sends me into orbit like getting a swift reminder of how despicably she was treated in the past. The evil she faced. Nothing.

"Did you have a choice when your stepfather bent you over and rammed his cock up your ass?"

"Rose!" I roar, seeing red.

Her chin lifts, her point made. "Don't tell me we don't have choices, Danny, because we went through hell alone and together to fight for them."

"You want me to sit around here waiting for them to come kill me?"

"Who?" she yells.

"Fucking everyone, Rose! The whole fucking world. If one man knows I'm alive, all the fuckers who ever wanted me dead will be crawling out of the woodwork to make sure I really am in the ground this time. You want that?"

Her jaw rolls, her frame quaking. "I won't let you go back. You'll be walking into a battle zone."

"But I'll win the fucking war," I say, and she screams, her frustration bursting out of her with force. She gets it. She doesn't want to, but she gets it. I can't sit here doing nothing. I've been blissfully dead for three years, but my time in paradise is up. I should never have trusted Spittle to keep my cover. I should have known the stupid fuck would fuck it up in one way or another. Greed is a nasty quality. But regardless, there are big fish moving in on my old town, and they won't risk me coming back to claim it. The attempt on Brad's life is the only proof I need, not to mention Kelly's intel. Whether I like it or not, I'm being resurrected.

Rose stares at me, trembling. "Please," she begs. It kills me seeing my warrior so exposed and desperate, knowing I'm the cause.

I shake my head, denying her. "We leave next week." I turn and walk away, out of the firing line, but also because I can't bear the distress on her face any longer. I take the handle of the door, set to go find some solace in a few Scotches, pull it open, and jump out of my fucking skin when something collides with the wall beside me, the crash deafening, glass spraying everywhere. "What the actual loving fuck, Rose?" I murmur, turning around, finding her heaving, her face red. I look down at the crystal glass bowl that weighs a fucking ton. Or did. It's a lethal weapon, and my wife just threw it at my fucking head.

I glance up, my blood heating. "I'm walking away now before we do some real damage to each other," I say, backing out of the room, keeping a close eye on her. Fuck knows what she'll launch at my head next. "Calm the fuck down, then come talk to me like the reasonable woman I know you can be."

She snorts, looking away, her hand going to her forehead and rubbing.

"Vera," I call, my eyes unmoving from Rose. Our house-keeper appears from nowhere, eyeing the mess of glass on the floor. "Clean it up, please." I rip my eyes away from my wife and walk away, taking a moment to gather myself. My Rose isn't a drama queen. She doesn't throw hissy fits over nothing, and she's not cracked me in the face for a long, long time.

This definitely isn't nothing, and she has every right to hate on me right now.

It hurts like hell, but I understand.

I need to sort this shit out and hope my marriage is still intact when I'm done.

2

ROSE

We've had some heated arguments in our time. We've fought, verbally and physically. It's how we're wired. Twisted? Probably. Unhealthy? Undeniably. But after what we've both been through, alone and together, it's no wonder. It's molded us into the people we are. The couple we are. Blackness like ours doesn't disappear. It fades, but it never truly vanishes. I've long accepted that the physical aspect of our clashes is our own fucked-up way of maintaining the proof we both need that we can hurt. Feel pain. But only we can inflict that pain on each other.

I leave Vera clearing the glass and lock myself in the bathroom, turning into the door and dropping my forehead to the wood, forcing my stressed breathing to calm. My body to settle. My heart to quieten. "Fuck," I whisper, clenching my fists and my eyes. We went through absolute hell to be free of our pasts. Today is just a reminder, a confirmation of my fears that we can never be free. Someone wants to kill my husband, and since he's already supposed to be dead, that's a bigger problem than a mere threat. The second he took a call from Brad last week and left the bedroom, I knew something was going down. I saw the flash of evil in Danny Black that drew me to him in the first place. The scar on his face seemed to glow. His icy eyes turned colder. The Angel-faced Assassin was back in that moment, and that scared the shit out of me. Not because he actually scares me. He doesn't. But what he's capable of does.

Who could be so stupid to poke a sleeping rattlesnake?

I hear the sound of the handheld vac start whirling and push away from the door. God, I missed him so much. In the three years we've been hiding out here in our own little paradise, we've barely spent three minutes apart. The past few days have been torturous. And now we're not talking.

I sigh and go to the sink, wetting a cloth and wiping between my thighs, wincing a little at the soreness he meant to leave behind. Then I set about cleaning the smears of blood from my face and chest. I tie up my hair, unhook my little white sundress off the back of the door, and pull it on before I leave the bathroom. "Thank you, Vera," I say, smiling, feeling shame grab me.

She gets to her feet and nods, leaving me, and I follow. "Fuck," I hiss, grabbing the wall and pulling up my foot. "God damn it." I clench my heel. It doesn't hurt. But the reason behind my injury does.

"Oh, Miss Rose!" Vera cries, dropping the vac and rushing over, her face full of apologies as she scans the floor, looking for the shard she missed. "I thought I'd got it all, I'm sorry."

"Don't worry." I take her arm and smile my assurance. It's my own damn fault for being so hotheaded and reckless. "Go, I'm fine."

I go back to the bathroom and sit myself on the toilet seat, pulling off some tissue and squeezing it around my foot, stemming the blood. He's barely been back a half hour, and we're both already bleeding. I pull my foot up to my thigh and try to squeeze the shard out. It's too deep.

Giving up, I hobble through the villa and break out onto the terrace, taking myself to the pool. I sit on the edge and plunge my legs in, watching as a drop of blood spreads, creating a pretty pink swirl. I rest my palms behind me and turn my face up to the sun, letting the warm rays bathe my skin as I gently swish my feet.

Calm. I don't feel like I've needed it more in the past three years.

I hear the patio doors to Danny's office slide open and the sound of his bare feet padding across the paving stones toward me. I return my eyes to the water, seeing his bare legs appear in my side vision. I look up at him, unable to see his face with the glare of the sun in the background. But I can see his bare legs and naked chest. And the sky-blue swim shorts that make his pale blue eyes pop madly. He lowers to the edge beside me, dropping his legs into the water, and finally his beautiful, damaged face comes into my sights. His dark hair looks shaggy, flopping across his forehead. His silver scar shines. My deadly masterpiece.

Holding out a tumbler, he smiles a little. A peace offering. "Have a drink," he says quietly, taking a slug of his own, though his is amber, not clear like mine. I accept and have a small sip of vodka, reaching for his thigh and resting my palm on the thickness. He takes my hand and squeezes, and it's silent, both of us just being. Settling.

Peace. We can only find it in each other.

"How's Daniel?" he asks, swishing his feet next to mine.

"Growing up too fast." I smile, but it's sad. Every time my son visits, I feel the wrench in my gut when he leaves. I have to repeatedly remind myself that he's not being stolen from me again. That he'll be back. "I asked Hilary and Derek if he could stay a few more days, but they have some family wedding." The people who bought my son on the black market after he was ripped from my arms have been quite open to Daniel getting to know me. It shouldn't be a surprise. The alternative would be to lose him altogether, but I could never do that to Daniel. They're all he's ever known. When he learned of my true identity, naturally he was full of questions. Not being able to tell him the horrible, nasty, painful truth was hard. But it was also necessary. I'll never expose him to the world I was once a part of. So according to my son, he was simply taken from me because I was unwell. Incapable of looking after him. It hurts. But not as much as he'd hurt knowing what I'd been through.

My eyes fall to the plaited brown leather strap around Danny's wrist. It's now threadbare, worn and faded, but Danny hasn't taken it off since Daniel bought it for him three years ago on his first visit to St. Lucia.

I look up at him, and he peeks out the corner of his eye, rolling his wrist, coating his glass in Scotch. "I'm sorry for throwing the crystal bowl at your head."

He sighs, hooking his arm around my neck and hauling me into his side, pushing his mouth into my hair. "I'm sorry for breaking my promise."

I swallow, going heavy against his hard, sharp torso, as I watch the ripples of the water, my feet rubbing with his. I take another sip of my drink, swallowing hard. "I can't agree to this." There's no way I can give him my blessing. I can't see him off to his old town with a smile and a wave, knowing why he's leaving me. I'll go out of my mind.

"Let's not fight," he whispers, brushing his mouth through my hair, saying what he wants to say without even saying it. I'm not winning this one. Not now, anyway. But I absolutely do intend on reassessing my battle plan.

"What happened when you were there?" I ask.

"Before or after I met The Enigma?" he says, and I frown at the water.

"The Enigma?" He's surely not talking about . . . I pull out of his embrace, looking at him with all worry I feel. "Is that who wants you dead?"

He smiles. "No, that's who told me I *wasn't* dead."

"How did he know?" Jesus, The Enigma? I've heard of him. Who hasn't? But, honestly, there was a massive question mark over whether he actually existed. Because while Danny Black, The Brit, The Angel-faced Assassin—AKA my husband—brandished his reputation unapologetically, the man dubbed The Enigma, for obvious reasons, did not.

"Spittle," Danny snarls, knocking back the rest of his drink.

"And The Enigma's in Miami?"

Danny looks at me, and I slowly lean back, not liking the nervous smile on his face. "No, he's not in Miami," he says, and I relax a little. "He's here."

"What?"

"He's here."

"Here where?"

Danny motions in the general direction of nothing. "In St. Lucia."

"Excuse me?" I splutter, my eyes darting around us. "You brought a stone-cold killer to our home?"

"And his girlfriend."

I blink, my hand losing the grip of my glass. It plops into the water, and I watch as it sinks to the bottom of the pool. *Sinking.* Dazed, I hear Danny call Keith, and I look at him, seeing him pointing into the water. I follow his pointing finger and see my tumbler on the bottom. "The Enigma has a girlfriend?" I ask, blinking.

"Well," Danny sniffs, pouting up at the sun, "this stone-cold killer has a wife."

He thinks this is funny? I get up, exasperated, and immediately regret it. "Ouch!" Dropping back to my ass, I clench my foot in my lap, scowling at the sharp pain radiating through my heel.

"What is it?"

"Vera missed a shard."

"For fuck's sake," Danny mutters, setting his drink on the ground and turning into me, taking my foot and inspecting it. He takes my foot to his mouth and licks the arch, smiling when I solidify. Then he sucks on my heel, hard, eyes on mine, thrilling in my condition.

"Why is The Enigma here, Danny?" I ask quietly, resting back on my hands, letting him do his thing.

"Because he wants to kill whoever wants to kill me."

"Why?"

"Because they burned his family alive," he says, so indifferent, focusing on the sole of my foot. "There's someone moving in on Miami. Spittle got himself in up to his neck, as usual. Been saying things he shouldn't be saying to people he shouldn't be saying them to." He gives me his eyes, and I positively hate what I see in them. Grit. Hate. "The Enigma is no longer an enigma. The Brit is no longer dead."

Chills glide down my spine. "Who is The Enigma?"

"James Kelly." He smiles. "British."

Typical. "All the good assassins are," I quip, and he laughs. He laughs so hard, dropping my foot and throwing his head back. It's the kind of laugh that takes my husband from devastatingly handsome to lethally handsome. I smile, despite it being wholly inappropriate, letting him get his jerking body under control. He eventually sighs, reclaiming my foot and taking it back to his mouth, sucking. I watch him watch me, just waiting for what I might say next. I have a million questions. I honestly don't know where to start. "So you've brought him here to devise your battle plan?"

"And so his girlfriend can recuperate."

"She's ill?"

"No, she got shot." He raises his eyebrows as I recoil. "She's a cop," he adds, as if I wasn't struggling enough to wrap my mind around this onslaught of information.

"A cop," I murmur. "A cop and a killer." Is he joking?

"Sounds like a fairy tale, huh?" He leans in and kisses my stunned face. "We're having dinner with them on Wednesday night."

"Dinner with the killer and the cop."

He pulls back, smiling mildly. "We'll skip the oysters," he says, and I shake my head to myself. In the three years we've been here, every dinner date involves oysters. We've both learned how to swallow. How to savor the taste. How to make the most of their aphrodisiac qualities. Not that Danny and I need stimulating in that area. Every encounter is explosive. Hot. Dizzying. We simply and sickly love reminiscing about that time when I was his prisoner. Being held against my will but, at the same time, not.

I frown and look down at the water. "What's her name?"

"Beau."

"Age?"

"Early thirties, I'd say."

"And she's a cop?"

"Was. She quit after her mother, also a cop, was killed by the same man that killed James's family."

"Fucking hell," I breathe, looking at him, stunned. "And I thought our story was a total fuck-up."

He smiles and pulls me into him again, hugging me close. "Our story is ours. Theirs is theirs."

"But they're here, and you both want the same man dead."

Danny says nothing, and I close my eyes, trying to brace myself for the worst. "You're not going back to Miami, Danny," I reiterate, automatically reaching down to my rings and turning them on my finger slowly.

"Take them off, we'll be having serious words, Rose," he warns, his tone deadly, his body tense against me.

I drop my finger and stare at the water, hating the long-lost feeling of helplessness rising from the deepest part of me. Danny would do well to remember that I will do *anything* to protect the people I love. Which means this isn't going to turn out well for either of us. "If you're going back to Miami, I'm coming with you."

"I know."

I withdraw, surprised. "What?"

"You think I'm leaving you here?" He laughs. "No. You'll be safer at the mansion."

My mouth falls open, my reality hitting me harder. "You're not going to let me leave the house, are you?"

"Nope," he says, straight up and completely unapologetic.

I swallow down the anger rising before it overcomes me and forces me into doing something really stupid. Like removing my rings. I've been free for three years, and he's going to make me a prisoner again? Has he even thought about where this leaves me and my son? As far as Hilary and Derek are concerned, I live a peaceful, uncomplicated life here in St. Lucia with my *normal* husband, who they know only as "Danny." I wake up each morning without fear. Without hurt. Without pain. My life is simple after endless years of agony. It's exactly what I *never* dared dream it could be. Calm. Undisturbed. *Safe*. Going back to

Miami won't only risk Danny's life and probably mine too, it could possibly destroy everything I've built with my son.

I wrench myself away from him and stand, furious. "Asshole," I spit, storming away.

"I hate you too, baby," he calls.

"Fuck off."

3

JAMES

If I didn't have a thirst for blood, I might be content staying here. It's a far cry from the recent chaos of my life. It's also surprisingly needed. A break from the bloodshed. A timeout from killing. A holiday I didn't know I needed.

I strike the match and sit back, watching the wood burn down to my fingertip. I hiss and drop the cindered stick onto my naked thigh, blinking slowly as I flick it away and push my fingertips together, staring out at the water on a deep sigh. The ocean is calm, the sun blazing, casting blinding reflections across the still planes. There's no breeze. Everything is so . . . still. So quiet.

It's the calm before the storm, but I must delay the storm. Entering a war with this much restrained hatred within wouldn't be wise. I've always operated on resentment. Let my fury be my fuel, but only I had been at risk of being hurt. Now, I have Beau, and I would've had our baby too, if she hadn't been shot.

I shift in my chair, gulping back my anger, dampening its

power. The Bear's demise was always going to be grisly after he ordered the death of my family. Now he's taken a part of my future. My skin tingles with a need that puts all previous needs to shame. I've lost count of the ways I'm going to kill him.

Just as soon as I find out who the fuck he is.

I was certain the safety deposit box would hold the answer. Was so sure Beau's mum had figured it out and put his name away for safekeeping. Along with mine. The box was empty. And we have the only key.

The Bear knows what I look like—he knows the name behind The Enigma—but he still doesn't know who I really am, or why I've spent years hunting him and his men. I look forward to enlightening him when I can look into his eyes. Or am I wrong? Does he already know? *The safety deposit box.*

We'll soon find out.

When I figured out The Brit wasn't dead, my next moves quickly fell into place. I don't feel guilty for dragging Danny from the grave, because I didn't drag him. He's been dug up by a mutual nemesis. A nemesis he's going to help me kill.

A thrilling shiver courses through me. *Control it.*

I look over my shoulder to the voile drapes hanging in the doors to the bedroom. Not until Beau is better. Stronger. It could be awhile. Her physical injuries will take weeks to heal, but the emotional damage? I'm not sure she can ever get over it.

I rise from my chair and go to the doors, pulling the drapes aside. She's still curled on her side, snoozing. Always so tired. Drained. A shadow of the woman I met, which is an achievement on Beau's part, because back then she was a whisper away from losing herself completely. Our whirlwind affair brought her into the light. Shady light, but light nonetheless. Now, I feel like I've pushed her back to the verge of complete darkness. I have to find her again. This isn't just about me and my need for vengeance anymore. It's about retribution for Beau. For the loss of her mother at the hands of the man who wiped out my family. And it's about us being able to move forward without our demons suffocating us.

I pad over to the bed and crawl on behind her, slipping my arm over her waist, being careful of her wound and the cast on her arm. I get as close as I'm comfortable with, which isn't close enough. I push my mouth to the back of her head and breathe in, closing my eyes. Finding my calm.

"I've decided," she whispers sleepily.

"Decided what?"

"Whether I hate you or want to fuck you."

I smile mildly as I open my eyes, and she moves slowly and carefully, turning over to face me. I reach forward and kiss her nose. "Tell me," I order softly. Her eyes. How I wish they would burn as intensely as they once did when I put my mouth on her. Anywhere on her.

"Neither." Her hand goes to my hair and drags through the waves. "I just want to love you and feel that love back."

"Done deal."

"Is it?" she asks, and I frown. "Because you seem distant."

"Do not question my love for you, Beau," I caution. "Definitely don't do that." Breaking away, I carefully ease her to her back. I straddle her thighs and start gently picking at the corner of the dressing on her stomach. I need to feel useful in a world I'm struggling to know how to exist. Look after her. Focus on her. Blood and death have to wait.

I peel away the gauze, flicking my eyes up to her every so often to check her face for discomfort. There's none. She's just watching me, quiet and calm.

When her wound is revealed, I'm forced to smother the rage it reveals with it. "I'm okay," she says quietly as I reach for the antiseptic wipes on the nightstand. She peeks down. "It looks better."

It'll never look better, not as long as it's there. I grunt and start tenderly cleaning around the area, and she relaxes on the pillow, going back to studying me. "What are you plotting?" she asks.

I don't look up at her, concentrating on my task. "Do you need to ask?"

"No. But I want to hear."

"All the gory details?" I cast the wipe aside.

"Yes."

"Savage," I murmur as I grab a new dressing. I haven't decided every detail. I keep thinking of more gruesome ways. "How does it feel?"

She sighs tiredly, making her annoyance known. She can express her displeasure as much as she likes. From now on, she's out of the firing line. "It feels like I've been shot."

I flick her a warning look, taping around the edges of the dressing. "We're going to dinner this evening."

"With?" she asks, but we both know she doesn't need to.

I humor her. "Danny and Rose."

"The Angel-faced Assassin and his wife." She looks at the ceiling. "And what will we talk about over dinner? How many people you've collectively killed? How many more you will?"

I push my fists into the mattress and lower myself until my mouth is hovering over hers. "You want to continue with the sarcasm?" I hitch a brow, and she rolls her eyes, relenting and pulling me down. I hold my hips high, avoiding resting on her wound. "No, Beau," I whisper hoarsely, my body coming alive, sizzling.

"Please," she begs, and it's crushing. I know our intimacy helps her, but she's so . . . broken. "I just need to feel a little bit normal." She reaches between us and seizes my dick, and I jerk on a groan, my head dropping, my breathing diminishing.

"I don't want to hurt you."

"Then don't," she whispers.

Fuck.

I push myself back, kneeling, and reach for the pain killers on the nightstand, popping two out. She opens her mouth, letting me put them on her tongue, swallowing them down without the need for water. Her good hand goes to her knickers and starts pushing them down. Insatiable. This is going to take some creative thinking.

I take over when they reach her knees, not wanting her to strain, dragging them off and casting them aside before pushing my boxers down. I roll her onto her side, getting a pillow and placing it in front of her stomach, before settling behind her and laying my arm over her body, testing the pad of protection. "Okay?" I ask, kicking my feet to get free of my boxers.

She answers by pushing her arse back into my groin. This isn't creative. This is a necessity. I reach for my cock and wrap a palm around the girth, drawing a few amazing strokes, every muscle buzzing with anticipation. It's been weeks since I've been inside her. I need to maintain my control.

Guiding myself to her pussy, I take in air, preparing, then I slip in slowly, easily, gently. She sighs, subtly bowing. "Are you okay?" I ask, my vocal cords tight, holding still, waiting.

She hums in answer, her shoulder blades pulling in. I dip and kiss each before sinking my face between them, easing out little by little, the friction mind-bending. "Jesus, Beau," I choke, biting down on my back teeth. "Okay?" I ask again, holding my body back, stopping it from doing what's instinctive.

"I'm okay," she grates, frustrated, her hand joining mine on the pillow and applying pressure, holding herself, and I know she's trying to stem the pain. Stop the blood flow there to kill the nerves. "Move," she orders.

"You're hurting," I mumble into her skin.

"Just move," she snaps, impatient, grinding back. "This is the only thing making me feel normal."

Her words trigger something in me. Duty. Love. I lick across her skin, finally allowing my hips to pump, steady and slow. Our collective moan is garbled and long. "Good?"

"It'll do," she whispers, and I smile.

It. Will. Do.

I maintain a consistent pace, my body moving slowly so she can move with me. The tighter her hand gets around mine, pushing into the pillow, the closer I know she's getting. I need to ensure she doesn't do herself any damage when she comes. Doesn't lose control. Make any jerky, sudden movements. That's not guaranteed. We all lose control in the throes of passion.

I gently lock down our arms over the pillow tighter, straining to keep the force, my muscles aching, as I split my attention between maintaining her pleasure and avoiding her pain.

"Shit," she gasps.

"Okay?" I ask urgently, my hips not getting the memo, grinding on.

"Oh God," she yells. "Oh God, oh God, oh God. I'm coming. I'm coming."

Just the sounds. The words. My eyes cross, my dick loads, and I hold on to her for dear life, my body in spasm, pouring into her, feeling the walls of her greedy pussy grab on and constrict.

"Fuck," I yell, jerking. "Shit."

"I'm okay," she cries, rolling her arse into me, her head thrashing on the pillow. I bite her back, fighting my way through my release. "I'm okay," she repeats, this time calmly. "I'm okay." She settles, breathing deeply, and I release her flesh and kiss it, moving my mouth across her back slowly. That was so good. Calm. Slow. But, as ever, immense.

She hums, her back tensing and relaxing under the attention of my mouth. "Have you spoken to Lawrence?" she asks, killing the moment. No, I haven't, but I've spoken to Otto every day to get an update on all things, Lawrence being one of those things. He still hasn't left his room at Danny Black's mansion in Miami. I've sent the doctors in. Depression was mentioned. Depression because of grief. Beau's uncle knows he's lost his husband. That was a given after Dexter took Beau hostage and put a bullet in her. Whether it was intentional or not, I couldn't give a fuck. But what Beau and Lawrence don't know is that Dexter is dead. And they can never know. That was a decision I was forced to make when Beau agreed to marry me and slapped down a condition: I must let her uncle's husband, the man who betrayed Beau, live. I agreed, but it was too late. I'd already killed him, and I can't say with any guarantee that things would have been different had he been alive at the time Beau stipulated her condition. He was dead the moment I found out it was him on the inside, feeding The Bear information that not only got Beau's mother killed, but also our baby. He very nearly took Beau from me too. So, yeah. That's a secret I'll take to the grave. As far as Beau and her uncle are concerned, Dexter has gone into hiding, and that's a perfectly reasonable explanation given he's got a pissed-off assassin hunting him. "He's okay," I say for the sake of it. Beau knows Lawrence is far from okay. "Why don't you try calling him before we go out for dinner?"

She's quiet for a moment, thinking. "The Enigma and The Brit walk into a bar," she murmurs, looking back at me, an ironic smile on her face.

I kiss her gently. "Very funny."

"It's not a joke, though, is it? You and Danny Black joining forces."

No, it's no joke. It's actually terrifying for all those involved, and even more terrifying for all those *not*. "It's a means to an end," I say, easing out of her carefully. "I'll turn on the shower." I climb off the bed and enter the bathroom, where white-washed driftwood dominates every inch. The vanity, the open shower, the walls. It's cloudy but crisp. Rustic but clean. *No glass.* The oversized shower head suspends from the ceiling, and I turn the knob, making it rain.

"Will it be busy?"

I turn and find Beau in the doorway, naked except for the dressing on her stomach and the cast on her arm. I look away from her quickly, the constant mars on her beautiful body taking my mind to dangerous places. "No," I answer, reassuring her. I made sure Black knew a quiet establishment was compulsory. Beau was doing so well in conquering her fear of chaos. Of crowds. The opera. The supermarket. But I'm well aware she only survived them because I was by her side. Calming her. Protecting her from what terrifies her. I feel like we've gone back twenty paces in that element of her life. I want her to relax. Leave no room for anxiety to move in.

So you're taking her to dinner with The Brit?

"What will I wear?" She lifts her scarred arm, and her throat rolls from her swallow. "No one wants to look at this when they're eating." I notice the cast on her other arm isn't an issue. Just the scars.

"Stop it." I go to her, taking her wrist and lifting it to my mouth, kissing it. I don't even see her deformity anymore. I hope she doesn't see mine, either. I turn away from her, giving her my naked, damaged back, reminding her that we're both imperfect.

"Are you going to dinner without a shirt?" she asks, reaching forward and stroking over the smooth but bumpy flesh. I glance over my shoulder, giving her a tired look. "Then your point is moot," she says, lifting her arm again. "I've nothing with long sleeves." She frowns. "And it's still really, really warm."

Claiming her shoulders, I lead her to the vanity unit and pick up the roll of cling film. "I don't want you to hide it," I tell her, starting to wrap her stomach to protect it from the water.

"It's a part of who you are." I lean in and kiss her forehead before helping her into the waterproof arm protector. "A part of who *we* are." And while we're imperfect, we're also really fucking perfect together.

"That's sweet." She pushes into my lips. "My assassin boyfriend has a romantic streak."

I scowl and pull away. "Fiancé," I correct her. "I'm your fiancé." Why do I have to keep reminding her of this? "Because you agreed to marry this assassin, remember?" I won't raise her condition. I hope we never have to speak of that again. She rejected me once. Not again.

"Remember."

I nod, satisfied, and finish wrapping her up. "You're good." I send her into the shower with a pat of her bum. "I have a few calls to make."

She nods, quiet, and I return to the terrace to call Black. He answers with silence, as I've become accustomed to. And then the sound of him taking a drag of a cigarette comes down the line. "I need your reassurance that Dexter will never be found," I say quietly, closing the terrace doors behind me.

"You never did tell me why Beau can't know about the mess you made of him."

I laugh lightly, taking a seat in the rattan chair and relaxing as much as a man who's lying to the love of his life can. "Beau seems to have grown a conscience," I say, raking a hand through my hair. "She agreed to marry me if I promised not to kill him."

"Oh," he says over an exhale. "That's unfortunate."

"Not if you can assure me his body will never be found."

"I can assure you," Black says with a confidence I can't ignore. "How's Beau doing?"

I look over my shoulder to the door. "Quiet."

"Mine too," he says, and then laughs a little. "Well, when she's not yelling at me or throwing deadly weapons at my head."

"That bad, huh?"

"I can handle her."

"I can't imagine she's going to be *my* biggest fan, then." I get up and walk down to the sand, scuffing my feet through the hot, silky grains. "The man who's dragged you from your grave." That's how his wife will see me. She'll want to blame someone, and I'll be that someone.

"You've not dragged me anywhere," he muses, thoughtful, and I nod. "Other powers have unearthed me. I can't sit around waiting for my past to catch up with me. If that benefits you, so be it."

I'm beginning to understand Danny Black. I'll expect no loyalty from him. I'll always be wary of him, but he's no need to be wary of me, and he worked that out very fast. I've no desire to become king of his old playground. That's the only reason I'm here at the pleasure of The Brit. I'm a means to an end for him too. We both want the same man dead, and two assassins is always better than one.

"Are you naked?" he asks, amused, and I frown, looking around me. I spot him in the distance, standing on the shore in a wetsuit, a jet ski bobbing on the water beside him.

"It's hot." I roll my eyes to myself, and he laughs, as I trudge back to the beach house. "See you at the restaurant."

"Look forward to it," he says. "And, James?"

"What?"

"Get some sunblock on. You don't want to burn that back of yours." He hangs up, and I look over my shoulder. He's still standing on the shore, his arm raised in a casual way. I raise mine in return, not feeling threatened by his comment. He's merely pointing out that we're the same. We're no longer hidden by death. We're no longer invulnerable. We have someone to live for.

And we need to be careful.

4

BEAU

I take off my arm protector and start unraveling the wrap that James so carefully applied around my stomach, naturally tense. And not just because of my wound.

Dinner.

And not just dinner, but dinner with The Brit. I'm literally having dinner with a ghost, a man thought to be dead. *And* his wife. What the hell are we supposed to talk about?

I drop the wrap in the sink and sigh. We'll probably talk about how many lives our men have taken between them. I can only imagine what kind of woman she is to be married to a man like Danny Black.

But then, if Rose Black is fucked up, I'm right there with her. Ex-cop turned gangster's mol. "Jesus," I breathe, glancing at the mirror. I look empty. Hollow. What would my mother say to me? What would she think? And yet I can't help but hope she would be egging me on. Encouraging me. Giving me a pep talk like no other, willing me to find the bastard who took her from me and end him. I've long accepted that I can't do that on my own. Her death goes way past a cover-up. It's led me into the deepest depths of the Miami underworld. It led me to James.

And James has led me to the truth. It's irony at its best. *Or worst.*

Mom wasn't only a talented cop, something she passed down to me. She was an intuitive woman. Strong. Determined. She never gave up on finding out who The Bear was. Or who James was, for that matter. The former had her blown up. The latter tried to save her. He failed, but he saved me, and in the process nearly burned himself alive.

I look down at my scars. Some might think from the mess of my arm that he didn't *save me* from the explosion. Nothing could have saved me from that destruction. But he did save me from *self*-destruction. From the moment James called me under false pretenses to paint his office, I was enamored. Mesmerized. Intrigued. Curious. Attracted.

I laugh under my breath. Fucked up *really* doesn't cover it. So perhaps Rose Black and I will find some common ground.

But what the hell am I going to wear?

I rub some face cream in as I go to the closet and scan the limited options. Sun dresses. Sarongs. Shorts. My shoulders slump, and I back up to the bed, dropping to the edge. I have nothing. My days in Miami were spent in ripped jeans and over-sized shirts with long sleeves that covered my damaged skin. The only dress I own these days is the dress James bought for our first date to the opera—where he assassinated a corrupt judge while I was handcuffed to a chair after he'd gone down on me.

I fall to my back, exasperated. Rose Black has nothing on me.

The door to the bedroom opens, and James appears in his boxers. We've only been here a few days and he's already sun-kissed. Bronzed. At least, the front of him. Not his back, which, like my arm, is constantly smothered in sunscreen. His hair is lighter, his blue eyes bluer. I pout at the Adonis before me. Soon, he'll get dressed. Probably put on a divine suit. Muss his hair. Spray himself with a cologne that'll send me delirious with pleasure.

And I can't even jump him.

My hand goes to my stomach, feeling at the white gauze. "I have nothing to wear," I grumble. "This was a terrible idea."

"Cover up," he orders, nodding to the sheets.

I frown and pull them in around me, concealing my naked form, as James stands back, opening the way. A man scuttles in with arms full of clothes and some strappy shoes dangling from his fingers. "What's this?" I ask, sitting up slowly.

"Miss Rose sent them," the man declares, stopping in the middle of the room, waiting for instruction. I'm stumped, so James directs him to the closet, where he hangs up various dresses while I look on. Once he's done, he nods and backs out of the room.

"Problem solved," James says, flicking through the vast selection.

I get up and pull the sheets in, approaching behind him. "Why would she send me clothes?"

"You can ask her at dinner." James pulls out a pretty cream dress that's decorated with gold stitching. "This one?"

I blindly take the hanger, lost for words. "I thought you wanted to see my scars?" I remind him, looking down at the long sleeves.

"I want you to be comfortable and relaxed." He drops a kiss on my cheek and goes to the bathroom, leaving me alone. Relaxed? That's laughable. We might be out of Miami right now, away from blood and death, but I'm under no illusion that it will remain this easy. We're here for me to recuperate. And for James to plot his next move.

I look at the dress, my eyebrows high. I don't know this woman, but she clearly has good taste. I lay it on the bed and go to the dresser to dry my hair, but I divert when my cell starts ringing. Part of me hopes it's Uncle Lawrence, but I honestly have no idea what to say to him. The man is ruined. Distraught. Riddled with guilt. He's also grieving for his husband, a man who had us all fooled for so many years. Whether Dexter's dealings with the criminal world was an accident or not shouldn't matter. He's the reason Mom's dead.

I reach for my phone and quickly retract when I see the screen. "Oh fuck," I whisper, looking over my shoulder. James is in the doorway, a toothbrush unmoving in his mouth.

I quickly look away, avoiding the bullets of fury being fired across the room, and reject the call. I have no idea what my ex-fiancé wants. Maybe to ask if I'm going insane. Whatever, talking to him when James is within a two-hundred-mile radius would be stupid.

I turn and face him. His toothbrush is still static in his mouth. "I need to dry my hair," I declare, going to the dresser, claiming the hairdryer. I focus on myself in the mirror, ignoring James's looming frame in the doorway, and start blow-drying my hair. When he eventually finds it in himself to back up into the bathroom, I breathe out, relieved. I've seen the killer in him only a few times. It's frightening. Ugly. I need to warn Ollie to stay away, or he might end up on James's shit list.

If he isn't there already.

He's *totally* there already.

I walk into the open living space, my clutch tucked between my cast and my body, and find it empty. No James. He left me in the bedroom applying makeup. I watched in the mirror, a mascara wand hovering in front of my eye, as he unhooked his trousers and shirt from the wardrobe and walked out without a word, still quietly raging. I'm not looking forward to this dinner. His mood isn't helping, but a drink might, so I go to the well-appointed fridge and pour myself a white wine, sipping it as I wander out onto the terrace to wait for him. The evening sun is still blistering hot, but the breeze, thankfully, is picking up, offering a breather from the constant heat.

I drop my purse on the table and lower to a chair, taking in the majestic sight of the sun setting, slowly falling into the ocean. I'd smile if I had it in me. James has *got* to learn to control his temper when it comes to my ex, because I can't change my past. I wish I could. So badly, I wish I could. But my ex is only a small reason why.

I sip, casting my eyes across the shore, wondering where the hell he's gone. My question is answered when I see him on the beach.

Standing on his head.

I lower the glass from my lips. He's balancing, trying to steady his mood. In his gray trousers and crisp white dress shirt. I sigh as I reach down to remove the gold heels before standing, wine in hand, and walking down to him. I approach quietly, taking him in from top to bottom. From his toes to his head. When I'm before him, I crouch, wedging my wine glass into the sand, and gently lower myself to my stomach, resting my chin on my cast, my face level with his. He knows I'm here, but his eyes remain closed. Focused. Dampening down the monster inside.

A few long minutes pass of watching him, until he eventually opens one eye, peeking at me. "I don't want to argue," I say, reaching forward and brushing a wave of his hair aside.

"Me neither." Slowly and with precision and control, he lowers to the sand before turning over to his stomach so he's nose to nose with me. His lip quirks, and mine quirks with it. "What did he want?" he asks.

"I didn't call him back." Why would I? I'm not stupid. Besides, we both know what Ollie wants. I have no idea why; I'm far from the woman he met, but for some unbeknown reason, he wants me back. And when he found out about James, even before he was aware that he's not your average man, he worked hard to turn me against him, along with Dexter. Their motives were different, but they wanted the same thing. James out of my life.

"I will kill him, Beau," he says calmly, with no menace or threat in his tone. It's just pure fact.

I exhale, reaching for his cheek and stroking it softly, the scratch of his stubble soothing. "I know you will." I find his eyes. The endless pits of darkness. "I love you," I whisper, and he nods, swallowing, inching forward and kissing me tenderly.

"We'll be late." He gets to his feet and helps me up, collecting my wine from the sand and taking a sip as he tucks me into his side and walks us back to the beach house. Sitting me down, he gives me my drink and crouches before me, collecting my heels. "You look lovely," he says, stroking across the instep of my foot, smiling to himself when I go stiff in the chair. He looks up at me, and I give him a warning look. His brow hitches. Another stroke.

I shake my head. We'll never make it to dinner. But I don't really want to go to dinner, so . . .

I place my wine on the table and push out of the chair, lowering to my knees in front of him. "More," I breathe, cupping his beautiful face with my good hand, moving in, kissing him reverently. "More, more, more, more." I rest my hand over his groin. He's locked. Loaded. Ready.

His groan is quiet but full of want, mixed with frustration. "I need to be slow and careful with you, and we don't have time for that," he mumbles, standing, dragging me up with him, our mouths still attached.

"Don't start what you can't finish." I lock my arm over his shoulder, pulling him closer.

"Oh, I can finish." Reaching back, he frees himself from my clutches. "But you'll have to wait for me."

I grumble my displeasure, and he kisses my scowl away before putting me back in the chair and slipping on my heels. Something deep and uncomfortable inside tells me there's more to his statement.

Wait for him.

How long will he dedicate to hunting down The Bear? How long will I have to wait for him to put that demon to bed? For both of us.

And what if he never finds out the true identity of The Bear?

What then?

James assured me that it wouldn't be busy. He didn't let me down. The seafront restaurant is quiet inside, and the decking outside is spacious and peaceful. We're shown to a table at the far side by an old, crooked brick wall at the top of a rugged cliff-side, with a sandy trail that leads to the beach. The view is breathtaking, the ocean sparkling under the orange glow of the sunset. The breeze is light. Parasols are scattered sporadically between the tables, and fairy lights on strings zigzag above, creating a glowing canopy across the entire deck.

A waiter pulls out a white rattan chair for me, and I lower to the bohemian patterned cushion. He lights the bowl candle in the center before handing me a wine menu as James takes a seat beside me.

"They're not here yet?" I ask, setting my clutch on the wall beside my chair.

"Danny texted me. They're running a few minutes late."

"A lover's quarrel?" I ask, curious. I can't imagine Danny

Black's wife is jumping for joy at the prospect of him returning to Miami. We all know what that means.

"Must be something in the air," James muses, plucking the menu from my hand. I pout, narrowing my eyes on him. "Wine?"

"Please." I settle back, taking in my view. Not the ocean. Not the sunset. Not the cute winding path to the white sand.

I stare at James. He looks insanely handsome. Casual. Easy. His collar open, his sleeves rolled up to his forearms. It's refreshing. This is James on vacation. I like it. Why we're here, however, isn't such a welcome thought.

"What?" he asks, not looking up from the wine selection.

"Nothing."

"If I'd known they'd be late, I would have indulged you."

I press my lips together, my eyes widening when his hand lands on my leg and slides up my dress to my thigh. His smirk is very real. So is my warning look. He laughs lightly and pulls away, his attention captured by the waiter approaching. James orders wine and nods toward the restaurant.

"They're here." He rises from his chair, and I follow his eyes across the deck to the back of the restaurant, rising too.

"Jesus," I whisper, taking James's hand to help me to my feet.

Danny Black looks plain deadly. Furious, in fact. A lover's quarrel? Good lord, he looks like he's on a mission to kill. And I remember. He is. His frame is imposing, his eyes cold yet sparkly. The whole restaurant is aware of his presence, attention pointing his way from every table. The scar on his face looks so sinister. And then a woman appears, clinging to his hand as he leads. Tall. Willowy. Piercing blue eyes and rich, dark hair. She's striking, her skin flawless, her cheekbones outrageous, her lips plump. I've never seen such a formidable couple.

"That's his wife?" I whisper, shocked to my core. I don't know what I expected. Perhaps a war-torn, sallow, hateful-looking woman. What I have instead is a woman worthy of a perfume ad.

I blink and look at James, feeling him staring at me. He cocks his head, and I shake mine.

"James," Black says, reaching the table. "Sorry for keeping you waiting." He pulls the exotic beauty closer. "This is my wife, Rose. Rose, James and Beau."

She smiles, but it's forced, moving around the table. Definitely a lover's quarrel. "Beau." She takes my shoulders and hugs me, but only very lightly, no force, no pressure. I smile over her shoulder at James, who's still holding my hand. I gently tug myself free from his grip, returning Rose's embrace.

"It's lovely to meet you," I say, letting her break away.

She looks down my front. "You chose the cream one."

I shift, so uncomfortable. "Thank you. I literally have no dresses here."

"Good choice," Danny Black says, and I look past Rose to see him shaking James's hand. He releases James, coming around the table, and Rose moves aside, giving him access to me. He kisses each of my cheeks. "You're looking better," he says quietly. "How have you settled in?"

"Great. Thank you for letting us stay," I say, although I suspect it's purely selfish. What does Danny Black care if I was shot? He needs James. James needs him.

"Anytime." He leaves me, pulling a chair out for Rose. "Darling," he says, gesturing to it on a slight smirk. She doesn't thank him, just gives him a knowing, warning, semi-filthy look. And then he dips and kisses the top of her head, lingering for a while before going to her ear and whispering something. You could cut the tension with a knife, and I'm sure it's not tension of the sexual kind.

I lower to my seat, peeking at James. I shrug when he smiles.

"So we're surrounded by deadly killers," Rose says quietly,

plucking the bottle of wine from the waiter before he has a chance to set it on the table. "It's a good job they're hot, or else why would we be here?"

I can't help my laugh, and something tells me I should.

Danny Black flashes his wife a look that suggests she's pushing her luck as Rose holds up the bottle, her head tilting at me. I nod. Yes, give me all the alcohol. I'm going to need it to survive this dinner.

"So what brings you here, Beau?" Rose asks, pouring us both a glass, not bothering to offer the men. She dumps the bottle in the middle of the table, takes her glass, and rests back, looking at me expectantly. "Except for needing my husband's services."

I sit back, wary, her bitterness potent. So it's me she's got an issue with? I flick my eyes to James and notice his tense frame, his laser stare on Black, as if silently telling him to rein in his wife. Black, lips straight, leans in and collects the bottle, pouring for him and James before setting his icy stare on Rose. "Forgive my wife," he says, slowly taking a drink, his jaw rolling. "She's not usually such a bitch."

I balk, James shifts uncomfortably, seizing my hand on the table, and Rose's nostrils flare. She throws back the whole glass of wine and slams it on the table, standing. "Excuse me, but I'm not all too excited about discussing the inevitable death of my husband." She pivots, sending her long hair wafting through the air, and marches back toward the restaurant.

As awkward as I've ever felt, I move my eyes across to Danny Black. He's staring at the table, obviously trying to gather his patience. He's seriously bristling.

"You weren't kidding when you said your wife has a stellar right hook, huh?" James says, nodding to Black's nose, which I now notice is slightly swollen.

Black blinks slowly, reaching for the bridge and pinching it.

"Excuse me for a moment," he says, pushing up from his chair. "My wife and I have some issues to iron out."

"Take your time." James squeezes my hand and Black leaves, pulling at his linen suit jacket as he goes. And I'm pretty sure he flexes his fists.

I turn to James. "You don't think he—"

"Not our business," he says, not looking at me.

"Excuse me?"

He turns into me, leaning close. "We're not here to offer marriage counseling."

"Of course we're not." I laugh. "Because we don't know how to be married."

"Not for long," he muses, his eyes running across my face, his thumb drawing a straight line down the index finger of my left hand. I shift in my chair, and he smiles darkly.

"Should I go check on her?" I ask, turning my hand over and gripping his.

He shakes his head, settling back and sipping his wine. "I know many things about Danny Black. Two things with unquestionable certainty."

"What?"

"He's a merciless killer," James says, looking in the direction Black just left. "And he worships the ground his wife walks on." He turns his expressionless face my way. "We're more alike than I want us to be." Releasing my hand, he collects the menu and scans the choices, leaving that statement hanging in the thick, tense air that's still lingering, even now that Danny and Rose have left the table. I look up at the restaurant doors, contemplating how to approach this when they return. *If* they return. I'm not looking for a friend, which is probably a good thing. I'm here for James. Period. James and me.

I've worked my way through my glass by the time they get back, and as I watch Rose weave the tables, I notice the obvious flush of her cheeks, and Black behind her discreetly adjusting himself.

She sits beside me, flicking me a small smile. "I'm sorry, I needed to get that out of my system."

"Which bit?" I ask without thought, the signs of her and her husband getting things out of their system splashed all over her face.

Danny chuckles. It's quite cute for a killer. And James rubs across his Cupid's bow, smiling mildly. It's sexy for another cold-blooded killer. "Shall we order?" Rose says, picking up the menus and handing them out. "The oysters are divine."

"Oysters?" I ask, taking my eyes to the choices. "I never know whether to suck, chew, or swallow." I jump out of my skin when Danny and Rose collectively burst into fits of laughter, and I look at them, stunned. Confused. Quiet. "Did I say something funny?" I ask, as they calm, Danny sending his wife a fond smile, taking her hand on the table.

"It's a private joke." Rose wraps her hand around his fingers, looking across the table to James. "So what do I call you?" she asks. "James? Kellen?" A sip of her wine, her smile small. "The Enigma?"

James looks down, not answering, smiling, and I relish the sight of his hair flopping forward, his lashes fanning his cheeks. He's saved by the waiter, not that he needed saving. He was never going to indulge her bold question. It's fucking weird, though. Knowing people know who he is, which means, technically, he's no longer The Enigma.

We all order and, oddly, the conversation flows. Not about murder or Miami, but about the island, what there is to do, where we should go.

As I sit back in my chair after our main meal, I watch James, fascinated to see him engaging, talking, smiling. This is so normal, it's fucking with my head. Two couples having dinner.

Chatting, laughing, eating. More than once, I catch James's eye and he gives me a reassuring smile, either topping up my wine or taking my hand and squeezing. He knows what I'm thinking.

I'm thinking this could be our life. Just us. Here. Being normal. We've never had dinner in a restaurant together, let alone with another couple. Tomorrow we'll go to the local store and pick up some groceries. Then check out the waterfalls across the island that Rose gushed about. James will go out with Danny on their jet skis. Rose and I, apparently, will chill on the terrace at their villa and have cocktails. No, I don't need a friend. But maybe I want one. Maybe I want this all the time, and the longer I'm sitting here with these strangers, the more I can understand Rose's earlier animosity. We've come here and disrupted her life. Disturbed her paradise, because that's what this is. It's paradise.

Killers in paradise.

"So you were a cop," Rose says, pushing her chair out, glass in hand, and crossing one leg over the other.

"In a previous life, yes." I look at James, wondering just how much he's shared about me. About him. About us. His elbows are on the table, a tumbler hanging from his grasp as he swirls it slowly, staring at the liquid, refusing to look at me. I lean over the table to take a piece of bread, not so keen on talking about my previous life.

As I do, my sleeve rides up, and I freeze, feeling all eyes on the monster scar peeking out of the lovely cream dress. I press my lips together and retreat without the bread. The silence is horrific, and it's in this moment I realize that not once throughout this dinner have I dreaded the conversation. Because it's been mindless. Free. Easy. That feels like it's changing now.

I take refuge in my wine, peeking up at James, shaking my head when I find him gazing at me with sorry eyes. *Stop it!*

Rose moves, and I frown when she lays her arm on the table. I see them immediately under the faint glow of the candlelight. Scars. Scars from many cuts. I move my eyes to hers, and she smiles. Then Danny's arm appears on the table, and he pulls up his sleeve. I inhale at the sight of the monster slashes all over his tan skin and glance at him. He smirks, stretching the unsightly scar that runs from his eye to his lip.

Swallowing, I turn my attention to James. "I won't remove my shirt," he says quietly with an edge of irony in his tone. And what do I do? I laugh. I laugh so fucking hard, and everyone at the table joins me. I've never laughed about my injuries. What the hell is this madness? But Rose's message is clear. As is Danny's.

We're more similar than we all probably want to be.

I don't think I've ever felt so full. Full of food, full of drink, and absolutely full to the brim with love. I watch James, which I've done a lot throughout a surprisingly pleasant dinner after what was a rocky start. He looks so relaxed. Even more handsome. I want to keep him here. It's getting easier to ignore the boiling desire for retaliation while we're here being . . . normal. It's like with the release of his true identity, some darkness has lifted too.

"Why don't you and Rose go for a walk?" he says, turning into me and kissing my instant frown away.

"Yes, show Beau the ocean at sunset," Danny adds, waving his arm for the waiter and ordering more drinks.

"I can see the ocean at sunset," I say, looking past him to the ocean at sunset. Danny falters, flicking his eyes to James, who's watching me closely. Silently. Warningly. The women are being dismissed so they can talk about all the ways they're going to kill. There's the end of my perfect dinner with my laid-back man. The darkness has resurfaced. The assassin is back. Although, what did I honestly expect? That a bit of sunshine and the magical sparkling ocean would strip James of the inner killer? No, I didn't, but this evening has given me a glimpse of what life *could* be like for us, and as fast as I embraced the notion, it's been robbed from me. I feel my teeth sink into the corner of my mouth, and I glance at Rose, gaging her reaction. She's contemplative, smiling but through pursed lips.

I'm guessing any protests from us might be met with force. I'm guessing Rose has grasped this too. It's why she's so obviously biting her tongue.

I look at my wine glass, a little huff of laughter escaping. Get the little women out of the way so the boys can talk business. Has James forgotten that this is my war too? Resentment starts to burn a hole in my stomach. "I'm not pregnant anymore," I say without thinking, turning a resolute stare onto him. "I'm no longer fragile, James. I'm not glass." I regret the words the moment they're spoken, my bitterness for the world, for our loss, speaking for me.

The look glued to me is undisputed rage. Rage mixed with a ton of hurt. "Do you think that escaped my notice?" he asks quietly, as if our company might not hear. I absorb his evident disgust. Take it all. I know I deserve it. "If you were still carrying my baby," he hisses quietly, "you wouldn't be drinking." He takes the bottle and tops up my glass to the very top, making a point. "So drink up, Beau. Make the most of it." He sits back, takes his vodka, and toasts the air. "Cheers, baby." And downs the lot, gasps, steam virtually bursting from his ears. Slamming his tumbler down, he cracks his jaw, heaving like a wild beast in his seat. "Go for a walk, Beau," he orders coldly and firmly.

I feel a hand lay over my arm, and I look blankly to my left. Rose is imploring me, lifting from her chair. I glance across to Danny. He's silent, studying me, quietly taking in the scene, which is basically me losing my shit, speaking shit, and causing shit.

Furious with myself, I stand and walk away. Rose is soon beside me, taking my hand and pulling me toward the back of the terrace. "Take your shoes off," she says, stopping us at an opening in the old brick wall, leaning down to unfasten her heeled sandals.

I do as I'm told, looking back as my fingers fiddle with the tiny buckle. Black is handing James a fresh vodka. I sigh, kicking off my shoes, and let Rose lead us barefoot onto the sandy path that'll take us down to the beach. The silence between us is awkward, and I hate that I've created it. I hate myself. James might be a killer, but he's *my* killer, and he's done nothing but take care of me. Indulge me. Give me something to finally live for.

"How can you love someone and hate them at the same time?" I ask absentmindedly, watching my toes sink into the sand with each step I take down the path beside Rose.

She laughs, but it's sardonic. "Were you at the table earlier?" she asks, inhaling and looking up to the hazy sky, smiling. "I love to hate my husband. I know he feels the same."

I think I can relate. I love James's persistent passion to right so many wrongs. I hate that it might break us. Already has to an extent. I swallow, forcing my hand away from my tummy when it instinctively reaches for it.

We step over a rock, hitting the beach, and Rose takes the hem of her dress and inches it up to her thighs. She casts a smile my way, and it's significantly more friendly than her half-baked attempts earlier. "Come," she says, dancing off across the sand toward the shore, pivoting when she reaches the water, walking backward. "Just stand here and stare out at the burning horizon. It feels like you're on the edge of the world." She turns and looks at her feet, the water lapping at her ankles. Her attempts to pacify me are commendable. She didn't ask for any of this, but it seems she knows her place, to an extent. I've known her only an hour or two, and I've fast learned that she keeps Danny Black on his toes. He adores her. She him. She accepts who she's married to and backs down when she knows she needs to. I can't help but think that James hopes I might learn a thing or two from Rose Black.

I pad down and join her, standing silently beside her, the sound of the ocean calming me.

"You were pregnant," Rose eventually says, reaching for my hand and squeezing, keeping her gaze on the water.

"Only a few weeks," I murmur quietly, an ache developing in my stomach. "Completely unplanned." I look across to her, and she smiles mildly before returning her attention to the ocean.

"Because who could possibly want a baby with a cold-blooded killer?" she muses, her hair whipping in the breeze. She releases my hand and pulls her locks from her face, looking almost sad. "I would." Her arms drop, her head tilting, as if waiting for the ocean to react to her statement.

"But you can't," I reply quietly, reading all the signs. And more than that, seeing nothing but devastation past the semi-strong façade.

She inhales and exhales slowly, gathering herself, and when she looks across to me, I see with perfect clarity the grief in her wildly blue eyes. This woman is fierce. Strong. How could she be anything else being with a man like Danny Black? She's absolutely my kind of people. More so because of the fragility hidden behind the armor. The beauty. The stunning dress and impeccable, flawless makeup. "I had a baby when I was fifteen," she says. "He was stolen from me. It was a pretty stressful birth and . . ." She swallows. "Well. That was that."

I have no idea what to do. What to say. I've never felt compelled to comfort anyone. But my recent loss, how it's unexpectedly made me feel, gives me a good sense of what Rose must live with daily. My chance of being a mother hasn't been stolen completely. Rose's has.

I move into her side and do what any compassionate woman would do. I put my arm around her, and she relaxes against me. It's now, here, dipping our toes in the ocean on the edge of the world, that I realize I'm not completely broken. Not so cold and damaged that I can't grasp another woman's struggles. "I won't try to dream up words in an attempt to make you feel better," I say. "It would be horse shit. Life isn't just a bitch, is she?"

"No, she isn't." Rose kicks the water. "She's a scorned whore."

I laugh, and it's pure and real. "Is Danny enough?" I ask.

"More than." Breaking away, she laces her fingers through mine, gripping hard, and tugs me farther into the water. "And James?" she throws back. "Is he?"

"Does it matter?" I ask, the bottom of my dress sticking to my thighs. I focus on the straight line of the horizon, breathing in the clean, salty air, filling my lungs. "He would never let me leave him anyway. So he has to be."

"But is he?" Rose murmurs.

"Of course he is." I turn a smirk onto her, and she throws one right back at me. "We bagged ourselves murderers. We're living the fucking dream, Rose."

She laughs, head tossed back, and I'm there with her. Because what the hell else can we do, except cry rivers of hopeless tears?

Tears that are fucking pointless in the world Rose and I have chosen to be a part of.

5

DANNY

"Sounds like we're both in the doghouse." I take a cigarette from my packet and light up, relaxing back in the chair as James watches the women head down to the beach. A solo singer is setting up behind us, and the sun is close to disappearing completely into the ocean. It's been a surprisingly pleasant evening, domestic spats aside. Mine and Rose's was resolved quickly in the ladies'. A failed attempt to slap me. A successful attempt to fuck her hard over the sink. I'm probably still dripping out of her now. I smile, exhaling.

"Beau's not the kind of woman that appreciates being told what to do." James rips his eyes away from the beach and sets them on the glass of vodka the waiter just placed down.

"So why don't you get yourself one?" I land the question like a bomb, taking another hit of nicotine and exhaling it over my glass. "Another woman, I mean."

James turns his tumbler left, right, then picks it up and downs the lot. "Because it wouldn't be Beau," he says, turning a stoic face my way. "I know I'm talking to a man who hears me."

I smile lightly, nodding mildly. "Loud and clear," I muse, thoughtful. I'm looking at a man who's walking in the shoes I once did. And it seems I'll be walking in them again soon. Except this time, I have my reward already. If she doesn't leave me.

"What's the latest in Miami?" James asks, circling the conversation back to what we're actually here for.

"I don't know," I flick my ash in the ashtray. "But I hear there's a shitshow of epic proportions about to go down." Part of me resents having to return. Another part of me, the sick motherfucker who's been dormant for a few years, cannot wait to see the faces of many men when they learn I've been resurrected.

"Tell me something," he says, watching his glass as the waiter tops him up again. I wait silently for him to go on. "Do you want to come back to life?"

I smile. "If my wife asks, no."

"Your wife isn't asking. I am."

"It never leaves you," I say, leaning forward. "You think you're going to kill your enemies and disappear off into the sunset and set up a life with Beau?" I huff, relaxing back, taking another drag of my cigarette. "There's always someone who'll want to exact their revenge. Someone who'll want you dead. I'm living proof, and I'm supposed to be dead and fucking gone from this world." Brad was right. He once told me that you don't walk away from this life. You can't. "Spittle tried to kill my best friend. My cousin. He did that for a reason, and we both know what that reason is." I give him a dark smile. "I'm not the kind of man to wait around for the danger to find me." I'll find *it*. And kill it.

"I'll take that as a yes."

I cock my head, looking down at the beach. I can't see Rose. But I always see her. "It's going to be messy," I say, not telling him anything he doesn't already know. Besides, I've seen him kill a man. Neither of us do things by halves, but there will be plenty of men to get through before we find who we need.

"I know nothing else," James says, tipping his drink to his lips.

"I never did extend my condolences."

"For what?" he asks, as I catch his jaw starting to pulse. "The massacre of my family? My baby? Or the attempted murder of my fiancée?"

"All of it."

"I don't want condolences." He sneers into his glass. "I want retribution."

I like this man more and more, and I am not the type of man to *like* a man. Only very few have ever had the honor of my approval. But James? He's understatedly immoral. And he's enamored by a fucked-up woman.

It reminds me of someone I used to know.

Still know.

"You haven't had kids." James looks up at me, and my drink falters at my lips.

"No." It's time to show him something of who Rose and I were. Who we might be again soon. "Rose was planted on me by an old enemy. Blackmailed to do everything he demanded, or her son would be killed. Probably her too."

"She has a kid?"

"When she was fifteen after being repeatedly raped by any man who desired her." My stomach turns, churning up the anger that lays sleeping in the pit of my stomach. "She had a boy. It was a rough birth." I shrug, like it's nothing, when it's every fucked-up thing. "She can't carry anymore."

"You saved her," James says with absolutely no emotion.

I fix my stare on him. "We saved each other. Sound familiar?"

He smiles, though it's mild. "And the kid?"

"I found him. He's thirteen now. Lives with his *parents* in Miami. He visits."

"And they're okay with that?"

"They don't have much choice. They bought the kid on the black market. They're lucky to be alive."

"I was talking about you. They're okay with him spending time with you?"

"They don't know who I am. I'm Daniel's biological mother's husband, who she met after moving to St Lucia."

"So what does he call you?"

"Mister." I smile, and I know it's fond. Daniel's a good kid. Smart, polite, accepting. I only wish I could give Rose more of him, but we're real. His parents are all he's ever known. His education is important. So is stability. Hilary and Derek give him that.

"What's your plan?" James asks, getting us back to business.

"First I'll take Byron's Reach. If there's anything going into Miami, it'll go through there."

"Take it how?"

"With force."

"And The Bear? How do you propose we get to him?"

"We put some piranhas in his pond." I roll the glowing red tip of my cigarette around the edge of the ashtray.

"Smoke him out."

"And kill him," I whisper, my tone as deadly as I feel.

"Is that the end?"

"There's no end when you're in this world."

"Meaning?"

"Meaning, if we go back to Miami, we set the bar. You don't walk away from the bar. You defend it, or you die. You need to be prepared for that. It's what you get for being prolific." When the waiter comes over, I take the two bottles from his tray before sending him on his way and topping us both up. "So the question is, James, are we going back to Miami?"

His eyes darken. "We're going back to Miami." Holding his glass across the table, he turns his stare onto me. "I'm prepared for anything."

I've seen many killers in my time. The one with the most vengeance in his stare was the one I looked at in the mirror every day. I could be looking in the mirror now, seeing an equal swirl of darkness and hate.

"To revenge." I hit my glass with his and throw back my drink, getting a flash of white in my peripheral vision. Rose is approaching, her feet bare, coated in sand. But no Beau.

She reaches the table and drops her heels to the ground, setting a hand on my shoulder to hold herself as she bends to dust off her feet. I turn my face into it and kiss her wedding ring, before laying my hand over hers. Rose catches James's questioning face. "She—"

"Wanted to feel the last bit of the sun on her face," James whispers, almost sadly, sinking back in his chair. "I've known what that woman has needed from the moment I set eyes on her," he says without looking at Rose, his gaze on the break in the wall that leads down to the beach. "Now . . . ?" He stands, and my eyes lift with him. "I need the restroom." Striding off, he pulls his phone from his back pocket, dialing on his way. He's a lost man. And again, I know exactly how he feels. Women do that to you. Fog your senses. Make you question your instinct.

"Are you ready to go?" I ask Rose, waving for the bill.

"I need the ladies'." She dips and kisses my forehead, and I smile, watching her go, leaving me alone at the table. Until Beau appears from the beach.

Approaching slowly, her sandals dangling from her fingertips of her cast adorned arm, she takes in my seated form.

"Restrooms," I say before she can ask. "Sit." I motion to the chair opposite, and Beau takes it, never looking away from me. I see the same resilience in her as I do Rose. The same fight. She's simply lost her way momentarily. "Can I ask you something?" I look over my shoulder, a solid indicator to Beau that this isn't something I want my wife to hear. Not until I know what the answer is, because it could change things significantly and, frankly, I don't want to give Rose hope that's wasted.

Beau doesn't answer, leaving me to go on.

"You used to be a cop."

"Yes. And now I'm the girlfriend of a murderer."

"There are worse things you could be." I feel my lip quirk, but Beau's face remains eternally impassive.

"Like what?"

"Like one of his enemies."

She blinks a few times, her eyes dropping to the table. "What did you want to ask me, Danny?" She reaches for her wine and takes a sip, refusing to look me in the eye.

"Can I be prosecuted for faking my death?"

Her glass freezes halfway back to the table, and I'm thrown when her face breaks and one corner of her mouth lifts. She finds my question funny? "Your wife beat you to it," she says, finally looking at me.

My head slowly tilts, her amusement making sense now. I laugh under my breath, shaking my head mildly as I trace the rim of my tumbler. "Rose has already asked you."

"She has."

"And?"

"It depends."

"On what?"

"Foul play." She sets her wine down, and I find myself moving in closer to the table, interested. "So long as there is no financial gain to yourself, life insurance, for example, then, actu-

ally, no. If you hate your life, you're technically allowed to engi-
neer an exit from it."

I nod, thoughtful, thinking this news would have pissed Rose
right off. She was looking for an out. Any reason to stop me
going back to Miami. "I signed everything over to Rose. There
were no policies involved."

"Then the FBI is powerless."

"What about my cousin? He identified me." I'm covering all
my bases. The last thing I need is to step back into Miami and
Brad or I get arrested.

"You drowned." She states it as a fact, telling me Beau knows
of my story, which isn't surprising, since she was a cop. I nod,
and she goes on. "How long were you in the water before you
were dragged out?"

"Three days."

She shrugs, not seeming in the least bit concerned. "A body
generally starts to bloat after three days. In the water, that can be
slowed depending on the temperature. Regardless, that long in
the water will produce drastic changes in the appearance of a
dead body."

"So you're saying they can't touch me."

"The FBI won't waste time looking for someone who wanted
to leave their life."

"I'm not just anyone, Beau," I point out. Fair enough, I get
that a person wanting to take a departure from their life with no
ill-gotten gains isn't worth the FBI's time. But I am worth their
time. "And I have committed plenty of crimes."

"Can they prove those crimes are yours?"

"No."

She nods slowly, tapping the stem of her wine glass. "Then
I'll start praying for Miami." She glances past me, and I look
over my shoulder to see James returning, Rose not far behind

him. "I want your word on one thing," she says, keeping her attention on James.

"What?"

"You leave Dexter out of your business."

"Who's Dexter?" I ask, my tone level, my mind quickly telling me to play it cool.

Beau looks at me, her eyes narrowing a little as she takes what appears to be a relaxed sip of her wine. "You know exactly who he is, but for the sake of clarity, he's the man who killed our baby."

"And nearly killed you," I point out. "So why would you want him left out of it, and why would you tell *me* and not James?"

"I want him left out of it because I have to believe there was a method to his madness. He's my uncle's husband. And I'm telling you and not James because I don't believe he can resist bludgeoning him." Her eyes lift the nearer James gets to the table. Fuck me, she knows her man well. Problem is, he's already bludgeoned Dexter, and I was the one who brought him to James.

The waiter lays the bill on the table. "I'll get it," I say, dragging it over, stopping James from pulling out his wallet. "You get the next one."

He nods and Beau stands, moving into Rose and hugging her. Their embrace is solid. They've connected. My wife has never had a friend, and seeing her with Beau, even if it kicked off a little prickly, eases the guilt riddling me. These two women are going to need each other, and as I look at James, I note he's watching them too, undoubtedly thinking along the same lines.

He catches my eye, and I nod sharply, extending my hand. "Jet skis tomorrow?" I ask.

"Sure." He shakes, and I stand when Beau approaches me. Reaching up, she kisses my cheek, lingering. Waiting for me to give her my word. *Fuck. Me.*

I loop an arm around her shoulder and pull her close. "You have it," I say quietly in her ear, lying through my teeth, and I take absolutely no pleasure from it.

"Thank you." She breaks away and joins James, and he's quick to tuck her fragile body close into his side. I watch them walk out as I lower to the chair, patting my lap for Rose to join me.

"I think there's some make-up sex on the horizon," she whispers as she settles, arms linked around my neck.

"I applaud him for waiting until he gets her home." I hold her with one arm around her lower back, reaching for my cigarettes and pulling one out with my teeth. Rose takes my Zippo from the table and lights it for me.

"She's got issues," she says as I take us back in the chair, getting comfortable.

"We all have."

"But I like her."

I smile to myself, the simple declaration providing endless contentment. "Does that mean you'll stop chewing my balls?"

"No," she whispers, laying her head on my shoulder and staring out at the ocean. "I still don't like this."

I look at her arm that's positioned under my chin, the scars bright on her gorgeous tan skin. I know how Rose has dealt with things out of her control in the past. I'll be keeping a close eye on her. Always. "Come." I tap her arse, she stands with me, and I hold my cigarette between my lips as I pull some notes from my trouser pocket and count some off, tossing them on the table.

I dip and collect her shoes, take her hand, and lead her to the opening in the wall. The sandy trail to the beach is dark now, the rocks poking up through the sand out of sight. "Get on." I drop to one knee and her leg appears over my shoulder, then the other, her hands on my head. I lay my arm across her shins and rise, walking us down the rest of the path to the beach. "Okay up there?" I ask, taking a drag of my cigarette.

"On top of the world," she says wistfully, her hands leaving my head. I know they're stretched up to the sky, her eyes closed, her head back. Rose. Peaceful Rose. She makes me a really fucking happy man, but in this moment, that happiness is being tarnished by what lies ahead.

I wander slowly, relishing my wife upon my shoulders, the waves lapping the shore gently, the moon glowing hypnotically. I'll miss this. But we'll be back. I couldn't go very long without it. I flick my cigarette away and hold up her sandals to take, laying a palm on each of her thighs under her dress. She squeezes her legs slightly, and I peek up, my smile small.

"I want to get married," she declares out of the blue, and I frown at the shore.

"You *are* married."

"Again."

The stretch of beach ahead curves around to the left, clusters of lighting dotted along the way from the bars lining it. "Why?"

"Because we're not technically married, are we?"

"We are according to me."

"But not according to the law. It's pretty impossible to marry a dead man, and since you're coming back to life, I want to marry you."

"You want a big, fancy wedding, baby?" I ask, slipping my hands inward, fingering at the seam of her knickers.

"Maybe," she replies coyly, tensing, taking hold of my head. "Can I?"

"You can have whatever the fuck you want, my queen." I stop just shy of a beach bar, hearing music, the decked terrace heaving with partygoers. Chainsmokers' *I Need You Right Now* starts, and Rose begins to sway above me, her hand sweeping through my hair.

I drop one shoulder, reaching up and pulling her down my front, and she squeals, looking faintly dazed when she finds her feet. I take her heels, throw them aside, and pull her into my body. Her palms meet my chest. Her eyes stick to my scar. "I fucking love you," I whisper, starting to move us slowly in perfect time to the distant track, my attention set firmly of my wife. My beautiful, resilient, warrior goddess.

Her hands slide onto my biceps and hold me, her face coming close, nuzzling, rubbing her nose with mine, her skin brushing over every part of my face as we dance under the moon, my legs slightly bent to keep our hips stuck together, lazily grinding, slowly swaying.

And it's how we stay until the music fades and there is only us, the ocean, and need. So much fucking need. She breathes in, moving her hand down to my groin, cupping me, biting at her lip. "You want me, baby?" I ask, rolling into her touch as she nods. "Here?" Another nod. "Now?" Her hand moves over my trousers, rubbing me to full hardness, her lips parted as she traces from my eye to the edge of my lip. "Answer me, Rose," I order gently, the air electric, my hunger for her going through the roof.

She smiles demurely, plainly loving what she does to me. But I do it to her too. I reach for her jaw and hold her face steady. "Say it," I whisper, reaching under her dress and slipping my finger past her knickers, groaning when I'm greeted by hot, throbbing wetness. "Say it, baby."

"Yes," she gasps, jolting, her hands flying to my chest, her fingers clawing, dragging the material of my shirt into her clenched fists.

I smile darkly, moving to her ear and latching on to her earlobe, grazing her flesh through my teeth. "Do you want my tongue fucking your sweet pussy?" Another convulsion of her body. "Plunging. Licking. Rolling." My mouth waters as I trace the shell of her ear.

"Fuck," she breathes, rolling her hips, tugging mindlessly at my shirt, pulling a few buttons off.

"Your clit is vibrating." Every inch of her is vibrating. "You want me to bite it? Nibble?" I roll my fingertip around the pulsing nub. "Suck it?" I ask hoarsely, a suppressed growl rumbling deep at the back of my throat. I pry her hands from my chest, guiding them down to her sides, and she fights me the whole way, wrestling with my grip, her eyes narrow but still bursting with desperation. "Don't touch me," I warn coolly, my forehead resting against hers as I reach for the bottom of her dress and pull it to her waist.

"I hate you," she whispers, pushing her head harder to mine, furious, but still compliant.

"Yeah?" I kick my shoes off and take her hands, walking her backward toward the shore, anticipation swirling within me. The ocean. Rose's pussy. Two of my favorite things. As soon as I feel the water, I stop us, place my hands on her shoulders and encourage her down. She inhales as her arse comes to rest on the wet sand, and I drop to my knees, pushing her to her back, and take the sides of her knickers, drawing them down her legs and tossing them into the water behind me. A gentle wave comes in behind us, and Rose inhales, her back bowing as the water gathers around her, splashing up onto her chest. The water. The white material of her dress. Her bra-less boobs beneath. I lick my lips at the sight of her nipples hardening to bullets, the dark areola showing through the wet silk. I flick my gaze up, my mouth open, my head spinning. She forces her chest up with another arch of her back, her hands sinking into the wet sand.

She's a vision. And I need a taste. I hook my hands under the backs of her knees and spread her, opening her up to me, and I lower to my stomach, immune to the cold when there's a fire blazing within licking distance.

I lock my mouth around her completely, closing my eyes and absorbing the salty freshness of her flesh. Her cry is broken. My moan is primal.

"Danny," she whispers, writhing in the sand, twisting and turning her body. "Oh, God."

I push the tip of my tongue past her entrance and lick through her slowly, feeling her clit twitch in my mouth. She convulses violently, forcing me to lay an arm across her stomach to hold her down. Her hands land in my hair, pushing me to her, gripping, circling, grains of sand feeling rough against my scalp. I pull back, drinking in air ravenously, setting my stare on her glistening flesh. Her clit is visibly twitching. Her lips are swollen. The muscles just past her entrance rolling. I dip and place a tender peck on her, so softly, but she still yelps to the black sky, trying to force my head down for more. I shake her hold off, sending her hands plummeting to the sand, grabbing at the millions of grains to hold.

"I want to see this." I go in and lick again, spiking a strangled yell. And again. Another yell, a jack of her body. And again.

"Danny!"

I smirk salaciously, running my tongue across my lips, lapping up her essence as I push two fingers inside. I watch her head thrash, feeling her internal muscles trying to drag me deeper inside. I've tortured her enough. And myself. I get some weight behind me and drive deep, and her soft walls welcome me home. A few licks, a hard suck, a light bite, and a precise swirl bends her, breaks her, and she comes all over my mouth on a desolate murmur of my name before going limp, her chest heaving.

I kiss every inch of her skin, easing her down, mesmerized by her body, by the sounds she's making, until she relaxes, sinking into the sand. Crawling up her body, I settle my weight, framing her head with my forearms. Her eyes are closed. "Open," I breathe, knowing what I'm going to see. Her lashes flutter, she inhales, and she looks up at me.

Tears.

"We're going to be okay." I kiss her between her eyebrows. "Do you hear me, Rose?" I have to make her believe it, otherwise we'll be fighting constantly. I've already resigned myself to the fact that I'm going to be looking over my shoulder constantly again. I don't need to be on my guard, watchful of my wife's tidy palm. Because that's how she's operated since she fell in love with the man who kidnapped her. When she feels threatened, when she fears something will threaten *us*, she naturally slips into fight mode. Frustration and fear are the fuel. I've always taken a backward pleasure from being on the receiving end of her physical lash outs. I'm the only man in this world who can anger her.

I'm the only man in this world who can love her.

Therefore, I'm the only man in this world who can hurt her.

Because true pain only comes from loving someone. It's a lesson we've both learned, and we both live by.

She's my beginning.

And she will be my end.

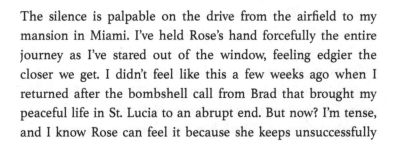

The silence is palpable on the drive from the airfield to my mansion in Miami. I've held Rose's hand forcefully the entire journey as I've stared out of the window, feeling edgier the closer we get. I didn't feel like this a few weeks ago when I returned after the bombshell call from Brad that brought my peaceful life in St. Lucia to an abrupt end. But now? I'm tense, and I know Rose can feel it because she keeps unsuccessfully trying to release her hand from mine. And there's why I feel different this time.

Rose.

On my last visit, she was in St. Lucia, miles away, being guarded. It became very obvious very quickly that keeping her there, out of harm's way, wasn't a long-term solution. Not when we have no fucking idea who we're dealing with, what exactly they know, and how we're going to handle it. So she stays with me. She's not happy about being here, and I'm not happy that I've been forced to bring her. So we're equally pissed off about the situation. Rose, naturally, more than me. I can't help but feel like life is going to be too fucking stressful for more reasons than one. My wife's temper is brutal. Unlucky for me, I'm the only poor fucker in this world who can spike that temper.

I'm the only man who can hurt her.

I glance across the car, finding her eyes nailed to the guy in the passenger seat. Nolan. He's Brad's new accessory. A good kid, by all accounts. I'm yet to find out. I crane my head to see what she's looking at when her eyes fall to his legs. A machine gun is spread across his thighs.

"It's a precaution," I say, shifting my hold of her hand so my fingers lace through hers.

"And what about the two cars up front and the two at the rear?" She doesn't look at me, turning toward the window. "Are they a precaution too?"

"Don't start, Rose," I warn. I do not need the added aggravation of my wife's sarcasm. She's got progressively more uptight since we left the villa this morning. The only person she's actually had any conversation with is Beau, and I bet my beautiful wife was slagging me off something rotten.

"Fuck you," she breathes, trying to pull her hand from mine again. I don't allow it, obviously. I see Nolan flick a wary glance up at the mirror, and I flash him a wry smile. It confuses him, I can tell by the slight squint of his eyes before he sharply turns his attention back to the road.

"Welcome home," I say quietly as we pull up to the gates. I get another jar of her hand for my trouble. I'm fast concluding that the only thing that seems to pacify my wife at the moment is when my cock is inside her. It would be a satisfying thought, one to savor, if it wasn't an impossibility. I'm going to be a busy man, and perhaps that's a contributing factor to Rose's mood. She's had me all to herself for three years. I've had her. Each day has been spent whiling in the sun, taking walks, eating indulgently. Indulging in each other even more. Miami is going to change the dynamic of our relationship. I don't like it, not at all, but, obviously, me ending up dead will change the dynamic a lot more. Rose knows that. She's just finding it harder to accept.

I glance across the car to her. She's looking at the two terraces leading off the bedrooms. There was only one terrace remaining when she left Miami three years ago. The other had been blown to smithereens. My blood runs cold, and my eyes clench shut, trying to push away the image of her dangling off the side, hanging on to the jagged concrete. Looking up into my eyes as she let go. She wanted to die. I gulp, the ramifications of my decision to return to Miami becoming starker by the minute.

The car comes to a gradual stop and Rose wastes no time opening the door, trying to escape me. I grab her upper arm, haul her back, and lean over, pulling the door closed on a bang, making one of the men on the outside jump back. "Let's lay a few cards on the table," I say, my fingers clawed into her flesh, stopping her fighting me.

She turns a ferocious stare my way. "You're shit at poker," she says through a pulsing jaw. She's right. Always have been. I smile on the inside, thinking back to that time in Vegas when I took her as collateral. She wants to think about it too, but her mood won't allow her.

"Maybe," I muse. "But I'm a champion at bringing my fiery wife to heel." I release her arm and place a palm on a breast, stroking my thumb in small circles over the sheer material of her silk blouse. I raise my eyebrows when her nipple solidifies, her hands clawing into the leather of the seat. "Are you going to argue with me on that too?" She can bring her all. I'm ready, and she knows it.

"You probably haven't got time to argue with your wife." Her words are broken, her back pressing into the seat, as I slide my palm down her front and cup her. The heat. I can feel it through her jeans.

Leaning in, I get my threatening face up close to her snarling one. "I'll always have time for you, Rose." I kiss her fury away, dragging her across the car onto my lap when she relents, whimpering. I flex up, making sure she feels me. And hears me. "You're my priority." That's not technically true. Keeping myself alive is my priority. The former is useless if I'm not physically able. I kiss her again. "It starts with you, and it ends with you." Brushing her hair away from her face, I look at her, waiting. "I'm backed into a corner, baby. I don't need you throwing flames at me too." I lift her and place her back on the seat next to me. "Wait for me in our room," I order gently, letting myself out of the car, unbending my body slowly, my eyes lifting up the front of the mansion as I do. I pull in my suit jacket and slip my shades on, feeling the eyes of many men on me, some old faces, some new.

The Brit is back.

"I'm not becoming your in-house whore," Rose yells, jumping out the other side and glaring across the car at me. "Your piece of ass to fuck when you need to let off steam after a hard day killing whoever the fuck needs killing." She storms off up the steps, and the men wisely move from her path.

"Fuck me," I breathe, blindly pushing the door shut. Yeah,

The Brit is back. And he's bought his impertinent woman with him. Trying to get this balance right might kill me with stress, if Rose doesn't kill me first.

I take one step, and the men around me move too, becoming more alert, more aware, some starting to look around, scanning the walls that surround the mansion. I freeze and cast an interested look their way. "Am I missing something, or has the national news announced my resurrection?" I ask.

"We're taking no chances." Ringo appears at the top of the stairs and, fuck, it's good to see his ugly mug. "Welcome home, Mr. Black."

"Shut the fuck up." I laugh as I round the car, this time ignoring the moves of the men around me, my arms lifting, beckoning him to me. His chest meets mine hard, and his big, murdering hands slap my back with force. "Good to see you, you ugly fuck."

"Is it?" he grunts, pushing me away, assessing me up and down. "St. Lucia suits you."

We start taking the stairs to the mansion side by side, and when we enter, Brad is emerging from the corridor that leads to my office. He spots Rose first, who's halfway up the stairs. "Rose," he sings.

"Fuck off, Brad," she spits over her shoulder.

"What did *I* do?"

"Breathe," she yells, and he recoils, looking my way.

I shake my head mildly as I go after her, ready to calm her the fuck down. I catch her wrist. Haven't I learned? She swings around, landing me precisely on the jaw, and I hear the men's gasps. Their horror. This woman is braver than any one of them.

I close my eyes, breathe in deeply, and exhale calmly. "Are you fucking determined to push me off the cliff of patience?"

She's trying so hard to hold back her tears, her jaw clenching fiercely, her waning strength pushing through. Her dainty shoul-

ders push back, her eyes passing me, taking in our audience.
She's smart and sophisticated enough to rein it in before it gets
really out of hand. Her gaze travels the room and comes back to
mine, and I reach for my jaw, making a point of cracking it, my
burning glare spelling out my mood.

Fuming.

Our spars, all of them, verbal, physical and sexual, should
never be aired in public, especially not in front of my men. "You
done?" I ask tightly. She looks away from me, pivots, and hurries
up the stairs, keen to escape the peanut gallery. *Oh Rose. My fiery,
savage, vulnerable Rose.*

I turn and take the stairs back down, noting Esther has
wandered into the foyer, wiping her hands on a tea towel. It
seems she's the only thing that's changed around here, her body
no longer carrying an insipid gray uniform, and is now adorned
in bright garments that do her complexion wonders. I've seen
her since we left, of course, but always in St. Lucia when she
visited. It never quite hit me how far removed she looked from
the woman Pops found all those years ago. But now, here at the
mansion, my past catching up to me, the backdrop as it always
was, she looks out of place. "Danny," she breathes, and it's half-
hearted, almost cautious. Worried.

"Hello, Mum." I go to her, dipping so she can get her arms
over my shoulders, but not before I take the tea towel from her
hand and cast it aside. Her hug is fierce. "I want to say it's good
to have you home."

"Then say it," I reply, letting her cuddle the shit out of me. I
can feel her unease. It's one more woman to try and appease. I
have a feeling my mother might be easier than Rose. She breaks
away and collects the tea towel from where I tossed it. I frown.
"Give me a moment with my mum," I say to the men over my
shoulder, and they all disperse, heading outside. "Come with

me." I sweep an arm out for her to lead, and she does, although obviously curious.

I open the door to my office for her, and she heads straight to my desk.

"The couch," I say, and she stops, looking back. "This isn't a business meeting, Mum." They say old habits die hard. They really do. I need to break her habit. Redirecting to the couch, she lowers. "What's this?" I ask, taking the tea towel from her again and holding it up as I join her on the couch.

"Now I know Carlo Black had you well educated, Danny." She cocks me a wry smile, and I roll my eyes. What is it with smart-mouthed women in my life? "I like serving you," she finally says.

I lay the towel over the arm of the couch, settling back. "I don't want you serving me. Those days are gone." The days when she pandered to my every whim, picked up after me, cleaned up my mess. It was Esther's way of trying to make up for leaving me with her piece of shit boyfriend who beat and raped me before Carlo found me on the streets of London. It was my way of punishing her but at the same time having her in my life.

"Are they?" she asks, reaching for my hand and holding it in both of hers. "I don't like this, Danny."

"Me neither," I admit, moving in closer to her, adding my hand to the bundle of limbs. "I'll be okay." I cock her a crooked grin. She doesn't appreciate it. "I might be back in Miami, Mum, I might be ready and prepared to kill, but I'm not prepared to have you waiting on me, or anyone else for that matter."

"I like—"

"I won't have it." It's non-negotiable. She is not here as a slave, not anymore. She's here because she's my mother. She's here because I love her dearly.

"I want to look after you," she says quietly, giving me imploring eyes. "I've been here the past three years in between visits to St. Lucia, and I've enjoyed my time keeping everything sparkly and clean. It's given me a purpose, to look out for you, even if you weren't here. But now you are. What else am I going to do with my time?" She pulls one hand away and indicates down her body. "There's only so much yoga and shopping a woman can do. Only so many cakes I can bake."

She needs a purpose. A job hasn't been necessary, and it only just hits me how lonely she must have been. Flush with cash and time, but incredibly lonely. And that makes me feel like shit. She's not glad I'm back in Miami. But she's glad I'm here. I need to find a balance for us—one that eases my conscience and gives Esther the purpose she needs. "Let me get a housekeeper," I say, and she starts to shake her head. "Listen to me," I order. "I'm not having you mopping up the mess of endless men around here. And believe it or not, I've become quite domesticated recently." She laughs, and I recoil, offended. "What's so funny?"

Chuckling, she reaches for my scarred cheek and cups it, looking at me fondly. "My sweet boy."

I'm a mafia boss coming out or retirement, for Christ's sake. But I let her have her moment. "The housekeeper is non-negotiable." I give her a look that dares her to object. "If you want to cook, fair enough. If you want to do some gardening, great. Take care of the dogs, feed them, but I draw the line at washing laundry and cleaning bathrooms." My lips straighten, forming a warning line. "That's the end of the discussion." I take her hand away from my face. "Moving on."

"To what?"

"Rose."

"Oh," she breathes, withdrawing. "She's not happy."

"Understatement of the fucking century." I reach for my jaw, stroking across my bristle.

Mum's lips purse, and I one hundred percent know what she's going to say. "She'll be scared, Danny. After everything you two have been through, the last place she'd want to be is here. Surely you can understand that."

"Of course I understand." But I also need to exact damage control. I get up and go to the cabinet, pouring a Scotch. I feel like I'm setting the bar with this drink. "I need you to keep an eye on her when I'm not here." Esther knows what I'm talking about. "I want all razors, blades, anything she can use to harm herself, gone." I knock back my drink. I know my wife too well, and at the moment that's an unfortunate advantage to have. Because it bends my mind, and I need to keep my mind straight. Ignorance really is bliss. I can't be ignorant. I need to keep my eye on the ball where my wife is concerned, and I need my mum to help me do that. I should speak to Beau too. Those two will undoubtedly be spending lots of time together.

Mum's silence speaks volumes, and I turn to find she's now standing. "Rose wants us to get married again."

Understandably, she looks confused. "Why?"

"I don't know. She wants a big, fancy wedding."

"When?"

"I'll let you know," I muse, thinking hard. "It'll keep her busy."

"While *you're* busy," she says, collecting that fucking tea towel, her expression knowing.

"Since you're so fussy about the mansion," I say, waving my empty around in the air. "I thought you might like to hire the help. You can do the interviewing." *Because I've not got time between killing many men and pacifying two women.*

"Sure, but I'm telling you now, none will be up to scratch." She wanders to the door, leaving me smiling behind her. That's a given, really. "I've made stew for dinner," she goes on. "A big one to go round. Let me know when you're ready to eat."

"Thanks, Mum."

She shuts the door, and I take myself to the desk, sitting in the chair. And so it begins. I scan the surface. Nothing's moved. The gold letter opener still sits precisely to the right, the leather-bound writing pad to the left. I pull a drawer open. Breathe in. Swallow.

Reaching in, I pull out the framed photograph of Pops and position it by the letter opener. This is how I remember him. My hero. Tanned, smiling, a cigar ready to pull on. Thick, silver hair and a malevolent twinkle in his shrewd eyes. Not the emaciated, weak, helpless old man who left me three years ago. I can't help but think that he's smiling right now. Smug. Cheering me on. Satisfied that I'm back here, in this chair, ready to command my troops and take back what was always his.

Miami.

Respect.

Fear.

I exhale and rest back, stroking over my Cupid's bow, lost in thought. I've gone full circle. And I know deep down in my heart now that I'm back, there will be no out until all threats, all enemies, old and new, are eliminated. That'll take time. I swallow, looking at Pops. The enemy never dies. Which means this isn't a temporary trip. I know that deep down. And I think Rose does too.

I'm yanked from my sobering conclusions when the office door opens and Brad walks in. He closes it behind him. Assesses me at the desk. In the chair. "We're reforming," I say before he can ask what the plan is. Although he knows. Of course he knows. There's only one reason I'd come back to Miami, and missing him isn't it. But I have missed him. My right-hand man. My best friend. My cousin.

"And there's me enjoying the quiet life," he quips, going to the drinks cabinet and taking a bottle of Scotch with two glasses before pulling out the chair opposite and dropping into it.

"Quiet? You had an attempt on your life."

He smiles, setting the tumblers down and pouring. "You worried about me?"

I reach across the desk and take a drink. "Maybe."

He grins. "And now you're here."

"And now I'm here," I muse, rolling the glass across my bottom lip. "I've told Esther to have all blades removed from the house."

His eyes narrow, and I see a watered-down version of my own anger. "That bad?"

"I don't know," I admit. "But I'm covering all my bases."

"What do I tell the men?" He reaches for his stubble and smooths down the roughness, a sign that no razors in the house isn't a problem for him. "Those who shave," he adds.

"If they object, tell them I'll happily give them a cutthroat shave." I pick up the letter opener and turn it in my grasp, my head tilted.

Brad laughs lightly. "Fuck me, Danny. Here's me thinking a woman and a quiet life has tamed you."

"Monsters can't be tamed, Brad." I can feel the dormant evil rising. "But they can hibernate and resurface more powerful." I'm ready to wreak havoc on this town. I'm ready to take it back and maintain my position, because I've had a fast lesson on what the alternative is.

And I'm not ready to die.

"Tell me about the men," I say, sipping my drink rather than knocking it back. "The new ones. You trust them?"

"Nolan's a street kid. Or was. He's young but keen."

"How old?"

"Twenty-one. Obviously angry, but that only fuels his thirst for blood. Good instinct, too."

I smile. "Remember when we were twenty-one?"

Brad snorts. "I remember whores and a fast lesson in what Uncle Carlo deemed acceptable levels of indulgence."

I laugh, and it's rich and happy. I recall the incident with perfect clarity. Pops couldn't locate Brad. I knew exactly where he was, where he had been for two days straight. The wrath of my father was something any man should avoid, even his son. Plus, I could never lie to that man. So I ratted Brad out, and Pops dragged him out of that hotel room and put a gun to his head, a firm reminder that women cloud your judgment. Brad didn't hold it against me. I know he would have done the same. "So what does Nolan do for you at the club?" I ask.

"Heads up security. He has a good eye for a troublemaker, if you know what I mean."

I hum, thoughtful. Not a bad position for a twenty-one-year-old lad. "And he's proved his loyalty how?"

Brad smiles. "You're not the only one with good instincts around here."

"Answer my question," I order. I'm trusting Brad. He's one of the only men I ever will, but I've been gone a long time and my instincts feel rusty.

"He's an orphan. Got no one. No place in this world." He knocks back his drink. "Now he's got a place, and I know a man who appreciates it." He points his glass at me. "As do you, Danny."

I can't argue with that. I was an orphan. Had no one. Then I had Carlo Black. "The others. Tell me about them all."

"Ringo, Len, and Bud couldn't take my call quickly enough. They're back with bells on. Turner and Dick have set up life on the West Coast. They're done."

I can't blame them. "Definitely retired?" I ask. Brad knows exactly what I'm getting at. Trust no one, and don't trust a man when he says he's done in this world.

"Definitely. I had Len and Bud tail them for a while."

"And the other newbies?"

Brad works through another few men, all new, all with

stories. And all to be trusted. That's fine, I'll accept it for now, but trust only comes from being earnt. I'll reserve judgment in the meantime. "All sensitive information remains between me, you, and the old men for now. The new guys know what they need to know. Got it?"

He nods. "And what about The Enigma?" He tops up his drink and takes a cool, casual sip.

"What about him?"

"What does he get to know?"

"Everything."

"You trust him?"

"I trust him," I reply, looking up as the man himself wanders in. "Your ears must be burning."

James closes the door and shakes Brad's hand before pulling out the chair next to him. "Wondering if I can be trusted? Whether I'll turn you over." His blue eyes glisten with amusement. "I'm trusting you and your men with Beau. She's staying here while we hunt down the boogieman. I'd appreciate the same sentiment."

I smile. It's wicked. "How is she?" I ask.

"Calmer than your wife," he retorts seriously, and Brad chuckles. I toss him a warning look that goes way over his head. He loves that my balls are in my wife's handbag. "You heard that, huh?" I ask.

"The whole of Miami heard it. We might not need to put the word out of your return."

"Speaking of which," Brad interjects, getting up and going to the cabinet, collecting a fresh glass and a bottle of vodka. "How are we breaking that news?" He places the tumbler in front of James and pours.

He's excited. I can see it in his eyes. "We should assume they already know." I'm not delusional. If they're as capable as we've concluded, they'll definitely already know. Time will tell on that matter. I flick my eyes to James, smiling darkly. "But they won't know about my new recruit."

"I'm no recruit," James retorts, deadpan. "I don't work for you, Black. I work for no one. I work *with* you."

I can feel Brad's cautious stare on me, wondering what I might say to that. It's an historical shift in the Black legacy. "There's a reason why I allowed you to walk into my office unannounced." I motion to the chair he's comfortable in. "Sit in that chair." My eyes land on the glass in his hand. "Drink my vodka."

James takes a long sip, watching me over the rim. "Then we're clear."

"Crystal," I agree, as Goldie, Otto, and Ringo all pile in. "Now, for the benefit of everyone here, let's have a recap of what we know."

James nods, wetting his mouth with more alcohol and motioning to Otto, who drops to a chair. Let's start unpicking this fucking mystery. And kill it.

"From the beginning?" Otto asks, looking overwhelmed by the prospect.

"Yes, from the beginning." I know a lot; James and I talked over many drinks in St. Lucia. And I mean, a lot. I felt like my brain short-circuited every time, the amount of information mind-bending. It's time to relay everything we know to Brad and Ringo, as well as refreshing me.

"We know he ordered the death of James and his family ten years ago," Otto says, sending wary eyes to his boss. James maintains his steely stare on my desk.

"Why?" Brad asks.

"James's father, Spencer James, fronted the biggest cocaine syndicate in the UK." Otto shifts uncomfortably in his chair. "His last deal was part of his exit plan. The Bear wanted England."

"And he got it," I muse, keeping a wary eye on James.

"He had The Snake fill Spencer's place over there," Otto goes on. "James got rid of The Snake in Miami over two years ago, the night FBI Agent Jaz Hayley, Beau's mother, was murdered. He found the order to kill her in a message on The Snake's mobile. It was sent to another burner. The receiving phone was switched off so we couldn't locate it."

"I tried to intercept the hit," James says, as I slowly turn my eyes onto him. "I saved Beau. I couldn't save her mother."

I nod, although he's not telling me anything I don't already know. He's simply building the big, bloody picture again. The mess of his back invades my thoughts. Beau's arm. "The only reason The Bear would want Jaz Hayley dead," I say, "would be because—"

"She figured out who he was," Otto finishes.

"And you," I point out, nodding at James. "She'd figured out who you were too."

"Who I *am*," James retorts.

"Sorry, yes." He's still a murdering bastard. "Except now you're not a paradox."

"Beau's mother held a safety deposit box under an alias," James says, rootling through his pocket and pulling out a key. He has our attention, and he knows it. There's only one reason an FBI agent would hold a safety deposit box under a fake name. "It was empty."

"And what did you think was in there?" Brad asks, as James places the key on the desk. All of our stares root on it. So small. But so significant.

"My real name. Who I am. Who my father was. And the identity of The Bear."

Brad and Ringo swing shocked looks his way. "Could it have been emptied before we got to it?" Ringo asks what we're all wondering.

"Find out who heads up that bank," I say to Brad, who's

eyeing the bottle of Scotch. This is not the time to find comfort in a bottle. We need clear heads because the web is only getting bigger.

"Beau knew something wasn't adding up when the police closed the inquiry into her mother's death," James goes on. "She started digging. I knew she was in danger."

"So you lured her to your den and fucked her seven ways to Sunday," Brad says, so casual. Stupid man.

"Do you want to die?" James asks, turning his deadly glare Brad's way, prompting him to hold up his hands in surrender.

"Beau's friend and Jaz's colleague, FBI Agent Nathan Butler," Otto continues, shaking his head at Brad, "started digging around when he found out Beau was seeing James."

"He obviously didn't like me," James mutters, deadpan.

"No idea why." Brad laughs. "I mean, you're one of the friendliest blokes I've ever met."

He definitely wants to die.

James's jaw starts to twitch, but he holds on to his temper, continuing. "Nathan Butler found CCTV footage from the night of Jaz's death. I was in the footage. He put two and two together and came up with ten. Assumed it was me who killed Jaz Hayley."

"Where is he?" Ringo asks.

"Dead. It *wasn't* me who killed him."

"The Bear?"

"Yes. Two officers pulled him over. He had Beau in the car. She got away. They shot him. He died later in hospital. I expect there's more to it."

"Like?"

"Like something similar to the Russian nurse I shot in Beau's room when she was in a coma."

"I assume she wasn't actually a nurse," Brad says, starting to look overwhelmed by the onslaught of facts.

"You assume right."

"And Beau was in hospital because her uncle's husband shot her?" he asks.

"Correct," Otto confirms. "Dexter Haynes. MPD. He carried out the hit on Beau's mother under instruction from The Bear and got rid of all the evidence, including the CCTV footage from that night showing James trying to save Jaz. Obviously, he recognized James from the footage when he met him with Beau."

"And in other news, Spittle told The Bear"—I wave a hand dismissively when James glances at me—"whether intentionally or not, that I'm alive. He then realized his fuck-up, panicked, and decided to take Brad out to try and avoid me finding out about his fuck-up."

"My brain hurts," Ringo mutters, dropping to the couch, rubbing at his head. "My fucking brain hurts so bad."

"You mean you have one?" Goldie says, shaking her head in a snarky way only a woman can achieve.

"And now you're in love with FBI Agent Jaz Hayley's daughter," I add, and James's unimpressed eyes turn onto me. "Women," I mutter. "My dad would kill me if he wasn't dead. So who is The Bear?"

"He has three arms," James says, and I smile. It's ignored. "First arm, the Irish. They deal in drugs. The Snake, the leader, as Otto said, is dead. The Eagle, his second-in-command, also dead."

Brad raises an eyebrow. He's not game to ask.

"The Alligator," James goes on, "their third-in-command, is inside awaiting trial. His name's Vince Roake. A bent judge was dealing with his case. He's also dead."

Brad looks at me with undeniably wide eyes. I give him a small wry smile. Yes. James has been a very busy boy.

"So what you're telling me is that we're dealing with a zoo," I say, amused, and so is James judging by the lift of his lip. "Funny how they're all named after animals, and yet I'm the biggest animal of all." I toast the air. "You come a close second, my friend."

James humors me, getting us back on track. "The Polish deal in women. The Shark is still out there. His second, The Fox, dead. The Hound, his third, alive."

Not for long. "And you've not located them yet?" I ask.

"I will," he assures me, and I trust him on that. "My apartment was compromised. All information I held has been wiped from the server." James digs into his pocket and pulls out a memory stick. "Bet you can't guess who deals in the firearms."

"I can tell you who *did*," I say, deadpan. "And he's back from the dead."

"Then the Russians should be scared."

"Russians?" I mimic, wary. "They're dead."

"Not this one. Sandy. He was sourced as a contact for me. Weapons. Turns out he's under The Bear."

"Fuck me," I say over an exhale. "Why The Bear? We've got snakes and sharks, so why would the illusive head of this web of crime and corruption go with something so . . . fluffy?"

Brad snorts. "Fluffy?"

I shrug. If I was going to pluck the name of an animal out of the air to instill fear into everyone, it wouldn't be a bear. "I'm just saying, kids take bears to bed and cuddle them all night."

"I've never understood that," Brad muses, kicking his ankle up onto his knee. "I didn't have a teddy bear. You?" he asks, and I shake my head. Stupidest fucking question ever. "You?" he asks, turning to James.

"Are we actually having this conversation?" James asks, looking between us in exasperation.

I smile on the inside. He had a bear. And that's where James and I are different. I was dragged up until I was ten. James must have had every luxury a kid could dream of, passing the days away on his country estate playing tennis, horse riding, and doing all the other things people from England who live on acres of land do. His father may have been a drug tycoon, but he was a lavish, bold man. I know because I looked him up. Of course I did. And I can't deny, reading about the assassination of Spencer James and his family made my blood run cold for no other reason than getting a hint of the anger and hate James harbors. Miami isn't ready for the both of us. But it should be thankful we're here, because the alternative . . .

Returning my attention to Brad, I get us off the subject of bears before James slams his head onto my desk. "What's the deal with Perry Adams?" We'll start with him.

"The mayor?" Otto questions.

"And ex bent lawyer." I raise my eyebrows and collect my phone. "We go back a long way."

"He checks out," Brad says. "Bank accounts all legit, no red flags, no extramarital affairs. Looks like he's finally being a good boy."

I nod and dial a number that's been etched on my brain since the day Pops formed an alliance with him. It's been three years since we've had contact. He answers without a word, and I click it to loudspeaker, placing my mobile on the desk. He's waiting for me to speak. Waiting to see if it's really me or someone else. Probably hoping on the latter.

"Chaka," I say quietly.

"Fuck me to Miami and back," he whispers, and I smile. "The fucking Brit?"

"I need guns." I get straight to the point, as I always did.

"Why would a dead man need an arsenal?"

"Because he's not dead anymore."

He laughs, and it's deep, rumbling, ground-moving stuff. "I'm not dealing in the States anymore."

"Then start," I say flatly.

"Too risky, my friend. And business is booming here in my fine African Nations."

"You once told me the meaning of your name, Chaka," I say, digging deep for anything that'll win me this battle. I need these fucking guns, and I can't get them from anywhere else.

"And?"

"And you told me it means 'king' in the tribal community where you were born." He's silent. He knows where I'm going with this. "So be a fucking king."

"Or?"

"Or the lions might prey on that peaceful community of yours, Chaka. You don't want that, do you?"

He laughs again, this time light. "Back with a bang, eh, Black?"

"Yeah, and I'd hate for you to be caught in the blast. Do we have a deal?"

"I'll be in touch."

I hang up. "How does the Jepson estate stand?" I ask Brad, knowing he'll have done his homework on that too, ready for my questions.

"Still in a trust until the kid is twenty-one."

"He must have a guardian. Find out who."

"Got it."

"And while you're at it, we need someone to run it when we've secured it."

"You sound confident."

"I am." I squint, thinking. "Why hasn't Byron's Reach been snapped up by some other criminal lord? It's the perfect place on the coast to bring in shit to the States."

"The place was crawling with FBI for a long time after you died, Danny," Ringo says from the couch, coming back to life, his brain still looking like it's hurting, judging by the mass of lines spanning his massive forehead. "No one in their right mind would go near it again."

"Then clearly I'm not in my right mind." I push my glass toward Brad, and he fills it. "What I want to know is, where the fuck are all these criminals smuggling in their drugs, women, and guns?" I look at James, noting his stretched silence.

"Just taking it all in," he muses, thoughtful. "But you forgot someone."

"Who?"

"Spittle."

Spittle. The name makes my skin crawl. "What about him?"

"He ordered Brad's death. He knows you're still alive. He was taking orders from The Bear, and he now knows who I am. He'll be reporting back to someone."

Brad laughs, and James glances across to him. "Spittle won't breathe a word."

"How can you be sure?"

"Oh, I'm sure." Brad grins, pulling up the screen of his phone and placing it on the desk. Both James and I lean forward to see the picture displayed.

"Well, that's one way to stop a man talking," I muse, staring down at the image of Spittle with his dick resting on a commercial meat slicer.

"You should just cut his fucking tongue out," James spits, unimpressed.

I nod, thoughtful, giving Ringo, Goldie, and Otto a moment of my eyes. They all get the message without the need to ask, getting up and leaving my office.

"How well do you trust your men?" I ask James the moment the door closes.

His eyebrow quirks, and I roll my eyes.

"Your people," I correct myself. Although the woman,

Goldie, certainly has animal traits in her eyes. I've seen it in endless men.

"I trust them with my life. Otto was my father's first for fifteen years. He saved my life. Protected me while I pulled my head out of my arse and found my calling."

"Killing." I state it as the fact I know it is.

"Justice," James corrects me coldly.

I nod. Same thing. "And the woman?"

"Honorable. Loyal. She'll never leave my side. Trust me on that one." He goes back to his pocket and pulls out something else.

"You got Mary Poppins pockets?" Brads asks dryly, as both our eyes fall to the photograph James places down.

"I don't know, have I?" He's back at his pocket again, and this time he pulls out a gun.

"I'm disappointed," Brad mutters, unfazed. "I was expecting a bazooka." He waves a finger flippantly at the picture. "Who's the dude?"

"Brendon Brunelli. I want him alive or alive. Last known location: London after being released from Wormwood Scrubs. I asked Spittle to look into it, but he's sidetracked at the moment having his dick shaved."

I chuckle, and it's unstoppable. "What did he do?" I ask, but I get nothing from James, just a look that's warning me to not push him on that. "Ring any bells?" I ask Brad, dragging the picture toward me.

"I'll ask around."

"Start with Eugene Connor in London," I say. "If anyone knows, he will."

"Thanks." James turns his eyes onto the photo of Pops on my desk, reaching forward and spinning it to face him. "I can see the resemblance."

Both Brad and I break out in uncontainable laughter, and

James looks at us both like we've lost our minds. "He's not my biological father," I say, relishing the usually unmoving face of James recoiling. "Maybe I'll tell you the story one day after a Scotch or twenty." Because that's how many I'll need to retell that tale. It would make a fucking brilliant novel.

"So, the plan," James says, getting us back to business.

"We buy Byron's Reach. Chaka gets us our guns. We kill The Bear." Once we find out who the fuck he is.

"All while keeping a wife and a girlfriend happy?" Brad asks seriously. "Good luck with that."

James sinks further into his chair, and I follow suit, both of us shrinking at the thought. Brad's right. I hate that he's always right. Now's probably not the right time to tell the boys that I've negotiated a deal with Rose that will give her the elaborate wedding she always dreamed of. Not when Miami is about to be ripped apart at the seams.

God help us.

6

ROSE

I'm not crying, but I'm close. I'm in my suite, the room he put me in after taking me from the Aria over three years ago as collateral. I wanted to hate him. Did to an extent. Then I started to chip through the lethal exterior and what I found scared me more than the man who bought me as a girl and controlled me for ten years. I found hope. I found hope in a notorious killer. And then I found love.

He's given me freedom, killed my demons, found my son, and he's going to take it all away. I love him. I hate him. I'm back to square one. Powerless.

I rest my hands on the terrace railings and look to my right. To his terrace. The room next to mine. That woman, the resilient, strong, impenetrable woman, survived being Danny Black's prisoner. And then married him. I love him with every fiber of my fucked-up being. I know he's stressed. I know he wouldn't choose this. I know I shouldn't be causing him more problems. And yet my deep, deep resentment for a world I've always hated won't let me lay back and accept the inevitable.

I sigh, returning my attention to the impeccable grounds of Danny's Miami mansion. So perfect. So colorful. But outside these walls?

I hear movement from the room next door. Danny's room. I bite my lip, knowing what I would see if I were a fly on the wall. My husband stamping around searching for me.

I creep back to the French doors, my eyes nailed to the other terrace, as I hear him curse me to hell. The sound of something hitting the wall sounds, and then he bursts out onto the terrace. His expression, one of fear and fury, tells me all I need to know. He thought I'd run out on him.

He finds me on the threshold of the doors, holding the frame, nervous as shit, although trying so hard not to show it. Fuck, he's angry. On the warpath. I find my shoulders pushing back as a result of that conclusion. I'm ready. Bring it on, Black. But unlike the times we've sparred and I've automatically pulled my armor into place, I don't need to do that anymore. I'm exposed. Vulnerable. But only to him.

He approaches the glass dividing the two terraces, his dark hair damp, curled slightly where it's meeting his nape. It's not the short, tidy cut he had when we met. But what's never changed is the fire in his icy stare. Whether he's livid with me, burning for me, laughing with me, there's always fire. He is fire. Danny Black is an unadulterated, uncontrollable inferno. "What are you doing in there?" he asks, slipping his hands into his pockets, probably to restrain them from strangling me.

"It's my room." I lift my chin, confident in my stance.

"*This* is your room," he retorts, jerking his head back in gesture to the space behind him. "*Our* room. Don't make me drag you back, Rose. I'm tired. Moody. I need a good fuck, a cuddle, and my mum's homemade stew."

"I'm not hungry, I'm not horny, and I don't need a cuddle." I must be out of my fucking mind pushing his buttons like this. Out. Of. My. Mind. The scar on his face deepens. It's my measure, my way of assessing what level of rage I'm dealing with. Right now, it's breaking the spectrum.

I see his body engage, and I back up, but before I've even made it past the door, he's cleared the railings dividing the terrace, catapulting his body over using one hand on the bar as leverage, and is coming at me like a bull. I don't bother running. I won't get very far.

Coming to an abrupt stop before me, his toes touching mine, he blows angry breaths into my face. My eyes narrow. Naturally, my skin prickles, heat washing over me, and it's got nothing to do with the heat of his anger. He snarls, reaching for my hair and fisting it. I smirk to myself, jarring my head, goading him. His snarl falters. A dirty, wicked smirk slowly forms. "Why'd you do it to me, baby?" He bends fast and hauls me up over his shoulder. "Don't answer that. I already know." Stalking to the door, he swings it open. "You want attention, don't you?"

I snort, and it's pathetic, because it's true. I've been spoiled for three years, been my husband's be all and end all, and now I have half of Miami's criminal underworld to compete with for his attention. That's pretty pathetic too, even having that thought, and yet here I am thinking it. I want to go back to St. Lucia and resume our bliss, not return to the blood, death, fear, and twisted clashes that brought us together in the first place.

"Excuse me," Danny says, and I wedge my hands into his lower back, looking up and trying to see through the hair covering my face. I catch a glimpse of Beau and James in the corridor, their backs against the wall to give Danny room to pass with me dangling over his shoulder. "My mum's cooked a stew if you're hungry."

"Thanks." James takes Beau's hand and leads her on, and she

looks back over her shoulder on a small, sad smile. She's not fully recovered, her stomach still tender, her spirit still dull. I know not because she's griped about it, nor even cried. But because I've observed her many times holding her tummy, falling into thought. Her despondency gives me a kick up the ass. I've not lost anything, and I won't. Not knowing Danny as I know him. But Beau has. She's lost so much.

God damn me.

I swallow, letting my head slump down, feeling ashamed of myself. I hear the door slam. Feel his hands on my hips. I'm lifted and tossed onto the bed, and I come to rest and brush the hair out of my face, finding him standing at the end, arms limp by his sides, his face impassive. "I'll be your punching bag, Rose. I'll take everything you have to give. In private." His hand comes up, his finger pointing at me. "But you will stow away your fists in public, you got it?"

I feel well and truly put in my place. "I'm sorry," I murmur quietly, my shame growing. Where the fuck is that woman who laughed in the face of threats? I'm having a hard time finding her. Perhaps because back then she was functioning on force. Accepting everything, taking it all without tears or complaint, because nothing would change. Now, I'm not forced to do anything. And everything could change. "I don't mean to lash out. Hurt you."

On a sigh weighed down with all the worry I know he feels for me, Danny rests on one knee at the end of the bed. "You don't hurt me. Not physically. But each time you plant one on me, Rose, it fucking hurts my heart, because you only lash out like that when you're feeling threatened. That hurts."

Why is he keeping his distance? I need him all over me. Lifting my arms, I beckon him into them. Another sigh, but he comes, sinking his face deep into my neck, sticking his lips on my throat. I'm here now. I may as well accept it and get on with it. The less hassle I give him, the quicker he'll deal with what needs to be dealt with and we can go home.

"How was your first meeting with the men?" I ask, rolling my eyes to myself, but short of asking how his day at work was, it's all I've got. I feel his lips stretch against my neck. He thinks my question is stupid too.

"Let's agree on some things," he says, starting to dot kisses across my skin.

"What?"

"We don't discuss business."

I laugh. It's not in amusement. My reasonable, pacifying mood has been turned on its head with one thoughtless, stupid statement, and this time it's not from me. "Oh yes, you don't discuss business with the latest whore you're fucking." I push into his chest. "Get off me."

"Oh for fuck's sake," he grumbles, not fighting back, rolling to his back tiredly. It's a further insult. "I didn't mean it like that. Stop being so fucking sensitive."

"Are you just going to lie there saying dumbass shit? I am your *wife*. I have a fucking right to know what the fuck is going on with my husband, more so when I know he's about to go to fucking war with God knows fucking who." I pick up a pillow and throw it at him with force, and he catches it, his knees coming up, his body folding in protectively. "I fucking hate you."

"You want to fuck?" he calls as I stomp into the bathroom.

"No. That's not the answer."

"Then tell me what the answer is, and I'll do it."

"We leave Miami." I know it's not that simple. God damn me, I know it more than I know I hate him right now. I slam the door, furious, and then burst into tears. I feel like my head could pop off, the stress, the worry, the anger, all coming to a head and compacting. We've never argued so much.

I stand in front of the mirror, looking at the woman I am. Searching for the woman I used to be.

Find her again, Rose. You need her.

I yell and swipe up the nearest thing I can lay my hand on and throw it at the mirror, shattering the glass. And I stare down at the razor-sharp shards littering the vanity, each one begging for me to take it and use it to release the pressure. To own my pain.

I'm halted when Danny charges through the door, nearly taking it off its hinges.

"Better than your face," I say calmly, feeling anything but, my tears streaming.

He says nothing, just walks coolly across to me and yanks me into his hard, warm chest, swathing me in his arms, holding me tightly. The silence is peaceful. His closeness so needed. "I don't know if I can do this." I tell him what he already knows, but I need to speak with words not actions.

"You can do anything, baby." He pulls out, holding my neck firmly, his eyes locked with mine. "Where's the woman I met?"

"She's got far more to lose now."

"You're not going to lose anything." He kisses my forehead lightly. "Only your mind if you allow it. I need you to be strong for me, Rose."

"Don't say that," I beg, my hands feeling him everywhere I can. "The last time you said that, you died."

"Baby, don't you know me at all?" His nose meets mine, his hands slipping to my cheeks. "I'm invincible."

I should argue. I won't. I've seen my husband in action. Watched him kill many men. He's merciless, always one step ahead. "I know you," I breathe, taking his wrists. "I'm sorry."

He hushes me and walks me back to the shower, reaching in and flipping it on. "Let's have a long, hot, intimate shower together." He places me safely to the side and starts collecting up the glass from the vanity, dropping the jagged shards in the trash while the shower warms. He checks the floor. The sink. Runs the faucet to get rid of any slithers he might have missed before collecting a hand towel and using it to brush down the counter, ridding it of any glass. Or weapons. Then he checks the floor once more before he begins stripping me down, starting with my jeans, and I watch him as he concentrates on getting me naked. I'm going to be his respite through this. His way to unwind. A reminder of why he's on this path. It's a job I'll take very seriously.

I start on his black shirt once I'm naked, unfastening the buttons and pushing it off his wide shoulders, kissing his chest as I move my hands to his pants and he kicks his shoes off. I can feel the vibration of his groan against my lips on his chest. I drop to my knees, pulling his pants down with his boxers and drop a peck on the very tip of his weeping erection. It twitches, throbs, and I'm pulled to my feet and backed up into the corner of the shower. His deadly, masterpiece of a body cages me in, water raining down on him. I lay my hands on his waist and gaze into his lazy, hooded eyes. "Ever call yourself a whore again," he whispers hoarsely, brushing our lips together, working me up, "I won't be so nice next time."

I reach down and seize his cock, and his eyes close, his inhale long as he pushes my hand away. A deep groan and a roll of his hips has him inside me, my back pinned to the wall enabling me to loop my legs around his tight waist. He goes deeper. I cry out. He grunts, starting to retreat and advance calmly, his pace languid. I'm hypersensitive to every slow stroke, my back slipping across the wet tiles with ease, and I reach for his face, pushing his hair away, holding him, watching his expression contort with a pleasure only I can give, and a need only I can sate. This beautiful, dangerous man. My absolute hero.

I rest my head back, keeping my unparalleled view, and let his expert ways wipe us clean along with the water. The strain on his face becomes more apparent after each advance, the pressure against my internal walls from his increasingly swollen length becoming firmer. His parted lips and his drowsy eyes are a glorious picture of my husband pre-climax.

I clamp my arms around his neck, hauling him in, and I kiss him with a passion that's natural, taking us both to the edge.

"Rose," he whispers jaggedly, jerking, coming, and I come with him, tensing every limb around his solid physique.

I strain to drag out the pleasure, every nerve in my body sizzling, pulsing, screaming. "Oh God," I whisper into his mouth, stiff in his arms, trying to contain the intensity. Every convulsion of his cock seems to trigger another spasm in me, making me twitch and tense, fighting to deal with the sensitivity.

Nipping my tongue, he relaxes into me, burying his face in my wet neck. "I could binge on you forever and never feel full," he says on labored breaths, and I smile into his shoulder, having a nibble of his flesh. I said that once, I'm sure of it. And I still feel the same. "Come, let me clean you."

I wince at the pull in my legs as I release them from around his waist, finding my feet, and stand quietly while he washes me down with the utmost care. Like I'm fragile. "You said you wanted to agree on some things," I say.

His movements falter, the washcloth pausing on my shoulder for a few seconds. "Right."

"I think that's a good idea."

"What do you want, Rose?"

"I want you to wear a vest when you leave the house."

"I'm assuming you don't mean a waistcoat."

"No, I don't mean a waistcoat." British lingo fucks with my mind sometimes. I turn so he can see how serious I am. "A bulletproof vest. I want you to wear one. So whoever you're sourcing your arsenal from, I want you to call them up and add it to your shopping list."

His smile is unsure as he leisurely soaps his torso down. If he even thinks about coming at me with some spiel about it being unnecessary, I might scream. "A bulletproof vest?"

"Yes," I reply. "The best on the market, please."

"Fine."

I hide my recoil. It's hard when I'm shell-shocked.

"Now onto some other things." He takes a towel and wraps me before seeing to himself.

Shit. Whatever he's going to demand, I can hardly say no now. "What things?"

"Our wedding." He drapes the towel over his shoulders and starts pulling from side to side, drying himself.

Oh? "What about it?"

"Well, since I'm a crucial guest, it would be nice to know when I should be there."

"Three weeks," I say casually as I saunter away butt naked, smiling as I go.

"Confirmed."

"No, but it will be. What are my boundaries?"

"No guests past our friends. Father McMahon will do the service, so we'd better check three weeks suits him. No wedding planner, no announcement in the local newspaper, and no moaning about it from you."

I stop in my tracks, my nose wrinkling. "This is going to be the most boring wedding ev . . . oh!" I'm hauled back and thrust up against the wall by his naked, hard, gorgeous, lickable, wet body. I blink, disorientated, gaining my focus. He looks mad. But he isn't. I push my face forward and lick a long line up his scar to his eye. "Can't wait," I whisper.

"You kill me." And he kisses me ferociously, grabbing at my breasts, pushing me higher up the wall. I yank and tug at his hair, urging him on, at the same time praying that I'm the only person in this world who *can* kill him. I become more frenzied at the thought. "I have to go," he mumbles around our manic kiss. "And whatever you're thinking right now, stop thinking it." He tears himself away, his labored breaths bursting in my face. He's got me, and I look away guiltily. Not for long, though, because he forces me back. "Understand?" he affirms with grit.

I nod as best I can with his long fingers gripping my face, and he kisses me, this time softly.

"Don't go," I beg, hating the need in my tone. I don't want to become clingy. I don't want to be that woman. And yet my hand still reaches for his softening cock, manipulation taking over.

"I'll be back later." His voice is strained as he knocks my feeling hand away and locates his jeans.

"Where are you going?"

"I don't discuss business with my wife." His lip quirks as he pulls them up his legs, and I scowl. "Anyway, you're busy yourself."

"Doing what?"

"Organizing our wedding."

Oh, yes. That.

After pulling a black T-shirt over his head, he strokes through his wet hair, and I all but dribble at the sight of my man looking casual. I smile to myself. He's not dressed to kill, so to speak.

He goes to the bathroom and appears a few seconds later with the trash can full of glass. "I'll put a call in to Father McMahon."

"I'll do it." I wander to the dressing table and sit down. "You're busy killing half of Miami."

A small, inappropriate, dark laugh, and the sound of the door closing. I stare into the mirror at my flushed cheeks. "And so my sentence begins," I whisper, studying myself as I think.

And think. He never mentioned that I couldn't, so I'm going to assume that I can. I go to the bed, get comfortable, and call my boy.

"Mom?" he says in answer, sounding surprised. And then he quickly corrects himself, and I know it's because he must be around Hilary. "I mean Rose."

God love him. The mom thing has happened naturally over the past three years of visits to St. Lucia, and I never once questioned it because Hilary was never around to have her feelings hurt. But the fact of the matter is, I *am* his mom. I deserve that title.

"Hey, kid," I quip, smiling at the ceiling, hearing scuffling and bangs in the background. "You okay?"

"No, my hamster escaped."

Oh? A rodent on the loose? I shudder. "How?"

"I don't know. I'm always careful to lock the door of his cage." More bangs. "I'm checking the kitchen cupboards. He likes cereal."

"Nice." I grimace. "You settled back into school?"

"Yeah, it's good."

"I can't believe you're in eighth grade." He's growing up too fast, the years rolling, and that sucks even more because I feel like he's only been in my life for a second.

Daniel bypasses it all. "When can I come visit again?" he asks, and I smile. Historically, I've only seen him every couple of months, but each year the visits are becoming more frequent, his eagerness to spend as much time as he can with us in St. Lucia the best kind of reward for his absence from my life for so many years. My fear that he would reject me was very real. I never dared hope that he would actually embrace me.

My smile quickly falls when I remember where I am. "You only just got home a couple weeks ago." I take no pleasure from how this must make Hilary and Derek feel. None at all. But for me? It's life.

"I've got to beat Mister on the water before I'm fifteen or I'll lose the bet."

I laugh. "You'll never beat Mister." Danny's been jet skiing most days for eighteen years. If he wasn't a mafia boss, he'd be a pro. "Tell me about school," I order.

"Really, Mo—" a beat. "Rose."

"Really. I want to hear if you're destined to be top of this class too." He's athletic, a total brain box and, of course, fucking beautiful. I dread to think of all the hearts he'll crush when he starts dating. *If* he starts dating. I don't want him to start dating.

"It's too early to tell," he says, blasé. "But I aced the soccer team tryouts and—"

I hear Hilary in the background calling him. "Okay?" I ask.

"Yeah, Dad's home. I've got to go." He sighs, definitely stroking my ego by sounding regretful. "I'll FaceTime you next week, okay?"

"Okay," I squeak, cringing. FaceTime. He'll see I'm not on the beach, or around the villa, or by the pool. "Love you, boy."

"Yeah, you too. Tell Mister I've asked if I can have some jet ski lessons down the beach at the weekends."

I laugh. "He'll be quaking in his wetsuit."

"He should be." He lowers his voice. "See ya, Mom."

My tattered heart repairs. "See ya," I whisper back.

After unpacking both of our clothes and calling Father McMahon, I head to the kitchen and find Esther stirring a big pot of something on the stove. "Stew?" I ask as I perch on a stool.

She turns around and smiles, dusting off her hands. "You look significantly calmer than when you got home."

I give Danny's mom a sorry look, reaching for the hand

cream that's in the middle of the island next to her purse. "I didn't think we'd ever come back. It's a hard pill to swallow." I squeeze some of the cream into my hand and start massaging it in.

"He'll have it sorted soon enough." She comes over and leans on her forearms opposite me, a happy twinkle in her eye. I don't understand it. I don't understand *anything*. "In the meantime, I believe we have a wedding to organize."

"He's trying to distract me." I'm not dumb.

"So you don't want to be married to my son in the eyes of God?"

I look at her tiredly. "Of course I do."

She claps her hands, and I jump. "Then let's get cracking." Esther magics a laptop from nowhere and takes a seat next to me, opening Google. "When?"

"Three weeks on Saturday."

"Wow. You mean business. Wedding planner."

"I'm not allowed a wedding planner," I reply, bored.

"Oh. Well, I'll be the wedding planner. Venues," she declares.

"Here."

"What?"

"It'll be here." I just know it. There's no way in hell Danny will risk having a big affair outside the boundaries of this house. No. Way. In. Hell.

Esther's lips purse. "Okay, guests?"

I prop my chin on my hands. "Danny, his army of killers, me, you, my boy, and Beau." That was easy.

She looks at me, cautious, and I raise my eyebrows. "Right, then." She goes back to the laptop. "Invitations."

"Esther, I could yell the time and date right now and everyone who can come would hear."

"What's the color theme?"

"I don't know."

"Then let's decide on that."

"Decide on what?"

We both look over our shoulders and find Beau at the kitchen doorway. I force a friendly smile, but only because she needs some friendliness. "The color theme of my wedding, which, at the moment, isn't worth having." I wince when Esther slaps my arm.

"She's overreacting," she says to Beau. "Come join us."

"Yeah, it's nothing." I wave a hand flippantly, and Beau gives me a side smile as she comes over, taking a seat at the island with us. "Where's James?" I ask, noting her stroking her arm, the cast gone.

She shrugs, giving me opens hands, as if to say, *"You tell me."* "Where's Danny?"

My nose wrinkles immediately. This is something we should get used to. Their absence. Just each other for company while our men are out doing hell knows what.

"Okay," Esther chirps, going back to her laptop. "The bachelorette party?"

"You'd better ask Danny." I smile sweetly. "We don't want it to clash with a murder."

Esther narrows impatient eyes on me. "Entertainment for the wedding."

"Probably prohibited." I sigh. "Is it too early for wine?" This is depressing. I don't wait for an answer, jumping up and going to the fridge. I pull down a bottle of New Zealand Sauvignon and twist off the cap. "Joining me?"

Beau raises her hand, Esther rolls her eyes, and I grin, taking down two glasses. I pour in plenty and hand them out, retaking my seat. "I have interviews for housekeepers to arrange," Esther says, snapping the laptop shut. "Enjoy." She leaves the room, and I turn my attention to Beau. She looks rested. It's good to see. "Will you be my bridesmaid?"

She blinks rapidly, and I hold my breath, surprisingly nervous of her answer. Does she think we're not close enough? "You serious?"

I shrug, like it's nothing, when it's everything. I'm grateful for her in my life, and not only because of the circumstances and timing. I hope she's grateful for me too. "Deadly."

She laughs. "Of course I will."

My body deflates, releasing air I didn't realize I was holding. Relief. "Good." *That's one thing I'm in control of.* "We'll go dress shopping." *If we're allowed.* "How are you settling in at Casa Black?"

"I want to say it's unnecessary." She grimaces and takes a sip of wine. "But I can't. It's a mess, Rose. The whole thing is a mess. My uncle is still in shock, we can't find his husband, James is on the warpath, and I'm here being useless."

I smile sympathetically. "I'm sorry for everything you've been through." It feels a bit lame, but what else can I say? "Danny told me that the man who wants him dead wants James dead too. He told me what happened to your mom. To James's family." Beau really has been through a lot. And James too. They're yet to conquer their demons and find their out. It's hard to accept that Danny and I can help them do that when our stabilized world is being rocked.

"And I'm sorry you've been dragged into the middle of it all." She pushes a hand toward me, and I take it, squeezing lightly. I don't want her to feel bad. Adding guilt to her mountain of woes would be unfair.

"Don't be sorry." I wave it off. "When you marry a man like my husband, I suppose you have to expect the unexpected." I chink her glass and drink some wine. "Tell me how you met."

Beau laughs, but it's uncomfortable. "You'll think I'm certifiable."

"Beau," I say, turning on my stool to face her, leaning in.

"Danny took me from a casino floor as an indemnity policy. He slapped my face within minutes of meeting me. I was supposed to bleed him for information and feed it back to my handler, a lovely man named Nox, who bought me from the man who took my baby and sold him on the black market. That man happened to be Danny's uncle." Her eyes widen with every unbelievable word I say. "I fell in love with the monster. If you're certifiable, I'm right there with you."

"Fucking hell," she breathes.

"I know." I drink more wine, frowning to myself. It sounds crazy. Utter madness. And yet it's all true, and that's not even the full picture. "So tell me. Or we could just carry on worrying about where our monsters are." I cock my head, and she laughs.

"Okay, are you ready?"

"No, wait." I take the bottle of wine and fill both our glasses to the rim. "Now I'm ready." I settle in, giving Beau my full attention.

"In a nutshell?" she asks, and I nod. She takes a deep breath. "Three years ago, I had a mom, a fiancé, and an amazing career as a cop. I aced my Phase One FBI exam, had a lovely apartment with my fiancé, Ollie, also a cop, and things were looking pretty fucking great. Except for my dad. He's a dick."

I recoil, and Beau shakes her head.

"He left my mom for a younger model. Amber. She's pretty unbearable. Anyway, my mom was an FBI agent. A great one. She took down many wanted criminals, but suddenly they started turning up dead."

"As in murdered dead?"

"Yeah."

A little piece clicks into place. "The Enigma," I gasp, quickly slapping my hand over my mouth. "James," I hiss.

"Yes. He was killing the most wanted men before my mom could get them behind bars, and it was driving her insane."

"Jesus," I whisper, sipping more wine, listening, both rapt and shocked. "And?"

"There's a top man. They call him The Bear."

"He's responsible for James's family's death too?" I ask, remembering Danny mentioning that. But . . . "The Bear?"

She nods, joining me when I slurp more alcohol. I'm not sure one bottle will be enough. "No one knows who he is. But James thinks Mom knew."

"Why would James think that?"

"Because she figured out who *he* was."

"Fucking hell." It's like something out of a crime thriller. "I'm sorry I keep swearing." I wave a hand for Beau to go on, blown away already, and I have a feeling I've heard nothing yet. It's sickly satisfying. "I didn't think two people could be more fucked up than Danny and I am."

Beau laughs, but soon stops, and she looks horrified with herself. Whatever is coming next, it's hitting her hard. My eyes fall to her scarred arm, which is covered with a sleeve. Always is.

"My uncle's husband, another cop, Dexter, somehow got involved with The Bear. He ordered Dexter to get rid of Mom because she figured out Dexter was corrupt. I think she also knew The Bear's true identity. I . . ." She stalls and clears her throat. "I went into a store to get some wine. We were painting her new apartment. It relaxed her." Swallowing, she lifts her sleeve, and I get my first full hit of Beau's scarred arm. "Mom was in the car. I wasn't."

"Oh Beau," I breathe, inching my stool closer.

She glances up, her eyes watery, and she smiles the saddest smile I've ever seen on a woman. "The police closed the case. Said it was a freak accident."

"What, a bomb?"

"They said Mom was smoking in her vehicle. She wasn't. They said there was a fuel leak. There couldn't have been because her vehicle was at the dealership a few weeks before. I kept fighting for justice, but I met a brick wall constantly. I know now Dexter manipulated all the evidence and destroyed the footage that proved it wasn't an accident. I quit my job, left my fiancé at the altar, and went deep, deep into depression. I painted. It relaxed me and brought me closer to Mom. Then one day I got a call from someone. Wrong number, he said."

"James."

"James," Beau counters. "He was just James then. A total fucking mystery, almost cold but, God, he stirred something inside, and it felt so much better than the constant hatred and bitterness. We got close. He said things that fucked with my head, but it all started slowly falling into place. Who he was. What he'd done. It was like he wanted me to know. He knew I was digging, and he knew it would have gotten me killed."

"A knight in shining armor."

"A desperate man." She smiles, and it's knowing. "He knew Mom knew who he was. He knew that if the police opened an internal investigation, his identity was at risk of being revealed."

"How?"

"He saved me," she whispers, turning her glass by the stem. "He tried to warn Mom that she was in danger, but he didn't get to her in time. He managed to pull me away." She lifts her arm, biting the corner of her lip, and my heart breaks for her. "Have you seen his back?" she asks, looking at me.

"His back?" I ask, confused.

She just smiles. "He was as broken as I was. And then we were fixed for a time," she murmurs, looking across the kitchen blankly. My eyes instinctively fall to Beau's stomach. "And now I feel like we're more broken than we ever were."

God help me, I must not cry on her. What do I say? What do I do? I have no idea, so I take the bottle and top up our glasses again. "Drink," I order, pushing her glass to her lips as I sip some of mine.

"More of a dinosaur shell than a nutshell, huh?"

I'm trying so hard not to look stunned. I know I'm failing. I feel like both of us are completely shrouded in devastation. Darkness. I can't allow us to just sit here dwelling on every tiny thing there is to dwell on, and there is a lot. "Right." I place my glass down, feeling all assertive. "Let's do something."

"Like?"

"I don't know. Tennis?"

Beau looks at her stomach, and I wince at my stupid suggestion. "I'm sorry," I breathe, exasperated with myself.

"Please stop apologizing, Rose. I blame no one except one man, and James and Danny are about to kill him."

"If they find out who he is."

"They will," she says, and it's with one hundred percent certainty. "I definitely wouldn't want to be him right now."

I laugh, nervous. I can't even think about it. And there's the problem. Hanging around here, scratching around for things to do, it gives us too much time to think. "Okay," I say, casting my wine aside. Walking into Danny's office armed with alcohol isn't going to do my cause any favors. "I'll be back. Don't move." I leave her, repeating a silent, encouraging mantra as I go, and enter his office unannounced. I immediately regret it. I should have knocked. Shown some willingness to be considerate. I cringe. "Sorry," I murmur, stepping back out and closing the door. I then knock and wait.

"Come in," Danny calls over a chuckle. Oh good. My gorgeous, chuckling god. He's more amenable than the growling monster, and I need amenable right now. I let myself back in his office. "What's up, baby?" he asks from behind his desk, looking all powerful and kingly. I never thought I'd see this Danny again. He looks as if he's never been away. Like he's slipped back into the role seamlessly. I shake away my resentment, feeling all eyes in the room on me. James, who's on the couch, Ringo, who's next to him. Brad is at the desk, with the young guy beside him, and the woman and guy who came in with James and Beau. Goldie and Otto. All quiet. All watching.

"Could I have a minute?"

With one nod from Danny, everyone starts to leave, and I smile, thanking each and every one of them, feeling like a massive inconvenience. "Make arrangements for me to meet this Leon kid," Danny says, and Brad nods.

I stop James, taking his arm. "You should stay. It involves you too."

His face falls, his tall body tensing. "Where's Beau?"

"She's in the kitchen. She's fine." I'm quick to reassure him, shutting the door, placing my attention on my husband and taking a few discreet confidence-boosting breaths. I'm well aware that I don't have only one man to get through.

Danny leans back in his chair, his fingers laced, resting against his torso, his face expectant, and James goes to the desk, perching on the edge, crossing his jean-clad legs at the ankles, folding his arms, his face interested. It hits me in this moment, standing here before them, who I'm faced with. Two of the dead-liest men to walk the planet. I'm not even exaggerating. It's fact.

I swallow and push on. "I wondered . . . maybe . . ." I move toward the desk, hoping their faces might soften the closer I get. They don't. "Maybe you'd . . . if . . ." I can't find the right words, as my brain's empty. I look at Danny's desk, searching my mind as I stare at an image of a man. I don't know who. Probably someone they're going to bludgeon. "Would it be . . ." I look up. "Could we—"

"No," Danny says flatly.

"Absolutely not," James adds.

My shoulders drop as they hold me in place with their

deadly glares. "Do you want us to go mad?" I ask, feeling defeated, with not much faith that I can convince them. "Come with us, if you must. Send a chaperone. Put us in bulletproof armor. But please, please, please, can we just go out somewhere?"

"Where?" Danny asks, perplexed, as if he doesn't get it.

"Shopping. I don't know, just somewhere other than here, where all there is to do is dwell on things." I turn my eyes onto James, making sure he's understanding me.

He snorts. "Beau can't do busy places."

"Then we'll go to the beach. The quiet part," I say, sounding way too enthusiastic, given I've not got a yes, and I don't look likely to get one either.

"The answer is no," Danny reiterates firmly. I look at him, hurt, and see the familiar, unmoving man I know too well. "Was that all?"

My eyes drop to the carpet, my small laugh one of disbelief. "That was all," I say, lifting my chin in an act of strength I'm really not feeling. I flick my eyes to James. He's on the exact same page as Danny. Same paragraph. Same sentence. Same fucking word.

It's a no.

"I'm sorry to have bothered you." I turn away, angry with him, with James, and with myself for the unstoppable sting in my eyes. But mostly angry with Danny. No flex whatsoever. I close the door behind me. "Asshole," I mutter, wiping at my eyes as I walk down the corridor, emerging into the foyer. I take a moment, sitting on the bottom step, to gather myself before returning to Beau in the kitchen. I can't tell her what I tried and failed to win for us. There's no need for us both to feel shitty. Or shittier.

On a sigh that Danny could probably hear from his office, I compose myself and take the gold rail to pull myself up but freeze when his office door opens. I hear his boots hitting the carpet. Then another pair.

They appear side by side, pacing determinedly, and my eyes follow them across the foyer until they're near. Danny comes to a gradual stop before me. I look up at him in question as James continues past the stairs in the direction of the kitchen. *Oh shit.* I stand, worried. "He can't be pissed off with Beau," I say, ready to go after him. "She didn't know I was asking for some freedom."

Danny takes my wrist, halting me, and I turn, ready to order him to call James back. "Sit," he says softly, lowering to the bottom step, pulling me down with him. He sighs, and it gives mine a run for its money. "I know I'm asking a lot of you, Rose," he says, looking at me, tortured. "But your safety is topping my priority list."

"I know," I breathe, shaking my head at myself. I don't really have a valid argument. I know of the world outside the enormous, carved wooden doors of this mansion. I lived in it for too long. "I just sat and listened to Beau's story." I reach for his hand, squeezing, feeling like I need to hold on to him. "So I understand why they're here, and I understand why you're now here too. I want justice for them." I smile at him. "And if there is anyone in this world who can help them find that, it's my husband." I stand and turn into him, straddling his lap on the stairs. I take his cheeks in my hands and kiss his scar, and he exhales, circling my lower back.

"You can leave the mansion," he says, almost reluctantly, and I pull back, shocked. "There are firm, non-negotiable rules."

"What?" I'll do anything.

"I know of your exact movements, if you're not with me."

"Done."

"You will have protection. Always."

"Done."

"And this." He reaches behind his back and presents me with a tidy silver handgun. "In your handbag at all times."

I look at the pretty accessory. "Okay," I agree. "And James was okay with it?"

"Like me, James doesn't want to be resented by the woman he loves. You know I'm not comfortable with this, Rose. But I also know I can't lock you up forever." He places a gentle kiss on my lips. *Forever?* "You'll be vigilant. I know your instincts are second to none. If anything is off, you act on it. Am I making myself clear?"

I answer him with a massive, appreciative hug. I'm not stupid. I know when I'm in danger. It's the advantage I have after spending most of my life *fighting* for my life. "Thank you."

He lifts from the stairs with me still attached to his front, reaching back to pull my arms away. He holds out my hand and places the gun in my palm, and I watch his face twist. He's hating this. Hating that he's having to go to these lengths. It's as clear as day that it physically pains him. "I love you," he whispers.

"Said no man ever while handing over a lethal weapon to his wife," I reply lightly, trying to soften his mood.

He huffs lightly, kisses my forehead, and wanders back to his office, and I watch him go, seeing the weight he's carrying on his shoulders. "The kid said he's asked for jet ski lessons so he can beat you before he turns fifteen," I call.

He chuckles lightly, but it takes some effort. "I'm unbeatable."

God, I wish that to be true in every way.

7

JAMES

I stand on the threshold of the kitchen watching Beau. She's in a complete daydream, unaware of my presence, and that bothers me more than it should. I know she has a lot on her mind. Trying to get a balance between fulfilling my mission, *our* mission, and doing what's right for Beau—*being her rock*—is still a fucking nightmare. We may have eradicated one enemy, but we're no closer to extinguishing the ultimate threat. I can only hope that resurrecting The Brit works, because I can't do what I need to do while watching Beau twenty-four/seven.

I eventually make my presence known with a light cough, reconciling myself to the unbearable fact that her senses are dulled at the moment. She doesn't feel my presence like she did. Doesn't know I'm close without actually knowing I'm close. It's not reassuring, especially after what I've reluctantly just agreed to. I need her on form. I need her to dig deep for the instinct inbuilt in her. The instinct she inherited from her mother.

She looks up, and the smile she gives me is half-hearted. It's an insult too. I know this woman inside out. She can't fool me, and she knows that. "Try again, Beau," I order lightly, going to her.

"Try what again?" she asks as I remove her from the stool and take her place, pulling her between my thighs.

"Try convincing me you're okay." I reach up and stroke the bridge of her nose, tapping the end lightly. It's breaking my fucking heart seeing her like this. She's always been broken. I knew it the moment I set eyes on her. But somehow, I've managed to break her even more, all while trying to fix her. It's a complete mindfuck. Defeating. But I mustn't allow the pain it spikes to rule me. I feel murderous already. Considering she could be forever ruined might burn my bloodstream until I turn to ashes.

"Is there any word on Dexter?" she asks. I knew it was coming. Danny clued me in on her quiet word with him at our first dinner in St. Lucia. Beau doesn't want him dead. She warned Danny of that too. I have to give it to him, he did well to keep his cool and not inadvertently hand Beau my balls on a shiny silver platter. I wish I could take that part of this whole fucking mess back. Only that part. I'd do things very differently knowing how Beau feels. I don't understand her compassion where her uncle's husband is concerned. He killed our unborn child. He nearly took Beau from me too. He killed her mother and covered it up. His death was ugly. It's the only murder I've committed and not had my head on straight, because when Danny Black delivered Dexter to me alive, I lost my shit completely. And in the process, I've risked losing Beau to something other than her darkness. So yeah, she can never know that I bludgeoned her uncle's husband. A despicable human that Beau thought was good to the core. An animal so deceitful he could watch Beau rot in despair, knowing he was the root of her agony. *Reprehensible.* He had all the answers to heal her but never gave her that cure. He watched her suffer. Watched her cry. Watched her hurt herself. *Bastard.*

I lied. I *wouldn't* have done things differently. Even now, weeks later, my head screwed back on, I would butcher the corrupt, immoral cunt.

Breathe, James.

"No word," I whisper, taking her nape and pushing her face into my shoulder, avoiding her sad eyes. I have no idea how I'm going to fix this. She'll always ask, and I'll never be able to answer truthfully. She'll never have closure. Therefore, I'll never have my Beau.

Fuck.

I slip my hands under her baggy shirt and feel her naked back. "Do you want to go out with Rose?"

"What?" She pulls out, looking at me in question. "Where?"

"Where do you want to go?"

"Back to St. Lucia."

"Within reason," I say tiredly. "The beach? The hardware store?"

"I have nothing to decorate."

That might be my temporary answer for distraction. Give her a project. It's been her relaxant since her mother died. Can it work now? I'm not sure, so much more has happened. "If I find you something to decorate, will you?"

A small smile, and this one is real. "All of my equipment is still in your glass box."

"Are you finding problems for all of my solutions?"

She gazes around the kitchen that sparkles as much as the rest of the house. "This place is perfect. Nothing needs painting." She sighs, and it's sad. "Where's Dolly?" Her mother's on her mind. Painting. Dolly.

"In the driveway," I say, and she looks toward the window, nodding.

"And the keys?"

"Are somewhere." *Where she can't find them.* I knew she's ask for Dolly. She can have her, but driving her? No. "I've got to go out." I need to go back to my *glass box* and fetch some things. Namely, my mini arsenal of weapons to see us by until Danny's contact delivers.

"Where?"

"My place."

"Can I come with you?" she asks, light lifting in her eyes.

"Why? You want to return to the place where you fell in love with me?" Who the fuck knows what I'll find when I go there? My home, my fortress, was infiltrated by the enemy when the shit truly hit the fan. I may have killed the culprits, but The Bear has more men. Slaying two won't have fazed him.

"Maybe." She shrugs, more light shining in her gaze. But I'm about to dilute it, and I hate that.

"Not today." I massage her shoulder blades, working my hands deep into her muscles. It's a tactic I'm not afraid to use. Soften her. Blind her. "But one day," I promise. "You've yet to finish my office."

"You've yet to compensate me for my time," she quips, and I smile, diving in for a kiss, swallowing us both whole with needed closeness.

"I'll pay you in abundance every day for the rest of my life." It's a vow I'll never break.

I look up over Beau's shoulder when I hear movement at the door, finding Rose hovering there. "Sorry," she murmurs. "I can come back."

"It's fine." I turn Beau between my thighs to face Rose, smiling at the small handgun in her grasp.

She looks down at it, purses her lips, and tucks it behind her back. "They're all the rage." She rolls her eyes, looking exasperated. The feel of Beau jerking a little in my hold, laughing, does inexplicable things to my heart.

"Then I must get one," she jokes, as I reach into the back of my jeans and pull out a matching gun.

I hold it out in front of her, and her head drops. "Didn't want you to feel left out."

Another laugh. "I'd think you're playing," she says, taking it from my hand. "But I know you." She releases the magazine and inspects it, before smacking it back into the chamber.

Rose's eyes widen. "Oh God, I bet you're an amazing shot, aren't you?" She wanders over, the gun looking plain awkward in her grasp. "I forget you were a cop."

"She's a great shot," I say, lifting us both from the stool. "I can attest to that." I give Beau a high brow, and her lips fall into a straight line. Any other man wouldn't have stood a chance. Lucky for me, I'm a fast ducker. Plus, she wasn't on true form, her broken wrist hampering her aim. On that thought, I check her now bare arm. She's constantly clenching her fist, always circling her wrist, as per Doc's instructions, trying to get some strength and movement back.

"You tried to shoot him?" Rose asks over a gasp. "You have to teach me." She looks down at the gun again. "The last time I fired a gun, I aimed at a forehead and took out an eye socket." Rose stills, frowning at her weapon for a few moments. "Ladies' lunch?" she breathes, looking up a little dazed. I catch Beau's curiousness. I bet that's a story about to be told. Good. I'll take all the distractions.

"Go get ready," I say, patting Beau's arse. "Check in every hour and be nice to your personal protection officer."

"Who's my personal protection officer?" she asks my back as I walk away.

"They'll meet you in the foyer in half an hour." Could be

longer. Goldie and Otto are still arguing over who gets the pleasure.

When I get back to Danny's office, I find what I knew I would. Goldie snarling at Otto. "I want to speak to HR," she mutters. "This is discrimination." As if to prove her point, she takes her gun from behind her back fast, disengages the safety faster, and has it aimed at Otto's head even faster than that.

He backs up, hands in the air. "Will someone put a fucking leash on it?" he asks, exasperated. One of Danny's men, Ringo, chuckles across the room. He pays for it, Goldie's aim quickly moving to his chest.

"Pardon?" she asks, her head tilting, daring him to mock her again.

"Didn't say a word." He waves a hand indifferently, taking a seat on the couch next to Nolan and Brad.

"Well, I'm out," Brad says. "I have a nightclub to run."

I take a seat, getting comfortable, feeling we might be here a while.

"Who the fuck's watching Rose and Beau?" Danny asks, his face displaying all the tiredness he's feeling. "Because they're getting ready to leave, and they're going to be pretty pissed off if we"—his finger waves between his chest and mine—"are forced to go back on our word."

Ringo sighs, moving into the middle of the room, just as Goldie does too. "I'll do it," they say in unison, throwing shocked looks each other's way. I don't give them a moment to reconsider or start bickering.

"Fine." I stand, motioning to Otto. "I've got a few things to do."

"Like?" Danny asks, interested.

"Like clear out my old wardrobe."

"Brad's arranged for me to meet someone to run the boat-yard," he says. "I thought you might like to join us."

"You mean that derelict piece of waste land?" I ask.

He grins. "Not for long."

"I'll leave you to do the interviewing. See you later." I pace to the door, eyeing Goldie and Ringo as I pass. I don't need to say a word. They see the look in my eye, the one that tells them I won't hesitate to kill if they let me down. They both nod. I don't know why the fuck everyone was arguing over it. They should have jumped at the chance to take the most important role going at the moment.

"Meet me at the club later," Danny calls, and I hold up my hand in acknowledgment, turning my attention to Otto. His beard has doubled in size since I left for St. Lucia. "You lost your razor?" I ask.

"Yeah, actually," he mutters, feeling at his chin on a frown. "What's the plan?"

"We need guns until Danny's contact delivers."

"*If* he delivers."

"He'll deliver," I answer, certain of that. "I'll drive."

The conversation isn't exactly flowing on our way across town to my building, but it's comfortable. "The safety deposit box," Otto says casually, turning the air con up.

"What about it?"

"When did he empty it and how did he manage that?" He's not asking me per se, more voicing his thoughts, so I remain quiet, letting him continue. "How long has he known your true identity?"

"You're assuming we're right in our assumptions that there was information held in it," I point out, although we both suspect that box at some point had some contents, and the flick of Otto's tired eyes my way confirms it. Jaz Hayley was smart, and she outright told me she was keeping the information on me as security. Along with some other interesting information. So if they got into it, how the fuck did they manage that without a key? "I guess we'll find out when Brad tracks down the bank manager."

"Don't you find it amusing that he had the face of the man hunting him all that time in the footage Dexter removed from the scene of Beau's mother's death?"

"Fucking hilarious," I mutter. And if he really did get to that safety deposit box and my name really was in it, quite frankly, I'd be pissed off I didn't get to see his face when he realized The Enigma, the man who tried to save Jaz Hayley, is the son of Spencer James. Really fucking pissed off, but along with accepting that I'd fallen in love with Beau Hayley, I accepted I couldn't keep *her* as well as my secret. I'm still The Enigma. But no longer *an* enigma.

We turn into the street and a heaviness descends, the silence shifting to a wary quiet, my eyes darting high and low, as do Otto's. I abandon the underground parking garage and continue down the street. "See anything?" I ask, swinging into a space.

"Nothing."

We both get out and round the Range Rover, meeting at the trunk, opening it and arming ourselves. I know Otto has constantly scanned the CCTV over the weeks, but these days I'm living by the motto that you can never be too careful. We lock and load, tucking our weapons into the backs of our jeans as we pace to the main doors of the building—shiny new doors after Butler ramraided the place. Otto pulls up CCTV as I unlock them, looking through the glass.

"Every floor clear," he murmurs, pulling out his gun.

I follow suit and step inside, listening. The whirring of the electric supply is all I can hear, the bank of surveillance screens on the desk the source. We pass them and Otto punches in the code to call the elevator, and the distant sound of the mechanisms kick in. I turn a questioning look onto Otto. I don't need to speak. He's thinking what I'm thinking. The elevator *should* still be on the first floor after we exited it weeks ago.

"When you came back to assist the guys replacing the doors?" I ask quietly.

"The elevator was here."

It requires a code, so how the fuck did anyone use the elevator? In perfect unison, we each move to either side, pressing our backs to the wall, guns poised. My eyes on Otto, his on mine, the sound of the elevator gets louder until it eventually pings its arrival. The doors slide open. We wait.

Nothing.

I nod to Otto, and he swings around, filling the doorway. "Clear," he grunts, disappearing inside.

"The shaft?" I ask, following him in and looking up.

"Clear." He shows me the screen of his phone.

"In the years we've been here, have you ever known the lift to travel up and down without someone using the code?" I ask.

"Never."

"Me neither." But why the fuck would someone be so stupid? "You said the surveillance has been clear."

"It has." The lift stops and we both edge to the side. Otto looks across to me. "I'm watching it live."

"And none of the sensors have been triggered?"

He shakes his head as the doors open, and I slowly crane my head, cautious, my heart booming. My apartment comes into view, and I scan every inch of it, searching for something, anything out of place. I don't tell Otto it's clear. I have a feeling. A horrible feeling. I step out.

"Wait," Otto barks, halting me, my foot in midair ready to place down. "Don't fucking move."

I freeze, holding my position as Otto fucks about on his

phone. "What the fuck are you doing?" I ask, splitting my attention between him and the open space before me.

With his eyes nailed to the screen of his phone, he slowly lowers to his knees. "Just stay exactly where you are," he whispers, turning his eye onto the space directly in front of my boot. He goes lower, onto his forearms, and it's then I see it. A wire. A wafer-thin wire crossing the air just outside the elevator doors.

"Fuck," I breathe, slowly pulling my foot back. "Trip?"

"Definitely." Otto starts to stand, rising deliberately slowly, scanning thin air. "Look." He holds the phone out in front of me, and I take in the footage he's got enlarged. It's live footage from an elevator.

This elevator.

And it's empty.

"Motherfuckers," I say on an exhale, lifting a foot and clearing the wire. "We get the guns, we leave."

"Take it slow," Otto warns, following the length of the line into a nearby cupboard. "Fucking booby traps," he mutters, revealing a pile of C-4 blocks. "We need to leave. They could have remote triggers; they could be watching us."

"Not before I have my guns." I can't fight a fucking war without an arsenal, and despite being sure that Danny's man will kit us out, who the fuck knows when that'll be. I stride through the open space, my eyes high and low, squinting, watchful.

"For fuck's sake, Kel," Otto mutters, coming after me. I stop at the foot of the stairs and check for triggers before taking them two at a time. Another check at the entrance of my bedroom. And another at the dressing room.

I pull out some bags and dump them at Otto's feet before rummaging to the back of my wardrobe and opening the colossal safe. You'd need to blow it up to gain access without a key or code, and lifting the fucker out would require a crane, so I had no concern whatsoever that my stash would still be here. I start passing Otto Glocks, VP9s, Berettas, machine guns, bullets, grenades, everything I have in my possession. The sound of them clanging against each other as Otto drops them into the bags is deafening. "Done. Let's go." I throw one of the bags over my shoulder, Otto takes the other, and we leave, taking the same route.

I come to an abrupt stop at the top of the stairs, and Otto warily skids to a stop too, looking at me in question. I back up, stopping at my office door, checking the entrance. Nothing. If there was anywhere I'd *definitely* go in my apartment if I returned, it would be my office. So why no trigger? I slowly lift my eyes to the bank of screens that dominate the wall, seeing every single one is illuminated, displaying the faces of many men. But not the men I'm going to kill.

I smile. It's twisted. It's dark. I see Brad. I see Otto. I see Goldie, Nolan, Ringo, and every other man I've set eyes on since digging up Danny Black from his grave. And, of course, the main screen, the largest, the one that holds center stage, has a picture of me and Danny. Not together, but . . . together. The two main targets.

"Fuck . . . me," Otto breathes from behind.

I start nodding slowly, running my gaze across the bank one more time before snapping a picture. "Cut the electric to the building," I order. "Do it now."

He goes straight to his phone and a few seconds later, a surge of power lifts and then dies.

"The elevator?" I ask.

"It's the only thing linked to the back-up supply."

I edge past Otto and take the stairs fast, my focus set, and walk straight through the trigger line outside the elevator. "They wanted us to see those screens. The line isn't to trigger the bomb. It's to let them know we're here." I smack the button for the elevator as Otto falls into the cart. "They'll have a remote trigger." The doors close, and we start moving, my eyes watching the floors tick down at a painfully slow rate. "He's going to call any second," I say, my stare rooted to the illuminated digits. "And listen to the explosion while he thinks I'm looking at the gift he's left me." I smile to myself as the elevator comes to a stop on the first floor. I can imagine the elaborate spectacle he would have made of it. Me, looking at my own face on the center screen where his unknown face should be.

I look at my phone when it rings, stepping off the elevator. I answer and put it on loudspeaker, adopting my historical tactic. Silence. "Kellan James," he purrs, using my real name like a weapon. And it cements what we all suspected. My identity *was* in that safety deposit box. My question now, though is . . .

Was *his*?

And how the fuck did he get into it when I have the key?

"I've missed you," I say flatly, striding through the lobby. "Lying low?"

He laughs, and it's truly gleeful. "I heard you've been making friends."

"Nice photograph collection." I push out of the doors, Otto on my tail, and lock them up again. I give him the nod to turn the power back on.

"Ah, yes. Are you looking at them now?"

"I am," I murmur, knowing that's exactly what will be appearing on the screens next. "Deceased," I murmur. "Nice touch."

"You like?"

I look at Otto, who shakes his head in disbelief. That's what happens when you spend years hunting someone. You start to think like them. "Beautiful," I say, stopping at the Range Rover and opening the boot.

"Since you missed the party I threw for your father, I thought we could have a belated one, just for you."

"You're too kind."

"Goodbye, Kellen." The line goes dead, and I look to the top of my building.

Fire bursts out of the windows, spraying glass into the air.

"Fuck," Otto yells, startling at the sound. And then we're both cowering, shards starting to rain down on the street. I quickly throw my bag into the back and jump into the driver's seat. "Jesus Christ," Otto barks, slamming his door, shrinking in his seat as the windscreen is pelted.

"Looks like I'm back from the dead now too," I say, pulling away fast, wishing I could call the fucker back and break the news that I'm still breathing. But I'll just have to keep playing the game.

"You're running out of lives, Kel," Otto retorts quietly, his mood dark. "Let's just get the fucking job done."

I head toward Brad's club, calling Goldie. "I've not taken my eyes off her," she says in answer. "Not for a second."

I wouldn't expect anything less. "Where are you?"

"A small beach in a cove not far from the boatyard Black wants. It's nice, actually. Peaceful. Sun shining, water still."

"You sound close to joining the girls," I say, feeling Otto's dark mood lift. I turn a look onto him, finding him highly amused.

"Got a bikini?" he asks.

"Fuck off," Goldie spits. "I'm still not talking to you."

"What's Beau doing?" I move the conversation along before these two start squabbling like kids again. If I didn't know better, I'd think there was some warped attraction between them, because they bicker like an old married couple.

"Standing on the shore."

"Face turned up to the sun," I add, seeing her in my mind's

eye doing that in St. Lucia every day. *Fighting to stay in the light.* My heart twists and turns in my chest, praying that one day she won't need to fight. "Has she got sunscreen on?" I ask, clearing my throat. "Complete block on her arm?" Because she forgets. All the fucking time, she forgets to protect her delicate skin. I know it's only because she's absorbed by the sunshine, and it's never truly been a problem because I've always been with her to rub it on when she forgets. I'm not in the sunshine now. Not in the light. Not unless you count the fireball that was my apartment billowing in the distance behind us.

"Her sleeves are down," Goldie says, and it's quiet, as if she knows what that means. She does. We went forward so many steps, even amid our crusade for justice. Now? Now I fear she's getting too close to the point of no return. I feel Otto's sympathetic expression aimed my way. "What's the deal?" Goldie asks.

I clear my throat. "My apartment is currently blazing."

"What?"

"A bomb. He triggered it, thinking I was in there." I take a left toward Miami Beach, hearing Otto muttering his curses.

"Fuck," is all Goldie manages. "He thinks you're dead?"

"Not for long." I can never return to being an enigma. Not now I've put us in the heart of the Miami underworld with the resurrected boss of that heart. "We're heading to the club. I want you to bring the girls there." I need Beau close right now. "Use the back entrance. I'll let Nolan know."

"Got it. See you there."

I hang up and breathe out as a screeching fire engine speeds toward us.

We're both silent as it passes, and I look up to the sun, willing it to keep shining for Beau.

8

BEAU

"I'm sure everything is fine," Rose says from the seat beside me in the back of the Mercedes.

I wish I could believe her. But I've gotten to know Goldie's facial expressions pretty well, and her face when she told us we were leaving the beach *now* was grave. I muster the energy to smile, albeit weakly, and accept Rose's hand when she lays it between us. She's gone out of her way to help me today. Moved mountains, literally, considering who our men are, so we could simply leave the elaborate Miami complex that's my temporary home. She's brought me to the light and let me soak it up quietly without a word. I'm becoming quite attached to her. Not dependent, like I feel I am with James, but attached. "I'm sure," I murmur, looking at my cell in my lap when it rings. "Oh God."

"What? Who is it?" Rose sounds worried, so I'm quick to ease her. I pick it up and show her the screen. "Oh," she breathes, lips pursing. She knows all about my dad. In fact, Rose knows just about everything there is to know about me now. No one will ever fill the void that losing my mom formed. The open, nonjudgmental friendship. Honesty. But despite the amount of time I've spent with Rose, I think her guileless acceptance may come close. A friend who knows all and loves me anyway. Just like a mother would. "Checking in?" she asks.

I laugh. "My dad doesn't check in. He calls when he wants something." But I just don't have the energy to hate him anymore. It's a weird feeling. So odd. But other forces are monopolizing my anger these days, and they are forces far greater than my egomaniac father. I brace myself and take the call, cringing my ass off. I haven't even told him I'm back in the country. "Dad."

"Darling," he says, and I roll my eyes. I feel a little bit guilty for my reaction. Perhaps seeing me half dead in a hospital pulled his head out of his ass. It's ironic, really. I've been half dead since Mom died. And now he cares? I remind myself of the supposed genuine dinner invitation from him weeks ago. The one that would involve his *friend*, Frazer Cartwright, who just so happens to be a journalist writing up a piece on the success of Tom Hayley, master businessman. I would have been there as a prop. Nothing more. And I know for a fact I was only invited because he'd deemed me more stable in recent times. I laugh on the inside. I've never felt more *un*stable. Add in the fact that James is now in my life, avoiding my dad feels more compulsory than ever. He'll want to know every tiny thing there is to know about James. His roots. His job. His ambitions. What the fucking hell do I tell him?

"How are you?" I ask. Small talk. Always is, always will be.

"Busy. How are you?"

I recoil in my seat, truly surprised. He never asks. "Good," I answer.

"About that dinner."

I look at Rose, my face twisted. "Dinner," I mimic. "Dinner

with you, or dinner with you and a journalist who's going to write a glowing article on how successful and humble you are? And what a fantastic relationship you have with your daughter."

"Now, Beau," he sighs.

I back down, but only because I'm too exhausted to be locking horns with him. And I'm still sidetracked by the fact that we're on our way to Brad Black's club and I don't know why. "Sure," I say over a sigh.

"Tomorrow?"

I only just stop myself from blurting a straight, *God, no.* I'm too beat to argue with him, but I'm also too beat to endure dinner with my father. "Maybe next week?" I need time to build some energy for this.

"Next week? Are you busy?"

No, never busy. He knows that. "I'm just . . . I have a few things to deal with." This is horrific. Plain horrific.

"Then I'll pop by Lawrence's place to visit with you."

My head drops back, my eyes closing, and I feel Rose rest a hand on my arm. Why has it only just occurred to me that I have no idea how much my father knows? I need to speak to James. "I'm not staying with Lawrence." In fact, the house is sitting empty, Dexter's missing, and my uncle, my dad's wayward, shameful brother, hasn't left his room at Danny Black's mansion yet. He won't talk. Wouldn't even look at me when I checked on him earlier. "I'm not there, Dad."

"Oh?" he says, curious. And then, "Ohhhhh. Him."

Him. That's all it needs, really. *Him.* I don't need my father's approval. I don't really want it, either. But if my near-death experience has brought on this long-lost, concerned, caring figure in him, it would just be a hell of a lot easier to have it. "James." I say his name clearly. "His name is James."

"And you're staying at his place? Moved in? It's a bit soon, isn't it, Beau? How long have you been dating him? What does he do for a living? I should know these things."

For fuck's sake. He deserves to know nothing. And if he did deserve information on my life, I could hardly tell him that my current address is a supposedly dead assassin's mansion. Don't even get me started on the occupation of my boyfriend who I've been seeing mere weeks. And if he knew I was pregnant? *Was.* I let my head drop to the side to find Rose, showing her the immense discomfort I'm feeling. "I'm staying with James, yes." It's not technically a lie. I *am* staying with James. But not at his place.

"Maybe I could stop by there to visit with you?"

I laugh, and it's unstoppable. "I don't think so." My head finds my hands.

"Then bring him to dinner," he suggests, making me balk. "I suppose I ought to get to know this man."

Jesus Christ. "Look, Dad, we'll do dinner." *Soon.* "I'll call you, okay?" Let's walk before we can run. I've spent years hating this man. Blaming this man. Wishing him dead instead of Mom.

"Okay," he agrees, if grudgingly. "But you should know, one of my latest investments is a beautiful luxury apartment block on South Beach. Let me buy you one. The penthouse, perhaps?"

This is too much. "We'll talk about it. I've got to go, Dad."

"Ok—"

I grimace and hang up. "Oh my God."

"He sounds really concerned about you."

"He does," I admit. And I have no fucking clue how to deal with it.

I've been so busy appeasing my father, I don't realize we're idling at the curb around the corner from the main strip on Miami Beach. Goldie and Ringo both look around, Ringo with his hand in the air in silent order for us to wait, Goldie with her cell to her ear. "Round the back," she says, motioning to a side street not far down the road. Ringo pulls away, and a few moments later, we're down an alley outside a pair of black iron doors. His hand comes up again, holding us in our seats as he answers his phone.

"Yeah," he says, as the doors open and the young lad who works for Brad Black appears. "Nolan's here," Ringo says down the line. "What do you want me to do with Rose?"

Rose shoots forward in her seat fast. "Are you serious, Ringo?" she asks, halfway between outrage and humor. I see Ringo flinch in his seat, and I catch his eyes in the rearview mirror. "I'm not his damn prisoner anymore," she goes on. "I'm his wife." Pulling the handle of the car, she slides out, throwing her purse onto her shoulder. "What will he do with me?" she mutters, marching into the back entrance of the club as I get out with Goldie, who looks amused, and Ringo, who looks thoroughly scorned.

"That told you," Goldie teases, closing in behind me, getting close but not physically moving me.

"Fuck off, wench," Ringo spits as he rounds the car, prompting Goldie to laugh her way into the club.

"Glad you two are getting along," I say dryly, feeling my stomach twist as I take in the decadent space swallowing me up. James wouldn't order them to bring me to a place he knows I couldn't cope with. I take comfort in that.

Rich blue wooden paneling lines the corridor with gold-framed portraits set every few sections, each displaying an old photograph of Miami. The battered wooden planks beneath my feet are polished, the ceiling scattered with gold spotlights shining a hazy, dim light on us.

Rose paces determinedly along in front, her glossy dark hair swishing across her back, her jeweled flat sandals clipping the wood rhythmically. Her pretty coral sundress makes her sun-kissed skin glow. I've thought it since the second I met her.

Perfection. It's hard for me to believe this woman was once damaged. I glance down my front, to my torn denim shorts and oversized shirt I've tried to pretty up by knotting the tails. I don't feel inadequate next to Rose. Actually, I feel hopeful. She's like a marker, an example of how I can feel.

If I get through this mess.

"Next on the left," Ringo calls from behind, making Rose slow in her determined strides. She stops outside a room marked OFFICE and takes the handle, pushing the door open.

"It's empty." She looks past me to Ringo. "Where are they?"

Silently, Ringo moves past us, gently but firmly moving Rose aside and entering the room. He holds the door, motioning us all inside, and then closes it and locks it behind us. I frown, looking around the office space. A desk. A bookcase behind it. A couch. A filing cabinet. "This way," Ringo grunts, pushing into one of the sections of the bookcase. I recoil when it pings open, revealing another room. He gets us all inside, closes the door, and puts a long code in on a wall-mounted control panel. The iron door on the other side of the room opens with a click, and Ringo pushes his way inside, revealing a staircase.

We all climb the steps silently, emerging into a huge room. "Wow," I breathe, standing stock-still on the spot, while Rose ventures inside, looking quite stunned too. There are four desks in this office, two corner couches, a private bar, a poker table, many men, and the back wall, spanning one side to the other, top to bottom, is glass with an unrivaled view of the club below. A smile creeps up on me. Glass.

I then realize the room's deadly silent and gaze around, finding all attention pointed at me and Rose. All conversation has stopped. James gets up from one of the couches and comes to me. "Hey," he says quietly, discreetly taking me in from head to toe. His relief is clear. What isn't, is why I'm here.

"What's going on?" I ask, uncomfortable under the scrutiny of all the men.

He hunkers, oblivious to the peanut gallery behind him, and caresses my cheek. "Apart from someone trying to blow me up?"

I withdraw. "You're not joking, are you?" I crane my head to see past his big body, noting the grave expressions of everyone, most of all Otto. He has a Scotch in his hand. A big one. And now I notice the mini arsenal of firearms scattered across the two enormous coffee tables in front of each corner couch. Grenades, pistols, machine guns. "Is that a harpoon?" I blurt as Rose approaches the table, casting an unsurprised gaze across the collection, before wandering to the foot of the glass wall and looking down into the club. I don't know why I'm shocked. I knew what James's collaboration with Black meant, but seeing it spread all over the tables, hearing James just escaped death, and observing the many men in this room, it's suddenly hit home.

War in Miami.

And my boyfriend has the biggest bounty on his head. I look across to Danny Black. He's running a close second, and his contemplative face, his relaxed but tense seated position at a desk, the Scotch before him, too, tells me he's mindful of this. Of course he is.

Danny blows out his cheeks and blinks, getting up from his chair and joining Rose by the glass wall. "We're done," he says over his shoulder, and the men disperse, leaving only us.

I look at James. "What happened?" I ask, seriously considering joining Otto with a strong, large drink.

"Did you have a nice day?" he asks, completely swerving my question. He's not real.

"You tell me you nearly got blown up and then switch to chit-chat of the normal couple variety?"

"We'll give you two some privacy," Rose says, pulling on Danny's arm and eyeing him.

"I don't need privacy. I need answers."

"You don't need answers, Beau," James says quietly. "You need peace."

I inhale, and it's long and deep. He *is* real. He's going to send me out on girlie days while he gets caught up in explosions. I wince, hearing a door close behind us. The room is empty, except for us.

James reaches for my damaged arm and strokes down the sleeve of my shirt, his eyes harboring too much sympathy. "Don't do that," I warn, shrugging him off and walking to the window. "Stop looking at me like I'm broken." I reach the glass. The club's dance floor is clear, the bar quiet, and I see Danny leading Rose across the floor.

"You've been broken since the moment I found you, Beau," he retorts, resentment rife in his words. "I'm not looking at you any differently."

"That's the fucking point," I yell, whirling around. "Yes, I was broken, but I didn't feel it when I was with you. When you obliterated everything, took me to that place you always do when we're intimate, I wasn't broken." I suck back a sob, my voice infuriatingly wobbly. "Now I feel more broken than ever." There's so much more shit to add to the pile. So many more answers I need, and the most horrific thing is that in order to get those answers, I need to let James go out there and find them for us. I have to risk losing the one and only thing that's given me any hope. I feel like I have my back pushed up against a wall.

"What do you want me to do, Beau?" he asks, his cheeks hollow from the force of his bite. "Tie you up? Stick things in your arse?"

"Yes," I choke over a sob. "Do whatever it takes, but please stop treating me like glass."

"You *are* glass," he murmurs. "Because I know better than

anything that if this breaks you, I won't be able to put you back together again."

I bite at my lip, my hands shake, and my arm feels like it's on fire. His face pains me. The mix of anger and sorrow. And I'm not helping him. By being like this, hollow and sad, I'm making James's mission harder, but I don't know how to be any other way. "I think I need to see a therapist," I murmur, trying to keep my words even and strong. "I think I need help." I must be strong. I need to be more like Rose. "I'm sorry."

James rakes a hand through his waves, cursing quietly, his blue eyes tortured. He stalks toward me with intent and yanks me into his chest far harder than he has in weeks. But it hurts way less than not having this part of him. The sure part. The dominant part. The part of him that I need the most. His chest, his solid arms around me, they're home. "Whatever it takes," he says, his mouth at my ear, and then he breaks away. Taking the front of my shirt, he rips it open on an animalistic grunt. Air leaves me on a rushed, shocked breath, along with my woes. The way he's looking at me now is exactly how he looked at me the first time he tied me up. With intent. This. This is what I need. This is what he's refused to give me because my broken body wouldn't allow it.

Fuck my body.

The cups of my bra are tugged down. My shorts yanked open then pushed down to my knees, and he whirls me around fast, pushing me into the glass. My breasts, aching and heavy, squish against the cold pane, and my breath steams the window. I gasp, my eyes darting across the club. But I don't stop him. No one can see us. This room is hidden, a secret space for mobsters, criminals, and assassins to conduct their business and spy on the people below. "More," I mumble, giving him that one word that signals my state of mind. Not that he needs it.

My wrists are seized, and I hear the swift slide of his belt out of his jeans. "More?" he questions, looping the leather around my wrists. "You want more, Beau?" He shoves my panties down, his hand between my thighs, stroking me tenderly. It isn't a sign of what's to come. I close my eyes, resting my cheek on the cool glass, letting my body soften and soak up the feeling of him playing, stimulating, stroking. I've missed this. Missed *him*.

His palm wraps around my neck, his front pushing into my back, and the scratchy feel of his scruff rubs across my cheek. I remain in my darkness, just feeling him. "If you want me to stop, say my name," he murmurs, licking up my cheek with his blazing hot tongue.

"Which name?" I whisper. "James? Kellen? The Enigma?"

"What do you think?" He tugs the bonds, testing them. The friction is instant. My healing wrist jars, and I inhale, soaking up the pain. "Don't fight the bond." It's a message. One I hear loud and clear.

"I won't," I say, wriggling my hands, desperate to break my skin and achieve the luscious burn, the soreness, anything to mask the other pain. I'm at the start of that road to nothingness. "I love you."

"Now's not the time for that, Beau," he says coldly, and then he rams into me with no warning or any scrap of mercy. I cry out, my eyes pinging open, my body tensing, trying to curb the brutal invasion. My mind instantly scrambles, and his name, all of his names, hang on the end of my tongue, waiting to be screamed. And it occurs to me that it's what he wants. His name. For me to stop this.

The thought has me thrusting my ass back into him, egging him on, and he groans, holding the bonds around my wrists with one hand, his spare on my hip. "Fuck, Beau," he breathes. He doesn't want to enjoy this. He doesn't want *me* to enjoy this.

My teeth grind, my hips roll, and I flex them forward, making him slip out of me, before I ram back again, absorbing the blow. But I need his power. His force. The ache, the burn, the deep, uncomfortable pain. "More," I hiss, peeling my damp cheek away from the glass and stepping out wider. "Give me more."

"No," he gasps, shaking behind me.

"Yes!" I slam back onto him, yelling at the glass, fogging it completely.

"God damn you, Beau."

"More," I goad. "More." Another desperate slam. "More, James."

"Fuck!" he roars, crushing me into the window, his hips starting to piston back and forth wildly. "You want more?" he bellows, smashing on, his force brutal, his pace inconceivable. I'm helpless, and it's exactly how I need to feel, because I'm helpless for the right reasons.

"More," I exhale calmly, my body out of control, jerking, banging into the glass, my insides in chaos, but my mind so incredibly calm. I close my eyes and float away with James pounding into me like a rabid animal, his shouts primal, a mixture of pleasure and despair. "More," I whisper, letting the ecstasy take me in their healing claws and indulge me. "More."

The force of my cheek to the glass doesn't hurt. The area of my gunshot wound doesn't hurt. My wrist doesn't hurt. My empty womb no longer hurts. My heart doesn't hurt. My scarred arm that always burns is scorching for another reason, along with every other molecule of me, as I accept James's punishing taking. I peel my eyes open and stare across the room to the tableful of weapons. And I smile. Because not one of them is as deadly as the man currently fucking me like an animal.

His passion-fueled yell of release is muffled, the feel of his cum filling me blistering hot. I exhale and hold my breath, ready to grab my orgasm and let it ruin me, but before I get the opportunity, he's pulled out, dropped to his knees, and pushed his face between my legs. "Shit." I gulp, the sensation of his mouth encasing me making my knees rickety. I fight with the bonds, my heartbeat frantic, my breasts slipping across the glass. It hits me like a wrecking ball, pleasure ripping through me unforgivingly, making me collapse against the glass. "More," I murmur, dizzy with the feel of his frenzied tongue lapping me greedily. It's too much, my nerves shot and sensitive. "James," I murmur, my voice broken. "James, stop."

But he goes on, hungry and deranged.

"James!" I yell, wriggling, fighting the leather securing me. "Kellen, stop!"

But he doesn't.

And I realize.

"Enigma!" I yell, and he immediately frees me of his torture, taking my hips and catching me when I fold to the floor. We're both breathless, both of our bodies rolling uncontrollably, and I ache. But my mind? That's clean. It's a temporary fix, we both know that, but it's a fix for now.

Enigma.

A reminder that he is still, in fact, the man I met.

"I love you," James whispers hoarsely, releasing me of the bonds and shifting to get his back against the glass. And then there's this new side to him. The soft side. He pulls me onto his lap. "With everything I have, Beau, I fucking love you." He forces my face to his, and I crumble on the inside at the sight of his anguish. "Broken, fixed, happy, sad, I love you. If you do anything, just remember that."

I nod as best I can in his hold, running my palm over his slick chest, my gaze following it, unable to sustain his eyes while they're so despairing. "I need to be stronger for you. Like Rose is."

"She's had far longer to heal, Beau."

"I know that. But I feel like I've put her back a few years." I look up at him. "She's still strong."

He smiles, as if I'm missing something, and it makes me wonder if he knows things I don't. Does Danny talk to him about things like that? Am I just seeing an exterior to the warrior queen? "My dad called me again." I rest the side of my head on his pec and let him hold me. "He's offered me an apartment in the new block he's building."

"That was good of him." The hostility in James is rife. "He doesn't even know who I am and he's trying everything he can to get you away from me. Imagine if he finds out I kill for a living."

I smile at his misplaced joke, nudging him with my shoulder. "If I'm going to be forced to endure my father, you have to endure him with me." I feel James's body harden beneath me, and I pull out to gage his expression. It's somewhere between smiling and grimacing. I purse my lips over my smile. "What happened between you two when I was in hospital?"

"You know what happened. Your ex threw around some careless statements, and now your father thinks I'm physical with you in ways that don't involve bonds and my cock."

I chuckle. That's misplaced too. I saw James's reaction to those careless statements. It wasn't anything to laugh about. "Not when I broke my arm. I meant when I was unconscious." *When I was shot. When I lost our baby.*

"Nothing happened." He looks away, and it makes me doubt him. "He showed up, we were civil, and he left."

I didn't see James when I was out cold, but I can't imagine he was civil to anyone. "I need you to humor him."

"I will." He kisses my forehead chastely. "When I can channel my energy into just that, I absolutely will." Putting his hand on my thigh, he rubs it, as if to reassure me that he's speaking nothing but the truth. I can't protest. To say James has a lot on his mind right now would be the biggest understatement in the history of understatements. "Until then, you should start building your bridges with him. Me showing up at your first dinner date will go down about as well as a cup of sick."

I burst out laughing, and every muscle I possess pulls as a result. I just catch his satisfied smile before my body goes limp and I fall against his chest. "He offered, actually. He wanted to visit us."

He stiffens.

"Don't worry, I put him off."

He relaxes.

Then James lets me be for a while, settled, sated, and getting a handle on the aftermath of my laughs as he strokes the inside of my thigh.

"Beau," he says after a time, his hand pulling away and turning over in front of me, revealing his palm.

His palm covered in blood.

"Baby, you're bleeding." He goes to move, and I make myself a dead weight, taking his hand and steadying his shakes.

"My period," I say quietly. "It's my period." I blink my foggy vision clear and snuggle deeper into his chest, feeling his arms envelop me tightly, his mouth resting on top of my head.

It's my first since I lost our baby.

And another reminder that I'm empty.

9

DANNY

I stand on the deserted shore, my feet inches away from the rolling water, taking in the cove. I've been back in Miami for over two weeks, and I'm still breathing. I'm also still married, another achievement, considering how things are progressing, which is basically slow. I assured Rose this would be dealt with quickly and we'd be out of here before she knew it. But really, I accepted the moment I agreed to return to Miami that there would be no going back, not unless we kill every enemy. Yet with each man killed, another is born. I've almost accepted that.

That's why I'm here at Byron's Reach, covering all my bases, watching our plans move into territory I didn't anticipate when I first met James. Plus, there's been no word from The Bear. No moves made on his part. I can only surmise he's letting the dust settle after removing The Enigma. Or, at least, *thinking* he's removed The Enigma. I thought *I'd* diced with death in my time. James is putting my attempts to dodge the Grim Reaper to shame.

Across the water in the distance where Winstable Boatyard once stood is a construction site, cranes and scaffolding dominating the space where I once operated from. I see Pops there. I see him wandering the derelict land that once stood empty. And I see the extravagant cabin he built when I was fifteen. The jet skis. The good times.

The guns.

I haven't yet told my wife about our imminent purchase of this land. Or about our plans to take back Miami. I'm more wary of Rose, her reaction and subsequent retaliation, than I am of a mass murderer on the hunt for me.

I hear the rumble of an old Jeep pulling away. "What do you think of him?" Brad asks, joining me on the shore.

"Well, he fits in around here." The kid, Leon, is all blond curls, bandanas, boardshorts, and pot. But he's smart. That was obvious very quickly.

Brad nods. "And this?" he asks, motioning in the general direction of everything.

"Perfect." That's exactly why we tried to buy it three years ago. Byron's Reach is a prime location to ship anything illegal into the country. It's secluded. Unmatched access. If I didn't know better, I'd ask why the fuck it hasn't been snapped up by a rival. Namely, The Bear. He deals in drugs, women, and guns. Or his minions do. But I *do* know better. After the massacre left behind three years ago when I sold my soul to the Russians and they turned on me, there's an understandable stigma attached to this area. The latest body was dragged out of the water only a few months back. Unidentifiable. The criminals know this place was on the FBI's radar. I should avoid it like the plague.

Should.

I won't.

James's offer to rent the land was snapped up by the legal

team managing the Jepson kid's estate. Now he's in negotiations to buy it.

I smile, casting my eye across the still ocean, taking my shades off to get the full force of the sun reflecting off the surface. There will be jet skis flying across this water in no time. A bustling cabin. An arsenal fit to kick off a world war.

I look over my shoulder, to what was a huge hole in the ground. It's shaping up to be a very useful and compulsory bunker. Or gun store. "Are we on track?" I ask Brad, taking in the cabling and pipelines. Chaka pulled through, unsurprisingly. The shipment arrives this weekend.

"Ahead of schedule. They'll be finished tomorrow."

"Impressive."

"It's come at a price."

"But cheaper than losing, eh?" An army of men are working through the night, and the fruits of their labor are plain to see. The extravagant cabin, a match of the one Pops built across the water but twice as big, is holding court, and the quay's complete. It took Pops two months to build Winstable. We'll have completed Byron's Reach in two weeks. Tough going, but essential, and not only because we have stock arriving imminently— both of the legal variety and *il*legal variety. We need to get this bunker concealed before we have any unexpected guests, namely the MPD or Feds. I've spent over two weeks lying low, letting the whispers of my resurgence be whispers. It's only a matter of time before the police catch wind of those whispers. Speaking of which . . .

"What's our friend Spittle up to?" I slip my shades back on and turn, starting a casual stroll through the site with Brad flanking me. "Still got his dick intact?"

"Len's on him twenty-four/seven. His house is on the market and his wife's in contact with a realtor on the West Coast. Sounds like we've pushed him into relocating."

I pull out a cigarette and offer one to Brad.

He waves me off. "You need to quit."

I light up and take a long, needed drag. "For a man who hates the obvious being stated, you do it a fucking lot."

"Fuck you," he mutters, and I laugh, pinching a sliver of tobacco off the end of my tongue. "How's Rose?" He makes a point of blatantly checking my nose.

"Rose is Rose." Glorious. Fragile but tough, all at the same time.

"You told her about this place yet?"

"She's distracted."

"The wedding," he sighs, showing his disapproval once again. "Bad idea."

"I had to give her something, Brad. Besides, while she's drowning in the logistics of that, she's not on my case. How's Hiatus?" I ask, steering away from yet another occasion when Brad has stated the fucking obvious. Of course the wedding is a bad idea, but I couldn't deny her. Give and take, and all that bollocks. "Ironic name for a club, by the way. Especially *your* club."

He laughs over an eye roll. "It's smooth. No shootings and no enemies. For now."

"You watching your back?" I ask, showing concern we both know is rare. It's pure luck Brad dodged Spittle's bullet. Nothing more, nothing less. We don't operate on luck.

"Like a fucking hawk, man." He holds out his hand. "Give me one of those smokes."

I smile and hand them over, looking over his shoulder when I see James pull up. Brad turns as he lights up, exhaling on a satisfied sigh. "I'm literally surrounded by dead men walking."

"Feeling left out?" I ask on a grin. "Because I can fix that."

He laughs. "Not much in life is guaranteed, Danny. But I can guarantee you'd never kill me. Your wife, on the other hand, is a different matter entirely. She's going to go into full-on demonic mode when she finds out about this place." He takes another drag of his cigarette, like a hit of nicotine can douse the nerves that thought spikes. "And do I need to point out that the reasons you and him"—he motions to James who's nearing—"are walking dead because you got yourselves a bit of ass."

"If she hears you refer to her like that, Rose will definitely kill you. Watch your words."

"Who's Rose going to kill?" James asks, obviously hearing the tail end of our conversation.

"That brave motherfucker." I point my cigarette at Brad before giving James my attention. "What do you know?"

"I know no one's in the market for a new supplier in armory." James takes his phone out and frowns at the screen.

"What's up?" I ask.

"Woman trouble," James mutters, and Brad chuckles, getting dark looks thrown his way from both of us. "You want to add me to the list of people who'll kill you?"

"Fuck me," Brad breathes. "You two are tetchy today. So no one's in the game for a new supplier?"

"Not for guns, not for drugs, and not for women." James gives me a look, *the* look, and I pout to myself.

Seems The Bear has all areas of criminal activity covered. "And you found this out how?"

"Vince Roake."

"Vince Roake?" Brads asks as I frown, the name familiar.

And it comes to me. "The one they call The Alligator?"

"That's the one. Started small time." A flurry of malice flutters through James's blue eyes. "Jaz Hayley arrested him before I could butcher him. He's been on remand ever since."

"Ah, the dead judge," Brad says, and then he frowns. "Why'd they call him The Alligator?"

"He was known to snap."

"What's with all these fucking animal names?" I ask. "It's like the set of fucking Sesame Street." They think they're animals? I laugh under my breath. They've not met me yet.

James smirks, and Brad coughs over his laughter. "So Vince Roake volunteered this information to you, did he?"

"No, his next-in-command did."

"Why would he do that?"

James sweeps his arm out, all chivalrous, his smile sick. "After you, gentleman," he says calmly, and I eye him, following his instruction, walking to his Range Rover. The boot starts opening before we make it there, and I round the car, finishing off my smoke and flicking it away.

We make it to the back of James's vehicle, and I balk at what I see.

"You. Are. One. Sick. Motherfucker," Brad breathes, taking the words right out of my mouth as we take in the sight, James leaning casually on the side of his car. I cock my head, nodding, counting the number of missing body parts. No fingers. No ears. Half a nose.

"Nice," I muse.

James joins us, leaning into the car and pulling off the man's blindfold. He's hardly breathing, but his eyes work, and they widen when he cops a load of me. "Hi," I say cheerfully, lifting my shades to my forehead. "Lost something?"

He garbles a load of fuck knows what, blood spraying from his mouth. No tongue. I look at James. "Well, he can't fucking speak now, can he?" And he also won't last much fucking longer.

James takes a leg and drags him out of the Range, and his body hits the gravel with a thud. "He's got nothing more to tell." Taking an ax from his car, James swings it casually as he stands over the half-dead guy. "Or have you?"

A moan. A weak cry.

"I think that's a no," Brad quips, flicking his cigarette at the man before stuffing his hands into his pockets.

"I got that too," James says, cool as a fucking cucumber as he raises and swings the ax, taking off the guy's right arm. I grimace and take a step back, but Brad virtually dives out of the way of the spraying blood.

"Fuck me, James," he mutters, brushing down the jacket of his suit. "This is bespoke."

"What am I missing?" Ringo appears between Brad and me, taking in the scene. His ugly face twists more, his huge nose wrinkling. Then Otto shows up too, circling the body like a vulture.

James steps over the guy, getting in position for his next hit. "What's my name?" he asks, bending slightly, putting himself in the line of what is certainly blurred vision. "Tell me my name."

A few garbles, but I definitely catch the tail end, deciphering it as "ma." The Enig*ma*.

"You say that to Beau when you're fucking her?" Brad asks, as James raises his arms ready for his next strike.

"You're next, Brad," he grunts, and I chuckle, along with Ringo, Otto, and Brad himself. But we all shut up and flinch when the ax comes down again, taking the guy's left arm. James exhales, looking up at us. "Don't send me psycho." He moves down to the guy's legs.

"You're not now?" Brad blurts, waving a hand dementedly at the mutilated body before us. "I think he's dead, by the way." There are no sounds now. But there's plenty of spasms, the guy's body jerking all over the dusty stones.

"As a dodo," Ringo adds, his face still repulsed. "Definitely as dead as a dodo."

But James isn't done, and we stand there, quiet, as he proceeds to take his legs too, until all we're looking at is a torso.

Like one of those freakish dummies people practice CPR on. But messier. James, finished, stands back and dusts off his hands.

"You forgot his head," Otto quips, and James immediately pulls his gun from the back of his jeans, aims, and fires, sending the bloke's brain spraying far and wide. We all jump back again, out of the firing line of blood and gore.

"And what did they call this one?" I ask, frowning at the sleeve of my shirt, flicking off what I expect is a piece of brain tissue. "The Worm? The Jellyfish?"

"The Dodo," James replies swiftly and coolly, and my eyes snap to his, along with everyone else's. James shrugs. *Is he fucking kidding me?* "Straight up." He points his ax at the remains. "They called him The Dodo."

After a few stunned looks passed around us, we all fall apart laughing, and it's the stomach-cramping kind. The bend-over, delirious, eye-watering, uncontrollable, body-jerking kind. "If you tell me there's one called Rex, I'm quitting life." I chuckle, struggling to catch my breath. "Get rid of him."

"Oh fuck," Brad whispers, and I turn, getting him in my sights. He looks stricken and confused, and I'm thrown by it.

"What?" I follow his line of sight until I have the source of his disturbed expression in view. "Oh fuck," I mimic, seeing all the men in my peripheral vision move back. Behind me. Out of the line of fire.

Busted.

Shit, I thought she had a dress fitting today. "Hey, baby." I slap on a cheesy smile and step in front of the dead body like I might be able to hide it from her. Not because she'll be pissed, but because, frankly, it'll give her nightmares. My wife has seen me kill many men. She's watched me decapitate the Romanian cunt who bought and handled her for years. She's watched me cut out my dad's cousin's tongue and force-feed him it when I found out he was the man who took her baby and sold him.

She's seen some disturbing things. But that was years ago. And I don't want her used to that shit.

"Hey," she says slowly, her scrutinizing eyes circling the men and where we are.

I'm bracing myself for the explosions. I don't know how she got here, how she knew I was here, but I'll find out once I've dealt with this unexpected situation. *And* if I come out alive. I point at the dismembered body. "That wasn't me. I didn't do that."

Her head tilts, eyebrows high, lips pursed. "It looks like a standard Angel-faced Assassin kill to me."

"It was James." I throw an arm out toward him, unhesitant and unashamedly chucking him under the bus.

"Where's Beau?" he asks, stepping forward, tense.

"In the car." Rose keeps me in place with her burning blues as James tosses the ax aside and marches off. "Who is it?" she asks, raising a limp hand and indicating to what's left of James's latest catch.

"The Dodo." I say it without thinking, and laughter erupts behind me.

No. Fuck, no, do not laugh.

My cheeks blow out, and I try so fucking hard to shut off any orifice that could let me down. The knobheads behind me aren't helping my cause, snorting and tittering in the background. *Death wishes, the lot of 'em.* It's no good. I lose my fight and bend at the waist, having to brace my hands on my knees to hold myself up. I haven't laughed like this since leaving St. Lucia, our life taking a swift turn from carefree and easy to serious and, frankly, fucking taxing. I need this release. Rose, however, looks like she needs to punch me in the face.

"You finished?" she asks, her posture threatening.

I focus on composing myself like my life depends on it, because it probably does. "Finished." Back to serious business. I raise a hand in indication for everyone to fuck off and leave me to handle this alone. "What are you doing here, Rose?"

"Me?" She looks at me like I've sprouted horns. "What are *you* doing here?" She motions around the site, to the diggers and cranes and piles of materials. She knows what's happening.

"No," I say firmly, and she recoils, indignant. "You will explain. How did you get here?"

"I drove."

"You gave Goldie the slip?"

"No one gives Goldie the slip."

Oh, for fuck's sake. "You held her at gunpoint, didn't you?" My lips straighten, annoyed. "I gave you that gun so you can protect yourself, not so you can brandish it at my men/woman when you feel like it." This isn't the first time this has happened. But it'll be the last. I stalk forward and grab her bag from her shoulder, rootling through. "Where is it?" I ask, looking up for an answer. I don't need one. It's on the tip of my nose. Literally. My eyes travel up the barrel to her hand, up her arm, across her shoulder, her face, to her eyes. The wicked glint is satisfaction personified.

"What are you doing here?" she asks calmly, pushing the tip of the gun into my flesh.

I move fast, dropping her bag and grabbing the gun, twisting so she spins into my chest. I lock down her arms, squeezing her hand until she drops her grip. I could have asked her for the gun; she would have given it to me. But where's the fun in that? My mouth at her ear, I growl, "How did you know where I am?" The woman infuriates me.

"I tracked you."

"What?" I don't like how smug she sounds. Not at all. She tracked me?

"When you were asleep last night, I shared your phone's location with mine."

"You did what?"

"You heard. I knew you were up to something, Black."

I release her and turn her to face me, my patience fraying. "You promised me you'd be wise." Leaving the mansion without protection isn't wise. "I'm fucking livid, Rose."

"And you promised me you'd wear a bulletproof vest." She reaches for my shirt and rips it open, revealing . . .

A bulletproof vest.

It's not the best on the market, but it had to do until Chaka delivers. Rose gasps, stepping back, and I tilt my head, my look expectant. Like, *give me an apology now before I fucking strangle you.*

She looks up at me. Her lip wobbles. "You listened to me."

"Of course I fucking listened to you." I'm a brave man, but my wife truly terrifies me at times. Not because I'm petrified she might pop me. Punch me. Rip a strip off me. But because she might leave me. I take her neck and drag her into me. "Don't take this as an amnesty. I'm still really fucking irate, Rose."

"So am I. Why are you here, Danny?"

"I'm recreating what Pops built." I don't try to fob her off. She needs to know, and hopefully she'll soon gather without me having to tell her that a quick exit from Miami is looking less likely with each day that passes.

She pulls out, and I quickly straighten my twisted face. It's times like this I wish I could play poker. Then maybe I would've had practice nailing my poker face. "The boatyard?"

I nod.

"Jet skis?"

I nod again.

Her head tilts. "Dealing?"

My lips press together. It's the only answer she needs but, surprisingly, she doesn't fly off the handle.

"You said we were here temporarily."

"I can't fight a war unarmed, Rose. I don't know how this is going to play out. They think James is dead and Miami has gone silent."

"Then let's leave," she begs, fisting my shirt and pulling my face down to hers. "We'll go back to St. Lucia. Beau and James, you and me. If they think James is dead, that's good, right?"

I take her hands from my shirt, peeling away her clawed fingers, smiling softly. Rose has spent plenty of time with Beau. As couples, we've had a few dinners over the weeks, trying to keep things relatively normal for the women. Rose knows that leaving Miami without killing the root of James and Beau's problems isn't an option. And is she forgetting that The Bear knows I'm alive? She's clutching at straws.

"Listen to me," I order, taking her nape and guiding her away from the corpse close by. "Remember how much you loved the boatyard?"

"Don't try and convince me you're doing this for me," she mutters.

"I wasn't going to." I stop us at the shore and point out to the water. "We had our first proper kiss somewhere over there."

"And don't start trying to be romantic. It's also where your jet ski blew up right after."

"Good times, eh?" I take her hand, bringing her rings to my lips and kissing them, eyes locked on hers. She's softening. I can see it past her deep blues. "Don't you think Daniel would love it here?"

She casts a look over her shoulder to James's handywork. "Sure," she says, as sarcastic as fuck. "Can't wait to show him."

"Let's FaceTime him, then." I seize her bag and pull her phone out, handing it over. "You've been avoiding telling him we're back for weeks, feeding him some spiel about your phone's camera being broken so you can't FaceTime with him." I know she's been hoping that she wouldn't have to tell him. That I'd take care of business and we'd be back in St. Lucia before Daniel had to know we were ever here. "We're not going home anytime soon, baby." I hate it, but I'm managing her expectations. "Daniel's less that ten miles away. Make the most of it." It'll be another distraction for her. I'm grabbing at them all, because I seriously don't want her worried or stressed.

Her dainty shoulders drop, her hand coming toward me to accept her phone, at the same time accepting I'm right. Acceptance still looks amazing on her. She dials and takes herself to a nearby rock, perching on it, holding the phone up and pulling a smile out of the bag. "Hey!" she chimes and, very quickly, she isn't forcing her happiness. I need to get back to that place in her heart where Daniel resides. The place that's reserved only for true smiles and genuine contentment. Nothing hurts me except for Rose's sadness.

"Where are you?" he asks immediately, obviously assessing the backdrop.

"I'm in Miami."

"What?"

"We took a little vacation. Thought we'd visit *you* for once."

"Mister's here?"

"Yeah, he's here." Her arm appears in the air, out of the shot of the camera, and frantically waves me over. Because she can't turn the camera around. I pull my buttonless shirt together as best I can and go over, settling on the rock next to her.

"Hey, kid."

"Hey, Mister." He beams at me, and it is one hundred percent life. Every time I look at this kid, I see every quality I love in his mum. Softness. Looks to kill. Acceptance. A massive heart and extraordinary resilience. Because this kid has had a bombshell, and he's taken it all in his stride. Shown Rose nothing but approval and love. Seeing him also makes me sad, because I can never give her kids. I can't give her a pregnancy without despair or fear. A baby, a toddler, a preschooler. She missed out on all of that.

Daniel's suddenly pouting, and it prompts Rose to speak up. "What's up? Did you find your hamster?"

"No. And I'm also not allowed to take jet ski lessons," he says, totally solemn.

I snort. Says who? The couple who bought him on the black market? "I've got a surprise for you," I say, lifting my shades.

"What? Tell me." The kid looks like he could pee his boxers at any moment, and Rose casts me a dubious look that I ignore as my phone rings in my pocket.

"I'll show you when you visit." I stand, dropping a kiss on Rose's head as I fish my mobile out. "I've got to take this. See you soon, kid."

"When?"

"I'll let Mum sort it." I walk away, taking Esther's call. "She's here," I say immediately, knowing she'll be worried.

"For Christ's sake," Mum breathes, rattled. "Has that woman got a death wish? Goldie's flipping."

"Where is she?"

"Zooming toward you, I expect." The second Mum's finished speaking, I hear the undeniable angry screeching of tires skidding down the track.

"She's here. Thanks, Mum." I hang up and look across to Rose, who is in the middle of saying her goodbyes to Daniel. She clicks off the call. "You're in big trouble," I say on a shake of my head.

"Save me," she sings, throwing the back of her hand to her forehead like some twisted damsel in distress. I grin. But I'll make damn sure it's gone when I face Goldie, who I can hear marching up behind me. I turn.

And nearly have my eye poked out by her pointing finger.

"Do not ever ask me to watch them again," she seethes, nostrils flaring.

I close my eyes and gather some patience. I know how fucking cunning my wife is. Goldie's mood is simply a reminder of the shit I have to deal with as a consequence. Looking over my shoulder, I find the object of my deepest affection and my deepest fucking frustrations, nibbling at her lip nervously. "See what you've done?"

"It was my fault," Beau calls, hurrying over and joining Rose on the rock, putting an arm around her friend protectively. Partners in crime, these two. Thick as thieves. I'm only marginally grateful in this moment, when I've got what I'm sure is a premenstrual black widow hissing at me.

James joins me. He looks about as happy as Goldie. "Never again," he practically growls at Beau. "Clear?"

Are they holding back laughter? God help them.

"A word," James says, tearing his warning eyes from Beau and walking away. I give Rose a look that suggests if she moves, I'll set Goldie on her. Then I follow James, giving Goldie a sorry look as I pass. She isn't happy. I can't blame her.

"It was bad enough when there was only one of them," she growls, going back to her car. Why am I not surprised that Beau gave her trouble as well? I'd say sorry, but Goldie would possibly shoot me for that too.

"What's up?" I ask, falling into stride next to James as he walks toward the shore.

He rakes a hand through his hair, showing a certain level of stress. I've not known James long, but in that time, I've figured out a few things beyond doubt. For starters, I like him. It's a rarity. He loves fiercely like me. His woman's peace is his end game. He hunts his prey and rips them limb from limb, literally. But I've also learned he doesn't show stress. He walked away from his obliterated apartment unfazed, so whatever's on his mind is heavy. "Beau's not letting it go." He turns toward me, flicking his eyes to the girls, who are still perched on the rock, looking too beautiful amid the construction site and graveyard.

"Dexter," I say, showing my understanding. "What do you need me to do?"

"Give me his body."

I throw a stunned look his way. I don't know what I was expecting, but it wasn't that. Maybe I thought he'd ask me to talk to Rose. Ask her to talk to Beau. I don't know, but having his decomposing remains dug up? "You serious?"

"She needs closure. For that, I need his body."

"Fuck me," I breathe, joining him with a rake of my hand through my hair. What a gift. "I'll see what I can do. How's her uncle?" The guy has practically barricaded himself in his room since he arrived at the mansion. The doctor's come and gone. The meds have rolled.

"Not good. I'm not his biggest fan, but he means a lot to Beau, so if I can fix that shit I will."

I blow out my cheeks, reaching for another cigarette. "I need a drink." I offer one to James on the off chance he might accept this time; he looks like he needs one, but he shakes his head and I get to pulling one out with my lips. "The men probably do too after your little rendition of *Texas Chainsaw Massacre*." I nod to the body. "The fucking Dodo," I mutter, walking away as I light up. I've only been back in Miami a few weeks, and hell knows I could do with a break from it already.

James motions to the bunker. "Ready to give me a tour?"

I smile, leading the way to what was a massive hole in the ground. "Waterproof, fireproof, and bomb proof," I say proudly, taking the steps down, James following. Once we're in the expansive room, where the walls are lined with a racking system to hold the arsenal that's on its way from Chaka, I point to the top of the stairs. "There will be a hatch there. The green container will sit over this. Will look like any other container in the yard."

He nods slowly, taking in the space. "Looks good."

It does. "You coming to Hiatus? I want you to meet someone." I take the stairs and the men lower the container over the bunker with the crane.

"Who?"

I turn, walking backward, lifting my shades, smiling ruefully. "I've got a private audience with the mayor of Miami." I can't fucking wait to see Perry Adams's face. Can. Not. Wait. I imagine it to be somewhere between haunted and petrified.

The new boatyard is nearly done. The guns will be here imminently.

It's time to get Miami talking rather than whispering.

The club is quiet, which is the *only* reason Rose is here. I even let her sit at the bar and have a glass of wine. Surrounded by men, of course, but still. It's relatively normal. The bartender, a unique human with every inch of his revealed skin tattooed, including his face, sets a bottle of white on ice in front of her before passing Brad a fresh bottle of Black Label. "On the tab," Brad says, waving for Nolan to come over.

He leaves the crowd of suited heavies and approaches. "Yes, boss," he says, as keen as ever.

"These men"—he indicates each one forming a semi-circle around Rose at the bar—"don't move. The doors covered?"

"Covered."

"The office covered?"

"Covered."

"Good man." Brad slaps Nolan's shoulder and points the bottle across the club. "We'll be in the office. Bring our guest when he arrives." Brad leaves, and I look up at the guy before me who's blocking my way to Rose. He's a giant, at least a foot taller than I am and ten times wider, bearded, and probably bullet-proof too. He wouldn't look out of place on the set of *The Vikings*. I tilt my head expectantly. He doesn't move.

"What's your name?" I ask.

"Tank."

I laugh lightly. Makes sense. "The woman behind you, that's my wife. Do not let anyone near her."

"She'll be safe, Mr. Black." He takes one side of his jacket and eases it back, revealing a Glock.

I smile. "Good man." I pull out a wedge of notes and slip them into his pocket. "It's a well-paid position. Great bonuses. Perks if you do a good job."

"What are the perks?" he asks, a subtle glint in his eye.

"You don't die."

He pales, just a little. "Understood."

"Good." He remains unmoving, like a dam that'll never break. "When I say don't let anyone near her, I'm an exception," I say, and he nods, moving one step to the side to let me pass. Once his big body is out of the way, I find Rose on a stool, a glass of wine in her hand, one leg crossed over the other, her expression knowing.

I don't entertain her curious look, settling on the stool beside her. "Enjoying your wine?" I ask, taking the glass from her grasp and helping myself to a sip.

"I was, yes." She claims it back. "Where's Beau?"

"James took her back to the house for a checkup with Doc."

"Why? Is she okay?"

"She's fine," I assure her, cupping her cheek, quick to put her mind at ease. "She missed her routine checkup yesterday because you two were wedding shopping. James rearranged for today and wanted to make sure she showed up."

Rose's lips purse. "She's been good. Not wincing as much, not lost in thought so often."

I smile, leaning in and kissing her. "You've helped."

She shrugs, blasé. "It's a good thing we get along. Anyway, I wanted to talk to you about the wedding."

The wedding. "What about it? Changed your mind?"

"No." She nudges me, but a sadness washes over her. "Who's going to walk me down the aisle?"

I withdraw, taken aback. I wasn't expecting *that*. "You want to be walked down the aisle?"

"It's traditional."

"We're not traditional," I point out. Traditionally, a father hands his daughter over to a man. Kind of like a transfer of ownership. "You'll walk yourself down the aisle. No one owns you anymore, Rose. That's the fucking point. Not even me." I lean in and kiss her deeply, feeling her smile around my lips. "But make no mistake, baby, you are unequivocally mine." I reach for her wine and place it on the bar before pulling her onto my lap, swathing her. "Are we clear?" I ask into her neck, mauling at her flesh, sucking, kissing, and biting.

"Clear." She giggles, wriggling, and as a consequence, my dick gets a firm grind of her arse. I groan. "We need to talk about my bachelorette party."

I freeze. We absolutely do not. Quickly withdrawing from the crook of her neck, I place her back on the stool. "I'm needed." I get up, plant a brief, pacifying kiss on her forehead, that I know won't pacify her, and move away before she can pin me down. Tank steps aside, I step past him, and he quickly steps back into place like a sliding automatic bulletproof door.

I give him a grateful nod. It's like he knew I needed a fast escape.

"I'm having one," Rose calls from behind him. "So you better find a way to make it happen."

Tank's lip quirks, his eyebrows high. I don't know what he's finding so amusing. As soon as I've got word that he's good people, he'll have to deal with her too. "Can I clone you?" I ask, sizing up the other men in the semicircle, knowing James will be on the same page as me. They all look capable, all stoic, all unmoving. But Tank? He is literally that.

He releases a low, hardly heard laugh, but doesn't reply, and I head toward the back of the club, giving Nolan a flick of my eyes. He joins me in a heartbeat. "Tank," I say, making him look over his shoulder. "What do you know about him?"

"Ex pro cage fighter. Criminal history. Father dead, mother in a residential care home."

"What's the history?"

"He decapitated the man who killed his father."

A mercy kill. He's *definitely* my kind of people. "Do you trust him?"

"Of course. He's honorable, Mr. Black. All the men we have here are certified loyal."

I make it to the corridor that leads to the office. "But I haven't certified them," I point out, and he nods, backing down. "You have some employees arriving." I nod past him, to the flurry of leggy women strutting up the metal stairs to the balcony bar where the dressing rooms are. "Tough job, eh?"

He laughs and gets on his way, and I look to Rose, knowing the appearance of an army of strippers is likely to draw a reaction. Problem is, I can't fucking see her past the mountain of a man shielding her. It's reassurance, and I need reassurance right now.

I head into the staged office and go to the bookcase, opening the way to the staircase that'll lead me to the men. I punch in the code, take the stairs, and when I walk in, everyone falls silent. I've always said silence speaks louder than words, but now? Now, I have no clue what this silence is saying. I slowly close the door, casting my eyes across everyone in here—Brad, Ringo, Otto, Goldie, and Bud. "Is anyone going to speak, or are you all just going to sit there and leave me wondering why you look like we have a problem?"

"Because we might have a problem," Brad says as he pours a Scotch. I have a feeling it's for me.

"Might?"

"I'm being optimistic." He slides my drink across the desk and necks his own. "We have a problem."

"Wha—"

The door opens behind me and James strides in, coming to a cautious stop when he sees us all looking his way. Silent. "What?" he asks.

"Good fucking question." I go to the wall of glass, where I have a perfect line of sight to Rose, Tank not quite towering to these heights. Beau's with her now, the girls drinking and chatting. I'd smile if I wasn't busy wondering, and worrying, what this fucking problem is. "Talk," I order, going to one of the desks and pulling a chair out, lowering, expectant eyes on Brad.

"The guy who heads up the bank where Beau's mother had her safety deposit box . . ."

"What about him?" James asks, settling beside me, his eyes lasers on Brad, waiting. "Fucking talk, Brad."

"His name's Kenny." Brad pours a vodka and pushes it toward James. He doesn't take it, his attention elsewhere. "Kenny Spittle."

I recoil, stunned, immediately turning my eyes onto James, who's resting back in his chair, the glass now in his hand. His expression. It's taken on an edge of psycho.

"Brother?" Otto asks, going straight to his phone.

"Son," Brad confirms, holding up a photograph, a picture of a very happy family by the sea. The Spittles. Father, mother, son, and, what I assume, girlfriend or wife to son.

"So the safety deposit box that supposedly has one key," Ringo says, "of which we are in possession, is held at a bank that's managed by the son of a corrupt, retired FBI agent who asked James to kill Brad and ratted out Danny?" He's taken the words right out of my mouth. It's too convenient to be a coincidence.

Brad nods, and I turn a look onto James. He's quietly seething in his chair, his fingers clawing the glass in his hand tightly. "Drink it before you shatter it," I say, reaching for the bottle to top mine up. "Whether whoever got into that box had a key is irrelevant. Either Spittle's son granted them access to the vault, or he took the contents of that box to them." Spittle must be having fucking kittens. It explains a lot. After his business with me three years ago, he would have avoided being trapped again. I'm a man of my word. When he fulfilled my final order, I got rid of the pictures that had held him to ransom for years. I didn't need them anymore, since I was dead. But now Spittle's involved with another player, and the other player—we all know who that is—has pulled Spittle's son into the mix. It's irony at its fucking worst. The man who helped me die has brought me back to life. Just to get me killed. And now I have fuck-all ammo to use against him.

"Find Spittle's son and bring him to me," I order. Not quite *no* ammo. "And call Len. Advise him of the developments and tell him not to take his eyes off Spittle. Not even for a second."

Ringo goes to his phone immediately, starting to pace up and down. James is still quiet. "Another drink?" I ask, undoubtedly interrupting him from planning what order he's going to take Spittle's limbs.

James says nothing and holds his glass toward Brad, who's quick to top him up. "We need to find out when that safety deposit box was breached." He looks at me, and I see the questions spinning in his warped mind. Finding out when that box was breached will also tell him how long The Bear has known that James, The Enigma, the man who has slaughtered dozens of his men is, in fact, Spencer James's supposedly dead son. Or *was*, since James is supposed to be dead again. He's survived two explosions. How many times can this man die and come back to life?

"I'm sure Spittle's son will tell you if you ask him nicely," I muse, assessing James's persona, watching as he gets more strung by the second. "How's Beau?" I need to distract him before he blows up and takes this office with him.

James frowns and looks across at me. "What?"

"Beau. How did it go with Doc?"

"Fine. She's fine." He returns his attention to the desk, back to seething. "How many men have I got to kill before I get to him?"

I blow out my cheeks and look at Otto. He's thinking the same as me, which is, basically, Miami had better hold tight. "Drink," I order, getting up, feeling like I need to stretch my legs. I go to the glass wall and check on Rose again. Tank hasn't moved an inch, therefore Rose hasn't either. There's a magazine on the bar. I can't see it from here, but I know what it is. They're scattered all over our bedroom. "When's Adams due?" I ask when Ringo's finished on his mobile to Len.

"Just pulled up."

I nod, my eyes still on Rose, hoping she keeps her back to the club. I don't want her anywhere near Adams. It's petty, especially for a man of my status, both in this world and in my wife's world. I have no competition. Still, the previously bent politician's dick has been inside my wife, and whether she enjoyed it or not, that fucking sucks. Being inside her is nothing short of fucking heaven. I can attest to that. No man could ever forget it. Every man in their right mind would want more. My eyes narrow, my teeth naturally clenching, and I look toward the entrance of the club when I see someone enter out the corner of my eye. I let out a little puff of laughter, watching as Perry Adams, briefcase in hand, heavies *to* hand, walks across the club floor like the king he thinks he is. A brush with death— AKA *me*—obviously didn't knock him down that peg for too long.

I watch him closely, not only to see if he clocks Rose at the bar, but to see if his famously roving eye even glances at any of the dancers parading around half-naked. His focus remains forward. I nod approvingly, taking some Scotch. Perry Adams looks composed.

Not for long.

I turn and find James still reeling in the chair, the desk before him about ready to crumble to cinders under his concentrated stare. "Ready?"

He inhales, slowly rising. The man is radiating fury. "Ready." Another long slug of his drink before he strides to the door, Otto not far behind.

"Hold him in the club until we've moved to the downstairs office," Brad says down the line as we follow. "Given the latest enlightenment, you still think Spittle doesn't know who The Bear is?" he asks quietly.

"I can't see it. Apparently, no fucker in this town knows who he is." And isn't that the most maddening thing. "I can't imagine he'd disclose his identity to a retired FBI agent who's got a mouth on him."

"The son?"

I shake my head mildly, my eyes on James's back. "I don't know, but I guarantee you who'll find out," I say, taking the stairs.

"I want a front-row seat," Brad grunts, his lip curling.

"Still holding that grudge?"

"Spittle, the prick, asked that mad fucker"—Brad's finger

comes up, motioning to James's back—"to bump me off. So yeah, I want popcorn too."

I laugh, eyes still on the mad fucker. With James around, I probably wouldn't need to get my hands dirty ever again. But . . . well, I like getting my hands dirty. "Third time lucky," I say quietly, entering the office.

"I need to associate with safer people," Brad mutters, pushing the shelving unit closed behind us and going to his phone. "We're good."

I join James on the opposite side of Brad's desk, our backs to the door, and pull out my cigarettes. "Do I need to cage you?" I ask in gest, offering James the pack. His eyes turn slowly onto me. He's in no mood for jokes. "Just let me lead this, okay?" I go on as he takes a smoke. "I know Adams. I know what makes him tick." I hold out my zippo to him before lighting my own.

"Knock yourself out," he grunts, exhaling as he gets comfortable. Trying to quit? Not while we're in Miami.

Brad appears in front of me, taking his chair, and I look over my shoulder to see Otto and Ringo looking cozy on the couch. I return my attention forward as the door opens, and I watch Brad's eyes move past me, his smile slowly forming.

"I'm honored," he coos. "The mayor of Miami making a special trip to my club."

"I've been wondering since you summoned me why," Perry replies. "Why would Brad Black, ex mobster now nightclub owner, want to visit with the mayor?"

"And what did you conclude?" Brad pouts.

"That he wants something."

"An extended license would be great," Brad says, and I smile. "Thanks, Perry."

"You'd have to apply."

"But I'm friends with the mayor."

"I'm straight, Brad. And we're not friends."

"Okay, I'm not your friend." His hand holding his glass extends across the desk, pointing to me. "But he is."

"He? Who's he?"

I slowly stand and turn, slipping my cigarette between my lips and sucking back a hit of nicotine, keeping my eyes up. His face. It's fucking golden. "Hello, Perry," I say over my exhale, sending smoke billowing into the room.

"Fucking hell," he whispers, frozen. It takes him a few minutes to find any more words, and I let him take that time, thoroughly entertained. "I'm completely legit now, Danny. I've got to be. The town is in order. Oh fuck, don't start creating anarchy."

"Me?" I ask over a laugh. "I've been dead for three years, Perry, and by all accounts, there's not been much peace around these parts."

"It's being handled."

"What's being handled?"

"The gangland killings. Criminals turning up dead everywhere. The police have it under control. It's quieted down."

Quieted down? *Yes, because The Enigma has been on holiday in St. Lucia and was blown up when he returned a few weeks ago.* For fuck's sake. "So there's no problem with drugs? Women? Guns?"

"This is America. There's always problems, but it's not an outright war out there."

Not yet, no. But Perry had better brace himself. He's also hinted to something that supports what James found out earlier. There's one person controlling Miami, and it isn't who the people elected as mayor. The Bear has woven a pretty solid web of crime, somehow getting every crook in this town to answer to him. Who the fuck is he? "Sit down, Perry," I order, and he scurries over to a spare chair, dropping into it. This is the Perry Adams I remember. Constantly shitting himself.

"I haven't cheated on my wife since Rose," he mumbles

nervously. I ignore James and Otto, who have both just inhaled loudly enough for me to hear.

"Never speak her name, Adams," I warn. "That's the first new rule."

"You gave me your word. I got you every scrap of information on that lawyer, Green," he rushes on, keen to detail his good deeds. "I cleaned up my act. You said—"

"Have I asked you for the thirty-five million you owed me?" I ask, and he shakes his head. "The photos of you with Rose are gone." I burned them while I shook with fury at the sight of another man's cock in my wife. "And I don't plan on killing you." I walk over, standing before him. "So I've kept my word."

"You're not going to blackmail me?"

Fuck me, how does such a pathetic piece of shit run this city? He's an embarrassment to men. "No, I'm not going to blackmail you, Perry." I smile, and it's dark. "I'm going to ask you very nicely for a few things from time to time, and you're going to give them to me because I'm your friend and that's what friends do for each other."

"Like what?" he asks, surprised but cautious.

"Well, first of all, I need a permit for the work I've had carried out at Byron's Reach."

"The work you've carried out? Already? Without a permit?"

"There was no time to apply. I'm sure you can get something sorted retrospectively, can't you, Perry?"

"What have you built there?"

"Just a cabin. There's a few containers." *A massive underground bunker that'll be full of firearms.* "And my new jet ski business."

"You need a permit for that too," Adams says, almost reluctantly.

"Then get me one," I fire back, my face serious. "That's all for now." I walk away and help myself to a drink from the bar, which is a piss-poor alternative to the well-stocked display in the hidden office upstairs.

"But you're dead. How do I make out official documents to a dead man?"

I turn and point my drink at James, who remains with his back to Perry. "Put them in his name."

"Who is he?"

"Danny James." The bloke's got more fucking names than the Queen of England, but he had a source who could get us a new identity quickly, and we needed a new identity quickly.

"But *who* is he?" Perry pushes.

"You don't want to know. Is that all?" I ask tiredly.

I know Perry Adams is actually the one wondering that question. Is that all I want from him? A few papers and an easy route to being legit. Or appearing legit. Perry will never know about the bunker. No one will ever know about the bunker.

Adams stands, a bit flustered, and edges his way to the door, eyeing everyone in the room, as if he's worried any one of us will pull a gun at any second.

"Nice seeing you, Perry." Brad beams. "Just forward the license when it's ready."

"Oh." Ringo slaps a palm on his forehead. "I forgot to pay those parking fines."

"I'll get it sorted," Adams says, looking to Otto, waiting for his demand.

"I'll have a cheeseburger and fries, please," he says, deadpan, and James shows his first signs of amusement since we left the boatyard.

I hide my smile and go to the door, opening it for Adams. "Good seeing you, Perry." He looks like he's been hit with a stun gun. Danny Black, The Brit, opening a door for him.

His men are waiting on the other side, and the moment their attention points this way, his shoulders rise, his chest expands, and his chin lifts. Fucking dickhead. I slam the door and exhale. "I still don't like him."

"Nothing to do with the fact he's fucked your wife," Brad says, standing.

"What's with that?" Otto asks, hands facing the ceiling. "Forgive me, but he's a bit of a pleb, and your wife . . ." He stalls, thinking better of it.

"Is hot as fuck, I know." I give the hairy, pierced fucker a slap on the shoulder. "I like you, Otto. Let's not change that."

"Who's this lawyer? Green?" James asks.

"Derek Green. He's the man who bought Rose's kid on the black market."

"Adams knows that?"

"Of course he doesn't fucking know that." Does he think I'm stupid? "As far as Adams is concerned, Rose needed legal representation after I died. That's what he knows." I feel like I need a head massage. And I'm fucking starving.

"We all set for the delivery?" James asks, looking onto the club, watching.

The guns. He can't wait to load the new bunker and declare his own resurrection. "Chaka called earlier. Tomorrow morning. Be ready." I leave the office, my direction automatic.

Rose.

When I reach the bar, Tank is still in position, along with the other men. "Can we lose the other men?" I ask, and he gives a short sharp nod. "And you might have noticed, but there's another female behind you now. Who do I need?"

He points across the club, prompting me to turn.

And laugh.

"Fuck me," I breathe, taking in the guy, a dead ringer for Tank in every way but slightly smaller in build. Only slightly though. "You're a twin?" I ask, giving him my attention again. He nods. "What do they call your brother?"

"Fury."

"Do I need to ask why?"

Tank shakes his head and moves to the side, giving me access to my wife. She's oblivious to my presence, lost in articles on cakes, table settings, balloons, and more. She can have whatever the fuck she likes, but I draw the line at a bachelorette party, and only because she'd refuse me an invit . . .

My thoughts drift off, and I tilt my head back to look up at the unit of a man guarding my most prized possession, smiling to myself. "You work for me now," I tell him, and he nods sharply. "My wife's well-being is your one and only concern." Another nod. "Every second I'm not with her, you will be." Nod. He's like a robot programmed to obey my every order.

"And when you *are* with her?" he asks, eyes forward.

"I'm growing to like you, Tank, but I'll never invite you into our bed for a cuddle. When I'm with her, you'll know when you're needed or not. I'll organize a room for you and your brother at my home. Do you drive?" Nod. "Your brother?" Another nod. "I'll organize cars." I move past him and get up close and personal with Rose's back, my chin on her shoulder. It's been a long fucking day, and I need it to end with food and a fuck. "You can have a bachelorette party," I whisper, and she stills, her fingers on the corner of the page ready to turn it.

"Why are you saying that like I needed your permission?" she asks, her tone even. She turns the page again, all casual and unflustered. I look out the corner of my eye to Beau. She's doing a shit job of concealing her smile, dragging her glass closer and pushing the rim to her lips in attempt to hide her amusement.

I was expecting a bit of gratitude. I should have known better. "Because you *do* need my permission, but if you'd rather go without . . ." I detach my front from her back and push her empty glass toward the tattooed-covered barman.

"I wouldn't," she blurts, flying around on her stool and

circling my midriff with her arms, squeezing her head to my chest. "Thank you, master."

Beau snorts over her wine glass, and I give her a warning look that goes right over her pretty blonde head. I don't know what she's so tickled pink about. I might have agreed to a party, but James hasn't agreed to let her join in the celebrations. "Don't push me, Rose."

She looks up at me, her face accusing. It throws me. "So when were you going to tell me that Hiatus is full of semi-naked women?"

"Hiatus is a strip club," I say coolly. "Perfect place for a bachelorette party."

"What?"

"I thought Friday night would work."

"The night before our wedding?" She balks at me. "I don't want a hangover on my big day."

"Then don't get drunk."

"Danny—"

"It's that or nothing, Rose," I say, making her nostrils flare. She knows the deal. She knows she can't go parading around town on a night out. What does she expect from me?

"And what about you?" she asks.

"What about me?"

"Are you having a bachelor party?"

I shrug, unbothered. "I'll have a few drinks with the boys."

Her shoulders drop, all fight leaving her. "Here. On Friday night too."

"Yes. Come on, we're going for dinner." I nod toward Beau, indicating that I mean all four of us.

"Where?"

"A little Italian place in the center of Miami." I quirk a brow at Rose, and her jaw drops open. "Rose and I had one of our first dates there."

"Awww," Beau coos.

"Yes," Rose breathes, her expression full of sarcasm. It's a sign of what might come next. "Danny murdered a man for appetizers, threatened to kill me during the main course, and then butchered an old enemy for dessert. It was so romantic."

I grin as Beau laughs, completely unfazed. "My first date with James was at the opera. He handcuffed me to a chair in a box and left me there while he disappeared to murder a corrupt judge." She toasts the air and finishes the last inch of her wine. "Where is he, anyway?"

I look over my shoulder and see him striding this way, and I break away from the girls to meet him. "Cooled off?" I ask.

"If you want Spittle alive, father *or* son, I suggest you make sure I'm not around when they're brought to you."

"Noted. See that guy behind me?"

James cranes his neck, looking over my shoulder. "The one who's as wide as the bar?"

"That's the one. Tank. I figured Goldie might have a problem with any further requests to watch them, so I've outsourced. There's one for you too." I point across the room to Fury, and James looks.

"You trust them?"

I see Brad emerge from the corridor with Nolan and wave them over. "He checks out." The others arrive. "I'm taking Tank," I inform Brad. "And what can you tell me about his brother?"

"He's got fists like boulders, and it's alleged he's bulletproof."

"His story?"

"Served time with his brother."

"Cozy," I murmur, taking in the unit before turning to James. "You good?"

"Good."

"I'm going to need to replace them," Nolan pipes up.

"Then replace them," Brad says, pulling Nolan toward the bar, talking quietly.

James leaves me and heads for Fury, motioning him to a nearby booth to talk. That's one issue sorted. I absolutely cannot be worrying about where and when my wife might turn up. I pull my phone out and go to the settings, shaking my head to myself at her sneakiness as I turn off the location sharing feature, looking at her as I do, waiting for the notification to drop on her phone. All I can see is Tank. But then Rose's head slowly appears, craning around his big body. Her face. It's thunder. I blow her a kiss, happy with myself, and lift a foot to join her o—

What the fuck?

Time slows to practically nothing, like one of those bad dreams that drag and drag and torture you by keeping you there, as I watch a group of men enter the bar, all lined up, all sneering, all looking pumped up on power. *Fuck!* The guns in their grasps all rise, and I swing my eyes to the bar, seeing the first signs of real movement from Tank.

"Incoming!" I bellow, reaching to the back of my trousers and pulling my gun, ducking at the sound of the first shot. It's not from me.

"Fuck!" Brad dives over the bar for cover, resting the nose of his gun on the wood, firing constantly as bottles on the optics shatter above him.

"Jesus Christ." I aim and fire, taking one of the men down, aim, fire, taking a second, my attention split between the gang and the bar.

"Get down," Tank yells to the women, moving fast, getting a grip of a nearby table and ripping it from the floor, the bolts holding it in place surrendering easily with a ping. He puts himself back in front of the women, holding the metal tabletop before him like a huge fucking shield.

Thank fuck.

"Danny!"

At the roar of my name, I instinctively drop to the floor and look up, just as another of the men is taken out. He flies back, hitting the deck.

"Stay down!" James yells, and I roll to my back to get him in my sights. He's stalking toward me, firing left and right, popping off men like coconuts off a shy. I see Ringo under a table, his lip curled as he shoots, and Otto with his back to a speaker, reloading.

James stops a few feet away from me, his gun still poised, his eyes darting. I turn over, checking the club. And then I see him. Backing out of the door, a sneer bigger than Miami coating his familiar face.

"What the fuck?" I whisper, starting to get up, my boiling blood starting to fry my veins. I stare at the entrance, struck.

No. It can't be.

"Where the fuck is Beau?" James roars, snapping me out of my trance.

I slowly turn my eyes onto Tank, who's gingerly lowering his shield. The relief that courses through me when he reveals Rose and Beau hunched on their stools over the bar, arms over their heads, is rampant. Rose turns and cautiously frees her head, peeking up at me. She nods at me and exhales, taking Beau's arm and shaking her. "Beau?"

She doesn't move, and my heart races as James sprints full-pelt toward her, taking her body gently and firmly. "Beau?"

She looks up at him, her eyes wide. "I'm okay," she says, her voice croaky. Her words don't satisfy him, and he starts patting her all over, lifting her shirt, checking her legs. "James, I'm fine."

"God damn *fuck*!" he yells, yanking her into his chest. "Who the fuck was that?" He's frantic. It's understandable. Beau's not long out of the woods, and here she is dodging bullets.

I find Tank with blood on the sleeve of his white shirt. "You good?"

"Just a flesh wound." He brushes me off with a wave of his shovel-sized hand, taking a nearby stool.

I raise my gun, pacing through the club, and when I make it to the entrance, breathless, I check left and right, searching the street outside. Nothing. But I saw him. And he didn't look very dead to me.

"Get inside," Brad hisses, yanking me back into the club and slamming the doors. I step over two bodies, my mind reeling as I head straight back to Rose. I pull her off the stool. James is still holding Beau to his chest, still looking like a restrained monster.

"It was Volodya," I say, starting to pull Rose through the club, tossing the keys of my Merc to Tank. "Let's go." How the fuck can this be? Spittle told me he was dead. He fucking told me!

"What?" Brad asks, audibly stunned.

"We're talking about the same Volodya, right?" Ringo asks, tailing us. "The same Volodya who shot you at the Winstable massacre?"

"Yes," I grate, still seeing his beady eyes in my mind's eye.

"He's dead," they say in unison.

"So am I," I remind them, pushing the door to the rear alley open with the head of my gun. Tank moves past us, opening the back door of the Merc, and I usher Rose in.

"Are you sure, Danny?" Brad asks as James appears, pulling Beau along behind him.

He gets her into the back of his Range and joins us. "Volodya?" he asks, as the pressure in my head builds and builds. "Russian mafia? You told me he was dead."

"Well, he obviously fucking isn't!" I explode, losing my shit and aiming at a pigeon on a nearby wall, blowing the fucker apart. I need to kill. Anything, I just need to fucking kill. On that thought, I stalk back into the club and work my way around the bodies, kicking each and every one. Finally, I get what I'm looking for. A murmur. I drop to my knee next to him, snarling in his face as he squints, blood trickling out the corner of his mouth. "Where will I find Volodya?" I grate.

He has a pathetic attempt to spit in my face, the saliva and blood spraying his chin. I locate his bullet wounds, one in his thigh, one in his stomach. "Talk," I demand, taking my thumb and shoving it into the hole in his belly, making him squeal. I twist and turn, the squelching sound fucking hideous. "No talking?"

I lay my gun on the floor and insert my other thumb into the bullet hole in his leg, giving that a few circles. He starts convulsing and jerking, his eyes rolling. I pull out my thumbs, my shoulders dropping in disappointment. He's passed out. Shame. If I thought Doc could save him, I'd have him taken back to the mansion to torture. But I know a dead man when I see one. I pick up my gun, push it into his eye socket, and blow out his brain. "Get Spittle," I yell, standing and pacing out of the club. "Now!" I circle the Merc and get in the back, slamming the door shut with force.

I feel Rose's worried eyes on me immediately, her hand going to my thigh and squeezing. And without thought, I reach up to my shirt and apply pressure to the old bullet wound below my collarbone from where that Russian motherfucker shot me three years ago.

No war in Miami?

10

ROSE

Esther is fussing around us like a hen, trying to keep our minds occupied with talks of tents, decorative topiary trees, and God knows what else. Beau looks rather engrossed. Me? I'm wondering what the point is, because if today is anything to measure things by, I won't have a fucking husband to marry.

The moment we returned to the mansion, Danny called Doc down to check out Tank's arm, James took Beau to their room to double-check every inch of her body, and the men all filed off to Danny's office. Poor Tank. He'd barely been in the job for a half hour before sustaining his first injury. And poor Beau too. James was not taking her word for it that she was unharmed. He wanted visual proof. She was exasperated, and James was a bull, physically carrying her away when she fought him.

I stare at the cup of tea Esther's made me. It's her go-to. Upset? Have some tea. Stressed? Have some tea. Angry? Have some tea.

"What do you think?" Beau asks, looking at me for an answer.

"Of what?"

Esther sighs, and I shrug. "I didn't hear."

"Come on." Danny's mom circles the island and joins me, presenting me with a catalogue. "The oyster or the blush?"

I consider the two dresses, both stunning, both silk, both undeniably Esther. I've learned many things about Danny's mom in recent years. She's incredibly soft but hard as nails. She's compassionate and patient. I've also discovered that she has impeccable dress sense since she's been living here as Danny's mother and not his housekeeper. "I love them both," I say, looking at the kitchen door. "How long have they been in there?" I peek at the kitchen clock. We've been back two hours, it's dark outside, I'm dog-tired, but I won't be able to sleep. I can't even begin to imagine the kind of carnage on the horizon. Well, actually, I can. And that is why I'm fucking petrified.

"I'll make some tea," Esther declares.

"You know, I think I'm going to go to bed." I can't stomach any more tea or pretending that I'm fine. I slip down from my stool and drop a kiss on Beau's cheek, and then Esther's. "Good night."

"Night," they both murmur as I trudge away on heavy feet, Tank tailing me. When I make it to the entrance hall, I stop, listening, seeing if I can hear anything from Danny's office. Nothing.

I sigh and take the stairs with effort, clinging to the gold rail to help pull myself up. My heels clink on the marble steps, echoing around the deserted space. Letting myself into our bedroom, I kick off my shoes and pull my dress up over my head as I pad the carpet to the bathroom. I drop it in the laundry hamper and put myself in front of the recently replaced mirror, reaching back to unfasten my bra. I set it on the vanity and rest my hands on the edge, leaning in, inspecting my drained complexion, staring into eyes that look as haunted as they did when he held me here against my will. I feel the same kind of overpowering suffocation and helplessness now. Except this time, I feel there really is no way out. Only by death.

I consider my toothbrush. The array of cosmetics I have to clean my face and remove my makeup. But I don't have the energy. I push away from the unit and go to bed, crawling under the covers. But I don't sleep a wink.

When the bed moves, I open my eyes, looking at the clock on the nightstand. It's two in the morning. He's been holed up in his office with his men for hours. His chest presses to my back, his hand stroking up my thigh, and then his lips are on my shoulder blade, kissing in slow, soft circles. My body lights up. Always does. I'll never stop my natural reaction to his closeness, but I don't respond, my mind having other ideas. "No," I say quietly, and his strokes of my leg stop, his lips unmoving on my skin.

"Rose?"

"I said, no."

A heavy, loud sigh, and he's quickly not touching me anywhere. The bed dips again, and a few seconds later, I see his silhouette move across the bottom of the bed toward the doors that lead onto the terrace. My eyes follow, and when he pulls the drapes back, allowing the moonlight to stream in, I permit my eyes to absorb every impressive inch of his naked body. I start at his feet, drift over his sturdy calves, up his legs, across his solid ass, his back, his shoulders, and eventually his neck, where his hair flicks out at his nape. He's an Adonis. A masterpiece. Still a deadly one, but also a devoted, fiercely protective one.

Danny Black. The Brit. The Angel-faced Assassin.

But more than any of that, my husband. My lover. My friend.

He pushes the door open and steps out onto the terrace, and I roll to my back, staring into the darkness. My mind circles.

Get some sleep, Rose. You're going to need some energy to keep resisting me.

Resist him. I couldn't then, and I can't now. *God damn me.* I get up and go to the balcony, finding him slumped in a rattan chair, his elbow wedged into the arm, the side of his head propped on his hand. A cigarette rests between his fingers, the end burning away, just inches from his hair. Troubled. He looks so troubled.

I don't want to add to that. It's twisted, backward, crazy, but I have to be here for him while he figures this out. He needs that familiar peace. He needs me, and I can't deny him what he needs, especially when I know I'm the only person in this fucked-up world who can give it to him. It's a blessing. It's a curse. It's pressure.

I go to him, putting my body in front of his, and he slowly lifts his eyes to mine, his face straight. I push my panties down and climb onto his lap, straddling him, lifting a little to hold his cock while I lower onto him, taking every perfect inch of him slowly, exhaling as I do. He remains impassive, the cigarette getting dropped, his hands taking my hips lightly. Our eye contact doesn't falter. But our breathing does. It's ragged, broken, strained. I start moving, circling, biting my lip as I take his shoulders for support, and his head drops back, his eyes hooded, drowsy with need, but every single thing I love about his icy blues is maintained. Fire. Passion. Love.

I begin rocking on him, taking in air with every grind, the friction wickedly good. There's no need for me to speak. To apologize. To tell him how I feel and how sick with worry I am. This man, this sick, murdering, twisted man, knows me inside out. As acutely as I know him. We need this right now. This closeness. Our crazy connection.

I move my hand onto his scar, focusing on it as I lift and fall gently, my head spinning with pleasure.

"My most important job is to protect you," he whispers, turning his face into my hand and kissing it.

"No." I fall forward and take his mouth. His gorgeous, absorbing, addictive mouth. "Your most important job is to stay alive." My kiss is firm. It's possessive. It's consuming, passionate, and rough. It embodies him. I taste Scotch. I taste nicotine. I flex my chest gently, moaning, the tingles building, but Danny gets there first, and he moans his release, his body tensing against me. For once, he'll leave me unsatisfied, but that's okay. This was for him. *His* release. *His* needs. *His* peace. "I hate you," I whisper around his lips, pulling away to get his face in my sights, stroking and feeling at his cheeks gently.

His forehead falls onto my shoulder, his sigh weary. "I love you too, baby."

With my hands stroking his hair, I hold him to me and gaze across the mansion's grounds. And I wonder, how long can he sustain the weight of this world this time around?

When I wake the next morning, I'm alone in bed. My mouth is dry, and I have a dreadful anxious feeling in my tummy. I feel around on the nightstand for my cell, at the same time circling my stomach with my palm. It's ten thirty. I can't remember the last time I slept past eight. There's a text message from Danny.

Morning, baby. I've got things to deal with at the boatyard. Back this afternoon. Let's do dinner tonight. Just us.

His words bring a small smile to my sleepy face, and then my phone pings and an image fills my screen. Of him. My beautiful, killer husband.

The Rolls-Royce of bulletproof vests. Happy?

My smile fades. Things to do at the boatyard. Take a delivery. I sigh. I'll never be happy that I must force my husband to wear a bulletproof vest. And last night at the club, the ambush, the confirmation of enemies far and wide, is why. I thought we'd kissed goodbye to the dangerous world that brought us together. The world we barely survived.

My stomach churns, and I groan, edging to the side of the bed and going to the bathroom where I'm in range of a toilet to throw up in if I need to. I flip on the shower to cool and get under the spray, willing this awful queasy feeling away.

I feel no better by the time I've washed my hair. Anxiety has never featured in my life. I couldn't let it. My walls were high, the bricks solid, but the moment I met Danny Black, cracks began to form, and bit by bit, the wall has come down, exposing me. I love it. I hate it.

I hear a knock at the bedroom door, followed by Beau calling my name. "Come in," I shout, pulling a towel down and wrapping myself in it. I step into the bedroom as she pushes her way into the room. I catch a glimpse of Tank and Fury in the corridor, practically filling it. "Hey," I say, taking a brush off my dressing table and starting to work my way through my wet tresses. "Have you been in the gym?" I take in Beau's sporty-clad body. She looks magnificent. Tight black leggings that enhance her shapely legs, a sports bra that makes her tits look phenomenal, and a washboard stomach that I could file my nails on. Her blonde hair is piled high, her face fresh, her eyes alive and shining. Whatever she's had, I want some. These past few weeks, she's come on in leaps and bounds, working out, chatting more, smiling more. But more amazing than how amazing she looks this morning and the progress she's made recently is the absence of sleeves. Her brutally scarred arm is out on full display for all to see. And as if she's noticed I've noticed—how could I not? —she lays a palm over her forearm, as if her dainty hand can hide it.

"Too much?" she asks, immediately making me feel terrible. I'm not staring because I'm shocked.

"God, no." I shake my head, ridding my hand of the brush. "I'm proud of you." So proud. It seems while Beau is taking steps forward, I'm going backward. "Did you put sunscreen on?"

She rolls her eyes, going to my wardrobe. "Yes, I put sunscreen on." She rummages through my clothes. "Come on, we have a busy day."

"Doing what?" I ask, perching on the end of the bed, suspicious, wondering if Danny's been in her ear, telling her to keep me busy. Undoubtedly.

"First, we have target practice," she says, huffing. "Do workout clothes exist in your life?"

Target practice? "I'm no gym fanatic, Beau. The closest thing I have to sports attire is a wetsuit, and that's back in St. Lucia."

"Then this will have to do." She whips out some yoga pants and a loose-fitting T-shirt. "Get dressed and get your gun." She throws my clothes beside me and pulls her cell out from the back of her leggings when it rings, sighing at the screen.

"Your dad again?" I ask, starting to dress. "How many calls have you dodged now?" She's doing anything she can to avoid seeing him, and I know it's because she's worried he'll knock her back a few too many paces.

"He's called every day." Gazing at the screen, she visibly inhales and answers. "Dad." She starts pacing, looking at the ceiling every now and then. "I'm sorry, I've been busy." She turns toward me and shows the ceiling one palm, cringing. "Yes, I'm good. No, I'm fine." Her hand meets her forehead. "Yes," she sighs. "Tonight. Okay." She tosses her phone to the bed and grimaces. "Can't wait," she adds to herself, looking at me with begging eyes. I don't know why. There's not much I can do to get her out of it.

"You can't avoid him forever."

She blinks a few times, seeming to completely lose the brightness she's gained recently.

"Beau?"

Shaking her head, she joins me on the bed as I pull on my T-shirt. "My mom said that to me the night she died." Looking at me, she smiles sadly. "She was desperate for me to make amends with him."

I reach for her hand and hold it tightly. She might be telling herself she's doing this for her mom, but I can see the lost little girl inside her. The one hidden behind the fierce cop and warrior woman. "How's your uncle?" I've still not met him. If I didn't know better, I would think he's a figment of Beau's imagination.

"Doc's coming over later." She pulls her hand from mine and reaches for her cell, tapping away at the screen before tucking it back in her leggings. "I honestly don't know what to do. He's a shell. It's like the roles have reversed. He's always been there for me, forcing meditation on me, trying to pick me up when I hit rock bottom, which was a lot." She shrugs. It's an offhand move that's far from offhand. "Obviously he's in shock, but I think it's the unknown too, you know? He's had no explanation from Dexter. No opportunity to try and understand. He needs closure."

So does Beau. Someone she loved, someone she trusted, not only betrayed her, but delivered a blow, literally, that killed her unborn child and put Beau in a hospital. She'll be lucky if she ever gets her head around that. "I hope you both find that closure." I pull my wet hair into a ponytail, unable to face blow-drying it.

"Are you okay?" she asks, frowning at me.

"I'm fine." I slap on a smile, unwilling and unable to offload my woes on my friend. Her strength is putting mine to shame. "Are you?" I counter, deflecting the question.

She eyes me suspiciously. "I'm fine. Doc checked me over this morning."

"But you had a checkup with Doc yesterday." Twice. Before and after the shoot-out at Hiatus. I shake my head to myself. A shoot-out. *For Christ's sake.*

"James is just being paranoid." She stands and pulls down the waist of her leggings a little, revealing her wound. It's no longer angry, the bruising faded completely. "Hardly notice-able," she murmurs. I wouldn't say that, and even if the visible scars fade to nothing, I know the hidden scars will always be there.

I find my purse, pull out my gun, and slip my feet into some sneakers. "Ready," I declare, holding my pistol up and posing Charlie's Angels style.

Beau laughs, mirroring me. "Never send a man to do a woman's job," she says, flipping me a wink. And just like that, I'm smiling with no effort at all. Beau is literally a godsend in my life, and I know she feels the same about me. An urge too powerful comes over me, and I throw my arms around my friend, hoping she appreciates just how much I appreciate her. "I feel the same," she says quietly, embracing me, both of us with handguns in our grasps.

"Watch where you're pointing that gun," I say, my words thick, the lump in my throat growing.

She holds me tighter. "We're not allowed to cry."

"I know."

"Then stop it," she orders, pulling away and catching the wayward tear trailing down my cheek.

"Sorry." I quickly brush at my face. "You do know what you've let yourself in for, don't you? I'm a terrible shot. Ask

Danny." We head for the door, and I swing it open. Tank and Fury turn, and both back up into the wall when they catch sight of the guns in our grasp. "Oh, crap." I shake my head, holding up a hand in surrender. "I'm not going to shoot you," I assure them, although I seriously wonder if a bullet would even penetrate their humongous frames. They both relax. "How's your arm?" I ask, pointing at Tank's bicep with my gun.

His hands come up. "Mrs. Black," he says, his voice pleading. "C'mon."

"Shit, sorry." I lower my weapon, and Tank relaxes once again. "We're going shooting."

"Where?"

"I don't know." I turn to Beau. "Where?"

"Somewhere in the grounds. It's big enough." She heads toward the stairs. "We're not leaving the mansion so no need for an escort."

I follow, as do Tank and Fury, ignoring her. "Strict orders," he grunts. "You won't know we're here."

I look over my shoulder as they follow us down the hallway to the stairs. They can't even walk side by side, they're so wide. "I doubt it," I murmur.

After bypassing the kitchen to each grab a coffee, we make our way to the gardens. Esther's on one of the pathways, talking to a lady I don't recognize. She shakes her hand, all very officially, and Bud takes over, escorting the woman to the gates. "Who's that?" I ask, pointing. With my gun.

"We seriously need to teach you some gun etiquette," Beau scorns, pushing my arm back down. "So, who was it?"

"I was interviewing her for the housekeeper position."

"Ohhhh," we both say, long and drawn-out. Something tells me it's another no.

"How many is that now?" I ask, smiling when Esther narrows her eyes on me.

"You think I'm being fussy."

I laugh. "I don't think you're being fussy." She's being *very* fussy. "What was wrong with that one?" My arm muscles engage again to point, but I manage to keep them under control.

"I haven't put my finger on it yet."

"Well," Beau says. "You better pull your finger *out*, because Danny will be hiring for you if you don't."

Her shoulders drop. "I wouldn't ask him to hire someone to do *his* job."

"What, kill people?" I ask over a laugh, which isn't at all appreciated by Danny's mother. Her warning look is fierce as I sip my coffee, backing away with Beau.

"Where are you two going, anyway?" she asks, eyeing our armed hands, and then our two personal protection officers.

"Shooting practice."

"Don't forget the tent company will be here later to talk about where it'll be set up."

"I won't."

"And the men's suits are ready to collect."

"Great."

"And your dresses will be delivered tomorrow."

"Super." A wedding, a celebration, doesn't seem quite appropriate now. I pout, my stomach turning again, dislodging that anxiety. So I drown it with coffee.

"Um, Rose," Beau says, grabbing at my arm.

"What?"

She starts backing up, her eyes round.

Confused, I locate the source of her wariness and find Danny's two Dobermans, Barbie and Cindy, before us, their thick necks extended, their eyes set. They're not growling. Not barking. But they're wary, their stance threatening. My confusion multiplies. They're used to me now, and they're used to

Beau too, so what's their problem? "Hey, girls," I coo, extending a hand for them to sniff.

They growl, and I quickly retract my offering. "Okay, don't move," I warn Beau, watching them closely, quickly weighing up our options.

"You want me to just stand here and wait for them to eat me?"

"They're not going to eat you."

"You sure? They're literally licking their lips, Rose. And dribbling."

They are, and it's weird. And then it occurs to me. I slowly look over my shoulder. Tank and Fury are stock-still behind us, shitting themselves. "Don't move," I warn them quietly.

They don't. Not their eyes, not anything on their colossal bodies moves a whisper. Fuck, I don't know how to handle this. "Sit," I order, but they don't sit. Instead, they start to growl and snarl. "Shit, I think they only listen to Danny."

"Where's Danny?" Fury asks from behind, his voice shaking.

"The boatyard."

"Great."

"Sit," I blurt. "Lay!" But they remain unmoving, their hackles up, their stare stuck to Tank and Fury. God damn it.

I'd take the mutts over you any day of the week.

Wise. They're less deadly than I am.

I smile at the memory. "Heel," I order, and the dogs are up like lightning, charging toward me and sitting at my feet like good little girls. I give them all the fuss they deserve, hearing Tank and Fury exhale their relief. "Away!" They dash off, barking, and I smile. Way less deadly than Danny, and yet I still wouldn't want to be on the receiving end of their bites.

"Are you okay?" I ask Beau.

"I'm fine. But I don't think they are." She nods toward Tank and Fury. The twins look plain terrified.

"I thought it was your job to protect us," I say, smiling and pivoting, wandering off, armed with my gun and my coffee.

"Your aim is completely ridiculous," I grumble, taking one step closer to the wall where every single one of the tin cans Beau set out for me is still standing. Every. Single. One. I peek at Beau's side of the wall. No tin cans. Because they're all scattered within a twenty-yard radius with holes in them.

"Loosen your grip. You're too tense." She aims and fires, barely lining up her shot. "Too tense, the shock jerks you and your aim will be off."

Tank and Fury both nod, agreeing. Feeling the pressure of my audience's close observations, I try again, closing one eye, holding my arms out straight but not stiff.

"And squeeze the trigger," Beau says quietly.

"Squeeze the trigger," I murmur, doing just that. A bang sounds, followed by a high-pitched ping, and a can flies off the wall into the air. "Ha!"

"See?" Beau comes over, taking the gun from me. "We're out of bullets." She looks across to the Vikings in silent question.

They both shake their heads in perfect sync. "Spoilsports." I pout, then I hear Esther calling me. I shade my eyes to try and see her, squinting. And when she comes into view, I gasp. "Oh my God."

"What?" Beau's quickly shielding her eyes from the sun too, trying to see what's got me panicked.

"My boy." What is he doing here? *How* is he here? I start hurrying toward the house, taking him in. God, he's grown more in the weeks I haven't seen him.

"Rose!" Beau yells, and I'm suddenly jarred to a stop, being dragged back. She turns me away from Daniel and takes the gun out of my hand.

"Shit," I murmur.

"Now you may go," she says, ushering me away, pushing both the guns into the back of her leggings.

I continue toward him, taking him in from head to toe. I do it every time. Assess every beautiful inch of him, every hair on his head, every fleck in his blue eyes. "Hey." He gives me one of those half hugs kids of his age do, a kind of push into the body and one arm around the receiver's back. He's gotten even taller. "Will you please stop growing? I can't keep up." He's nearly overtaking me.

He points back at the mansion. "Whose house is this?" he asks, looking stunned.

My lips press together, and I glance to Esther for help. It's actually mine, since Danny signed everything over to me on his death. But, obviously, I can't tell him that. "We're renting it."

"Who are all the men everywhere?" He looks past me, his head retracting at the sight of Tank and Fury.

"They work for Danny." Shit, this was a bad idea. The questions are just going to keep coming. "How did you get here?"

"Esther picked me up from school."

"She did?"

Esther smiles, tilting her head at me. What is that? What's going on, and why don't I know about it, especially when it's concerning my boy? "I'm doing burgers for dinner," she says, ignoring my questioning face. "Do you want one, Daniel?" She just can't help it. There will be no new housekeeper. She relishes her . . . what does she call it? *Faffing* too much.

"Sure," he says, distracted by the mansion. "It's massive, man."

"Daniel, this is Beau, my friend."

"Hi, Daniel."

"Hi," he says without even looking at her, transfixed.

"Hey." I poke him in the shoulder. "This is my friend Beau."

Ripping his attention away from the house, he smiles awkwardly. "Nice to meet you."

"You too." Beau backs away, keeping her back, where our two guns are tucked away, out of sight. "I'll catch you later. I'm going to check on my uncle." She reaches behind her and turns stealthily, keeping the guns concealed.

"Hope he's okay," I call as Fury passes us, shadowing Beau.

"There's a delivery for you," Esther says, motioning toward the drive.

"For me?" I ask.

She says nothing and makes her way to the house, and I throw my arm over Daniel's shoulder, starting to walk him back. It's so good to have him here, so good to see him, but I'm really not sure if it's a good idea. I push my lips into the side of his head, breathing him into me.

"Where's Mister?" he asks, tensing slightly at my affection.

"Just dealing with some business." I glance at the sky, giving it a pained look.

"Jet skis?" he asks, hopeful.

"Yes, jet skis," I chirp. "He deals in jet skis."

"Speaking of which." Esther comes to a stop up ahead, arms up, like *ta-dah!*

I stop in my tracks, stunned, as I stare at a Jeep tugging a trailer up the long driveway, two jet skis on the back.

"Sick!" Daniel gasps, breaking away and running toward them. "Oh my God, this is sick!"

I take in the two sparkling machines as I kick my legs to life, approaching the trailer as it comes to a gradual stop, while Daniel dances along the side, "oh my goshing" all over the place. Both are black, both Sea-Doos. I round the back and locate what I'm looking for, and my heart squeezes. One has "Mister'" scrolled across the back. The other "Kid."

Matching jet skis for my man and my boy.

I look at Esther, and she smiles softly, before entering the house. "Surprise," I murmur, completely shook.

"This is epic!" Daniel continues to leap and jump by the side of the trailer, looking about ready to pee his pants. "When can I take it out? Oh my God, I'm definitely gonna beat Mister now." He dives at me, throwing his arms around my useless form. "Thanks, Mom."

"Welcome." All I can think about is guns. Bloodshed. Murder. I break away. "Go help Esther, okay? I'll be in soon."

He prances off as a young lad hops out the driver's side, his long hair held back by a bandana, his shorts halfway down his ass. "I think he likes it," he says, running a palm down the side of one of the jet skis.

"Who are you?"

"Leon." He grins. "You must be Rose."

"I am. What do you do for my husband?"

"Help run his jet ski business, of course." He pulls out a smoke and lights up, kicking his dirty Converse back and leaning against the Jeep. Of course. The *jet ski* business.

I bend down by one of the jet skis and tap the side. It doesn't sound hollow. It's a good start. I rise, thinking, feeling eyes on me. I peek to my right and find Tank watching me closely. "What do you think?" I ask, motioning to the machine.

"Sick," he grunts, and I laugh, then hear the sound of the gates sliding open. A convoy of cars drive through one by one, Danny's Merc and James's Range Rover in the middle of the long line.

"Not conspicuous at all," I grumble, folding my arms over my chest. The cars come to a stop, and Danny emerges, looking like the absolute god he is. Strong. Powerful. Respected. I take him in from top to toe, his beige chinos, his crisp white shirt, as he slips on his shades.

He falters in his movements when he finds me. "Am I in trouble?" he asks, as all the men disperse.

I motion to the trailer. To the house. To Danny standing by enough flashy cars to make up a fleet to escort the president. "Daniel's here."

"I know."

"And you think that's a good idea?"

"I know it's a bad idea for you *not* to see him." He approaches slowly, perhaps a little wary. "You look off." His palm lays across my forehead, his face concerned.

"I feel a bit queasy," I admit. "It might have something to do with endless men wanting my husband dead or . . . dead."

"I've told you before, I'm invincible." He swings an arm around my shoulders. "You've met Leon then."

I raise my brows at the boho kid. "He looks like he'll fit right in," I murmur, and Danny laughs, knowing I'm not talking about the gun side of his business, which is exactly why Leon's been hired. He slots right into the façade. But my question is, does Leon know what else goes on at the boatyard? Of course he knows. He must have been there today when Danny's delivery arrived.

"I'll get these back to the yard, D-boss," Leon says, turning another cheeky smile my way, bowing. "It was nice to meet you, Mrs. Black."

"You too, Leon," I say, watching him, full of beans, hop back into the truck and pull away.

Danny starts walking us into the mansion, Tank on our heels. "What have you been doing this morning?"

"What have *you* been doing?" I counter, holding his hand where it dangles over my shoulder.

"You know what I've been doing." He pulls his glasses off and looks down at me with high, warning brows. "Now answer my question."

I pout. "Beau's been giving me a master class in shooting."

"Oh?"

"I'm still quite shit."

He laughs, and it's my favorite laugh from him. Pure. Real. We enter the kitchen and find Daniel with his sleeves up, ready to plunge his hands into a bowl of ground beef. "Hey, Mister," he chirps, his eyes lighting up when he sees Danny.

"Hey, kid." Danny pulls a stool out and pushes me onto it, going to the fridge and fetching a bottle of water. He ruffles Daniel's hair as he passes and drops a kiss onto Esther's cheek as she chops onions. "What did you think of the skis?" Danny settles on a stool opposite my boy, holding my thigh with one hand and drinking his water with the other.

"It's so sick, man." Daniel's hands plunge into the meat and start mixing in the onions as Esther scrapes them into the bowl off the chopping board. "Thanks, Mister."

"Welcome. Maiden voyage soon?"

"When?" he asks, as keen as I knew he'd be. "Now?"

Danny laughs, while I break out in a sweat. Daniel at the boatyard? "Maybe next week," I say, appeasing him, feeling Danny's amused stare rooted on my profile. I'm glad he's finding this funny. "Danny's busy." *Plotting death.*

I peek at Esther. She's smiling at her onions. This was a terrible idea. Why am I the only person around here who seems to realize that? And what the hell did Hilary and Derek think about my mother-in-law showing up to collect Daniel? They must have been full of questions. Unless . . .

I look at Danny next to me, my eyes narrowing. He looks out the corner of his eye as he slugs back more water. Obviously gun smuggling and murder is thirsty work. "What?" he asks.

"You didn't kidnap him, did you?" I whisper.

He rolls his eyes. "No, I didn't kidnap our boy."

Our boy. The circumstances of Daniel's arrival is suddenly forgotten. He's *our* boy. My heart squeezes, happy and sad. I want him here, of course. All the fucking time, I want him here, and yet I know that's impossible.

My cell rings, and Danny looks down at the screen. "The gate?" he asks.

"It'll be the tent company." I answer and instruct Bud to direct them to the main house. "I'll meet them on the drive." Hanging up, I set my eyes on my husband. "I'm glad you're back," I say, and he peeks at me with a little fear.

"Why?"

"I need help deciding where the tent will be." I definitely detect a miniscule drop of his shoulders. "Come on," I say quickly before he can object, getting up and heading for the kitchen door. I'm met by Ringo and Otto, their frames filling the doorway, halting my escape. They look straight past me to Danny, and I glance over my shoulder, seeing him nod mildly and get up. "You said you'd help," I whine dejectedly, deflating.

"No, *you* said I'd help."

"I'll help," Daniel chirps, his fingers slathered in sticky meat.

"And me," Esther pipes up, a blatant move to placate me. It's all good and well, but I'm not marrying Esther and it would be quite nice to have my husband involved somewhere in the planning.

"See," Danny murmurs as he approaches, sinking his fingers into my hair and kissing my forehead, trying to appease me too. "It's covered." He pulls away, and I swallow, unable to look him in the eye. I feel like I could cry. How stupid.

"Okay," I relent, breaking away and turning, hiding my face, but I only make it one step before I'm tugged to a stop. I look at his big, lethal hand wrapped around my forearm. "I said okay."

A swift tug has me facing him, but I keep my eyes low, willing the glaze to fuck off. A tent, for fuck's sake. What's gotten into me? The tips of his fingers grip my chin and lift, but I resist, making it as hard as possible for him to make me look at him.

"Rose," he says, low and threateningly. I swallow and look up. His glacial eyes are annoyed slits, but his grip soon softens, as well as his stare. He breathes in deeply, nodding. "Give me half an hour," he says, eyes on mine, and for a moment I think he's told *me* to give him time, but then Ringo and Otto back out of the kitchen, and I realize he's talking to them. He dips and bites my cheek. "Come on," he whispers, curling an arm around my neck and hauling me close. "Let's go talk tents."

I smile, settling into his side. He chose me. "I won't be long, Daniel," I say, looking back at my boy. He doesn't even acknowledge me, his focus on his burger mixture. He clearly loves being with Esther, who is totally in her element being on Grandma duty.

When we get to the front drive, I greet a man who's staring up at the front of the mansion. "You must be Franz."

"Rose," he says, taking my hand.

"Thank you for coming at such short notice."

"No problem. You were lucky we had a cancelation."

"This is my husband, Danny."

"Nice to meet you," Franz says, offering his hand. "Husband-to-be, right?"

"Right," Danny replies, accepting and shaking, sizing up Franz. "Local?"

"Naples, actually."

"Quite a drive." Danny releases and stuffs his hands in his pockets. "Shall we?" He starts wandering around the side of the house. "I was thinking by the pool."

"You've been thinking about it?" I ask, following with Franz.

"It's off the main patio. Makes sense." He looks back at me. "Did you have somewhere else in mind?"

"No."

"Then off the main patio it is." He comes to a gradual stop and points to the lawn. "There."

"Great." Franz gets a tape measure out and starts taking notes. "I assume electric is accessible."

"Over there," I say, pointing to an outside socket.

"Perfect. We'll need access the day before to get everything ready."

"No problem." Danny perches on the low wall that edges the patio.

"What kind of lighting were you thinking?"

"Over to my wife," he says.

"Wife-to-be," Franz corrects him, and Danny peeks at me, a small smile tickling the corner of his lips.

"Right," Danny agrees quietly, hardly heard. "Wife-to-be." He crosses his ankles and gets comfortable, and I swing into action, confirming all the plans —lighting, tables arrangements, chair dressings, everything, while Danny gives the dogs some fuss.

"You could at least pretend to be interested," I mumble, muscling my way in between Barbie and Cindy.

He sends them away and looks over his shoulder when Ringo approaches behind us. "I really have to go now." He stands and kisses my cheek. "You've got this." He wanders off, talking quietly with Ringo as he goes.

I've got this. Have I? Have I *really* got this, because I'm losing my grip more each day. I wait until they've disappeared around the corner before following, peeking around the house when I get there. A car pulls up, and Brad gets out, going straight to the back. And a few seconds later, a man is dragged from the back seat, wailing his protests. It's the detective who came here when Danny was missing. The one who asked us to identify his body. Spattle. Spittle. I thought he and Danny were good.

"For God's sake," I mutter, watching as he's manhandled into the house by Brad, who has a gun wedged into the man's temple. "Not fucking cool." God help any man here if Daniel sees anything he shouldn't see.

"Rose?"

I bite down on my teeth and pluck a smile from nowhere, turning to face Tank. "Yeah, okay," I mumble. "I'm spying on my husband."

I make my way back to Franz and walk through the rest of the plans, my mind elsewhere, my stomach back to churning terribly. Once we're finished, and I've handed him over to Bud to see out, I hurry back into the house, bypassing the kitchen to avoid Esther and Daniel. I feel sick to my stomach. "I'm fine," I call back to Tank, who's following my hurried pace. I burst into our room, dash across the carpet, and the second I'm in the bathroom, I throw up everywhere on loud, body-jerking wretches. "Jesus," I gasp between heaves, yanking off some toilet paper to wipe my mouth.

"Still fine?"

I swing round and find Tank in the doorway, grimacing at the toilet. "Keep this to yourself," I order harshly. The last thing I need is Danny thinking I'm not strong enough to deal with everything. *I hate this* . . . but I have to endure it. I have to stay strong. "God damn me," I whisper, locking myself in the bathroom and drawing on every ounce of strength to pull myself together before I go downstairs to be with Daniel.

I need to appear okay, not just for the sake of my husband.

11

JAMES

"Where are you holding him?" I ask Brad as I follow him into Danny's office, the thirst for a kill overwhelming me.

He laughs his way to the drinks cabinet and pours himself a Scotch as I shut the door, an unmoving sneer fixed on my face. "I'm not telling you." He turns, smiling at my barely contained rage. "Maybe you should burn off some energy in the gym."

I drop into a chair. "I'd rather burn some energy on Spittle. Why is he still alive?"

"Spittle is one of those things in life that everyone hates but serves a purpose so we have to keep it." Brad throws back his drink. "Like toes. We all hate them, but we need them."

My fingertips start drumming my jean-clad thigh, my mind planning all the ways I'm going to kill Spittle, because one way or another, today or tomorrow, he will die. Brad takes the seat beside me, passing me a tumbler. I can sense some pacifying words on the horizon. There are three things I know about Brad Black: he has a sick sense of humor, he's a coldblooded killer, and he thinks really hard about his kills. A bit like Danny Black. And me. A thoughtful killer is the deadliest killer. A killer who plays with their prey. Extends their torture. Prolongs the thrill. Although thinking seems to be beyond me at the moment. Has been since Beau became the end game. I just want to kill every fucker who poses a threat and be done with it. Move on. Seal the peace that is eluding Beau and me. I'm technically still dead. It won't stay that way for long with Danny causing ripples in the underworld.

"Take a breath," Brad says quietly as I throw the vodka down my throat. "Or a drink."

The door opens behind us, and we both crane our necks to find Goldie hovering on the threshold. "What is it?" I ask, and she opens up the way, revealing Beau. The sight of her balances me, and I exhale, taking in her lithe body coated in Lycra. I've eased her gently into exercise, made a point of it, and her well-conditioned body has handled it well, her muscle memory helping.

I flick my head for her to come in as I rise, meeting her in the middle of the room. "What's up?" I ask, cupping her head in my hands and pushing my lips to the top of her head, inhaling, closing my eyes, relaxing. I expect the smell of sweat. No sweat, just her intoxicating fruity scent. *Calm.*

"I need some more bullets," she says, simple as that, straight-up, no hesitation.

I still, and my eyes snap open. I see Goldie hovering on the edge of the office with Fury, both doing a terrible job of hiding their amusement, and I hear Brad behind me outright chuckling. Yes. Fucking hilarious.

I pull away, although I'm evidently reluctant, and cautiously peek down at her. She's doing a terrible job of hiding her smile too. Taking my wrists, she pulls my hands down from her face. "Good day?" she asks.

Me? "I'm more interested in yours."

"Rose and I did target practice."

My entire being seems to deflate, and Beau starts massaging at her wrist. "Take it easy," I warn, replacing her working hands with mine, rubbing gently as I guide her to the couch and nod for her to sit.

Otto and Ringo walk in, and Brad stands. "He's been dragged into the garden," Ringo grunts. "Something to do with the wedding."

"Fucking wedding," Brad mutters. "Worst idea he's ever had."

"Apparently the suits are ready," Otto says, prompting Ringo to glance down his front.

"I don't know what's wrong with this one."

"It's not a tux."

Ringo looks across to Goldie. "You got a new suit?"

When I expect her to go psycho on him and his incessant, unexplained need to rile her, Goldie instead lifts her chin. "No, actually. I have a dress." Her eyes quickly turn to slits, daring any man in the room to question her. So, of course, they don't. Ringo's learned his lesson. Almost.

But . . . a dress? Goldie?

Beau laughs beside me, and I turn an interested look her way. She shrugs. "About those bullets."

"I'm living in a fucked-up version of Little House on the fucking Prairie," Brad snaps. "I'm going to smack some balls over the net. Let me know when Romeo's finished pacifying Juliet."

"Say that to Rose," Beau shouts on a laugh.

"No fucking way," he calls back, pushing his way through the men. And woman.

"So, the bullets."

She really wants those bullets. It's the third time she's asked, and I'm worried, especially after she nearly shot me when she found out I was there the night her mother died. *Nearly*, being the operative word here. If Beau hadn't been sporting a broken wrist, I wouldn't be sitting here now. And since she's not averse to getting trigger happy with me, perhaps I should rethink my desire to ensure she can protect herself. Being in a relationship with Beau Hayley is perilous in every way. "No bullets," I say, looking up and giving Goldie and Fury a nod. I've got this for now.

Goldie pulls the door closed, and I return my attention to Beau. "How's Lawrence?"

She wilts before my eyes, which tells me all I need to know. Not that I need Beau's reaction. I have it from a good source—namely, Doc—that Lawrence is still in his suite here at Black's mansion. He's not eating. Not speaking. "I don't know," she says on a sigh. "He won't let me in his room today. He's locked himself in. I don't even know if he's taking the meds Doc has prescribed."

"We'll find out. Come o—" I catch a wave of uncertainty pass across her face.

"I've agreed to have dinner with my father tonight."

I make sure I hide my grimace as I know she'll be dreading it. He doesn't like me, and I can't say I'm his biggest fan. He's been absent from Beau's life for too long, not there when she needed him. He thinks showing up at the hospital when Beau was shot, throwing his weight around, making demands, would heal the years he's been lacking? It won't. Now he's just another cause of stress for Beau, and that makes me dislike the egomaniac even more. The feeling's mutual, of course. But I couldn't have handled things at the hospital differently if I'd tried. Couldn't have been civil. Not to him, not to anyone.

"I want to know where, what time, and who will be there."

She's not surprised to hear my demands. "He's texting me."

"Good. Let's go check on Lawrence." I go to stand, but she pushes me back to the couch and clambers onto my lap, straddling me. Oh? "Beau," I warn roughly. This isn't the time or the place. I've got Danny on the warpath, Brad sulking, Lawrence hiding, Spittle waiting for me to mutilate him.

"What?" she whispers, feeling down my torso to my jeans and unbuttoning the fly.

I hold my breath, scrambling for some willpower to resist her. "I have shit to deal wi—" My back cracks, arching, as she slips a hand into my boxers and seizes me. "Oh fuck." My legs straighten, black spots hamper my vision. Of course, I can't deny her, never will. She's been doing so great in recent days. Who am I to hamper her progress?

So I take this precious moment to be close to her, the tip of my finger running along the waistband of her workout leggings. Her hands on my chest, she leans into me, eyes flicking all over my face. "I want to look at you for a minute." She kisses the corner of my mouth, and every drop of blood inside sizzles. "Feel you."

"Working out suits you."

She gives me an impish grin. A telling grin. She's got me, and she knows it. "I'd prefer to work out with you." Her smooth palm glides down my shaft with beautiful ease.

Since Beau's epic meltdown at Hiatus, sex has definitely cranked up a notch or twenty. But I'm still careful. Still cautious. Still worried about the long-term damage. And yet when she looks at me the way she's looking at me now—her eyes lazy, full of sex, her body literally blowing my mind—the animal inside growls his want. "You want to work out?" I ask, lifting from the couch, Beau attached to my front. I hold her under her arse with one hand and take her to Danny's desk—God forgive me—swiping a few things off before sitting her on the edge. "Here?" I ask, pushing into her chest, sending her down to the wood. Her breathy, desperate "yes" is hardly decipherable amid our heavy breathing. "But you just had me this morning." I take her sports bra and shove it up, stretching it over her head until the tight elastic has her arms restrained by her ears. "Open," I order, smiling when her lips part. I push the fabric into her mouth. "Bite."

She clenches down, her eyes wild with satisfaction, as I cup her soft, gorgeous tits. Her back bows, offering them, so I lower and take a nipple between my teeth, biting down lightly as I squeeze and mold her flesh. Her muffled moan saturates the room, her sounds of need fueling my own. I grip her leggings and pull them down to her calves, then push her legs up, draping her bound feet over my head. I take her all in, every mind-bending pore of her stunning body, my mouth watering for a taste, my skin singing to touch, my eyes hungry to watch her squirm and writhe, my ears desperate for more of those moans. And my nose bombarded by the heady scent of her desire. I pull my dick out, lay a palm on each thigh, and tug her down the desk until the aching, swollen head of my arousal meets the warm, pulsing flesh of her pussy. She jerks, and I shake, easing gently into her. "Fuck," I hiss raggedly as her eyes widen, the material of her sports bra springing from her fighting the bond. "You feel incredible." With the backs of her legs flush against my chest, her arms restrained, she is at my mercy, and it is exactly where she wanted to be. Lost. Reminded. Pushing back the darkness. That thought gets my hips moving, thrusting, pumping, sinking into her over and over until I'm out of my mind on only Beau. It's safer. For everyone. I close my eyes, tilt my head to the ceiling, and let nature take over, thrashing my body against hers, driving high and deep, sucking back air repeatedly. I'm gone. Out of my mind. My body's on autopilot, searching for the release, my gasps constant.

I come on a strained bawl, my groin slapping against the backs of her thighs, and I snap my eyes open, blinking repeatedly, my stomach muscles clenching. Her stifled yell signals the end for Beau too, and I collapse forward, practically bending her in half, battling for air. "Jesus," I whisper, my face finding its place in her sweaty neck. "You okay?"

She hums, sounding sated and happy, her thighs limp around my torso. "Were you hoping someone would walk in on us?"

I lift, getting her in my sights. She's staring at the ceiling, panting, so I nuzzle her cheek to win her attention. She looks so drowsy. Spent. "I don't feel the need to be seen anymore." I kiss her hard and deep, with all the passion I feel for her and her alone. "So long as *you* see me."

"I see you." She bites my lip harshly, dragging it through her teeth, and I hum, eyes on hers until my flesh pops free. "Is there any news on Dexter?"

The biggest passion killer, if ever there was one. "No." I slip out and dip from between her legs, pulling a Kleenex from the box on Danny's desk and wiping her clean before pulling her leggings back up. "There's been no breakthrough." My mind is feeding words to my mouth, and I have no control over them. Getting Dexter's body back was a priority. Then we found out Spittle's son heads up the bank where Beau's mother held the safety deposit box and the Russian's ambushed Hiatus. Naturally, the latter two moved to the top of our priority list.

I pull Beau up and help her get her sports bra back down. "Come on." I dip and start collecting up the few things I swiped from Danny's desk, and Beau joins me.

"Who's this?" she asks, collecting up the photograph of Spittle and his family, studying it.

"That's no one." I plunk it from her grasp and slide it onto the desk, and then take her hand, leading her from the office.

"Sure it is," she mutters.

I ignore her and bypass the kitchen to pick up the master key from Esther, and by the time we make it to Lawrence's room,

Beau is silently apprehensive. I unlock the door but when I try to open it, it doesn't budge. "Lawrence?" I call, putting some weight behind me. "He's pushed something against the door."

"What?"

I strain, pushing my shoulder into the wood. "For fuck's sake."

"Lawrence!" Beau yells, starting to panic. "Lawrence, let us in!" She starts banging on the wood next to my head. "Lawrence!"

Her urgency fuels my own, but for the life of me, I can't get the fucking door to move. What the fuck has he put behind it? "When was Doc here?" I ask her.

"Earlier."

"Need help?"

I look down the corridor, seeing Fury emerging from his room. "Yes, get this door open." I kick it with my boot, pulling Beau out of the way of the bull that's about to charge.

"Hurry," Beau orders, frantic, her voice cracking. "Please, hurry."

"Hey." I spin her into my chest, holding her close. I look at Fury over Beau's head, my eyes telling him to get it done, and get it done fast. Something's not right. "It's fine. I'm sure it's fine."

Fury backs up as far as the corridor will allow, and he stomps forward fast, his shoulder meeting the wood with a deafening bang. The door doesn't budge and, as inappropriate as it is, I'm relieved, because if the unit that is Fury is struggling, I don't need to lift those extra weights as I thought. He looks across at me on a frown, obviously thinking along the same lines as me. What the fuck is behind the door?

"Bro?" Tank rumbles, appearing at the end of the corridor.

Yes. Two battering rams. And if they can't shift the door, I'm going to have to break a window and climb up the face of the house.

"Help me," Fury orders, waiting for his brother to join him. They run at the door like rhinos, crashing into it, knocking it off its hinges. A collection of bangs sound from inside the room as Fury takes the door and lifts it out of the doorway, propping it up against the wall. A pile of furniture greets us, wardrobes, chests, chairs.

"What the fuck?" Tank mutters, walking through the heap, shifting it aside, like a snow plough clearing a blocked road.

"Oh my God, what?" Beau breathes. "What is it?" She tries to go after him, but I grab her, a nasty feeling falling.

"Beau." I pull her back, looking to Fury. "Get Doc," I order, and he stomps off at a steady jog. "Wait here." I give Beau eyes to suggest the consequences will be dire if she ignores me.

"Fuck you, James." She dips, dodging my reaching hand, disappearing into the room. "Oh my God, no!"

"Fucking hell," I hear Tank gasp.

I'm in the room like a bullet, and find Lawrence on the bed with a plastic bag over his head, his lifeless body surrounded with pill pots.

"No!" Beau screams.

"Shit. Get that bag off!" I grab her and haul her out of the room. "Rose!" I yell, restraining Beau's flailing arms and legs. I don't even know if Rose is up here. "Rose! Beau, calm down." I hear footsteps up ahead, and Rose appears with Esther, both out of breath. "Rose, please, take her," I beg as Beau wails and screams in my arms, hitting my chest repeatedly.

"What's happened?" she asks, racing down the corridor, her face horrified by the state of Beau. "Beau, babe, come on. Come with me." Rose looks at me, alarmed, eyes questioning, and I turn my stare toward Lawrence's bedroom. Rose gasps, catching sight of Beau's uncle. "Shit, fuck. Okay. Beau, I need you to come with me." Rose doesn't let Beau's fighting body deter her, grappling with her arms, enduring the constant, deranged hits.

"Beau, listen to me," Rose shouts, and Beau stills, but her breathing is shot. She looks up at her friend on a despairing sob. "He's going to be okay," Rose says, leading a now compliant Beau to her room. "I promise." She looks at Esther, who watches on, stunned. "Will you make sure Daniel's okay?"

Translated: Keep the child away from the fucking carnage happening all over this house.

I blow out my cheeks, dragging my palms down my face. *He's going to be okay.* I think Rose just made a promise she can't keep. "Fuck," I yell, punching the door that the twins just charged down, knocking it to the floor. I brace myself, trying to get my head on straight. Beau's being taken care of. Now . . .

I stalk toward the bed, seeing Tank with his ear to Lawrence's mouth, his fingertips on his wrist. "Well?"

"He's breathing but has a weak pulse."

I exhale, relieved, scanning the scene and trying to assess exactly what we're dealing with. Endless pill pots. Photos scattered everywhere. "I'm here," Doc announces, racing in with his case, Fury following with another two hefty bags of equipment. "Oh goodness." He gets to work immediately while Tank and I stand back, useless. I haven't seen Lawrence for weeks. He was a slight man, all arms and legs, but the weight loss is dramatic, his limbs now bony. It's a shocking sight, and one I take absolutely no pleasure from.

I force my eyes away and start pacing the room, wanting to get back to Beau so much, but not without the news I know she'll need. Doc won't insist on a hospital. He knows that isn't possible, both Danny and I made that clear when we brought the retired doctor into our world, and he accepted on the condition that we provided everything he could possibly need for every eventuality. He got it.

"I'll need to pump his stomach," Doc says, hooking a bag of fluids to the headboard.

"Will he live?' I ask, my tone as blunt as my words.

"He'll live," Doc replies, pulling a length of rubber pipe from one of his bags and applying some kind of gel to the length. "I saw him only a couple of hours ago." He nods to the piles of furniture by the door. "That barricade would have taken him some time to build, and he hasn't vomited."

I nod, backing out of the room. "Would you two mind?" I say to Tank and Fury, indicating the wide-spread remains of Lawrence's barricade. They nod and get to work. "Update me." I make my way to Rose and Danny's room, entering without knocking. Beau is huddled on the bed sobbing, Rose's arm around her. She looks up at me through glassy eyes. "He's going to be okay," I say quickly, hoping to ease her worry. But I can't see a way forward without having Lawrence watched constantly, and I'm not letting Beau be that person.

She releases a pained whimper and gets off the bed, coming at me and pushing her body into mine. I hold her, feeling her relief all over me, as well as her tears soaking through my T-shirt. I can only thank God that we found him in time, and I know Beau will be crucifying herself over this. I had her on Danny's desk for at least ten minutes. Both of us lost.

While Lawrence was attempting suicide.

I swallow down the anger before it consumes me. Beau's been doing so well. Worried about her uncle still, yes, asking after Dexter, yes, but her lost spirit has been awakening more recently, and it's been a comfort to my ravaged soul. This will set her back, and I can only resent Lawrence for that. "Come on," I say softly, gently detaching her from my front, giving Rose a nod of thanks. She waves it off with ease, smiling, though it doesn't touch her dark blue eyes. The situation, naturally, could be the cause for that, but now I'm more together, I notice she looks a bit pasty. I cock her a questioning look, and she once again waves it off. "I'm going to take Beau to lie down," I say, leading her from the room.

"I'm here if you need me."

I look back, seeing her heading for the bathroom. She shuts the door and a couple of seconds later, the toilet is flushing. Way too soon for her to have used it. I'm suspicious, but now is not a good time to question her, so I file my observations away ready to mention it to Danny. "Rose is in the bathroom," I say to Tank as we pass. "Tell Fury Beau's lying down for a while."

"I want to see him," she says, resisting me.

"No." I scoop her up and lock her to my chest. "You'll let Doc get him comfortable, then you can see him." I enter our room and place her on the bed, pulling her trainers off and the sheets back. Her eyes are puffy and squinting, signs of a headache from crying so much. "Get in."

She does what she's told, and I crawl in behind her, spooning her, cuddling her close.

Over an hour passes before her breathing changes. Her body goes heavy against me, twitching every now and then. I lie with her a little longer before carefully easing myself away when I know she's sleeping deeply.

I head straight for Lawrence's room, meeting Doc in the corridor outside. "He's conscious," he says, pulling the zipper on his bag closed. "I would like to say it was a cry for help, but . . ."

"I hear you." I work on fixing my irregular breathing before I enter, my anger building. "Thanks, Doc." I gently knock before pushing slowly through the door, and I find him awake on the bed. When he turns his eyes my way, his lip wobbles. "Come to tell me what a selfish bastard I am?"

"Yes," I reply, closing the door. "You must have known what this would do to her." He's an intelligent man.

Lawrence looks away, ashamed. I'm not prepared to let him hide, so I round the bed, putting my big frame in his field of vision. "Your husband shot your niece." My voice raises of its own volition. "He killed my . . ." I suck back air and suck in some control. I cannot lose my shit. "He killed our baby, Lawrence."

He closes his eyes, hiding again, but he can still hear me, I make sure of it, pulling a chair up by his bed and getting close. Not threatening, but certainly in his space.

"You don't have to like me. I don't want or need your approval. But I do want and need you to pull your shit together for the sake of Beau." I swallow. "That woman, *my* woman, has been through hell. She lost her mother. Her father is a self-serving, power-hungry womanizing wanker, who's showed no interest in her, not past what she could do for his public image. You, Lawrence, were all she had, and she might have me now, but she still needs you. So I'm going to ask you nicely, just this once, to pull your fucking head out of your arse and stop mourning the man who nearly took her from us. Look at what's in front of you and make the fucking most of it, because we're all learning pretty fucking fast that life is too short." I clench my eyes shut, grappling for calm, blindly feeling for his emaciated hand and squeezing. "I'm begging you, Lawrence." I open my eyes and find his glazed gaze on me, his hand constricting mine weakly. "I can't let her return to those dark places again." She's done so well, even after a mountain of more shit being piled on top of her. If she breaks, I'm breaking with her, and that's going to cause all kinds of chaos for Miami.

He whimpers, sniveling. Any other man I'd condemn outright for being so weak and pathetic. But Lawrence? I can only feel pity, and my wrath won't solve this. Look at him. I'd break him in two with a flick of my little finger.

"I don't know how to be without Dexter," he whispers.

"You'll be honorable, Lawrence. You'll be loyal and real. You'll be everything he wasn't."

He eyes me with a weak, wry smile. "I never had you pinned as a shrink type."

"When someone matters to you, when they're your world, you be whatever you need to be to make them okay."

"A killer too?"

"A killer too," I confirm, not beating around the bush. He's heard things, many things. There's no getting away from that.

"You told me at the hospital that you'd kill Dexter if you find him."

I can only nod. What a fucked-up situation I'm in, and once again I wish I could turn back the clock to the moment I snapped and finished Dexter. I've never lived with many regrets. Since Beau ambushed my life, they seem to be coming thick and fast.

"But Beau's made me promise not to," I add.

He shoots his eyes my way. "She did?"

"She won't marry me otherwise."

"Oh . . ." Lawrence breathes, eyes darting, my bombshell sinking into his head. After a few, silent seconds, he looks at me again. "Who's The Bear?"

"I don't know," I confess, realizing I'm still holding his hand. And yet I can't bring myself to pull it away when he's clenching it with force, like a lifeline. "He's at the top of the Miami criminal pecking order. I think Jaz figured out who he was and that Dexter had been corrupted, hence—"

"He had her killed." Lawrence shows me the first sign of anger, and I can't help but think it's a good thing. He needs anger to extinguish the grief. Anger will help. So I fuel it.

"But it was Dexter who made it happen, Lawrence. It was Dexter who tampered with the evidence and hid the footage that proved it wasn't an accident. It was Dexter who killed Jaz and nearly Beau too." I do something I hadn't planned, standing and releasing his hand. I turn and pull my shirt up, showing him the mess that is my back. His gasp is weary, weak, and as shocked as it should be.

"You tried to save them," he whispers.

"I will find out who The Bear is. I *will* kill him, Lawrence." I drop my shirt and face him, our talk stoking the anger within. "I need to be on my A-game and worrying whether you're going to try and top yourself again and distress Beau isn't going to help me. So do whatever it is you need to do—put your stockings on, your makeup, your fucking wig, I do not care, but now's the time to pick yourself up."

I see something lift in the frail man, something significant, and yet I can't cling to it. Not yet. Not until I see him make moves to rectify this shitstorm he's caused. A sharp nod. A sniffle. A rough wipe of his eyes. He can't give me much more in this moment, only an execution.

"I'll leave you to rest," I say, giving Lawrence space to mentally stock up on strength. I take a few moments outside his bedroom to cool my hot head before picking up my feet. I pass Esther on the stairs, a tray in her hand. "She's resting."

"This is for Lawrence. Doc said some tea and toast would probably go down well. Daniel's eating his dinner with Rose."

I smile. Tea. A good old British cup of tea, and Danny's mum makes a cracking one. "Thanks, Esther."

"You're welcome, James. I'll check in on Beau too. The men just went into Danny's office." She continues up the stairs, and I go find the men, bowling into Danny's office . . .

At the exact moment he swipes a machete and takes off the head of a man.

I stop where I am, avoiding the spray of blood, and watch as the head rolls across the carpet. It slows, doing a little twirl, before coming to a gradual stop at my feet. Eyes on me.

I look up at Danny. "Feel better?" I ask, stepping over the dismembered head, hearing the muffled sound of retching. I peek out the corner of my eye and see Goldie barely containing her need to throw up all over the place. I smile to myself, dropping to the couch. "What did I miss?"

Danny holds out the blade and Ringo is quick to relieve him of it. He looks down at his shirt, flicking at the spots of blood. "Well, Spittle's dead."

"So you obviously decided what to do with him." I look across to his head, thinking Spittle might have been better off letting *me* at him. "You sure Doc can't work his magic?"

Danny smirks, dark and dirty, and pulls his cigarettes out, lighting one and exhaling over his words. "He was no good to us anymore." He toes Spittle's body with his dress shoe, his lip curling. "Otto got into his bank accounts. A deposit landed yesterday. Two hundred grand."

I nod, thoughtful. "Payment for services rendered, or services *to be* rendered?" I muse, wondering—or knowing—if Spittle's failure to advise Danny that Volodya is still breathing may have also contributed to his gruesome death. "How?" Danny's had him watched like a hawk since he kindly removed his cock from the meat slicer. How stupid can a man be? Or desperate.

"Otto disabled his mobile phone," Danny says. "So when he was seen talking on one, it roused suspicion." He swipes up a clear plastic bag from his desk, and I lean forward, trying to see what's in it.

"A mobile?"

"Spittle, God bless his heart," Danny muses, taking another drag of his cigarette, "tried to hide it when he saw Len coming at him. Hid in a cubicle of the men's restroom at the restaurant he was in. When Len kicked the door in, no mobile phone."

"He tried to flush it?" Otto asks.

"No. He rammed it up his arse." Danny smirks, glancing around the room, seeing everyone wince, no doubt their arseholes clenching like mine. "Apparently we need to do internals on our prey now."

Everyone steps back.

"Are you telling me he was fucking himself with a phone?" I ask, grimacing.

Danny laughs, and it's a full-on belly laugh, his palm landing on his desk to hold him up. That's a psycho laugh. I've heard my own enough to recognize one. He composes himself, wiping under his eyes. "The question I have is how many calls did he make?" He holds the bag up again, and the tension in the room thickens, everyone's eyes snapping to each other, wondering which lucky fucker is going to have the honor of handling it to find out who Spittle's been calling. "Any offers?" Danny asks, giving everyone a moment of his eyes. "No?"

Brad steams through the door in full workout gear, his muscles still pulsing, his forehead pouring sweat. The toe of his trainer nudges Spittle's head, sending it rolling a few feet across the floor. His eyes widen. "For fuck's sake, Danny."

"Good workout?" Danny asks, resting his arse on his desk.

"He's ex FBI, for Christ's sake."

"He's a fucking snake." He pushes the butt of his cigarette into an ashtray. "He told The Bear I'm still alive." He holds up the bag again. "He's been making calls right under our fucking noses, and he ordered a psycho assassin to murder you, Brad."

"Don't talk about me like I'm not here," I quip, resting back, enjoying the show.

"For fuck's sake." Brad yanks a towel from around his neck and wipes his face.

"You're just pissed because *you* wanted to end him."

"Yeah, I fucking did." He snarls down at Spittle's head, draws his foot back, and kicks it across the room, the power giving it some height.

"Fuck." Danny ducks, and Spittle's head ricochets off the

wall behind him, leaving a sizable blob of blood on the paint-work. "You dickhead."

Oh, Spittle. What a fucking mess he was in. "So what has The Bear got that we haven't got?" I ask, resting an elbow on the arm of the couch, propping my head up, thinking. "Because there's got to be an explanation for Spittle being so fucking stupid." Everyone turns their eyes onto his head, looking at what being stupid gets you when you're stupid around Danny Black. "I need to burn off some steam." Balance. I need to stand on my head to clear my head. I get up and move toward the door.

"I'll hold the pads first," Danny says, dropping the phone back on his desk. "I don't care who gets into that phone, but I want answers by tomorrow." He looks at Brad. "Coming?"

"No, I've got to get to the Hiatus." He pulls his T-shirt over his head. "I can't fucking believe you've murdered Spittle without me."

"Stop crying about it," Danny says tiredly. "And someone find me his fucking son." He catches up with me, and we walk side by side down the corridor to the foyer. "What's going on with Beau's uncle?" he asks.

"Stupid fuck tried to kill himself." We reach the staircase. "Do I have a body yet?"

I don't like the expression on Danny's face. "Yeah, about that . . ."

"What about it?"

"They gave it to the sharks."

That answers that, then. "Shit."

"I'm sorry, mate. I did say I'd make sure no one finds it, as per your instruction."

I shake my head, hoping to God my message has gotten through to Lawrence. "I need to check Beau. Meet you in the gym."

"Sure," he replies, heading for the kitchen. "Mum, can you take Daniel home?"

I take the steps two at a time and find Fury in the corridor.

"She's awake. She went into his room," he says, motioning to Lawrence's door. "About five minutes ago."

I nod and take the handle, pushing my way in quietly. She's sitting on the edge of her uncle's bed, holding his hand. When she looks up at me, I expect to see tears. Instead, I see hope. And then she smiles a little. "He's okay," she says over a swallow.

"Glad you're feeling better." I join Beau by the bed, taking a chair, then check my watch. "You have dinner with your father in an hour. You'd better get ready, you'll have to leave soon."

"Oh, I'm going to cancel." She shakes her head vehemently, returning her attention to Lawrence. "Uncle Lawrence needs me here."

I peek at Lawrence out of the corner of my eye, and his lips purse. He's thinking exactly what I'm thinking. He's thinking Beau just found the perfect excuse to cry off doing something she's been avoiding for weeks. "Lawrence is fine." I reach forward and knock her arm lightly, and she looks at me, cautious. She's cottoned on that I've cottoned on. "Aren't you, Lawrence?"

"Fine," he agrees, sitting up, the effort it takes him painful to watch. He clasps both of Beau's hands. "You must go."

"I don't want to."

I inhale some patience, but I keep my mouth shut, hoping Lawrence can solve this without me throwing demands around. It's no secret that I think Tom Hayley is a prick. But once again, I'm willing to overlook that for the sake of Beau. It's another demon of hers that needs crushing.

"For me?" Lawrence pleads, and I slowly sit back, my focus shifting to Beau, watchful. It's below the belt, but I'm not about to call him out on it. Right now, Beau will do anything to help

Lawrence, and if that means he manipulates his position for the sake of Beau's peace, I'm all in. "It would make me so happy for you to reconcile with your father. I know my brother is . . . challenging, to say the least, but he does love you, Beau, even if he has a hard time showing it." He offers a weak smile. "It's not his fault he's an emotional defect."

I laugh to myself. *Well played, Lawrence. Well played.* You'd refuse to believe Lawrence and Tom Hayley were brothers if you didn't know them. Chalk and cheese.

I see the subtle lowering of Beau's shoulders. "Fine," she relents. "But if any journalists show up, I'm leaving."

Tom Hayley better not disappoint me. "Go get ready," I order gently, not giving her time to overthink this. "I'm going for a workout."

She's suddenly acutely aware, running a scrutinizing gaze up and down my form as I stand. She's searching for evidence of a kill. "Not me," I confirm, my eyebrows high and knowing. "He's waiting for me."

She nods slowly, contemplatively, but she doesn't ask questions, leaning up on her tiptoes and pressing a kiss on my cheek. I push into it, swallowing. She's checking if I smell of murder too. "Don't you trust me?"

Her mouth moves to my ear, and it forces my body to lock up. "I trust you to do whatever it takes, and that might mean lying to me," she whispers, discreetly reaching for my groin and cupping my balls. My eyes shoot to Lawrence, who's looking at Beau fondly. She squeezes, and I suppress a low, pained growl. "You won't lie to me, will you?"

There's my girl. "I believe you have me by the balls, baby," I murmur.

"Don't forget it." She clenches down harder, and I cough. Fuck me, what is she doing?

"Beau," I warn, spiking a coy, satisfied smile as she releases me and steps back. *Fuck*. I turn and leave before Lawrence catches sight of my groin area, exhaling as I go. "She's having dinner with her father," I say to Fury after I've pulled the door closed. "He's a megalomaniac, so expect hostility."

"You got it."

"And no matter how many dummies he throws out of his pram, do not take your eyes off Beau."

He nods, and I slip into our room to throw on some workout shorts before making my way to the gym.

I walk in and find Danny raining holy hell on a punchbag, battering the ever-loving shit out of it. When the door closes behind me, he stops, virtually hugging the bag, panting. "I work out alone," he heaves, and we both smile as I lower to a mat and get my arms in position, ready to find my balance and, hopefully, a clear head. I slowly bring my feet from the mat, my knees to my chest, and start extending my legs until I'm as straight as a pole, the rush of blood to my head familiar and needed.

I zone out, my mind clears, and I float in a bubble of quiet nothingness. I walk my way through my kills, reassess their purpose, mentally cross them off the web that sprouts from The Bear. The Irish, the Polish, the Russians. Drugs, women, guns. Animals. The Snake, The Shark, The Ox, all leaders of their division but foot soldiers of The Bear.

My eyes snap open.

"Seventy minutes, James." Danny's distant voice is muffled and grainy. "Your head must be fucking throbbing."

I lower my feet to the floor and blink, feeling the blood rush back into my body. "His son." I turn my eyes onto Danny.

"What?"

"Spittle's son. Why haven't they found him?"

"Otto said he's not been at work and no one at the bank will talk. I've pushed the search wider."

I start to pace, circling the mat, thinking.

"You're making me fucking dizzy." Danny grabs a bottle of water from the fridge and swigs ravenously. "Tell me what the fuck you're thinking before I beat it out of you."

"I'm thinking The Bear has his son. It's the only explanation for Spittle doing something so fucking stupid."

"You mean taking money, shoving mobile phones up his arse, or crossing us?"

"All of the above, but something tells me he's been even more stupid than that." I get up, grab my phone, and jog out of the gym, Danny on my tail.

"James, for fuck's sake, talk."

I make it to Danny's office and push my way in, finding Len clearing up the mess. Dropping to my knee, I scan Spittle's body, feeling at his jacket, working my way down the buttons. I find exactly what I knew I would. I pull the button, and a wire follows. I look up at Danny, my eyes telling him to keep his mouth shut. His face. Fuck, he's raging. I yank at the wire, cutting the reception.

"The fuck?" Danny breathes.

"It was a trap. He wanted you to bring Spittle here." I toss the wire aside and rise. "What was said before you decapitated him?"

He walks over to the Scotch and pours himself a large glass, his workout sweat becoming an angry sweat. "Fuck, fuck, fuck!"

"Did you mention me?"

And as if my phone has heard me, it rings, and we both turn cautious eyes onto my hand where it's held. "I'm going to assume that's a yes," I say, making Danny's nostril flare. *So he knows I'm alive now?*

I answer my mobile, my jaw rolling.

Silence.

I look at Danny, seeing the monster drop into his eyes.

Silence.

I hit the loudspeaker icon.

Silence.

I will not be the first to break it.

"How's Beau?" he asks, and then he hangs up.

"Fuck," Danny yells, throwing his glass across the office.

I'm gone like a bullet, tearing through the mansion at break-neck speed. "Everyone," I roar, crashing through the doors and leaping down the steps. I fall into the nearest car and feel around at the ignition. "Keys!" I get out, moving to the next car in the long line of Mercs, flinging the doors open one by one. "Get me some fucking keys!"

"Here," Danny yells, racing to the Merc at the front. "I'm driving."

I don't argue, sprinting to the passenger side and falling in. I go straight to my phone to dial Fury, seeing a text message from him. Ten minutes ago.

The restaurant is below ground. Reception spotty. I won't move far from Beau.

"Fuck!" I slam my fist into the dash, dialing Fury anyway.

"What is it?"

"Bad reception." It goes straight to voicemail, and I curse my head off some more as Danny skids out of the gates onto the main road. The sound of a phone ringing fills the car, and I glance down at my screen. It's not mine.

"Tank," Danny says, taking the call through Bluetooth. "Now's not a great time."

"We just dropped the kid home. Rose and your mother are insisting on stopping off somewhere."

He stares ahead, his hands flexing around the wheel, his already terrible mood getting some stress added to the mix. "Where?"

"Some workshop near the airport."

"Workshop?"

"I think it's supposed to be a surprise, so I'm feeling a bit backed into a corner here, boss."

"Text Len and tell him where you are so he can join you." He hangs up and scrubs a hand down his face.

"Put your fucking foot down, Danny," I order, dialing Fury again.

Breathe. Breathe. Breathe

No answer.

I reach forward and pull open the glovebox, dragging out the Glock I find and checking the magazine. "You know what this means, don't you?" I say to the gun, my veins burning, my trigger finger twitching.

"Yeah," Danny whispers. "It means we're both back from the dead." He turns cold blue eyes my way. "I will fight you to the death for this kill."

"Then I'd better find him first," I murmur, my eyes constantly passing between the clock, the speedometer, and my phone.

12

BEAU

An hour. For one whole *long* hour I've sat here listening to my father talk non-stop about himself. His investments, his unbearable girlfriend, and the development of new apartments he's building on the marina near South Beach. Maybe he's nervous. Or perhaps he is simply *that* egocentric. The only thing pleasurable about dinner with him so far is the food. And the surroundings are quite lovely too. The Mexican downtown is traditional and quaint. The food is delicious. For that alone, I'm glad I didn't turn away at the door when I realized Dad had failed to take into consideration my issue with busy spaces. Although, really, it wasn't all that busy in the main restaurant. I've faced worse in recent times, but James isn't with me tonight.

My father seemed oblivious to my building stress as we stood on the sidewalk outside, his eyes fixed on my exposed scar. I think I saw regret in his eyes. Regret and pain.

"I can't eat here, Dad," I'd said quietly. It was in that moment he clicked. He apologized profusely, held me by the tops of my arms, and begged me to let him fix it. He didn't let me down. We've been seated downstairs, away from the main restaurant upstairs. It's quiet down here. Just us. No journalists, no girlfriend, and no anxiety on my part. But the presence of Fury hasn't gone unnoticed, my dad recoiling when he caught sight of the mountain shadowing me as I got out of the car.

"He's a friend of James's," I'd explained simply. And he hadn't pressed. I expect he wasn't prepared to face the consequences. Smart man. And so, yes, it's been okay. I can cope with it. My father, on the other hand, blows my mind at every turn. I don't even know what he's rambling on about now, his lips moving, his arms swinging around animatedly between forkfuls of his pasta.

"What do you think?" he asks, taking a mouthful of his wine, waiting for me to answer.

"Great," I murmur, lost, my compassionate side unwilling to let me rain on his proud parade by telling him I've not been listening. Just nod. Smile. Agree every now and then, and this will all be over very soon.

"Excellent." He smiles, holding up his glass for the waiter to fill. "I'll make the arrangements."

I nod, clueless, and glance at my phone. Still no service. I look to Fury. He shakes his head. I'm getting progressively more restless, my thoughts increasingly difficult to keep in check. There's been no mention of James from my father, the man he thinks abuses me. He's not asked after Lawrence. Not that I can share much, of course. And the need to bring up my mother is becoming overwhelming. Here's my father, laughing, jolly, boasting about his high-flying life, and where is the woman he abandoned? The woman who was by his side when he was nothing. The woman he discarded when he became something.

Dead. Murdered.

He's so fucking blissfully unaware, it's crushing. But it's not his fault. I have to keep telling myself that, or I'll melt with a rage that's being channeled on the wrong person.

"I'm just going to use the restroom," I say, getting up, prompting my father to rise too. "Excuse me." I dab my lips with my napkin and walk away from the table, Fury on my heels. My eyes are on my screen, searching for just one bar that'll give me some coverage so I can check in on Lawrence and also call James, because I know he'll be fretting. Nothing. "Damn it," I breathe, pushing my way into the restrooms. I wander around the small space, arm in the air, willing my cell to pick up a connection. Nothing. I pull the door open. "I need to go upstairs for a second," I say to Fury, skirting past his enormous body. I won't settle until I speak to Lawrence and James.

I reach the stairs, take the handle, but my foot stops just shy of the first step when I see someone coming down them. My heart begins to beat double time, my head quickly swimming, as I back up into Fury's chest. "What the hell?" I whisper, quickly and instinctively moving behind the nearest thing that'll hide me. Fury. He looks over his shoulder to me, his big, bearded face frowning.

"Who's that?" he asks, hand on his hip.

I look past him, just as Ollie reaches the bottom of the staircase, his expression alarmed by the beast before him. "My ex-fiancé," I breathe.

"Should I kill him?"

"What?"

"Should I—"

"No, you shouldn't kill him. Why would you ask that?"

"Because I'm pretty sure that's what James would tell me to do."

I close my eyes, my meltdown very real. Not only because Fury is right. "Fucking hell." All is suddenly *very* clear. This is a trap. A ploy. A joint effort to reel me back into Ollie's affections. "We need to leave."

"Stay there," Fury orders, one arm moving out to hold me behind him, the other remaining under his suit jacket where his gun is holstered.

"You don't need your gun, Fury."

"You might know him, but I don't."

"He's an FBI Agent."

"And James is a mass murderer so I'll take my chances, thanks. Ready?"

Oh God.

"Beau?" Dad's voice comes at me from the side, and I cautiously peek at him.

"Why?" I ask. "Why would you do this?"

"Do what?"

He astounds me at every turn. Is he that thick-skinned? I move out from behind Fury and face the situation. My ex.

Ollie raises a hand in hello, but his eyes are set firmly on my muscle-bound guard. I can only imagine the conversations between my father and Ollie. It's worrying. Ollie was there when Dexter held me at gunpoint. He heard what was said, and in a moment of panic, I try my hardest to remember exactly what that was. *And* if Ollie was even conscious when it was said. I can't be sure. I can't recall. It was a frantic situation, most of it a blur, and the next thing I knew I was waking up in The Brit's mansion. But what I can be sure of are the damaging statements that Ollie flung around when I broke my wrist. Dad definitely heard that. So now what? They've formed an alliance?

"Why did you bring Ollie here?"

Dad recoils, moving closer, his neck craning to see the bottom of the stairs. "Ollie?" He smiles immediately. "What a nice surprise."

God, give me strength, does he actually expect me to buy his horseshit? "Dad, give me some credit." I move forward, but quickly get tugged back by Fury, obviously getting too close for his liking. His hand's still on his gun, his eyes still resting on my ex. He doesn't break his stare, simply shaking his head, and because I trust him, and perhaps because I want my dad and ex to come out of this alive, I listen, remaining where I am.

"Beau, darling." Dad comes to me, arms open. "I had nothing to do with this."

"Then why is he here?" I look to Ollie, for the first time noting how forlorn he appears.

"I saw Tom this afternoon," he says. "I asked after you, of course, and he mentioned your dinner plans. Since you're not taking my calls and I can't seem to get close to you . . ." He turns his eyes onto Fury, who moves in closer to me, his massive chest pressing into my shoulders. "Beau, I don't know what kind of trouble you're in, but—"

"Is it that man?" Dad pipes in. "Are you talking about that man? James?" Dad comes to me. "Has he hurt you again?"

"No, and I'm not in any trouble," I grate, going to the table and grabbing my purse. "Everyone needs to stop interfering."

The panic on Dad's face as he rushes to me pierces my heart. "Beau, don't go. We were having such a lovely time."

"I'll call you," I say passing him, just as an almighty bang comes from upstairs. "Oh fuck," I whisper. The sound of charging men pounding through the restaurant is deafening, and he crashes down the stairs like a wrecking ball, landing at the bottom, armed, his face nothing short of raw, burning rage. And as if James wasn't enough, Danny speeds down behind him. Both are in workout gear. *What the hell is going on?* I watch, pensive, as James's gun swings back and forth from my father to Ollie, as if he can't quite decide who to kill first.

"What on earth?" Dad cries, arms held in the air, moving back.

Ollie remains silent, backing up into a wall, watchful eyes on James, whose breathing is off-the-charts heavy. I would like to think the mere fact that my ex is here *isn't* a good enough reason for James to be charging in on my dinner with Dad, brandishing a gun. But I know James. He hates Ollie. Yet something isn't sitting right, and with Danny backing him up?

"What's going on?" I ask, splitting my attention between them. "Why are you here?" Neither appear prepared to talk, both silent, both looking pretty fucking murderous. "James?"

He doesn't look at me, his focus elsewhere. What is he thinking? For a man who's been encouraging me to make amends with my father, he's not exactly helping matters.

"Fine," I snap, pushing my way past them, done with this. With *them*. I get two steps up before I'm hauled back and pulled into James's chest, his gun now set on Ollie.

"You take your hands off my daughter!" Dad bellows.

"Dad," I breathe, willing him to shut the hell up. Now is not the time to wield his ego. "Please."

"What are you thinking, Beau?" he goes on, waving a hand at James, deranged. He looks at Danny. "And who the hell is this? His partner in crime? Another wannabe gangster?"

Oh Jesus. Dad really doesn't want to know who *this* is. He doesn't want to know anything. "James is not a gangster." *He's a murderer. An assassin.* He's The Enigma, and I know my father will have heard of him because his dead wife was chasing him down before he left her for another woman.

"That there is Danny Black. Better known as The Brit," Ollie says, his face unmoving, as if he's heard the whispers of Danny's resurrection. "And him," he goes on, turning his eyes onto James. "There's no record on him. Nothing. Nowhere."

"Who the fuck are *you*?" Danny asks, moving forward threateningly. "Inspector Gadget?"

"Danny, please," I beg, feeling James's white-hot gaze on the back of my head. "He means no harm."

"Do you, Ollie?" James asks, his voice ice. "Do you mean any harm?"

"I'm not standing around listening to this. Seeing this," Dad yells, yanking his jacket off the back of his chair, his disappointed gaze landing on me. He has no right to feel disappointed, and yet it still stings. "This is absurd." He stalks away without another word, and I watch, annoyingly disheartened. "This isn't the last you'll hear from me," he yells back. "I'll have you thrown in jail."

Danny's suddenly moving fast, and he seizes my dad, throwing him against the wall, wedging the gun in his cheek.

"Danny," I yell, scrambling to get free from James's tight hold and failing.

"This is definitely the last we'll hear from you, Mr. Hayley," Danny whispers menacingly, moving his hand to Dad's throat. My father's eyes widen and fear falls into them.

"Danny, stop."

"The only reason," he hisses, "you're not dying now"— Danny moves the gun to my father's temple, and Dad flinches— "is because you're Beau's father, and I have a really fucking annoying fondness for your daughter." He shoves him away. "So fuck off before I misplace my morals."

My head goes into my hands, my brain about to explode. That's it. I can kiss goodbye to any kind of happy families I might have secretly hoped for. It was one thing Dad suspecting James was physical with me. I could have proved otherwise. But there is nothing I can do to erase the past five minutes of weapons being flaunted and deadly threats being thrown.

"Beau," Ollie says quietly. "Beau, I—"

"Just go, Ollie." I exhale, begging him with all I have. "Go before they kill you."

I back up toward the ladies' restroom and disappear through the door, going to the mirror and roughly wiping my eyes. I have around two seconds alone before James charges in. "Don't," I warn, furious, unable to appreciate the immense ball of rage burning wildly before me. He's caused me untold stress by barging in on my dinner. And himself, for that matter. As well as Danny. My father might have been shitting himself while Danny held him at gunpoint, but once he's out of reach, his ego will kick in and he will be moving mountains and using his influence to get James and Danny thrown in jail. I would like to think he'd be doing that for me too, and he'll no doubt play that card, but I know my father. It'll be for his image more than anything, because God forbid anyone finds out that his ex-cop daughter is wrapped up in the criminal underworld of Miami.

"You've made this even more hard fucking work than it already was, James." I move past him fast. Obviously, he makes a grab for me, but this time I don't let him win, stealthily twisting and locking his arms, sending his gun to the floor. I rush up the stairs.

"Beau!"

I ignore him, marching through the restaurant, seeing all the tables are now without diners. There's no staff either. Empty. But then, seeing two men like James and Danny charging through with guns would explain that.

"Beau!"

"Fuck off, James," I yell, pushing my way out of the door, looking for Dad. I see Ollie pulling away and Dad getting into his car up the street. "Dad!" I can't leave things like this. I can't let him think I'm a doormat or even a victim. "Dad, wait." He stalls at his car, watching me hurrying toward me. "Dad, please," I say, coming to a stop, a little breathless.

"Beau, my darling, come home with me," he pleads, his face soft, his worry real as he massages his chest.

"I can't do that, Dad."

"You can," he insists, constantly looking past me to the restaurant, wary of what's going to come charging out of the doors at any moment, gunning for him. "I'll take care of you."

I smile, but it's sad. It's like he's brandishing words he thinks I need to hear. Problem is, even if they were the right words, it's too little too late.

His phone rings, and he curses, taking the call, grimacing as he continues to rub circles on his chest.

"Dad, are you okay?" He looks ashen.

"Beau, for fuck's sake," James bellows, and I look back, seeing him and Danny piling out of the restaurant, still fucking armed.

"God damn it," I mutter, torn between holding them back and seeing to my father.

"Just give me a minute," I say to Dad, heading back toward James, set on calming him the hell down. *Why the fuck are they here? Especially together.*

I walk with intent, like no woman should walk toward two deadly men.

"Beau," Dad calls, holding the side of his car, his body hunched.

I stop, worried. "Dad?"

"I'm fine," he wheezes, trying to straighten himself and failing.

"Jesus." Has my boyfriend given my dad a heart attack?

"Beau!" James yells, winning my attention.

Boom!

The front of the restaurant seems to swell, the sky lights up, windows shatter, glass sprays, and the sound pierces my eardrums. I scream, bringing my hands over my head to protect me from the flying debris. I stagger toward a nearby wall to lean on, my hands holding my ears with force, suppressing the exposure to the never-ending roar of noise. The flashbacks. The screams. The burning, unbearable heat. I see Mom's car. I see her face the second before it blew up. "No!"

I look up, spinning on the spot, disorientated. The ringing in my ears is unbearable, my vision foggy. It's all too familiar, but I can't feel the blackness setting in. I can't feel the pain. "James?" I yell, frantically searching the street. Panic pushes my shock aside. He was closer to the restaurant. Oh my God. "James!" I scream. The smoke is thick, car alarms wail, people scream. "James!"

"Beau."

I gasp and move toward his voice, cutting the plumes of dense air with my body, coughing into my hand. The heat. God, the heat. "James?"

"Here," he says. "I'm here." He emerges from behind one of Danny's Mercs, holding the side to hold himself up. All the windows have been blown out, the hood littered with broken bricks and glass. James's face is smudged with soot, and he has a horrible hacking cough.

"Fuck me," Danny splutters, getting up from the ground, his hands braced on his knees as he coughs his guts up.

"Fury," I murmur, scanning the area. "Where's Fury?"

Both James and Danny look to what remains of the restaurant, the flames billowing inside.

"Oh no," I whisper, my hand coming up to my mouth. "No, no, no."

"Beau, we need to get out of here," James barks, seizing me.

"But Fury!" I wriggle and squirm in his hold, trying to pry his hands from around my waist as he drags me away.

"He's here," Danny yells, disappearing behind a mountain of rubble and emerging a few moments later with Fury staggering along beside him, hacking and choking. "Get in the car!"

My relief gets the better of me, emotion catching up, and I let out a wracked sob. It's short-lived. "Dad," I blurt, starting to fight James's hold again. "My dad." I'm suddenly facing the other direction, James having swung around, and I see my father holding on to the side of his car, looking completely stunned. He's in shock. I break away, running toward him. "Dad," I pant, making it to him, holding his suit-covered arms. "Dad, are you okay?"

"Beau, we need to go," James barks.

"I can't just leave him!" He's a zombie, completely out of it.

"Fuck," James curses, taking my father's arm and guiding him to the passenger side of his car. "Where are your keys?"

Dad blinks rapidly, patting at his pockets absentmindedly. "I don't know. I had them."

I scan the sidewalk where he was standing and spot them in the gutter. "I've got them." I dip, collecting them and throwing them across the roof of the car to James.

"Get in," he orders me.

I do as I'm told and watch as James rounds Dad's car, signaling to Danny up front, and as soon as he's behind the wheel, he screeches off, throwing me back in my seat.

"Get your belt on, Beau," he demands harshly, catching up to Danny as I slowly pull my belt across, shaken to my core, my ears ringing, my attention split between my raging boyfriend and my traumatized father.

Until I hear sirens.

I peek out the back of Dad's car and see various emergency service vehicles speeding into the street from the other end. "You knew something was going to happen," I whisper, turning back around. James is supposed to be dead, so what the fuck is going on? He looks up at the rearview mirror, finding me. "Are we just going to skirt past the fact that someone just tried to blow you up again?"

He doesn't say anything.

He doesn't have to.

The Bear's moves are becoming bolder.

And death seems to be getting closer.

It's complete chaos outside Danny's mansion when we pull through the gates. Otto and Goldie look about ready to tear each other's heads off, Ringo between them, Brad's just getting out of his car, and Rose is being held on the steps by Esther and Tank.

I peek at my father, who hasn't breathed a word for the whole journey, his gaze set firmly forward. And it isn't because he's scared of the man beside him. I don't think he's got it in him to be *anything* at the moment, other than frozen from shock.

As soon as James rolls to a stop, I get out, rounding the car to open the door for Dad. He looks at me blankly. My smile is weak as I offer my hand, and he accepts, letting me help pull him out. I shut the door and motion the way, seeing Rose flying down the steps and diving into Danny's waiting arms. She checks him everywhere, kisses every square inch of his face. And then slaps him.

I watch, tense, as everyone waits for his reaction. He cracks his jaw. Rolls it. Gives Rose a murderous glare. And then she dives back into his arms on a broken sob.

"Beau," Dad says, turning into me. "Where are we? What on earth is going on?" He looks up and around again, before grabbing my arms and getting close. "We must leave. You'll be safe with me."

I can only smile dejectedly at his naivety, taking his hands and holding them. "I'm safest here," I assure him. "I promise you."

He deflates before my eyes, as if it's just this moment finally sunk in that I'm here of my own free will. "I don't understand."

He shakes his head, frowning, looking as if he's trying to unravel it all here and now. "Why?"

"Because I need to know who killed Mom," I admit, the words just coming. It's time to give Dad some of the information he needs so he can wrap his mind around my life. "And because I love James."

Dad's frown deepens. "Your mother died in an accident."

It doesn't escape my notice that he's completely swerved my final statement. "It was no accident."

He recoils, his eyes flicking to James. "What are you talking about?"

"One day, Dad, I will tell you everything." I tuck an arm through his and start leading him toward the house. "But just know this," I say, looking at him. "James is saving me."

He shakes his head, a clear indication that he doesn't understand and probably never will. "I should call Amber," he says, reaching up to his chest again, massaging.

"Dad, I want Doc to check you over first," I say, not liking his chalky complexion.

"Who's Doc?"

Esther approaches, her friendly smile as friendly as always. I can't help returning it because I know what's coming. "I'm putting the kettle on," she says.

"Would you mind showing my dad to the kitchen?" I ask. "I'm sure he could do with one of your famous teas." I pass him over to Esther as his head bats back and forth between us. "Esther will take care of you. I'll be there in a minute."

Esther, ever on the ball, whisks him off, away from the brewing showdown on the driveway, without giving him the opportunity to protest. And like she knows him inside out, she starts distracting him from the army of murderers behind him with compliments.

I sigh, seeing Fury limping toward the house. Rose is still

attached to Danny's front while he talks to the others, obviously detailing what just went down, and James is sitting on the hood of Danny's mangled Merc, arms and legs crossed, watching me.

I wander over and lower my ass next to his. "Why were you there?"

"Because I got a call."

"From?"

"The Bear."

"What did he say?"

"Your name."

I swing my eyes to his, not panicked, not worried, just surprised. "So he lured you there and you fell for it?" God, he must have been in his element with Danny Black there too. Two birds, one bomb. Did he know The Brit was there?

"Fell for it?" James laughs over his breath, and there's not one scrap of humor in it. "What did you want me to do, Beau? Carry on with my workout and hope he was joking?"

My eyes drop to the ground. I don't know what the hell I want. I just want this to be over. I rub at my temple, hearing Otto and Goldie still bickering. "What's wrong with those two?"

"Otto was hanging out at Hiatus with Brad. Goldie wasn't best—" Pulling up, he takes my arm, stroking over my scar. I look down and see a long cut, the blood drying. "You're always injured."

I know what he's thinking, and it doesn't sit well. So I pull my arm away and move in front of him, roughly pushing his thighs apart and getting in between them, my arms draped around his neck. "I'm okay," I assure him. The cut? It's trivial. It's nothing in the grand scheme of things. We've both sustained so much worse.

I reach forward and brush my fingertip lightly over his cheekbone, where a tiny shard of glass is glimmering in the sunlight. "Keep still," I whisper, leaning into him and placing my mouth over the area, sucking gently while running my tongue across his skin. When I can no longer feel the shard grazing my flesh, I pull back and pinch the shard off the end of my tongue.

"I'm okay," he whispers, gazing so deeply into my eyes.

And because we understand each other's language, I take his hand and lead him into the house. To our room. To our bed.

To that place where there is only us, electricity, and a ferocious need that can never be sated.

I'm stripped, tied to the bed, blindfolded, and gagged.

"Oh my God," I breathe when I feel his tongue sweep through my pussy. "More."

13

DANNY

If this is the welcome home I'll get each time, I might try and get myself blown up every day, the slap aside, of course. My blood has gone from being charged with adrenalin to charged with need. Need for her.

Release.

Clear my head.

I'm certainly not thinking straight, because every fiber of my being is demanding me to go on a shooting spree until some fucker tells me who the fuck The Bear is. He's laying traps down all over Miami, and we're walking right into them. *Release.*

"Baby, I can't breathe," I whisper, reaching back for her arms and forcing them away. She loosens her hold but compensates by climbing up me and wrapping her thighs around me too. "I'm going to take a shower," I say to no one in particular, carrying Rose up the steps as Tank moves aside, nodding.

I take the stairs and wander through the mansion, and the

pressure builds and builds in my head, questions running in circles. I have no answers. I don't even feel close. Spittle is dead, his son is missing, and we don't know who the fuck The Bear is. One thing is clear, though. The Bear succeeded in intercepting the safety deposit box before anyone else, which means James's suspicions were correct. Beau's mum really did figure it out. Forgive me, but it's a massive fucking ego crusher knowing that a law-abiding FBI agent unraveled the mystery, and we're nowhere near fucking close. I growl to myself, my concern for our situation growing by the hour. No one is talking. No one is dealing with us. Everyone in Miami appears to be under his control. Everyone except us.

And that's a problem for him.

I let us into our suite and go straight to the bathroom, lowering Rose to the vanity and flipping on the shower. I put some music on, strip down, cast my filthy gym clothes aside, and move into her, taking the hem of her jumper. "Arms up," I order, lifting it over her head and throwing it on top of the pile of laundry.

"Tell me what happened," she says quietly, as I reach behind her and unhook her bra.

"No." I drag the lace down her arms and drop it to the floor, moving to her jeans. "I don't want to talk, Rose. Lift."

She pushes her hands onto the counter and raises her arse. "So I'm just here as a form of relaxation for you, am I?"

I discard her jeans, then her knickers, and take her ponytail in my fist. Hard. And because Rose is Rose, she pulls against my hold, showing me that the woman I fell in love with is still here. "No, you're here as a form of purpose." I loosen my hold and tighten it again, my eyes fixed on hers. Her palms splay on my pecs and stroke down my torso, through the dust and grime sticking to my clammy, post-workout skin. She reaches my groin, intent swirling in her dark blue eyes. I let my heavy head drop, my forehead meeting her shoulder, a strangled groan saturating the bathroom when she curls her hand around my cock. "Stroke," I order, biting down on my lip, the veins in my dick throbbing. "Stoke me slowly." My hand tightens in her hair, my spare finding the counter, anchoring me. "Slowly," I whisper, every muscle hardening as she glides up and down my length lazily. My hips begin to circle, my mouth drying from my heavy pants. "Easy," I murmur, turning my face into her neck and latching on, sucking and biting at her flesh. "Make me come, Rose."

"Soon." Her hand drops, and I growl, yanking at her hair. "Now."

She jars her head, hissing with pain. "Soon." Her palms push into my chest with force, and I stagger back, dazed.

"Now," I grate, blinking my vision clear. "Do it now, Rose." My throat is suddenly in her hand, her small frame walking me back into the shower. My back hits the tile. Her front meets mine. The steam and water drench us. She squeezes my throat, and I swallow, searching her wild eyes. "What are you doing?"

She drops to her knees, looking up at me, her tongue running across her lips. Then I'm in her mouth—so fucking deep—and I bark at the ceiling, my fists balling.

I suck air through my teeth, my knees immediately wobbling. Her fingers find my arse and claw, digging in harshly. "Fuck!" She slides back, circles, kisses, and yanks me back into her mouth. "Jesus!" My hands go to her head and hold on for dear life, my hips thrusting to meet her manic pace. The tip of my cock hits the back of her throat repeatedly, her teeth grazing my shaft, the friction dizzying. I mumble her name over and over, feeling utterly blindsided by her mercilessness, my body locking up in preparation. Completely dazed, I drop my head and my eyes. She's watching me, her head bobbing, her hold of my tense arse brutal. Blood surges. Nerves sizzle. "I'm going to come." My words are strained.

She pulls away. "Soon," she rasps, rising and pushing her face into my cheek, biting the area of my scar. I exhale. It's shaky and strained, my dick twitching against her stomach.

"Rose." Her name on my lips is a warning.

"Danny," she whispers, taking my shoulders and pushing into them. "Down." And because I'm a fucking slave to this woman, I go down, kissing my way across her taut, wet stomach, through her strip of hair, and into the white-hot heat of her pussy. "Oh, yes"

I lick, suck, kiss, bite, slipping my fingers inside and fucking her as my tongue caresses her. I look up through the water raining down on us. Her head hangs limply, her palms braced against the wall. I place a hand on her arse and squeeze hard.

"Yes," she breathes, smacking the wall with a fist, and when I think she might come, she hauls herself back, gasping for breath, leaving me on my knees, my watering mouth ravenous for more.

"Rose," I warn, reaching for her thigh. She moves back. "Don't make this violent." Another step back. My nostrils flare, my desperation going through the roof. "Come here."

Her smile is salacious as she pads toward my kneeling form. She cups my head in her palms, looking down at me. "Do you want me to fuck you, Danny?" she asks, bending, getting her mouth to my ear. She licks behind my lobe, instigating a whole new level of shakes. They ripple through me, from my brain to my toes, and I hiss, forced to pin down my dick before it explodes. "Ride you," she whispers. "Grind onto you. Scream your name."

"I'm a patient man, Rose, but you're pushing me."

"What are you going to do?" She licks the shell of my ear, humming, satisfied when I jerk. "Kill me?"

"Why are you testing me?" She knows what I need. *Stop denying me.*

"Because. I. Can." She shoves me down to my back and straddles me, lifting and seizing my dick. Then she levels us up and sinks down on a moan, her head falling back.

Lord have mercy, the sight, the feel. She shifts her legs, placing the soles of her feet on either side of my chest, leaning back and anchoring herself with her palms on my shins. I reach up to her throat and stroke down between her breasts as she rises and smashes down, our flesh slapping. "Fuck!" I grab her knees, and she goes again, up and down with force. My head rises and falls back to the shower floor with a whack. A roll of her hips, a grind, a sharp rise and fall. And then she's in her flow, bouncing up and down on my lap, her head tossing from side to side on constant cries of pleasure. I lift my head again, but this time fight to keep it up, looking down my tense torso, watching my cock sink into her constantly. My neck muscles strain, my thighs rigid, my stomach aching. But the view. The view is so worth it. She gasps, I roar. She moans, I hiss. The sensations, the friction, the rush of my release charging through me. I need more.

I shoot up, circling an arm around her, and take her down to her back, sinking in quickly and thrusting frenziedly, my hands pressed into the shower floor, my arms ramrod straight, holding me up. "Danny!"

"Because. I. Can," I yell, shaking some water out of my eyes, never faltering in my pace. Her hands grapple at my pecs, fly over her head, sink into her hair. And then they're on my face, her fingers dragging across my lips, feeling, her eyes drowsy but alive. She's going.

I pull out on a bark and spin her onto her front, ramming

back inside of her. My biceps bulge, holding me at half height as I bite at her wet back, powering on. My body's hurting. Every muscle's pulling. My mind's gone. Pound after pound, I give it to her. Scream after scream, she begs me for it.

And when we go, we go together, and it's fucking loud.

I bellow at the ceiling as her walls grab on and wring me dry, her body twitching beneath me, her voice broken and hoarse. I collapse, dazed, breathless, and more in love with my wife than I thought possible. "I hate you," I pant, pushing my face into her wet hair.

"I hate you more." She can hardly speak. Can't move. So I force myself up with some effort, slipping free on a wince. My dick's still pulsing. Jesus, that was good. And so fucking needed.

"Stay there." I reach for the shower gel, squeezing some across her back, and straddle her arse, starting to work her muscles back to life as I watch her profile, her cheek resting on her folded arms under her head. Her eyes are closed. Her lips parted to find air.

"You weren't wearing your vest," she says, remaining in her darkness. "You promised."

"I don't think a bulletproof vest would have saved me from a bomb, baby." I push my thumbs firmly into her spine and work them up to her neck, her body rolling with them. "And there wasn't time."

"Why?"

My escape has been short-lived. "The Bear knows James is alive. James got a call."

"What did he say?"

I feel her muscles harden under my touch. "Relax," I order, massaging deeply. "Nothing. Only Beau's name." I swallow, watching my touch move across her shoulder blades. "He knows she's James's weak spot. As you are mine."

She moves to turn over, so I get off her, resting my arse on my heels. "Is she okay?"

"A few scratches. She was on the street. We were *nearly* on the street."

"Why wasn't Beau with you?"

"She and James had an argument. Her ex was there when we charged in, so James's already boiling blood bubbled over. Beau stormed out. We were a few too many paces behind."

"So you only got out alive because James and Beau had an argument?" she asks, and I nod. That's the crux of it. Although we only made it out by the skin of our teeth. "Danny, I feel like he's getting closer and closer." Her worry is warranted, and I won't insult her by claiming otherwise. I puff out my cheeks, taking her hands and standing us up.

I get under the spray and soap myself down. That's enough. "How was your day *shopping*?"

"Fine." She sighs, frowning as she starts shampooing her hair. "We need to talk about Daniel."

I still, worried. "What about him?"

"He's a smart kid, Danny. There's only so long we can keep the truth from him." Her worry slips into a small smile. "He loved his jet ski, Mister."

I nod, like it's nothing. "Good," I say gruffly, rinsing. I seize her jaw and her hands freeze in her hair. "Don't worry about Daniel," I order, kissing her hard. She should know better. I'll protect that kid as vehemently as I protect her. "Now the boat-yard's nearly finished, he can try out his new ski."

"I'm not comfortable with him being at the boatyard, Danny."

I suck my bottom lip between my teeth as I step out and reach for a towel. I can't claim being with us is the safest place for Daniel to be when there are bombs going off left and right.

"You know me, Rose. I won't allow him to see anything he shouldn't see." It's a stark contrast to *my* childhood, where I saw all the things I definitely shouldn't have seen.

She sighs. "I should check on Beau."

I laugh a little. "Not tonight." I dry off, our bed calling. Sleep calling. "We're going to bed."

She smiles, but it drops as she takes a soapy hand to her stomach.

I falter drying myself with the towel. "What's up?"

"Nothing." She shudders. "I feel like I've been pounded by a very hard, very large dick."

I grin. "You're welcome," I quip, satisfied and semi-sated. "I could binge on you forever, baby, and never feel full." Her nose wrinkles as she steps under the spray to rinse her hair. "Meet me in bed. Naked." I grin. "And let's see how long you can resist me."

I slept like a baby, but I don't wake feeling refreshed and revitalized. Sitting on the edge of the bed, I drag my palms down my rough face, exhaling heavily. Rose is sprawled beautifully across the sheets. So peaceful. At least, she looks it. I fear she's as churned up inside as I am.

Leaving her sleeping, I shower, dress, and make my way downstairs, texting Tank as I do, my face in my phone as I take the steps. I frown at the missed call from Leon ten minutes ago and call him back. "What's up?" I ask, frowning harder when he starts to explain.

"You serious?"

"Dead serious, D-boss."

"I'm sending Len over. When he gets there, you help him put the fucker in the yellow container." I hang up and text Len as I hit the marble.

Look up.

And freeze.

What the fuck? I immediately move a step back. Actually, *who* the fuck? I take in the back of a slight, tall figure of the woman, her masses of blonde, tumbling curls cascading down her back, skimming her arse. Her sequin-embellished catsuit is blinding, her platform stilettos skyscrapers, putting her at least half a foot taller than I am. The new in-house whore?

I frown. She has rather large feet. And, come to think of it, wide shoulders.

I inhale, ready to ask her who the fuck she is and what the fuck she's doing in my house when she swirls around.

I recoil, my mouth snapping shut.

"Oh hello," she sings, dramatically flicking her hair over her shoulder. "And who might you be?"

I don't like the cheeky smile, or the delight in her eyes. Like a goldfish, I stand there, blank, my feet automatically taking another step back. "Danny," I murmur like a twat, looking around, before turning my wary eyes back onto her. Him. The man. The woman. *What the fuck is going on?* "And who might *you* be?" I ask, tilting my head, my persona no doubt nervous. I don't do nervous, but it's the way she's . . . he's . . . looking at me. Like I'm lunch.

"I'm—"

"This is my aunt Zinnea," Beau says from behind me.

She's coming down the stairs, her hair wet, an amused smile on her face. Aunt? "Ohhhh," I breathe, clicking, wondering why the fuck no one thought to tell me. I would have been more prepared. Less obviously shocked.

"I didn't think she'd be visiting for a while, or I would have mentioned her." Beau passes me, still amused, and joins her uncle. Aunt.

"I'm a drag queen, darling. Don't be alarmed." Zinnea rests

her weight on a hip, her hand there too, her long talons a vivid shade of pink.

Beau's barely keeping her laughter in check. I roll my eyes, looking back when I hear more footsteps behind me. James plods down, fastening the two buttons of his polo shirt. He too has an amused smile on his murderous face. I curl my lip at him. *Dickhead.* He *definitely* could have told me. Returning my attention back to Beau and her uncle . . . aunt, I smile. I know it's dark. "Well, I'm a murderer, so no judgments from me."

He . . . *she* gasps dramatically, her hand slapping her chest. "This is your house?"

"This is my house," I confirm, passing them. "I hope you're enjoying your stay at my pleasure." I turn and walk backward. "How's your father?"

"I'm just going to check," Beau says, motioning to the kitchen. "Your mom was making him tea."

"He stayed the night?"

She shrugs. "I wanted Doc to check him over."

I laugh under my breath. The only thing wrong with Beau's father is a serious case of wanker-itis. "But he's going today, right?" Because I can't promise I won't kill the fucker if I bump into him.

"Yes," she assures me, a knowing glint in her eye. "I would have asked, but Tank said you were busy."

"Wait," Zinnea yelps, turning into Beau and grabbing her checks. "Tom's here?"

"Yeah."

"Oh my." He . . . *she* pirouettes on the spot and flounces off toward the kitchen. "Brother!" she sings as she enters.

"What the hell is *he* doing here?" a loud, gruff voice barks.

Beau sighs, turning to kiss James. "I'd better go." She jogs off, and James catches up to me.

"I've been thinking," he says, focused forward.

"Me too." I open the door to my office. "I think we need to pull our fingers out our arses before we end up dead." I smile. "For real."

"Great plan," Brad agrees from the couch.

"What the fuck are you doing here this early?" I ask, scrutinizing his bedraggled form.

"I stayed the night so I could be here this early," he says as Goldie, Ringo, and Otto all pile in. It's not even eight and my house is full. I need to start charging rent. "What the fuck happened?" Brad asks, getting up and pacing.

I drop into my chair and gaze around the office. "Something's different," I muse quietly, not quite being able to put my finger on it.

Goldie coughs, and everyone's attention turns to her. She taps the carpet with the tip of her boot. "New carpet."

"Oh yeah." I lean across my desk and crane my neck, taking it all in. "Blue. I like it."

"It was the only color available off the shelf."

"You laid it too?"

"Yes, I laid it too," she grates, daring me to make a big deal of it.

"Ringo moved the furniture for her." Otto's face is deadpan as Goldie swings toward him.

"Are you ever gonna shut that fucking trap of yours or do I have to carve your tongue out?"

I press my lips together. I want to keep my tongue. "All right, children," I sigh. "Good job, Goldie."

"Thanks, Boss."

"Thanks, who?" James asks, and she shrugs. I chuckle, and James drops to a chair, exasperated. "Let's get on with it."

"I don't know where to fucking start," I admit.

"Maybe here," Otto pipes up, coming over. He throws a picture on my desk. "I believe you know this man."

I stare at the image, almost afraid to ask. "I do. That's Rose's kid's dad."

"Biological?" Otto asks, and I shake my head, feeling James's eyes on me. He knows the story, but I won't be going into details with anyone else. "He's a lawyer, yes?" Otto asks, and an uncomfortable shiver slithers down my spine.

"Yes, he's a lawyer," I confirm. "Will you get to the fucking point?"

"He's representing Vince Roake."

The room falls silent, and James shoots a shocked stare Otto's way, as I try to get my head around what I'm hearing. "The Alligator?" I ask. The Irish fucker who's rumored to be taking the place of The Snake? "Hilary and Derek are respectable people."

"Who bought Rose's kid on the black market," James says quietly, telling everyone in the room what I *didn't* want them to know. I flash him a threatening look, and he tilts his head, his eyebrows high.

"Be real, Danny," Brad says. "James is right."

"There's not a cat in hell's chance he'd represent someone like Vince Roake," I say, agitated. "Known criminal, drugs dealer, and murderer?" I laugh. "No way."

James shrugs. "Not unless he's being—"

"Blackmailed," I whisper. *Fuck!*

We all jump when Rose bursts in, breathless, panicked, out of her mind. "Daniel," she blurts, her eyes welling. "He said he's not allowed to see me anymore."

"Oh fuck," Brad breathes, immediately starting to pace. "Oh fuck, fuck, fuck."

The rage is instant, it's hot, and it's going to erupt. "Get him here," I demand, standing from my chair. "No, fuck it. *I'll* go to him." I round the desk and stalk toward the door, stopping when

I reach Rose, taking her wet cheeks in my palms and kissing away her tears.

"What's going on?" she asks, taking my wrists. "Do you know why?"

"Am I going to fix this?" I ask, resting my nose on hers. She nods, sniveling. "You bet your sweet arse I am." I push my lips to her forehead and leave her, walking through the mansion with purpose. "Get me his office address," I call back to whoever's following me. "And my machine gun."

"Danny." Tank appears, looking a bit bewildered. And worried.

"She's in my office," I snap, my pace not faltering, my purpose unwavering. "Why didn't you know that?"

"I did know that."

I stop in my tracks, and all the men behind me grind to a halt too. So why the fuck is he looking so worried? "I'm in the middle of something here, Tank."

"It's important."

Important? "As in, it concerns my important wife?"

He nods, his eyes flicking to the men behind me, prompting me to turn too. They're all silent, uncomfortable, and I realize that whatever has Tank looking worried isn't because he briefly misplaced my wife.

"I'll meet you at the cars," I say and, of course, there's no contesting. They all file past, Brad giving me a look to suggest I should keep my cool no matter what I'm about to hear. Likely. James comes out of my office with a machine gun in each hand, looking as murderous as I feel. "She still in there?" I ask him.

"Opening a bottle of vodka," he says, handing me one of the guns.

It's eight o-fucking-clock.

"I've called Beau down," he adds as he walks on, obviously reading my mind.

"Thanks." I give Tank my attention again. "Talk."

"She's throwing up. All the time."

I back up, my head tilting, my mind refreshing the memory of her in the shower last night circling her tummy, looking mildly uncomfortable. "Since when?"

"That I know of? Yesterday morning."

"Why am I only finding this out now?"

"You were a little sidetracked yesterday."

When we took a call from The Bear and left the mansion like missiles. "Does she know you know?"

"She warned me not to tell you."

"Why?" I ask like a dick, as if Tank might know the answer. Of course, he doesn't. *For fuck's sake*. I slap his beefy bicep. "Good man." I leave him and burst into my office, finding Rose on the couch with the vodka in her hand. I narrow my eyes. "When I get back, we're going to have a little chat."

"What about?"

"About your vomiting episodes."

Her jaw hits her lap. "He told you?"

"Yes, he told me. Because he works for *me*, Rose. Me!" I point the machine gun at her, this situation doing my other situation no favors. Why is she throwing up? Is she ill? Obviously, I'm thinking the worst, and that only serves to bring my already terrible mood down to the gutter. "Be here when I get back." I turn and leave, slamming the door behind me.

"Where the fuck do you think I'll go?" she yells.

I snarl my way down the corridor. "Watch her," I order Tank as I pass, seeing Beau hurrying out of the kitchen.

She looks at me with the machine gun in my hand, her face a picture of disbelief, and she quickly backs up to the kitchen, pulling the door closed. I couldn't give a fuck if her father's here. "Did you know she's been throwing up?" I ask, hostile and threatening.

She recoils, a filthy look passing over her pretty face. "Who the fuck are you talking to?"

"You! Did you know?"

"Calm the hell down," she shouts, just as James walks back through the door, obviously wondering what the commotion is all about.

"What's going on?" he asks, eyes swaying from me to Beau.

"He's being a prick," she snaps. "Do I know *what*?"

My jaw rolls, but I do my best to rein in my temper. "That Rose is puking her guts up," I say calmly, feeling anything but.

Beau pulls up, thinking. "I did think she looked a bit pale yesterday."

"She did?" She did. Why didn't I pay more attention to that? I recoil at my own thought. Am I a terrible husband?

"Yeah," James says, and I blink, wondering if I asked that out loud. "She disappeared into the bathroom pretty sharpish after we'd found Lawrence."

I *am* a terrible husband. And that's the fault of all the criminal bastards out there who are monopolizing my attention. I'll kill every single one of them. Even more slowly than I'd planned.

"Is she still in your office?" Beau asks, and I nod. "Where are you going?" She moves around me.

"To kill someone," I grate, marching on. "Fucking slowly."

"Don't get blown up," she sings.

"That's not fucking funny, Beau," I shout back, emerging into the sunshine, slipping on my shades. I stop at the top of the steps and scan the line of cars in the driveway, a man at the driver's door of each.

"Not fucking funny at all," James hisses, joining me.

"Your girlfriend is about as hilarious as a nasty rash on my dick," I say, checking the gun as Otto approaches.

"The address," he says, as my phone pings. "Blue Lagoon, just south of MIA."

"Nice," I reply, knowing the district well.

"He moved in two months ago."

"From where?"

"A very unassuming, cramped place Downtown." Otto raises his eyebrows, twirling the piercing in his lip.

Interesting. "Let's go." I take the steps and point to the third car back with my gun. "We're in this one."

"I'll drive." Brad falls behind the wheel, I take the passenger seat, and James slides into the back.

What the fuck is wrong with my wife?

His office block is impressive. Very impressive indeed. The giant glass structure sits proudly on Blue Lagoon Drive, casting a shadow over the water. Palm trees line the front, the sun reflecting off the endless windows, making the building glimmer. It's quite a step up from his *unassuming, cramped* office Downtown.

I slip out of the car and remove my jacket, laying it over my machine gun. "I'm good from here," I say to the glass entrance.

"Not a fucking chance," Brad scoffs, brushing past me, heading into the building, covering his own gun with his jacket.

"Why's he being such a bitch these days?"

"The only bitch I see around here is you," James grunts as he follows Brad.

They disappear into the lobby, and I sigh, going after them, leaving the rest of the men with the cars. The foyer is as impressive as the exterior, all cream marble, glass, and pale furniture. "Floor?" I ask.

"Fifth." James points to the elevator.

"Can I help you?"

I turn at the sound of the voice, finding a middle-aged woman behind a large marble desk. I flash her a smile. She recoils. "We know where we're going." I take a leisurely stroll to the elevator and board with Brad and James, all three of us lining the back wall.

"Do we have a plan?" Brad asks, hitting the button for floor five.

In answer, James tosses the belt that feeds his gun over his shoulder.

"Subtle," I muse, smiling as the doors close. They don't meet in the middle, a man's suit-covered arm appearing and stopping them. They reopen, and he looks up, smiling, stepping inside. It falls when he clocks us lined up against the back wall. "Going up?" I ask.

With wide eyes rooted to James's bullet belt, he backs up. "I'll take the next one."

I nod, hitting the button again, and we ride in silence to the fifth floor. When the doors open, I step out, glancing around the fancy reception area. "This must cost a pretty penny," I say quietly, taking in the clean space, the white and glass at every turn offset with potted palms. "I'm here to see Derek Green," I say to the lady behind the glass desk.

She glances past me, to Brad and James, and I look back, seeing James has covered the belt with his jacket. So it's clearly only our presence that's the problem. "We're," I correct myself. "*We're* here to see Derek Green."

"Do you have an appointment, sir?" she asks, going to her computer, clearly anxious.

"No."

"He's in the boardroom. A meeting."

I glance past her, to the walls of glass forming a corridor, rooms on either side. "That way?"

"Um . . . yes."

"Thank you." I flash her my sincerest smile, which I know will still be sinister. "Some tea would be lovely," I call back as I wander down the corridor casually, slowly glancing each way as I go, checking the occupants of each room I pass, all smaller offices. The final room reveals an extensive boardroom, with an enormous white table and gray leather swivel chairs surrounding it. I count thirty chairs, but only five are in use, and at the helm, Daniel's *father*. He projects quiet power. Unassuming, unlike his surroundings.

He looks up.

Sees me.

Drops his pen.

I pull back my suit jacket, revealing my machine gun, and then slowly twirl my finger in the air. *Wrap it up.* Darting his eyes to the table before him, he swallows hard. His persona, the fact that he clearly knows who I am, tells me more than he undoubtedly wants me to know.

"Is he supposed to recognize you?" James asks.

"Nope." I move back, away from the door, my eyes unmoving from the flustered, flat-out panicked form of Derek Green. "Speaks volumes, doesn't it?"

His mouth moves, forcing some smiles, and the men at the table start gathering their laptops and files, leaving the room, every one of them recoiling when they spot us waiting outside. As soon as the room is empty, except for Derek, I stroll in, taking the seat at the far end, opposite him. James takes the chair directly to his right, Brad the one on his left. He eyes them both. Then me.

My lips straight, I place the machine gun on the table. His eyes land on it and stick. "Nice office," I say, taking my time to gaze around. "What do we have here?" I muse. "Maybe five thousand square feet. Premium spec, unrivaled location, so maybe thirty bucks per square foot a year." I pout, looking at the ceiling.

"We're talking twelve and a half thousand dollars per month." I blow out my cheeks. "That's a massive leap from the . . . what? Fifteen hundred you were paying a few months ago?" I reach for the machine gun and swivel it to the left, and then back to the right. "Business must be booming, Derek." I look at him. "Care to explain?"

His sweat is very real. So is the fear in his eyes, so if he tries to play dumb, I can't promise I won't rape him with this gun. "It's been a good year." His words shake, his hand instinctively reaching for his tie and loosening it.

James, as hotheaded as I've learned he is, picks up his gun and rests it on the desk, aimed at Derek. He flies back in his chair, hands up.

Brad chuckles. "You're playing with the big boys, and a little machine gun makes you shit your pants?"

"I don't know what you're talking about."

James releases the safety and loads, the sound making Derek flinch. "You sure?" he asks, moving a fraction to the right and firing, obliterating the wall-hung TV behind Derek. The sound is earsplitting, as round after round sounds, the belt jumping across James's shoulder as it feeds the machine gun. James? He's motionless, expressionless, a fucking robot. Derek? Oh, poor Derek. His arms go over his head, his body folding over the table. I can see Brad laughing. Can't hear him, though. Fuck me, my ears are bleeding. But I let James at him, knowing how he feels about any poor fucker who's stupid enough to get embroiled in The Bear's business.

James finally relieves us all of the noise and relaxes back in his chair, eyeing the glass wall into the corridor. "Tell them you're okay," he says quietly.

I look to see people on the other side of the glass, some stock-still in shock, others running scared. "Do it now," I order. "Get up and reassure your staff that all is well." I watch, amused, as Derek stands on shaky legs and more or less stumbles to the door, swinging it open, sweat pouring. "And if anyone calls the police . . . well, I don't think I need to spell it out."

"No need to panic," Derek says, sounding pretty fucking panicked. "We're just . . . um . . . acting out a crime scene to . . . um . . . yes . . . to corroborate some evidence." He coughs. "Back to work." He shuts the door, presses a button, and the room is suddenly private.

"Acting out a crime scene," I say, thoughtful. "Very good, Derek."

His forehead meets the glass. "Why are you here?"

Why am I here? I brush my lip slowly with my middle finger. "You've upset my wife," I say quietly, and he peeks at me. "Therefore, you've upset me." I stand, walking around the table and claiming Derek's arm. I manhandle him back to his chair, pushing him down. "Take a seat, Derek. You're gonna need it."

"I've done what any decent father would do," he cries, his arms thrown into the air.

"You're not his father," I point out, crouching beside him, my glare deadly. "You're the man who paid handsomely for a baby who was ripped from his mother's arms. Unlucky for you, the victim in all this happens to be my wife. I could have ended you three years ago, Derek. But I did the right thing by Daniel because I knew that was what Rose wanted." I get up closer, making him lean back. "She's done everything right, and now you're saying she can't see him? Do you understand the consequences of your actions, Derek? Do you *really* understand?" I reach for James's gun and turn it a fraction, so it's aimed square at Derek's forehead. He inhales. "Now this can be solved pretty easily, and you know how." I rise to my full height, slip a hand around the back of his head, and smash it down onto the desk with force. He cries out, grappling at his bloodied nose, his glasses bent and broken. "So fix it, because I won't be so nice next time."

The door knocks and opens, and the lady from reception appears with some tea. I slap on a smile and go to her, relieving her of the tray. "Thank you, very kind."

She can only nod, her eyes glued to a bleeding Derek Green behind me.

"He's a great actor, eh?" I chuckle, holding up the tray. "Thanks for the tea. We were just taking a break from acting out that crime scene." I step forward, forcing her to retreat. She quickly shuts the door, and I take the tray to the table, lifting the lid off the pot and stirring. "Now let's move on to Vince Roake." The staff may have indirectly been told not to call the cops but, let's face it, who wouldn't?

Derek glances up, his nervous form becoming more frantic.

"A client of yours, I believe. On remand. Found guilty at trial, has appealed, fired his attorney, and hired you. Of all the people in the world, Derek. He hires *you*." I pour the tea, a cup for each of us. "Milk?" I ask the tray, getting a grunt from James, a "please" from Brad, and nothing from Derek. "Do. You. Have. Milk?" I look at him, and he nods jerkily. So I add milk. "No sugar for me." I smile at him. "Obviously." I proceed to spoon sugar into Derek's cup, one after the other, until the bowl is empty, and Derek's tea looks like toffee. "Drink up." I slide it toward him and hand out the delicate cups and saucers to James and Brad, taking my own and sipping. I hum, holding the cup up and inspecting it. "You know, no one makes tea like my mum."

"No one," Brad agrees, joining me and testing. "She's not passed on that talent to you, Danny." He grimaces, placing his cup down.

I take another sip, just to test it again. "What do you think?" I ask James, who's contemplating me with a poorly concealed smirk.

"It's average."

"It's average," I mimic, returning my attention to Derek. "I'm wounded. How about you, Derek? Do you like my tea?"

With shaky hands, he lifts the small cup of goo to his lips and practically chews his way through half of it, his skin turning a fetching shade of green, fighting to suppress his heaves. "Very good," he coughs.

My nose wrinkles. "Don't lie to me, Derek. I hate liars." I slip the cup and saucer onto the desk, move the guns closer to him so the ends are touching his chest, and retake my seat at the end of the table. "Bear that in mind when I ask my next question." I push the tips of my fingers together, resting my elbows on the arms of the chair. "Who do you answer to?"

He wipes at his nose again, exhaling, any fight he had in him leaving his body. "The Bear."

I only just control my surprise. "Directly? No middle man?"

"No middle man."

"How does he reach out?"

"Email."

I note James goes straight to his phone, texting Otto. "On his way," he confirms, resting his mobile on the table.

"What has he got against you, Derek? What's he black-mailing you with?"

"What do you think?" he asks, exasperated. "He knows we didn't obtain our son legitimately."

"You realize this is one mighty big fucking coincidence, don't you?" I can't assume The Bear doesn't know who Daniel is to me. And I won't. "Have you mentioned Rose?"

"God, no. But you understand why I have to stop Daniel seeing her. And you! For fuck's sake, he'll think I'm in your pocket."

"You *are*, Derek. From now on, you most certainly are."

His head falls into his hands. "Oh God. I knew taking on the Dorn case was a mistake."

I frown. "What's the Dorn case?"

"First-degree murder." He waves a hand in the air. "Hedge fund kid with a psychotic personality disorder. The evidence was circumstantial, but you'd have to be a fucking dumbass to believe he didn't do it. Apparently, lucky for me, the jury was full of dumbasses. Dorn walked free, I made a name for myself, as well as a few bucks, and now I'm first port of call for any fucking murderer in Miami who needs a lawyer."

Brad peeks up at me, as well as James, both clearly thinking what I'm thinking. Could it really be a coincidence? Could it really be that simple? Because if The Bear knew Daniel was my wife's son, surely he would have utilized that tool before now.

Time will tell. Until then . . .

"This is what's going to happen," I say, just as Otto walks in. He takes in the carnage behind Derek, the state of Derek's face, and then grimaces at his half-drunk cup of tea. "You're going to give Otto here all the email communications you have from The Bear."

"He'll kill me. Jesus, he already impaled Daniel's hamster on our porch railing."

I recoil, swinging my eyes to James. "And there's us thinking he's fond of animals."

"I haven't encountered one called The Hamster yet." He shrugs. "Maybe he has an aversion."

"Rodents." Brad shudders. "I hate rodents."

I smirk, edging forward in my chair and laying my forearms on the table. "Derek, you have to trust me on this," I say, as James and Brad both reach for their guns, caressing them like they could be working a woman's body. "I am *not* the lesser of two evils in your life right now." I push back in my chair and kick my feet up on the table. "I know you hear me. So you will continue to represent Roake. You will forward any information you have to me, no matter how small or insignificant."

Derek shakes his head, straightening out his broken glasses. "Do you know what you're dealing with?" he asks, looking at me as if I just don't get it.

"Do *you*?"

He swallows, looking away. "The extent of that man's power, the size of his web of corruption. Politicians, police, lawyers, criminals. They're all making a living because he allows it. Literally anyone who carries any clout in this city and beyond is ruled by his silent fist."

"I'm not," I say quietly. "And I carry a lot of clout, Derek."

"Yes, so I can see why you're a big problem for him. I'm not a gambling man, Mr. Black, but I would bet that coming back to life is one of the worst decisions you'll ever make."

My fist hits the table hard, the bang echoing around the room. I'd like to think it's inherent anger at his audacity and nothing more, but there's an irritating slither of frustration mixed in there too. Jesus, what the fuck would Pops make of this? He'd find the root of his problem and kill it. End of story. So that's what I'll do. "Me being raised from the dead could be the only thing that keeps you alive, Derek. Remember that."

I look at Brad, because I just can't be arsed to get up and walk the length of the room again. He reaches across to Derek's head and brings it crashing down onto the table with a thwack. He yelps, holding his beaten face. "I don't want Daniel to see you like this," I say, my lip curling at his shaking form. "So I've arranged for someone to pick him up from school." I stand and grab my machine gun. "He's going to stay with us for a little while."

"What?" He shoots up. "You're kidnapping him?"

I look at him like the dickhead he is. "Derek, that kid is more mine than he is yours. I'm married to his real fucking mother, you deluded fuck. She's played fair so far, let you spin your story about adopting him, let Daniel believe every word to save your integrity." Really, it was the only way without giving Daniel the gory details of Rose's traumatic history. She didn't want to scar him with that. She doesn't want him to believe the world can be so cruel. "And you repay her by trying to stop her seeing him?" I laugh, and there's not one scrap of amusement in the sound.

"How will I explain that to Hilary?"

"I don't give a flying fuck what you tell your wife. Lie. Whatever."

His shoulders drop. "And what will you tell Daniel?"

"He's coming to stay with his mum for a while. Nothing strange about that." I pull out my cigarettes. "I bought him a jet ski. I'm sure he's told you. We'll have a few day trips, spend some time on the water. He loves cooking with my mum too."

Derek gets up and goes to a nearby console table, pulls a Kleenex out of the box, and dabs at his nose. "I always wondered about you." He exhales, looking at me. "Why there were no pictures of you from his visits to St. Lucia."

I pout. "I'm camera shy."

"And supposedly dead."

"When did you figure out who I was?" I ask, my curiosity getting the better of me.

"My client. Roake." he sighs. "I was asked to deliver an envelope to him on one of our meetings about his case." He shakes his head, wedging one hand against the wood and leaning on it, his body visibly heavy. "Inside was a photograph of you."

So my mug shot is being passed around the recruits? Not a surprise. "So you took a peek before handing it over to Roake? Very naughty, Derek. And you recognized me how?"

He nods at my hand, and I look down, seeing the leather band on my wrist that Daniel bought for me from a market on his first visit to St. Lucia. Well, damn. "Daniel still has his too," Green says, sounding rather sad. "He didn't shut up about your matching wristbands and jet skis for weeks after he came home."

I bet Derek had a heart attack when he figured it out. And now I bet he's wondering what he's done to deserve this. To be entangled in this web of crime, blackmail, and exploitation. And it's not because he bought a kid on the black market. No one in Miami knows that Rose is Daniel's mother. That's circumstantial. What Derek actually did was win a high-profile court case. He made himself useful to The Bear, and lucky for that illusive fucker, Derek had some skeletons in the closet to hide. Something juicy to blackmail him with. And now he's useful to me too. "Was there anything else in that delivery we should know about?"

"Like what?"

"Pictures of anyone else?"

He looks at Brad and James. "No."

"I'm injured," Brad mutters, as James sits, looking too thoughtful for my liking. We know why there was no picture of him. Because The Bear thought he was already dead.

"Well, I think that's business concluded, for now," I say on a dazzling smile. "I bet it's nice for you to finally put a face to the name. We'll be in touch." I slide my gun off the desk and leave, Otto, Brad, and James following me. "All this in three fucking years, and no one, not one fucking person, knows who he is?"

"Someone did," James mutters, hitting the call button of the elevator with the tip of his machine gun.

"Yeah, great. She's dead. Very useful."

"Don't piss me off, Danny."

"Sorry," I mumble, actually feeling it. James knows I don't hand out apologies freely. "Rose mustn't know about this." She'll lose her mind, and I have enough to fucking deal with right now.

We board the lift and the doors close, as James's phone rings. He answers. Peeks across at me, frowning.

"Where?" he asks, his body visibly tensing. "Watch them." He hangs up. "Two men just pulled up in a Chevrolet. Two men that don't look like they belong in this building, if you know what I mean."

"Men like us?" I say on a laugh.

He looks up at the small screen above the door and then back to the screen of his phone when it pings. "They're waiting for the elevator. Heading for floor five."

"Convenient. How do you know that?"

"Goldie asked them."

I laugh, slipping a cigarette between my lips, lighting it, and lifting my machine gun, aiming it at the door. "Ready?"

They all mirror me on grunts of agreements, and the doors slide open, revealing two men. Their eyes widen in unison, they back up, but they're not stupid enough to reach for the belts that I can see poorly concealed under their jackets. Not when faced with four men, three of which have machine guns pointed at them. "Turn around," I say nicely, and they both slowly turn. "And let's walk ever so calmly out of the building."

James steps out with me, each of us pushing the tips of our guns into their lower backs.

"Excuse me, sir, this is a no-smoking premises." I look past the men before us, seeing a security guard approaching, young, built, and probably bored out of his mind for ninety-nine percent of his day. I bet my cigarette is his biggest drama today.

I flick it at his feet and nod to Otto, who wanders over and stuffs a wedge of notes in his jacket pocket, giving it a friendly pat. "Apologies," he says, smiling through his overgrown beard. "What's your name, chap?"

"Jerry."

"Jerry," Otto muses, pulling a card out and slipping it into his pocket with the cash. "I think you're grossly underpaid. Give me a call, and I'll fix that."

He nods, his hand over his pocket as he steps back. "Have a good day, gentlemen."

"You too." Otto swings round. "Let's go."

Yes, let's go. I have something to clear up with my savage wife.

14

ROSE

"You've been staring at that bottle for over an hour," Tank says.

Over an hour? Is that how long it's been since Beau left me in Danny's quiet office to shake off my supposed headache? It wasn't a lie. I *do* have a headache. A headache from thinking too much. Worrying.

I slowly move my eyes from the bottle of vodka to Tank. His eyebrows rise but remain a bushy straight line rather than a curious curve. I blink and return my stare to the clear glass. I can only assume he is getting bored of watching me in my silent turmoil. That's too bad for him. He should have kept his big mouth shut.

"Are you going to drink it or not?" he asks.

The print on the label starts to blur, the reds and blacks blending messily from staring so hard. "Not," I murmur, slipping it onto the nearby table, feeling a weight lift from simply not having it in my grasp any longer. I inhale and rise from the couch, brushing my front down. "Where did Danny go?"

Tank looks at me in a way that suggests he thinks I think he's stupid.

I roll my eyes and glance at my cell, desperate to call Hilary and plead for her compassion. But I need to have it together, and I feel anything but at the moment. We've always been so cautious. I knew bringing Daniel to the house was a terrible move. God knows what he's said to Hilary and Derek.

I walk to the door on heavy feet, and Tank pulls it open for me. "Thanks." I make my way to the kitchen. "Hey," I say to Esther's back. "Where's Beau?"

"She's with her father in the lounge." Esther places a dish on the counter and tips a bag of raisins into it. "Doc's checking him over." She pushes the dish aside on an exhale of tired breath. "What's going on, Rose?" she asks, and I frown.

"I don't know. Ask your son."

"I mean with you. What's going on with *you*?" She collects a loaf of bread and dumps it on the counter heavy-handedly. "You're . . . off."

"I'm fine."

"Then why are you throwing up?" She starts buttering the bread, her attention split between me and her task. "Danny's called me to make sure Doc's available when he gets back."

"Why, is he ill?"

"Don't be smart."

I let my head fall into my hands, massaging my scalp. What can I say? I'm stressed? Worried? Anxious? No. No signs of weakness. I can't give any clues to suggest I'm struggling to deal with this world. I'm a joke. Because anyone with a pair of eyes can see the turmoil I'm in. I want to be strong. I want to be everything Danny needs me to be. Three years ago, no problem. Now? God, it's so tough, maybe because I've had a taste of normality. Well, normality with Danny, anyway. Danny and I will never be truly normal. We'll always be fire and ice.

Hot and cold. "I'm fine." I release my head and offer a meek smile.

The look pointed at me by my mother-in-law is a picture of incredulity. "The guy from the workshop called. He'll deliver your gift for Danny the morning of the wedding, but it'll be early. We'll need to find somewhere to hide it."

"Hide an ice sculpture?" I ask. "I'm more worried about making sure it remains ice."

"Otto found the perfect spot. Shady and minimal air circulation, as the sculptor recommended."

"When did Otto become an expert on ice sculptures?"

She shrugs, and I turn on my stool when I hear footsteps behind me. Beau wanders in. I feel like a terrible friend for not asking about her father when she sat with me in Danny's office for an age trying to wring a reason out of me as to why I'm throwing up regularly. Truth be told, I feel a bit pathetic. She's more together each day, even with bombs being thrown at her. I know the appearance of her aunt Zinnea has helped. Beau has told me a lot about her uncle . . . *aunt* . . . but nothing really prepares you for that first moment when you meet Aunt Zinnea. Or Zinnea Dolly Daydream, her stage name. And such a transformation from the skeletal, near-dead uncle I saw only a day ago.

I smile as she joins me at the island, reaching for her hand and squeezing. "I'm much better," I assure her before she can ask. I ignore Esther's light snort. "How's your dad?"

"Insufferable." She cranes her neck to see what Esther's making, reaching across and plucking a raisin out of the dish. "Doc thinks he had a mild panic attack."

I laugh under my breath. That's not surprising, given what's happened.

"You heard from the guys?" she asks.

"Nothing." I look down at my cell again, my heart naturally

picking up pace. I'd like to think Danny's destination *wasn't* Hilary and Derek's house. Not when he walked out of here with most of his men and a small arsenal of machine guns. And yet I know Danny. He takes no prisoners. But I also know his adoration for my son is limitless. He wouldn't storm in with guns, literally, blazing, not with Daniel around. But . . . Daniel wouldn't be home. He's at school, and Derek would be at work. "Oh God." My head goes back into my hands, hurting, but shoots back up when my cell rings. I scramble to gather it up, deflating when I see it's the gate calling. "Hello."

"Rose, it's Bud. I'm on the gate. There's a visitor for Beau. I've tried calling her but I'm getting no answer."

"She's here," I say, handing my cell to Beau. "Visitor for you."

She frowns, accepting and taking it to her ear. "Yes?" She stiffens. "What?" It's Beau's turn to rub at her forehead. "Yes, sure." She hangs up and hangs her head. "Fuck."

"What?"

Pushing my cell onto the island, she gets up from the chair. "My dad's girlfriend is here."

"Oh." I know how Beau feels about her. "Just smile sweetly and it'll all be over very soon."

"You've not met her. She's unbearable." She wanders off, muttering under her breath.

"I'll come rescue you. Just call."

She throws a small smile over her shoulder, and I return forward, finding Esther now plonking slices of buttered bread in her dish. "I'm going to lie down," I say, getting up before she can resume grilling me.

"Okay," she replies quietly. Thoughtfully. I pass Tank at the doorway. "Is it necessary for you to follow my every move around the house?" I ask, sounding grumpy.

He doesn't answer. He doesn't need to. He's been following

me around since the moment he was appointed my personal shield. Today is no different, I'm just being snappy.

I see Beau closing the doors into the TV room, and I take the stairs, each step I'm climbing seeming to drain me more. It's an effort to simply walk. I make it to the top and drag myself toward our bedroom, scanning the bright abstract paintings lining the corridor.

I slow to a stop when I hear the front doors open in the distance.

"Where the fuck is my wife?" His voice echoes around the mansion, and I whirl around, panicked.

"Oh shit," I murmur, glancing up at Tank. His lips are straight, his hairy face expressing all the wariness I'm feeling. "He doesn't sound happy, does he?" I murmur lamely.

"He's sounded better."

"This is your fault," I fire accusingly, creeping to the top of the stairs.

"He pays me to do a job."

"Someone needs to remind my husband that he signed everything over to me when he died, so it's actually *me* paying you."

"I dare you to tell him that." Tank chuckles.

I flip a quick evil look over my shoulder before returning my attention forward as I approach the top of the stairs, seeing two men being manhandled toward Danny's office. His eyes land on me like a pair of wrecking balls, and I find my spine lengthening in an act of feigned strength I know deep down won't wash.

James moves in close to his side, flicking a cautious look my way. If he's trying to silently warn me that my husband is in a rotten mood, it's wasted. I'm practically disintegrating under his fiery stare. I've never wished Danny would be too busy with work to give me his time. Except now.

James speaks, Danny nods, eyes unmoving from mine, and

then James walks away, following the two men who've been practically kicked into Danny's office.

"Today's catch?" I ask cockily, lifting my chin.

"Don't change the subject, Rose." He climbs the stairs with purpose, claiming my elbow and pushing me toward our room. I don't put up any resistance. I'm not a complete idiot. "Take a break," he snaps at Tank as I'm hauled past his mountain of a body and thrust through the door.

"Sit down," he orders, so I go to the bed obediently and lower to the mattress, hands in my lap. He can't hide his surprise. Subservience isn't something he's used to or expects from me, and it's obvious he doesn't know how to handle it. But, truth is, I'm too drained to fight him.

He starts pacing up and down before me, his eyes on his feet, his mind obviously whirring, and my gaze follows him back and forth at least a dozen times. What's going on? Where's the attack? The monster? The threats to strangle me if I don't comply. I'm feeling as lost as he looks.

Danny eventually stops. Inhales. Looks up. I withdraw at the swirl of regret in his icy eyes. "Am I a bad husband?" he asks, throwing me even more for a loop.

"What?"

"You heard me." He comes to me and drops to his knees, his hands squeezing my thighs and pulling them apart so he can move into me. "Am I a bad husband?"

What is this madness? "Well, you're legally not a husband at all."

"Small technicality that'll be remedied in a few days. Answer my question."

"Why are you asking me this?" My hand reaches for his overgrown dark waves and pushes them back from his face.

"I'm just trying to figure out why everyone else seems to have noticed you're throwing up, but I didn't."

"I'm fine."

"Rose," he says, low and full of warning. "Why are you throwing up all the time?"

"It's not all the time," I say over a laugh, like he's being dramatic. He is. "A few times, that's all."

"Why?"

"I'm worried," I blurt. Sick with worry. Worry for him, for Daniel, for me, for us. I'm simply out of my mind with worry.

"Why?"

"Really, Danny? You're asking me that?" I try to brush his hands off my thighs and get precisely nowhere, his fingers curling into my flesh. I hiss, throwing him a filthy look. Here he is. The hard-handed monster. "You got shot at a few days ago. You walked out of a burning building yesterday. Today, I've been told I can't see my son."

"Daniel's sorted."

I tilt my head. "How."

"Some polite persuasion."

A bark of laughter erupts, and Danny glares at me. "Polite? You?"

"Always."

"You walked out with a machine gun, Danny."

"But I didn't use it."

Oh God. "So I can see him?" Do I care what Danny did, what he took, what he used, if it means I get to see my boy?

He pushes himself up, resting his weight on my thighs, and leans in, biting my cheek. "He's coming to stay with us for a while." He heads to the bathroom, as if he hasn't just landed a bombshell, leaving me on the edge of the bed, struck dumb. A statue. Coming to stay?

Snapping to life, I go after him. "What are you talking about?" I enter to find him standing at the toilet, his dick in his hand. And this is how warped I still am because every time I see him taking a piss, I smile, being taken back to the very first day he took me from a casino floor and slapped me.

I quickly shake my untimely reminiscing away. Daniel can't stay here. And surely Hilary and Derek wouldn't have agreed to that. Especially now. I pull up. *Especially now, what?* "What happened?" I ask. "Why did Daniel tell me he wasn't allowed to see me anymore?"

Danny flushes and goes to the sink, flipping on the faucet. "I expect because Derek found out who *Mister* is." He raises his eyebrows.

"How? We've always been so careful."

"Rose, baby, we're back in Miami."

"Don't remind me," I grumble, backing up into the doorjamb when Danny stalks toward me. My back hits the wood, his fingers claw my jaw, and his face comes close. "How long did you think we could be here without them finding out who I am?"

"Which begs the question why they've agreed to let Daniel come stay with us. First, I can't see him. Now, he can live with us?" I narrow my eyes. "What did you do? And don't say polite persuasion."

"I held a machine gun to Derek's head."

I balk at him, reaching for his hand and pulling it from my face. I don't know why I'm surprised. This is my husband I'm dealing with. I shove him out of my way and go to the toilet, lowering to the seat. "They'll take him away forever."

"Will you let that happen?" Danny asks. "Because the Rose I know wouldn't."

I look up at him, confused, and he exhales, coming and crouching before me. "Derek isn't the standup man you thought he was, Rose."

"What?" I whisper.

"He has a client. One of The Bear's men."

My mouth drops open. "Jesus. That's too close to home, Danny."

"I know. Derek was legal counsel for a high-profile case a couple years ago. He got a lot of media attention, which led to The Bear moving in and hiring him to take the case of one of his men, a man called Vince Roake."

"But what if—"

His hand lands over my mouth, silencing me. "If The Bear knew Daniel was my step-son, don't you think he would have taken him by now?"

It's hard to think rationally in the face of such a potential nightmare. "What about school?"

"I don't have all the answers yet, Rose. I can't allow him to go to school until I can guarantee he's safe. We'll have him home-schooled while I deal with this."

"But—"

"Have I ever failed you?" he asks, looking at me expectantly.

"No."

"And I never will, baby. In my world, I do what I need to do to survive. You and Daniel are a part of me, so I will do what I have to do to keep you both safe and keep my sanity. You've played ball for three years. You've protected Daniel by dancing to their tune." Placing a gentle kiss on the edge of my mouth, he whispers, "It's time to stop dancing and start fighting again. No second chances, baby."

I whimper, taking his shoulders and hauling him into me, cuddling the grizzly bear like he's a teddy. He is sometimes. I know he's right. I've been more than understanding of Hilary and Derek, more than flexible. All for the sake of my son. And how have they repaid me? They've tried to push me out of Daniel's life. Do they have any idea of the world they're in? The safest place for Daniel is here with me. His mom. I realize that now. I wouldn't trust anyone to keep him safe like I trust Danny, and with that thought, all of my anxiety transforms into relief. He's safe. My boy will always be safe, and I trust my husband to make sure of that.

A knock at the door disturbs us, and Danny pulls out, smoothing over my skin with his fingertip. "That'll be Doc." He gets to his feet.

"What?"

"He's come to check you over," he calls back as he goes into the bedroom, and just like that, I'm all anxious again. "Don't even think about fighting me on this. It's non-negotiable."

"It's my body," I shout, outraged and, frankly, worried.

Danny's back at the door in a heartbeat, his expression deadly. "Wrong," he grates, his scar seeming to flash like a warning beacon. "Anything more to say?"

"Yes, fuck off."

"Oh, baby, you're one of the only people in this world I would never kill, and yet I want to kill you the most."

"Make it bloody," I practically snarl, and he laughs under his breath.

"Fond memories." He winks, and it absolutely doesn't suit his murderous face. But it's still sexy as hell. God damn me. "Come," he says, jerking his head. "Let's get this over with. I have men to kill." He smirks and leaves, and I drop my head to my knees, staring at the floor where my hair pools around my bare feet.

"Mr. Black."

I peek up at the sound of Doc's old voice, digging deep for the grit I need to appear fine, when now, more than ever, I feel the sickest.

"Rose," Danny calls, sounding all too happy about my impending examination. I don't even want to ask what he thinks I might be hiding from him. Am scared to. Like I'm scared to seriously ask myself. I drag myself to the bedroom, finding Doc setting his medical bag on the end of the bed.

"Hi, Doc," I sing, way too happily, dropping to my back on the mattress.

"Mr. Black said you're feeling under the weather." He pulls his stethoscope out and taps the end before hooking it around his neck.

"He's worrying over nothing." I keep my eyes off Danny, avoiding his displeased look, but I see him lower to a chair by the bed. So he's going to supervise?

"Well let's put his mind at rest, shall we?"

"Yes, let's." I smile sweetly and drop my head to the side to get Danny in my view. "He's busy mutilating men."

Doc laughs as he plucks a thermometer from his bag. He actually laughs. I don't know if it's genuine humor or nerves.

I keep my potent stare on Danny, who's silently observing, the side of his finger thoughtfully brushing across his lips as Doc takes my pulse, checks my heart, my temperature, and flashes his pen light in my eyes. "These waves of sickness," he says, packing his stethoscope away. "How frequent and how long do they last?"

"They're sporadic. Some last longer than others." *Depending on the level of stress I'm being subjected to.*

"Headaches?"

"Sometimes."

He packs his things away and snaps his bag shut. "A virus, I'd say." He reaches for his gray beard, stroking it thoughtfully. "Nothing to worry about."

"Good." Danny rises from his chair and appears above me, his face hovering close to mine. "Wasn't so bad, was it?" My nose wrinkles. "And now you have a content husband who can get on with business worry-free."

"Good for you."

He takes my cheeks, squeezes, and slams a kiss on my lips. "What are you doing this afternoon while I'm working?"

"What time will Daniel be here?"

"He's at soccer practice. I've got eyes on him. My man has his instructions."

"Will I be able to take him soccer practice?" I ask, not at all hopeful, so when Danny smiles and nods, it's all I can do not to squeal my happiness. Such a simple thing, but at the same time *every*thing. I know I'll have Tank a few paces behind, and I know we'll be driven, but it still delights me. "I'm going to Walmart to buy him a soccer net. Maybe some new cleats. And a ball." The grounds will be the biggest and best soccer pitch ever. He'll love it.

"Okay. Do you have money?"

My eyebrow curves of its own volition. "Yes, I have all of yours."

He smirks dirtily and straightens, pulling his phone out when it rings. A quick glance at the screen. A definite narrowing of one eye. Then he slowly turns and leaves, taking it to his ear. But he doesn't speak. Not until he's out of the room.

I flop back onto the bed on a sigh. "Okay," Doc says, perching next to me. "Let's speak frankly now Mr. Black has left the room."

"Pardon?"

"Rose, I have been a doctor for forty-five years. I ran my own practice for forty of those."

"What are you saying?"

"Are you pregnant?"

I recoil, so much so, I shift a few inches up the mattress. "God, no. That's impossible."

"How?"

She's hemorrhaging. She'll need a transfusion.

Will she be able to carry again?

Unlikely.

I push back the brutality of my past and sit up. "Doc, you need to trust me, it's not possible."

"As you wish," he says quietly, taking his bag from the bed and walking slowly to the door. "Enjoy your shopping trip, Rose." He leaves, and I close my eyes, immediately wishing I hadn't when I'm bombarded with flashbacks. I hold my head, fighting away the faces of evil. "No." I slam my fists down and jump up, set on going to find Beau.

I swing the door open. Tank's back. For such a mammoth guy, he disappears and reappears like magic. "I'm going shopping," I tell him as I pass.

"I know. I'll get the car ready."

"Beau still in the TV room?"

"Sure is."

"Thanks." I take the stairs fast and approach the doors, tapping at the wood delicately. She's been in there for way longer than I know she's comfortable with. It's time to save her.

"Come in," she calls.

I smile at the wood as I push my way in, her high-pitched, relieved tone giving her away. Her face says a thousand words, part pained and part pleased to see me.

"Is it that time already?" she asks, jumping up.

"Yes, we'll be late."

"Dad, I'm sorry, I promised Rose I'd help her with something."

The man on the couch cranes his head to look back at me. I don't miss the contempt he's doing a terrible job of concealing. "Nice to meet you," I chirp, my curious eyes falling to the fake blonde sitting next to him, who is yet to bless me with a hello or even her face.

I bite at my lip, flicking an interested look Beau's way. She subtly shakes her head, exasperated. "I'll see you both out."

"Yes," her Dad says, standing. "Come on, darling." He puts a hand out and helps the woman up from the couch.

And then she turns.

And I stagger from the weight of my shock.

What the fuck is she doing here? She must have balls bigger than any of Danny's men.

"Rose?" Beau says. "All right?"

All right? Am I? I'm staring at the woman who not only once served as the in-house whore here at Casa Black, but the woman who also held me at gunpoint when she realized I'd won Danny's affection. It was a shock to me—Danny's affection, not so much her reaction—so I can only imagine how *she* felt. Oh God, what the hell am I supposed to do with this? And more to the point, what the fuck does *Amber* expect me to do? Keep a dignified silence in the presence of Beau and her father? She must have lost her damn mind. Why the hell did she come here? I don't know. Like I thought, *massive* fucking balls. One thing I do know, though, is that she's more likely to come out alive facing me rather than Danny. The more I'm thinking, the angrier I'm getting.

"Amber." I glare at her.

"Rose," she says, smiling, like she's seeing a long-lost friend. "It's so lovely to see you again."

I look at her like the crazy bitch she is.

"You know each other?" Beau's father asks, his attention jumping back and forth between us. "How?"

I laugh, and it's unstoppable, as Amber shifts nervously from foot to foot. "Just old friends," she says, linking arms with him. "We'd better get you home now that the doctor has given you the all-clear."

Yes, get him home before I expose you for the gold-digging whore you are. "Why would you even come here?" I ask, my mouth out of control. "Do you have a death wish?"

She swallows, flicking her eyes around the room. "Tom insisted," she murmurs.

"Then make an excuse."

"Why would she do that?" Beau's dad asks. "I called her to come pick me up. I can't drive. Too shaken after the ordeal I've been put through. She was worried."

I blink my disbelief and come back to the same question, because it's not making fucking sense. Why the hell would she come here? It soon hits me, but before I can unravel it and make my brain catch up with what's unfolding, Amber speaks up.

"I was so sorry to hear of your loss."

"Loss?" Tom says. "What loss?"

I close my eyes and inhale. I should be worried. I'm not. Everyone will soon know Danny's alive and kicking, so what's one more person? "My husband," I breathe, giving Beau apologetic eyes, knowing she's doing her best to keep the information her father has to hold against her to a bare minimal. "My husband died."

"You remarried?" he asks, confused.

"No, I haven't remarried."

"Then who's that man out there with Beau's antisocial boyfriend? The one who threatened me with a gun? Beau said he's *your* husband."

He's sounds so accusing. Like I'm responsible for my husband's killer hands. "That's my husband."

And as if he's heard me summon him, he bursts in unceremoniously with Brad and Ringo flanking him.

"Oh great," I murmur, dropping my head. This couldn't get any worse.

I'm wrong. Esther appears in the doorway with a tray of tea, all smiles. Until she spots Amber. "What is that tramp doing here?"

"I will ask you not to speak to my girlfriend like that," Beau's father says, pulling Amber close, who is lost in a mixture of shock and embarrassment.

"I've got it, Mum," Danny grates, his eyes boring holes through Amber's struck form.

"Danny?" she breathes, clutching her purse to her chest.

Danny leers, looking her up and down before turning his steel stare onto Beau's father. "I suppose you're with her for her wisdom and shining personality, aren't you? Did you know she's not a real blonde?"

I wince, glancing across to Beau. *Sorry,* I mouth, but she waves me off on a roll of her eyes. We all know why Tom's with Amber, and we definitely all know why she's with him. She's younger than Beau, for God's sake. I shudder. But I can't wonder how she stomachs an aging, overweight man pounding clumsily into her every day. I was there once. Difference is, I did it for survival. Not money.

"Would someone explain what the hell is going on?" Beau's father barks.

"Dad," Beau says, going to him, arms out, all pacifying. She stops just short, something seeming to come to her. She looks at Danny. "Where's James?"

"Busy," he grunts, eyes still drilling into Amber.

Beau inhales, going back to her father. "Let's sit down."

"Let's not," Danny grunts, striding farther into the room. "Let's give your father a few home truths so I can get back to work."

"And what exactly do you do?" Tom asks. "For work?"

"Jet skis," Danny barks. "Ask your girlfriend what *she* does."

I suck my lip, nervous for Amber, despite hating her with every fiber of my fucked-up being.

"I know what she does," Tom says, motioning to the subject at hand. "I know everything about her."

"Let's hear it then," Danny says, moving to a couch and getting comfortable.

"What's going on?" Beau whispers in my ear. "You know her?"

"Yes, I know her. I'm so sorry."

"She was raised in New York by her parents," Tom says proudly. "A heart surgeon and an eye doctor."

"Oh, really?" Danny looks genuinely surprised, looking over to Amber who is dying right there on the spot.

"Yes. She graduated from medical school six years ago." Tom smiles, and I cough over my tongue, restraining my laugh. Esther doesn't bother, falling apart, being forced to set down her tray of tea. "What's so funny?"

"I hate to piss on your bonfire, Tom," Danny says, amused too, "but Amber here is about as qualified in medics as I am in sainthood."

"What are you talking about?"

"She's a whore." Danny says it quietly and clearly. "A gold-digger. She fucked her way through this house, one man after the other."

"And once pulled a gun on me," I pipe in, like a pathetic snitching school girl. I don't care. The audacity of this woman is off the charts, whether she thought Danny was dead or not. I don't know what her game plan was. Maybe she hoped a new mob had moved in and she could charm her way back into their beds. Maybe she was just curious about what I might be doing with myself now. Or maybe she's simply a brazen hussy. What-ever, Tom has been enlightened. There's no bed for her here—over my dead body—and I doubt there will be at Tom's house now, either.

"How does it feel knowing your precious, medical student girlfriend was once little more than a hooker?"

Poor Tom's face is blank, and Beau's eyes are wide, wary, and maybe a little sorry for her father. "Amber?" he says quietly, turning to her. "Tell me they're lying."

"They're lying," she rushes to say, grappling at his suit jacket. "Don't listen to them, Tom. It's jealousy."

"What am I jealous of?" I ask, flummoxed. I've had my fair share of screwing out-of-shape, middle-aged egomaniacs. I wouldn't go back if my life depended on it.

"Remove her now or I'll do it myself," Esther declares, brushing her hands off and marching out.

"I think it's time for you to leave," Tom says, looking at Amber with sorry eyes.

"What? No, Tom, please."

He shrugs off her touch and moves away, as well as looking away, and Amber's body deflates, an air of indignation finding her. She pulls her purse onto her shoulder. I notice it's *Saint Laurent*. And then she walks, head held high, out of the room on her skyscrapers. I notice they're Jimmy Choos.

"Make sure she leaves," Danny says, pushing up from the couch. "Back to business." He walks out with his men, and Tom flops to the couch, his head in his hands.

There could be two reasons for his utter despondency. First, his enlightenment, although how he ever thought a woman in her twenties would be genuinely interested in him is beyond me. Maybe Amber is as good an actress as I once was. Second, his realization of the true web of unlawfulness his daughter is tangled up in.

"Dad?" Beau moves in beside him. "Are you okay?"

"I feel like such a fool."

"Don't. It could have happened to any wealthy man."

I don't know how she's being so compassionate. Tom left her mother for that tart. "And guilty," he murmurs. "For everything I put you and your mother through."

She physically recoils at that, obviously shocked to the core.

"Okay." Looking uncomfortable, she stands, clearing her throat. "Do you need a ride home?"

"I can drive," he sighs, standing, glancing around the room. "I can't convince you to come?"

"No, Dad," Beau says, shaking her head.

"Why are you here?" He goes to her, his voice begging. "I don't understand."

"James," she says simply, detaching his hold from her, refraining from detailing everything else. The Bear, the explosion, her uncle's husband. And a whole heap of other shit. The man's dealt with enough today already. "I've got to go. I'll call you, okay?" She drops a kiss on his cheek, leaves the room, and I follow quickly.

"Shopping?" I ask, linking arms with her.

"Anything," she says, her tone begging.

"Did someone say shopping?"

We both look up the stairs, finding Beau's uncle in all his drag queen glory. "Only Walmart," I admit. "I need to pick up some soccer supplies for my boy."

"Oh, Beau can't do Walmart. Not at this time of day."

I wince, throwing her an apologetic look. What time of day it is slipped my mind.

"Yes, I can," she declares, thanking Fury when he opens the door for her. "Because you'll be with me, Aunt Zinnea."

I look at Lawr—Zinnea and smile, seeing how elated he is by Beau's statement. "Ready?"

He motions down his sparkly form. "Born ready, darling." He struts down the stairs like it could be a catwalk, cocking his arm out when he reaches the bottom. "Do you think Walmart is?"

I laugh, letting him lead me out. He's found his armor. His medicine. Alter ego or not, he's better, and that's a weight off Beau's mind.

15

JAMES

"What did I miss?" Danny asks as he enters, eyeing the backs of the two men in the chairs before me. I can tell by the look on his face that he's surprised they're still in one piece. Or alive, even. "Not much, apparently," he muses. "Still no words?"

"They're Russian." I drag a chair over and sit on it back to front, resting my forearms on the backrest.

"How'd you know?"

"Well." I reach behind me and slide a gold letter opener off Danny's desk, twirling it in my hand while admiring it. "When I stick this in one of their legs . . ." I flip the solid gold piece of stationery, catch it by the handle, and plunge it into one of the men's knees.

"Blyad," the man barks.

"That happens." I twist and turn the blade, and the Russian starts to dribble and mumble. Then I yank it out. "Translated: whore. Or *fuck*. Whichever you prefer."

"That's my pops's letter opener," Danny says, collecting his own chair and joining me.

I look at the blood tricking over the gold. "Sorry." I press the length onto the Russian's bloodied jeans and drag it slowly, wiping it clean. Both sides. He hisses, jolting in his chair, his hands fighting with the cable ties. I place the letter opener back on the desk.

"It wasn't a dig." Danny claims it and does his own inspection, smiling fondly at it. "I was just saying, it was my father's." He tosses it, catches, stands for that extra bit of power, and sinks it into the other guy's thigh.

"Pizda!"

"What does that mean?"

"Pussy. Cunt. Vagina. Take your pick."

He pouts as he sits again, reaching for the handle and ramming it down some more until it hits the wooden seat of the chair. More dribbling. More hissing. "Is that a new rug?" Danny asks, looking at our feet to the oriental piece of rich reds and golds that's rolled out beneath our prey.

"Easier to replace than the whole carpet," Goldie says from the couch, not glancing up from her phone.

Brad chuckles, heading for the Scotch. "Drink, anyone?"

"Here." Danny raises his hand, as do I. "May as well get comfortable. It could be a long afternoon."

The unmistakable widening of the Russian's eyes makes me smile. "Know any translators?" I ask, accepting the crystal cut tumbler that's half full.

"Yes, actually. I just had one call me."

I look across to him as he necks half of his drink. "Which one?"

"Our friend Volodya." Danny waves his glass at the two men. "He didn't mention you two, though. So I'm thinking—"

"Sandy," I muse.

"Either or, bad news for these guys. Do you think they can understand?"

"No idea."

"I think so," Otto muses, tossing a burner phone on the desk. "They seem to be able to text in English."

"Oh good." Danny smiles brightly at the men. Bright but dark. "As I was saying, bad news for you two. You see, I did a deal with Volodya a few years ago, but he got a bit pissed up on power. Decided I should die. And Sandy? He sent some Russian whore into James's"—Danny points his glass at me—"girlfriend's hospital room to kill her." He reaches for the blade and yanks it out, then cranes his head, looking at the rug being pounded by a steady flow of blood. "Shit, I think that hit an artery. That seriously limits the time we have to torture information out of you."

"Torture," I whisper. "Not how I'd like to spend my last half hour." I put my hand out to Danny, and he graciously surrenders the letter opener. "I don't think they're going to talk." I stand and move in behind the Russians, holding my hand out to Otto. He drops a pair of pliers in my hand.

"Ouch," Danny says, as I pry open one of their mouths as he jerks and squirms, doing everything he can to hamper my intention.

Too bad for him, I've done this countless times. I clamp down the pliers on the end of his tongue and yank it out, resting the tip of the letter opener somewhere in the center of the slippery organ. His mate in the other chair looks on, horrified, bleeding out all over the rug. Danny stands and pulls the belt from his trousers, folding it in half and taking a seat again, threading the leather through his fingers. "If I wrap this belt around your thigh, you might live. If you talk now, your mate might live."

"Okay, okay!"

"Ah!" Danny chimes. "It speaks."

"Hallelujah," Brad mutters, perching on the desk behind Danny. "Get on with it, I have a club to run."

"You have to promise us protection," the one able to speak says, his accent thick but his English perfect, as his mate tries his best to shake his head, objecting. So we have a squealer and a loyal advocate. I chose the right man's tongue.

"I don't have to promise you anything," Danny grates. "If the information you provide is any good, I might consider it." He flicks his eyes to me. Danny knows these two men aren't walking out of here alive. Even if they lead us directly to our prey.

"Volodya and Sandy work together," he spits urgently. "They head up the gun side of the business. The Polish deal with the women. The Irish in drugs. It's been peaceful. The only issue was The Enigma."

I look at Danny incredulously. So it really is one big happy family?

"Oh, I've heard of him," Danny says, getting up and going to pour more Scotch. "Another one, James?"

"Hands are kind of full at the moment." I give the Russian's tongue a little yank, pushing the blade in a fraction, not piercing his flesh, but as close as I can get before drawing blood. "You don't know who The Enigmas is?" I ask.

"I think he's above their pay grade," Danny says, joining Brad on the edge of the desk.

"The Bear," I say. "What do you know?"

"Nothing."

For fuck's sake, someone has to know who the fuck he is. "So how the fuck does anyone do business if they don't know who they're dealing with?"

"He emails. Only ever emails."

"Oh for fuck's sake," Danny snaps, slamming his glass down on the desk and lunging forward, ramming the letter opener through the tongue I'm still holding. The scream is blood-curdling. It also gets the other Russian talking again, although what the fuck he's saying is a mystery. I expect he's praying. He should be. I release the clamp and move over to his dribbling, whining form.

I hold the pliers in front of him.

"He emails the three at the top," he blurts. "Only ever them."

Well, that's not true. He also emails Green.

"The Ox leads the Russians. Volodya and Sandy answer to him. Then there's us below them."

"Oh," I muse, moving around the front of him and taking Danny's chair. I circle the pliers for him to continue.

"The Shark. Polish."

"Deals in women," I say, and he nods. "And below The Shark?"

"The Hound and The Fox. The Fox disappeared. The Hound has a tattoo covering his right cheek. Some writing in his native language."

"Where is he?" Danny asks.

He shakes his head. "I don't know, I swear. But I can tell you the Irish lost The Snake. The Eagle and The Alligator are . . . *were* below The Snake. The Eagle's dead. They're trying to get The Alligator out of jail to take over the drugs side. The Dodo is also missing."

I hear Danny and Brad shift on the desk behind me, and I glance across to see Otto, Goldie, and Ringo all looking rather bored. "So what were you doing at Derek Green's office?" Perhaps with a shortage of Irish to swing by Green's place, they sent some Russians instead. *Happy families.*

"We were told to give him a gun."

"Why?"

"I don't know!"

I look at Danny. He's thoughtful. What the fuck is happening in Miami? The Irish can deal and kill, the Polish traffickers can buy, sell, and rape women, and the Russians can open fire wherever the fuck they please, but it's okay because everyone gets along. Peace in the city, he said. What a shame we're fucking with their plans. *Fuck this shit.*

"Thanks for the chat," I say, turning and putting my hand out to Danny, who places the belt in my hand. The Russian deflates before me, relieved. "Problem is, you've told us a whole lot of what we already know."

His eyes widen, his back pressing into the back of the chair.

"The Snake, The Eagle, The Dodo, The Fox . . ." I slip the belt around his head and use the ends to pull him forward. "All me."

"No," he whispers, his eyes widening.

"Yes."

"That can't be. The Enigma's dead."

Danny laughs. "You get the feeling people have a problem with us being alive?" he asks from behind. He's being a real comedian today. I'm not sure what people should be more wary of, the joker or the deadly, short-fused monster.

Both. In equal measure, because after every joke, there's a move that's going to be grim. So I shift slightly to the right, just as he flies past me, taking the bloody tongue of the non-squealer with his fingers and pulling it out, inserting the letter opener over and over again.

"So we're just going to kill you now," I say calmly, turning my stare back to my man, tightening the belt until his eyes start bulging and his face turns red. I look straight into his eyes, making sure he can see me, my whole miserable history parading through my mind in slow motion, cruelly reminding me of every dismal detail. My father's happy face the last time I saw it at the dinner table, his family surrounding him. My mother's priceless pearl necklace that she constantly fingered while engaged in deep conversation. My sister's crafty smile when Mum slapped the back of her hand for helping herself to the Eton Mess before Dad. She loved Eton Mess. My family. Wiped out.

I blink back the flashbacks, tightening the leather. Vessels start to burst in the whites of the Russian's eyes, tiny red cracks visibly branching. I see it clearly, like a close-up, like the growth of roots being recorded and sped up. His lips turn blue. His body jerks a couple of times before going limp. I don't realize I'm holding my own breath until I release the belt and exhale heavily, starting to heave on my chair. I thrust him back violently and stand, filling my hands with a glass and a bottle, pouring and necking.

"You okay?" Brad asks, killing the silence.

I gasp and slam down the vodka and tumbler, bracing my hands on the edge of the cabinet. "Never better." Pulling myself together, I face Otto. "Get in that phone and send a message confirming delivery of the gun. Call Green and tell him to be in touch the moment he finds out why the fuck he's been sent a gun."

"Done."

"Anyone else feel like we need a diagram of this web?"

Every man and woman in the room spring to life. "Yep," Danny says, coming to me and rubbing at my shoulder, not saying a word, but just . . . acknowledging where I'm at.

"A diagram." Brad coughs, grimacing as he passes the dead guys, reaching past me for the Scotch. "A diagram and a drink."

"I'll get some paper," Ringo adds, starting to rummage through the drawers of Danny's desk.

"Who's playing artist?" Otto starts pulling chairs from everywhere in the room, positioning them around the desk.

"Me." Goldie takes the paper from Otto and collects a pen. "Women are better hand writers than men."

"You want to be a woman when it suits you," Ringo mutters.

"Shut up or I'll stab you in the eye." Goldie sits down, and we all join her as she draws a circle at the top of the page and writes —very neatly, it must be noted—*The Bear* in the center. Then three lines from there. In one, *The Snake (Deceased),* in another, *The Shark*, and in the final one, *The Ox*.

Irish, Polish, and Russians.

Drugs, women, and guns.

"These three," she says, pointing her pen to the animals, "answer to him." She points to The Bear at the top.

"Could be a woman," Ringo says casually. "I'm deeply offended by your assumption."

I hold back my chuckle, feeling the stress leave me. Every other man in the room, however, does not.

I pluck the pen from Goldie's hand before she follows through on her threat and sinks it into the eye socket of any one of her tormentors. I rest it on The Snake and draw a line down from there, adding a circle at the end and writing "*The Alligator AKA Vince Roake. Incarcerated*" in the middle, and another line from there. "The Dodo. Deceased," I say quietly.

"So the drug supply must be down," Brad muses.

I pull a line down from The Shark, adding *The Fox Deceased* and *The Hound* reaching for the paper and pointing at The Ox. "We know Volodya and Sandy are under him."

"And this is just the tip of the fucking iceberg," Brad says, exasperated. "What about all the minions sprouting off all these circles of animals? I mean, he took James's family out in London ten years ago, for fuck's sake."

I rest back in my chair, thoughtful, running over so many of my hits. "He took them out. He didn't need to be anywhere near London to order the kill. He likes bombs. He wants rid of me because I threaten him." I look at Danny. "He wants rid of you because you threaten his empire. He had police inside. Might do again now. He didn't buy Byron's Reach. Why? He's got the Russians, the Poles, and the Irish under his control. Fuck knows how many others outside the country."

"You've spoken to him," Brad says.

"He uses a voice distorter," Danny confirms. "Which means he's worried his voice, his accent, might give him away."

I squint, thinking hard. The reach of his organization is even vaster than I gave him credit for, and I silently gave him a lot of credit. I've killed many of his men. And I'm beginning to feel like I've not even touched the sides. "The only person The Bear speaks with directly is—"

"You," Danny says, stroking the edge of his desk with his fingertips. "Makes you pretty special. It also makes me wonder what the fuck he has on all these men to receive their compliance."

"And he killed the one woman who can give us a name." Brad blows out his cheeks and runs a hand through his hair.

I glance around the desk, seeing a crowd of bewildered faces. And now it's silent, everyone deep in their own thoughts. Until Danny's phone rings and everyone shoots their eyes to him. "Perry," he answers, sounding as pissed off as he looks, placing his phone on the desk on loudspeaker.

"I have your permit."

"Good boy."

"Is that it?" he asks. "Just the permit?"

"No, where's my cheeseburger," Otto grunts. "And Ringo's pardons on the parking tickets?"

My smile is private as I watch Danny. He's thinking. What's he thinking? "What are you doing two weeks on Saturday?" he asks Adams.

"Ummm ..."

"I'm getting married. You're invited. I'll forward the invitation." Danny hangs up and stands, and we all look at him, bemused.

"Anyone found Spittle's son yet?" he asks, his eyes passing over all of us. The silence gives him his answer. "I need a break." He heads out of the office, a pile of frowning faces following him. Mine included.

"What the fuck, Danny?" Brad yells.

"I'm going out on the water."

I could do with clearing my head too, but water isn't what I have on my mind.

"She's gone shopping with Rose," Danny calls from the door, obviously reading my mind.

"What kind of shopping?"

"The kind that happens in Walmart."

I frown. It's too early for Beau to even entertain entering a Walmart. Not without me. I look up, trying not to appear injured. "And no one thought to tell me?"

"I'm telling you now." Danny smiles, his expression telling me not to worry. "Come, the water's calling, mate."

"I'm going back to the club." Brad skirts past the two dead bodies.

"I'm going with Brad," Otto declares.

"Me too," Ringo adds. "I'll get someone to clean up this mess."

"What about me?" Goldie stands, looking as indignant as any woman could look.

"Should have gone shopping with the girls." Ringo gives her a cheesy, slap-worthy grin that does nothing to improve his looks.

"Get off her back," I warn him seriously, making him shrug, showing the ceiling his palms. "I mean it."

"I don't need you to defend me." Goldie storms past us, shoulder barging me as she does. "I'll drive you to the boatyard."

"Feeling optimistic?" Danny asks, looking across at me as we follow Goldie out of the house.

"Optimism gets you nowhere. Actions do. We still don't know how the women, drugs, and guns are getting into the country."

"Patience, James," he says quietly. "I feel like enlightenment is on the horizon. His army is dwindling. We're killing off his soldiers faster than he can replace them. He's panicking. Making moves he shouldn't. The Russians delivering guns for the Irish, case in point. It's only a matter of time before someone higher up puts a foot wrong."

He's right. There's a cat among the pigeons. Or a herd of lions.

I just hope that the enlightenment Danny speaks of comes sooner than the next bomb.

The still, calming water is a poor alternative to finding peace in Beau. But beautiful, nevertheless. The breeze feels good on my face, the sun blazing, warming my skin. I close my eyes and look up to the sky, walking back in my memory to a time that feels like centuries ago but was only weeks. St. Lucia. The quiet. Watching Beau stand on the shore enjoying the sun on her face. Her peace has become mine, and despite the progress she's made, I need those untarnished moments back. I need them to become a constant, consistent part of our lives.

"Watch your back," Danny calls.

I look over my shoulder, finding him in his wetsuit holding the drawbar of a trailer, rolling it down to the water. He's not even straining. "Maiden voyage?" I ask, moving aside. The trailer hits the water, and he wades to the back, negotiating his new jet ski off the back.

"I've missed it," he says, an excited glint in his eye. "You coming in?"

I wander to the front of the trailer and grab the metal, dragging it back up the sand. "Are these things loaded?"

He smirks, slipping his shades down to cover his eyes before jumping on. "Go get changed. You need a timeout." He starts the engine and revs, the sound thrilling. Danny's passion has fast become a passion of mine. It really is something else being on the open water, reveling in the speed as we cross the small waves.

I make my way to the cabin, hearing him roar off behind me. *Cabin*. The label completely undersells the impressive wooden structure built on the shore, with a balcony spanning two sides over the water and a jetty stretching into the ocean. A few jet skis line the wooden quay, all docked, ready to be tested. The inside space is quiet, word yet to spread through the jet ski community that this little gem is here. It won't be long. Not only is the setup fucking remarkable, so is the timeframe in which Danny made it happen. This place has been built in his head for many years.

Leon, the young lad hired to manage the place, is behind the shop counter scanning through spreadsheets as he chews on a pen. He suits this place, all free-spirited, shaggy-haired, board shorts, bandanas, and beaded man jewelry. He doesn't, however, suit the spreadsheet. But this wild kid was set to become an accountant before his love of the ocean won over pen-pushing his way through life. And perhaps his love of a joint every now and then. He was a good find. "How's recruiting going?" I ask as I pass.

"Interviewing this evening, J-boss." He chucks his pen down and snaps the laptop shut. "You going out?"

"Yeah."

Leon falls into stride next to me. "Which ski? I'll get it ready for you."

His footwear catches my eye. Because they're filthy, the once-white Converse high tops as grubby as hell. "The black Sea-Doo."

He falters, falling a few steps behind. I know if I glance back he'll have a look of horror on his face. "I have three strict instructions," he says, pulling me to a stop at the men's changing room door. "First rule, no one goes near the green container. Second rule, if the Feds show up, smile."

I turn, my own smile threatening. *Really* good hire. "And the third?"

"Only D-boss and his kid ride the black skis. So, you see, we might have a prob—"

"I was fucking with you, Leon." I push through the door and go to my personal locker. "The gold one's mine." I pull my wetsuit out and grab my gun from the back of my jeans, slipping it inside.

"Don't pull that shit, man," he grumbles, freeing my hands of my suit so I can strip down. "I still haven't decided whose bad side is worse."

"Mine," I say, hanging up my jeans and T-shirt. "Always mine."

"Funny, D-boss said the very same thing. How do you two know each other, anyway?"

"Rule number four." I claim my wetsuit and pull it up to my waist. "Don't ask too many questions." I cock my head and his proud nose wrinkles.

"But I can ask some, right?" His smile is cheeky. I shake my head to myself and head out to the water.

"Are you getting my ski, or what?" I get no answer, making me stall at the door. Leon's a statue by my locker, his eyes wide. "What's up?"

He gets his lax mouth under control and rakes a hand through his beach waves, diverting his stare, becoming flustered. "Um . . . nothing. Nothing's up."

I frown. And then I click, looking out the corner of my eye to where my scar begins on my shoulder. "War wounds," I mutter, picking up my feet.

"You went to war?" he asks, full of zeal, coming after me as I head for the containers. I slide the doors open, revealing my backup source of relaxation. I smile to myself, stroking down the side of the glimmering paintwork. "We're *at* war," I murmur, reaching the back.

"Huh?"

"Nothing. Fucking beauty, right?"

"Right, J-boss. Total beauty."

My eyes drop to the stern. "Motherfucker," I breathe over my light laugh, crouching and running my fingers across the text.

"Sounds mysterious. What's the story?"

"What's rule number four?"

"Ah, J-boss, come on."

"Get the Jeep," I order, hearing him sigh and trudge off, muttering claims of unfairness. "The Enigma," I whisper, tracing the text, my eyes following. *Smart-arse. Bastard.* It's ironic. I'm not an enigma anymore.

I push myself up and round the ski, grabbing the drawbar of the trailer and pulling it out of the store as Leon backs up in the Jeep. I hook it up and smack the side, starting to pull my wetsuit up my torso as he gets *The Enigma* into the water. I look out across the ocean, seeing Danny zigzagging across the sparkling cove.

"Ready," Leon calls.

I wade into the water and ease my jet ski off the back, calling out, "We're good," when I'm done. I board, start her up, and inhale the clean sea air.

"Have fun," Leon yells as I chug slowly into deeper water, and the moment I reach the buoy, I yank at the throttle and stand, crashing across the water at breakneck speed. The buzz is instant, the roar, the crash of water, the salt spray on my face. Fuck, it feels good. Needed.

I fall into the rhythm of the machine's motion, my body moving up and down smoothly as I skim the water, the growl of the engine pitching higher every time I break the swell, leaving the water before hitting it again with a thud.

I smile, a distant Danny getting closer, and when I'm just a few yards away from him, I turn sharply, laughing when he tries to shield himself from the bullets of water my move makes. "You fucker," he yells, his jet ski slowing to a stop.

I go in for the kill, circling, turning, attacking him with the water, not giving him a moment to get his bearings and retreat.

"Who's king of the water?" I yell, smirking when I catch sight of the evil glint in his eyes that I've come to know.

"Me, you fuck." He's suddenly racing away, gaining a good distance, before he slows and chugs around to face me again. I grin. A face-off. What a fucking pair of kids. I rev my engine, edging forward, staring at him in the distance, hearing the distant sound of his intimidating throttles too. *Game on, Black.*

His engine bellows, and I yank on my throttle and speed toward him. I will not be the first to turn. Never. And I know he won't either, which basically means our shiny new skis are going to be smashed to smithereens in a few seconds.

"Come on," I yell, my adrenalin pumping, Danny getting closer.

Reckless. But I need to let off some steam, and I know Danny does too.

Closer.

I hear him shout over the rush of wind and water, his body rising from the seat.

Closer.

I see his intention. He'd rather take the hit himself than let his precious ski get damaged.

"Come on, you murderous wanker," I say quietly, engaging my muscles, my arse lifting from the plush padded seat. "Let's do this." I launch at the exact same time Danny does, leaving the ski and sailing through the air toward him, and our hard bodies collide on a powerful crash. I grunt on impact, wrapping my arms around his neck as his go around mine. We're literally hugging in mid-fucking-air.

"Fuck." He coughs as we sail a few meters through the spray before hitting the water with a slap, sinking deep. I kick my feet, pushing my palms into his chest to break away, fighting my way to the surface. I break the water on a gasp, seeing Danny emerging a few feet away.

"Yeah!" he bellows, slapping the water with his palm, laughing his fucking head off.

I sweep my hands through my hair and shake my head. "You crazy fucker."

"You started it." He smirks and lunges forward, dunking me. The Brit fucking dunked The Enigma. What are we, five?

I cough and splutter, jerking my head to shake my hair from my eyes. "Get the fuck off," I mutter, shoving him away, laughing.

"Fuck."

My amusement dries up, our childish game ending abruptly. "What?" I pull my arm out of the water, seeing the key where it should be on the end of my wristband, thinking an AWOL ski is the cause of his alarm. I swing around. The jet skis are fine, bobbing on the water nearby, the engines cut. Then I spot his problem.

"Play time's over," Danny says, front crawling to his machine and climbing back on. He looks toward the shore where the black BMW is parked, a suited man leaning casually against the side. "That's a cop if ever I've seen one," Danny's mutters.

"Know him?" I ask, swimming over to my ski and climbing up, reattaching my key.

He lifts his glasses. "Can't tell from here." He smirks. "So they've finally heard I'm back."

He looks delighted by that. And sickly, I know he is. "Ready to say hello?"

"Oh yes."

We start a steady pace back side by side, taking our time, Danny clearly not in any rush. I take in all of the buildings on the shore, some fully built, some half built, some with only foundations dug. Developments are flying up everywhere. It's a shame. This little cove is a beauty.

It takes everything in me and more not to laugh when we get to the shore, seeing Leon looking at the cop with a shit-eating grin on his face. Even the kid recognizes a copper when he sees one.

"I don't believe it," Danny says quietly, getting off and wading to the sand.

I follow, watching the cop's lip curl to the point it distorts his face. "I take it you know him."

"Higham," Danny sings, reaching behind his back for his zip and pulling it down. "You been promoted?"

"It's Agent Higham to you," he grunts, reaching into his inside pocket and pulling out his badge, flashing it like a status symbol.

"Ooh, fancy." Danny pushes his suit down to his waist. "To what do I owe this pleasure?"

I keep my eyes on the cop as he turns his beady eyes onto me, looking me up and down before pushing off the side of his car and strolling forward casually while I dismount and join Danny on the shore.

"You realize faking your own death is a crime, Mr. Black."

I laugh under my breath, walking to a nearby wall and

taking a seat, removing the top half of my suit. If Danny could be arrested, he'd be in cuffs already and there would be a hell of a lot more cops here.

"Did I fake my death?" Danny asks, putting his hand out to Leon, who swiftly fills it with Danny's cigarettes and Zippo. The kid looks bemused. Awestruck. Excited.

Higham's curled lip twists. "So where have you been for the past three years?"

"Lying low. I'm sure you heard that my boatyard bore the brunt of two gangs' rivalry. If I was presumed caught in the crossfire and killed, that's your problem, not mine."

"And Agent Spittle's."

"Then you should be speaking to him."

"He's missing."

"Oh?" Danny lights up and joins me on the wall.

"I think you're sniffing around the wrong dog," I say, holding Higham in place with a stare he should feel threatened by. "Spittle was bent as fuck."

"Who the fuck are you?"

"Your worst nightmare," I say darkly, sounding as dangerous as I mean to.

He becomes flustered. "Brad Black identified the body."

Clutching at fucking straws. He knows it. "Brad was looking at a bloated, decaying corpse that had been mauled by sharks." Danny practically sighs. "You got a warrant?"

"No."

"Then fuck off."

Higham's chest puffs out slightly, his ego dented, but he just about manages to hold up his hard façade. "I can get a warrant."

"On what grounds?" I ask as Danny comfortably puffs his way through his smoke, and Leon's head swings back and forth between us, rapt.

"Things have been calm around here," he says, waving a

hand at Danny. "*He's* back from the dead, you show up, and suddenly bombs are exploding all over town."

"I wasn't dead," Danny says. "Sorry to disappoint."

Quiet in Miami? For fuck's sake. I rise, moving in intimidatingly close. Higham stands his ground. *Dickhead*. "Some advice," I say quietly, my mouth close to his ear. "Stay out of our way, and we will stay out of yours."

"Is that a threat?"

"No." I sniff, looking out the corner of my eye to him. "Just advice."

His eyes fall to my shoulder, his nostrils flaring, his lip twitching, desperate to curl again. "Have a good day, gentlemen." A long, hard, intimidating stare before he trudges back to his car and wheelspins off, having the last say with a screech of his tires.

"Nice bloke," I muse, joining Danny again, putting my hand out for his Marlboros. "Give me those."

He hands them over. "Two beers, Leon."

"Coming up." He dashes off, leaving Danny and me perched on the wall.

"What are you thinking?" Danny asks, after we've sat in a comfortable silence for a few minutes.

"I'm wondering where Spittle's son is. I'm wondering when the next bomb might land." I take one last drag and flick the butt away as Leon returns with two beers. We knock bottles and swig. "What went down with Beau's dad?" I ask, not wanting to broach that subject with Beau herself.

"His girlfriend, you met her?"

"No."

"She used to be the boys' plaything." He shrugs. "Mine from time to time too."

"Does Rose know that?"

"Yes, Rose knows that." His nose wrinkles. "Hence, fireworks in the TV room. I had to take care of it, or we would have had two dead Russians *and* a dead whore."

Hearing a car behind us, we both look over our shoulders. A beat-up old Chevy coughs and splutters its way across the gravel, and I smile, picturing Beau's dilapidated old Mustang. "What's he doing here?" I call to Leon, who's moving gas canisters off the back of his Jeep.

"Otto said I've got to give him a job." He heads over as the young lad from Derek's office block pulls his big body out of his car. "I'm thinking tow truck," he adds, and Danny chuckles. "Oh, and your phone's been ringing, boss."

We both stand. Look at each other.

"J-Boss," Leon yells.

"That'll be you." Danny slaps my shoulder as I jog off, undeniably twitchy. I make it to my locker, retrieve my phone, and breathe out my relief when I see it's not Beau or Fury. I call Otto back.

"Where the fuck have you been?" he barks.

I ignore his irate tone, looking up when Danny walks into the changing room. I click to loudspeaker. "What's up?"

"I've traced back the emails Derek Green sent us to an IP address."

"Where?"

"Internet café off Biscayne Boulevard."

Danny frowns, moving in. "Are you watching the account?"

"Yeah, I'm watching."

"The second an email lands, I want to know."

The sound of pumping music suddenly filters down the line, and I frown. "Where the fuck are you?" I ask Otto.

"Right now?"

"Yes, right now."

Danny's eyebrows rise, and we wait, curious. "Right now, I'm staring at legs that go on for years wrapped beautifully around a shiny silver pole."

"Unbelievable," I mutter, as Danny laughs his way to his own locker and strips out of his wetsuit. "Enjoy." I hang up and join him getting dressed. "You heard from Rose?"

His smile is knowing as he fastens his jeans. "Stop worrying."

"I'm not worrying." I'm really worrying. Trying my best not to, but with bombs and bullets firing at us from every which fucking way, it's a challenge. "I'm not worrying," I affirm when his eyebrow cocks. I yank my jeans up, slipping my gun back into place.

"We can't keep them locked up."

I laugh, my head thrown back. "Coming from the man who kidnapped his wife? Your relationship with Rose has Stockholm Syndrome written all over it."

"Oh, we're talking fucked-up relationships, are we?" he asks, and I brace myself for the hit. "From the man who tied his girlfriend to a chair in an opera house so he could slip off and murder a judge."

"How the fuck do you know that?" I grab my T-shirt and thread my arms through the sleeves.

"Women talk, mate. And apparently ours never shut the fuck up when they're together. Which is how I also know that you're partial to a self sex tape or two."

I still, my head caught in the neck of my T-shirt. *What the fuck?* I can hear his silent laugh. Slowly pulling my T-shirt down, I eye his smirking face. Women talk, okay. But do they show? Those tapes are private. They're for me and me only, because I'm the only person who should see Beau's naked body, especially during the throes of passion. "If you tell me you've seen those tapes, I can't promise I won't shoot you here and now."

"I've been shot at for less."

I reach back and pull out my gun, disengaging the safety and aiming it at Danny. "Don't piss me off."

Hands up, he laughs, moving back. "I've not seen the fucking tapes, mate. Chill the fuck out."

I snarl, stowing away my weapon. "I know you know shit like that ain't funny," I mutter, stomping out of the changing room. "And the reason I know is because you killed one of your own men for daring to touch Rose." I look back, hitting him with a grin to match the ones he keeps tossing around. "They really do talk."

He does a terrible job of concealing his surprise, and an even worse job of hiding his anger. "Fucked any women while their husbands watch lately?"

"Past life," I hit back, unmoved, carrying on my way. "Burnt your wife's hand on the toaster recently?"

"What the fuck?"

I smile as I pass through the café, seeing Leon showing the kid around. "J-Boss," he sings. "This is Jerry. Jerry, this is J-Boss. Oh, and here's D-Boss." I look back and see Danny stalking out of the changing room, his face like thunder. "D-Boss, this is—"

"We've met," Danny barks, making Leon and Jerry recoil. "The toaster was a point."

"What about the stinger of a slap the night you met her?"

He's getting progressively more wound up and, sick fuck that I am, I'm enjoying riling The Brit. "Another point."

"Parading her around naked in front of your men?"

His mouth falls open. "I'm going to sew her fucking mouth shut." His finger comes up. "That woman has caused me more damage than I'll ever cause her."

I slap his finger away. "Chill the fuck out," I say over a laugh, watching as his scar gets deeper and deeper, his eyes colder. I note the clenching of his fists. The roll of his jaw. Leon and Jerry wisely step back, out of the danger zone. "And would you mind putting my razor back?" I add.

My final blow is the final straw, and he launches a right hook that nearly takes me off my feet. *Jesus.* "Go fuck yourself," he yells. "Or burn yourself."

Oh, he did not. I charge, tackling him around the waist, sending us crashing to the ground, our phones scattering along with the loose change in my pocket. I straddle his waist and punch him square on the jaw. "Fucking pussy," he spits. "Rose hits harder than you." He shoots up, taking me to my back, and we roll and squirm around on the floor, our flying fists out of control, only the odd one connecting.

"Phones!"

I still. I'm on my back, Danny's palm's around my throat, while my palm's splayed and pushed into his face. The sound of two mobiles ringing fills the silence. In unison, we each give up and frantically search out our phones. I spot mine, Danny spots his, and we scramble on our hands and knees across the café floor, seizing them and answering.

I roll to my back. "Hey beautiful," I puff, knackered.

"Hey, baby," Danny chirps, landing next to me.

"Why are you panting?" Beau asks as I lick the corner of my bottom lip, recognizing the warm, coppery taste of blood. I check Danny, who has a tidy scuff on his cheekbone. "Just got in from the water."

"Just got in from the water," Danny mimics, turning his eyes onto me, grinning. "No, not yet. He's being taken to the house."

I punch his bicep and get up, going to the fridge and grabbing a water. "How's your shopping trip?" Isn't she coping? Is that why she's calling, because she needs my voice to help her make it through the trauma?

"Struggling," she admits.

"I'm on my way," I say, heading out.

"No, wait. Zinnea needs this."

I halt, listening to her, but I'm not happy about it. *Zinnea needs this.* "Want me to stay on the phone?"

"For now, yes. She's full on. What have you said to her?"

"Nothing."

"I don't believe you."

I shrug. "Don't believe me then."

Beau sighs. "What are you doing, anyway?"

"Just hanging out."

She laughs lightly, and it does nothing to ebb my urge for her. "The Enigma and The Brit. Just hanging out?"

I look across to Danny, just as he reaches for his cheek and grimaces. He finds me across the café. Snarls. Then pulls his gun, aims at my head, and fires.

I duck, the bullet sailing past me and sinking into the wall. "James!" Beau yells, sounding frantic.

Yes, The Enigma and The Brit, just hanging out. "I'm fine," I say, smiling. "Danny's doing target practice. I think he needs some tips from you."

I get the middle finger before he stomps out, Leon and Jerry moving aside hastily to let the raging beast through. He slams the door behind him, I laugh, and Leon puts his hand out to Jerry, smirking. "When can you start?"

16

BEAU

I hang up, taking my phone to my mouth, contemplative. "Is everything okay?" Zinnea asks, dropping a windchime into our cart.

I smile and inhale, ready to take on another aisle. "Yeah." *Deep breaths, deep breaths.* I swallow, cautiously glancing around. The number of shoppers seems to be multiplying by the second. And it's hot. Stifling. *Breathe, breathe, breathe.*

I need James.

Breathe.

I don't need James.

Deep breaths.

Fuck, I need James.

My heart rate goes from stable to frantic in a few panicked crashes, and I hold the side of the cart, trying so hard to talk myself down. "I think I should wait in the car," I say quietly, looking up at Zinnea. Her face. I feel like a total letdown. "Will you let Rose kn . . ." I pause, frowning, searching the vicinity. "Where's Rose?"

"She went that way." Zinnea points behind me. "Something about cleats for her son."

I turn, searching for her, panicking now for another reason. No sign of Rose, but Tank is behind me, his gigantic frame hardly visible past the piles of soccer equipment loaded into Rose's cart. "Why are you here?" I ask.

His searching eyes land on mine, his face furious. "I'm going to kill her," he barks, stomping off.

Instinctively, I jog the other way. "Wait there," I call back to Zinnea.

"Beau," Fury yells, but I ignore his warning, turning a corner, then another, going up one aisle, down another. "Where the hell are you?" I say, my eyes scanning every nook and cranny as I pull up her number and call. It goes to voicemail, and I curse her ass to hell and back, running up and down aisle after aisle, hearing Tank and Fury yelling our names at the tops of their voices, neither bothered about the attention they're attracting.

With my heart in my mouth, I push past people, dodge carts, calling her name. Nothing. I check every department. Every corner of the store, and when I've searched for ten minutes and found no sign of Rose, I finally relent and do what I've dreaded having to do.

Call Danny.

"Shit." I cringe and hit his name, starting to make my way back to Zinnea. My mouth is dry, my throat sore, my chest tight.

He answers quickly. "Beau?"

"Hey." I close my eyes briefly and inhale some bravery.

"You okay?"

"Yeah . . . um . . . Rose is . . ." I fade off, halting in my tracks when I spot her up ahead. Air leaves my lungs faster and louder than I planned, my palm slapping my breastbone.

"Rose is *what*?" he asks, sounding ominous.

"Fine," I squeak, quickly—and probably stupidly—hanging up. I pace toward her static form. "Jesus, Rose, don't do that to me."

She seems to snap out of a daydream and whirls around, a smile appearing like she could have just pulled it off the shelf and slapped it on her face. "Oh, hey."

Oh, hey? I've been running around this store like a jerk for over ten minutes, and all she's got to say is *oh hey*? "Tank's losing his shit."

"I forgot something."

"What?" I ask, scanning the shelf of ladies' cosmetics. No kids' cleats in sight.

She quickly snatches some shaving cream down and holds it up, but it starts to lower slowly, her smile falling. "Are you okay?"

Am I okay? No, I'm not fucking okay, but not because I'm up to my eyeballs in frantic shoppers. "I'm fine. I thought . . ." I don't know what I thought. "I was worried." I sigh, pinching the bridge of my nose, trying to screw my head back on.

"Well, I'm fine." Rose marches past me, and I frown, following her path, just as Tank comes charging around the corner like a rhino. "I'm here, I'm alive," she sings sarcastically. "Call off the search party."

Tank looks about ready to rip her head off as I follow them, wary, until we make it back to Zinnea. "There you are!" she screeches, rushing over and checking me from head to toe. "What happened?"

"Drama over nothing." Rose claims her cart and heads to the checkouts. "I forgot my shaving cream, that's all."

"Sorry," I say to Fury as I pass him before he has a chance to lay into me, my eyes never leaving Rose's back. She starts loading her things onto the belt as Tank moves to the other end, and Zinnea reluctantly heads to the next checkout. "Will you help my aunt?" I ask Fury, who proceeds to mentally gage the distance between Zinnea and me.

He eventually plods off, and I move in on Rose. "Here, let me help." I dip into her cart and collect the shaving cream. "Just what a woman needs when her husband's confiscated all blades within a ten-mile radius," I say just loud enough for her to hear. Lips pursed, she avoids my eyes, so I continue, dipping back into the cart, my hand landing on a box.

Rose seizes my wrist, and I still, looking up. Her focus is set firmly on me. She smiles. "I've got it."

I shake off her hold, moving a soccer ball, revealing a . . . "What the fuck, Rose?" I whisper, snapping my eyes to hers.

"Shhhh," she hisses, grabbing the pregnancy test and putting it on the belt under a bunch of sport socks. "I need you to go to the other end and make sure Tank doesn't see this."

I stare at her, a million questions parading through my mind, none of which I can ask now. So I do as she's asked and go to the other end, making sure I'm in front of Tank. As soon as the cashier scans the box, I snatch it from her hand and stuff it in a bag, smiling awkwardly at her alarm. "Thanks." I peek cautiously out the corner of my eye to Tank. He's oblivious, his attention split between the mundane task of packing and Rose at the other end of the checkout. Peeking the other way, I find Zinnea chatting happily to her packing partner, Fury. I don't know how I'm going to keep my mouth shut until we get home.

Rose pays, then claims the bag containing the test, and smiles meekly, stuffing it in her purse. "Thank you."

"Rose, what—"

"Ready, darlings?" Zinnea sings, pulling the cart as Fury pushes.

I bite my tongue, giving Rose a look to suggest we're not done. "Ready," I breathe as she bowls past me. I rush to catch up. "Rose, you have to tell Danny," I whisper, keeping close to her side, peeking back to make sure the Vikings and Zinnea are out of range.

"I'm sure I'm worried over nothing. I didn't want to say anything to you."

"Why?" I ask, injured. "I'm your friend."

"You've been through so much." She shakes her head mildly, and I fold with guilt, hating that she's shouldered this bombshell on her own.

"This isn't about me. It's about you."

"I'm sure it's nothing." She smiles mildly. It's a bit of an insult. "I can't be pregnant."

I return my attention forward, trying so hard to look casual. Normal. It's hard when my head's reeling. "Then why—" I snap my mouth shut when something catches my eye across the store, just entering. Or some*one*. "Shit," I murmur, fighting to maintain my pace.

"What?"

"That man," I say, not pointing. "The one in the royal blue suit by the entrance."

Rose does a stellar job of appearing uninterested. "What about him?"

"There was a photo of him on Danny's desk." I keep us walking, trying to split my attention between the Vikings and Zinnea behind us, and the man I recognize up ahead.

"I saw a photo on Danny's desk," Rose says quietly. "That's not him."

"They probably have a drawerful of photos, Rose." All men on their list. It's not like James can keep them on the screens in his apartment anymore. I reach into my purse and feel around for my cell, pulling up the camera when I find it.

"What are you doing?" Rose hisses, nervously looking over her shoulder.

"I'm taking a picture." I curse under my breath, the image too grainy. "I need to get closer."

"Are you insane?" Rose tries to steer me toward the door, but I'm persistent. "Beau, for fuck's sake, he could be anyone."

"I just need to get a little closer."

"Yes, great. Let's get closer so he sees us, recognizes us, and kills us."

"Stop being dramatic," I say, my eyes rooted to the blue-suited man. "What's he doing?" He's hovering by the Minute Key kiosk, looking a bit twitchy, a bunch of keys being tossed in his hand.

"Why don't you go ask him?" Rose mutters, her body pushing into mine as I continue to try and direct us closer, my phone ready to snap a picture. It's definitely him. Mid-thirties, short, slick black hair, a patchy beard.

"Beau," Fury calls from behind, and I wince, weighing up the merits of ignoring him.

"Just grabbing something," I call back, scanning the area for anything I can actually grab.

"Oh my God, we're going to die," Rose whispers.

"Rose!" Tank yells.

Jesus, will they stop shouting our fucking names?

"Coming," she calls. "Beau, for Christ's sake, James will kick your ass."

"Rose, fuck knows how long the list of men they need to kill is. The quicker they get it done, the quicker we get out of here and back to St. Lucia." I stop and look at her. "Don't you want that?"

Her mouth opens and closes a few times, as my words, all true words, sink in. I see an air of determination creep into her. I see her hand go to her stomach. It's instinctive. If Rose turns out to be pregnant, she'll want to leave even sooner and even more. "Do not get too close."

I nod, quickly linking arms with her, hearing Fury and Tank cursing behind us. I know exactly what I'm doing. This is someone of importance, someone James is looking for, I know it. The cop in me, this instinct, will never die. "Just a bit closer," I say, trying to focus on my camera and aim, all while being discreet.

And then he looks directly at us, and we both freeze. I feel Rose's stiffness against me. "What do we do, what do we do?" she hisses, as we're literally charged from behind by what feels like a massive boulder.

"What the fuck are you two playing at?" Tank grunts.

The man frowns, his eyes darting across all of us, finally resting on me. I quickly break our eye contact, reaching for the first thing I can lay my hands on. I move toward a self-checkout and tug a bag off one of the holders. "Rose's bag's broken," I blurt, words just toppling out of my mouth. The man's frown deepens, and he becomes twitchier, his already strung body definitely tensing more. Not looking at him, I go back to Rose, taking the bag in her hand and slipping it inside the new one. Her eyes are wide as she looks at me, and I silently plead with her to look normal. "You'd make a terrible cop," I whisper, as Tank tuts his displeasure beside us. "What's he doing?"

"Looking through his keys."

I peek over my shoulder, see he's distracted, and quickly take the photo I need. "Done," I say, seizing Rose and plastering a smile on my face for the Viking's benefit. "Let's go." I guide Rose out.

"What's going on?" Zinnea asks, tottering along beside us.

"Nothing," we sing in unison, heading for the cars, my back rolling constantly, my skin cold.

"Beau?"

I stutter to an abrupt halt, bringing Rose to a stop too, my skin getting colder. "No," I whisper.

"What?" Rose says, confused, looking around us.

I see Fury in my side vision reaching for his holster, his face a picture of threat. "My ex-fiancé," I mutter.

"Ohhhh," Rose breathes.

"It's Ollie," Zinnea sings, and my shoulders drop, exasperated. "Beau, look, it's Ollie."

Why does she sound so pleased to see him? Has she forgotten he held James at gunpoint? *Oh God.* I inhale and face him. He's frowning down at his watch, undoubtedly wondering what I'm doing in Walmart at this time. I absolutely do not want to do this. So I won't.

"Get in the car," Fury grates.

"With pleasure." I swing the back door open and slide in, leaving the others to put the bags in the trunk. I quickly pull up the photo and text it to James with a question mark, then notice Zinnea swinging her eyes back and forth between me and Ollie, while Rose tries to coax her toward the car. Fury stands silent and threatening to the side, and Tank loads the shopping. I can see by the look of my aunt's face that whatever Ollie is saying isn't helping. I can imagine. Talk of bombs and God knows what else. Lawrence knows a lot. More than he probably should and, in fairness, he's been quietly accepting of my decision to be here. To be with James. I do not need Ollie stirring more shit into the already overflowing well of shit. I start to get worked up, and I'm out of the car before I can stop myself.

"In the car, Beau," Fury barks, moving his big body to shield me. I muscle my way past him, determined.

"Back off, Ollie," I warn.

"Do we have a problem?" A man, suited, an FBI agent if ever I've seen one, joins Ollie, giving everyone a tactical flash of his gun by casually pulling one side of his jacket back.

"I don't know," Ollie murmurs, turning his narrowed eyes onto Fury. "Do we?"

I can see it now. Ollie's revenge on the horizon. His ego set to be restored. "We don't have a problem," I grate, taking Fury's arm and trying to move the unmovable man. Of course, he doesn't move.

"Do you have a license for that firearm?" Ollie asks, now refusing to look at me.

I close my eyes and inhale some patience. Ollie knows what he's doing, and a second later, his partner has drawn and aimed at Fury. "Get your hands on the roof of the vehicle," he bellows. "Do it now."

I turn my condemning stare onto Ollie's sneering face. "Don't do this, Ollie."

"Why? Will your boyfriend and his friends attack me again?"

"Hands on the car!"

"Fuck this," Fury mutters, drawing and aiming too, prompting Ollie to quickly arm himself as well, followed by Tank.

"Oh shit," Rose whispers.

"Stay where you are, Zinnea," I order, feeling her meltdown brewing, her gasps constant. "It's okay." I glance past Ollie and his partner, seeing the man I recognize from the picture exiting the store. "Fuck," I hiss, just as my phone starts ringing. "I need to answer that," I say calmly.

"Don't move," Ollie's partner yells, his forehead glistening with sweat. "Do not move."

"I really need to take the call." I hold up my cell, showing them, before slowly lifting it to my ear. "James."

"Where are you?" he asks, his breathing strained.

"Walmart. We have a situation."

"Put the phone down, Beau," Ollie orders, his nostrils flaring.

"Is that Burrows?" James asks.

"Yes."

"The guy in the picture?"

"Leaving the store." I just get my words out before Ollie lunges forward and snatches my cell from my hand. "You do not want to make enemies of them, Ollie," I say quietly, and because I know him, I recognize the hesitation in his eyes. I divert my stare to the exit doors of the store again, scanning, searching, as my cell rings persistently in Ollie's hand. I see the blue-suited guy getting into a silver Audi. *God damn it.*

I could draw my own gun and add another to the mix. Or . . .

I move fast, throwing my arm out and disarming Ollie, ignoring the shooting pain that flies up my arm. I spin the gun and aim it at his chest, and he staggers back, stunned. "Not lost my touch, huh?" I say through my teeth. "Now there are four guns, and three of those are aimed at you two. Be wise," I warn, and Ollie's partner sensibly lowers his to the ground by his feet. I dip and pick it up, tucking it in my purse. "And your car keys."

"Beau, come on," Ollie yells.

"Do it!"

Nostrils flaring, his chest expanding from his inhale, he dips into his pocket and pulls out his keys, tossing them at my feet. "Rose, Zinnea, get in the car." I collect them up and move toward the Range Rover, opening the passenger side door as they both scuttle toward me and slip into the back. Fury and Tank, guns still aimed, get in the front. "My phone," I say, holding out my hand, eyes on Ollie, daring him to refuse.

His chest puffing, his jaw tight, he lays it in my palm. I get in the car. "Let's go," I order, relaxing slightly as I sit forward, putting myself between Tank and Fury upfront. "Follow that silver Audi."

"What?"

"Do it," I order, answering James's call.

"What the fuck is going on?" he barks.

I don't know where to start. "I think I might be a wanted woman," I say, prompting a huff of sardonic laughter from the

Vikings. "So if we could go back to St. Lucia sooner rather than later, that would work for me."

"Beau," he retorts, full of warning. "Talk."

"I didn't know what to do," I say, going into defense mode. "The guy in the picture was leaving and Ollie and his partner pulled their guns on the twins."

"What did you do?"

"Disarmed Ollie." I cringe, waiting for him to yell at me. "And now we're following the guy in the picture I sent you."

Quiet. I don't like it. I look nervously between Fury and Tank, noticing they look as tense as I feel. "Burrows?" James asks.

"I took his keys."

An inhale. "I'm not happy," he says calmly.

I knew he wouldn't be. "We're keeping a safe distance."

"Pull back," he orders, so loud the whole car hears. "Now."

Fury's foot eases off the gas immediately, and the distance between us and the silver Audi grows. *God damn him.* There's little point trying to convince my personal protection officer to ignore James. I'm sure he has a strong desire to keep breathing. "Who is he?" I murmur, despondent.

"Put me on loudspeaker."

"Who is he?" I repeat, my dejection converting into impatience.

"Put. Me. On. Loud. Speaker."

"Fine," I grate, clicking the icon. "It's not like he couldn't fucking hear you." I fall back in my seat, my eyes laser beams on the Audi getting farther away, my mind spinning.

"Location," James barks.

"North West Twelfth heading downtown," Fury answers obediently, rolling to a stop at a red light as the Audi sails through. I feel Rose's hand rest on my knee, feel her eyes on my profile, as well as Zinnea's.

"Go back to the house."

"Copy that," Fury says, checking his mirrors and signaling.

I breathe in deeply, exhaling calmly. "Who is it, James?"

"The manager of the bank where your mum held her safety deposit box."

"What?" And he's just going to let him get away because of some misplaced, fucked-up need to keep me out of harm's way? No.

"We'll find him, Beau."

"I've found him," I grate, jumping out of the vehicle. I throw my bag over my shoulder and sprint across the road, dodging the traffic, tucking the gun into my pants. "Beau!" Rose yells, sounding distressed, but I focus forward, my attention split between the fading Audi and the cab across the street. Car horns blare, the twins bellow. I cut James off and jump into the back of the cab. "Drive," I order shortly, looking out the back window. Fury's stomping down the road, a face like thunder, cars screeching to a stop around him. "Drive," I yell.

The driver, looking startled, pulls away fast. "Okay, ma'am."

"The silver Audi up ahead. Follow it." I find it again, pointing, and I don't take my eyes away. "Keep two cars back."

"You got it," he practically sings, now sounding excited. "Cop?"

"Yeah," I murmur for the sake of it, killing the conversation and any potential further questioning.

He follows as instructed until we make it Downtown, and when the Audi signals left into a side street, he looks to me for guidance. "Slow down," I order, shifting to the left of the car so I can keep the Audi in my sights. It rolls to a stop, sitting idle at the curb halfway down the quiet street.

"I think someone's trying to get hold of you," the taxi driver says as my cell rings persistently and the cab comes to a standstill.

"I think someone's probably having a hernia," I murmur, taking the handle and letting myself out. I can't even begin to imagine the mood James is in, but he needs to come to terms with the fact that I will never be a glass girlfriend to go with the rest of the glass in his life. This isn't just about him. His history. His heartache. His justice. I need this as much as he needs this, but now for many more reasons. Not just justice. Not just peace. But so I can move forward with James. "Can you wait?" I ask.

"Sure."

"Thanks." I pace down the street to the Audi, sure and determined, reaching into the back of my jeans and pulling the gun I seized from Ollie. I check the magazine. Smack it back in. Release the safety. My heart is thundering in my chest, my adrenalin booming. Keeping my gun by my thigh, I pass the car slowly, looking inside, seeing the man engrossed in his phone. I round the hood, putting myself in front of the Audi. He looks up. Blinks his surprise.

I aim.

He shoots back in his seat, hands up, and we stare, him undoubtedly recognizing me from the store, me wondering what the fuck I do now. My phone won't stop ringing, my heart won't stop racing. I'm not a cop anymore, keeping the streets of Miami safe. I'm a woman fighting for my life. Fighting for eternal peace. And this feels fucking good. I'm not broken. I'm not despairing. I'm not passive. I'm making shit happen.

He moves, and my decision is made for me. I fire, shattering the windshield, and round the side, opening the passenger door and getting in. "Do not move," I say calmly, feeling anything but.

"Who the hell are you?"

I keep quiet and reach for his phone that he's dropped into his lap. "My name is of no consequence. What you can tell me is." I ram the gun into his temple. "Let's talk about the safety deposit box that belonged to Agent Jaz Hayley."

"Oh shit."

"Yes, oh shit."

His eyes clench shut, his back plastered to the back of his seat. "Who are you?"

"I'd say I'm your worst nightmare, but that wouldn't be true."

His eyes turn but his head remains stuck to the back of the seat. I can see it in his stare. He's scared to ask. So I'll help him along the way.

"The Enigma," I whisper, almost menacingly. "I believe he's vying for your blood too."

His intake of breath is sharp. "No." And then he's moving fast, swiping his arm up and knocking me away before reaching under his seat. I lunge forward, cuffing his cheekbone with the handle of my gun. "Fuck!"

I ram my palm into the side of his head, wedging it against the window, re-aiming. "Let's be sensible."

"Okay, okay."

I release him, holding my gun steady, and reach under his seat. I pull out a gun. "Who told you to get the box?"

"I don't know."

"How did he tell you?"

"Text."

"What did he threaten you with?"

"My father's life."

"Who's your father?"

"Frank Spittle."

I still, hiding my frown. Spittle. I've heard that name. My cell starts ringing again, and I glance down, seeing James's name filling my screen. And then the sound of screeching tires fills the side street, and my heart turns in my chest. I don't know who should be more afraid. Him or me. "Don't move," I say, letting myself out of the car. The Mercedes races toward me like a bat out of hell. I can literally feel the anger in that car from here. I don't bother asking myself how he knew where I am. "Good luck," I murmur, to both of us, lowering my gun, ready to bear the brunt of James's temper. The smell of burning rubber saturates my nose, the Merc screaming to a stop, James and Danny jumping out, both armed, both furious.

I soak up the fire in James's glare, standing firm, shoulders back, chin high. I don't give him a chance to tell me to get in the fucking car. I pace over and slip into the back, settling and watching as Danny yanks the guy from the driver's side and thrusts him against the side of the Audi, his face lethal, his lip curled, his gun pushed into his throat.

James, however, maintains his deadly glare on me. I break the connection and go to my cell when it rings. I take Rose's call, if only to escape the silent wrath of James. "I'm alive," I say, looking back when I hear another car skid into the street. "The cavalry has arrived."

"Jesus, Beau."

"Does the name Spittle mean anything to you?" I ask.

"Spittle? Yes. He's the one who let on that Danny isn't dead. Ex FBI," she says, and I nod to myself. I knew the name was familiar. MPD. FBI. It's my old life. "I saw them dragging Spittle into the house," Rose goes on.

And I bet he didn't leave. At least, he didn't leave breathing. "The guy we were following is his son."

"Shit. I seriously wouldn't want to be in your shoes right now."

I laugh a little. "I'll see you back at the house." I look across to James, who's now manhandling the man over to Otto's car. "If I'm not dead." I disconnect and wait for the men to finish their business, using the quiet time to cool my temper. James was prepared to let one of his wanted slip away because of his misplaced worry for my well-being. It's probably childish, but that pisses me off. Frank Spittle's son is an obstacle in our way. I had a chance to remove the obstacle, and I took it.

I pull my belt on as James and Danny stomp back to the car, swing the doors open, fall in, and slam them. I'm sure a thorough telling off is coming from both sides. So who's going to be first?

Danny swings around in his seat and pins me in place with livid, icy eyes. But he says nothing, probably out of respect for James. And yet I bet he has plenty to say, none of it pleasant. I make sure I hold his stare. I'm not breaking. He eventually growls and returns to the wheel, starting the car, but before he can pull away, James fills the space Danny just freed. He doesn't look at me as his hands start patting at my body forcefully. I know what he's looking for, so I let him go ahead and find them. He pulls a gun from between my thighs, then leans forward more to reach behind my back, roughly yanking the other free. And I remain still and accepting. I'm not, though. *Choose your battles.* His mood now won't allow him to see reason, so I'll sit on my grievance until he's calmed the hell down. The buildings around us are virtually shaking with the tremors of his rage.

When he's found what he's looking for, he returns forward. Except he's missed one. So I reach into my purse and pull out the gun that I took from Ollie's partner, letting it hang from my finger as I hold it between the two front seats.

He looks at it out the corner of his eye, snarls, grabs it, and then Danny roars off, taking his anger out on the Mercedes rather than me. James doesn't have that outlet. Which means I'm in massive trouble when we get back to the house.

17

DANNY

I've seen silent rage on James. I've seen his eyes glaze, his body shake, his jaw twitch. But all of those times pale in comparison to now. I know how *I* feel, which is fucking incensed, and she's not even my woman. She's playing fucking kamikaze.

When we pull through the gates of the house, I cast a wary look across to James. The car feels set to explode with the weight of his anger, and Beau's out before I come to a complete stop. She slams the door and paces to the house, ignoring more animosity from Fury as she passes him on the steps. James remains in the seat next to me, his breathing audible. I let down my window when Otto approaches. He eyes James. Looks at me. "Take him into the office," I say, scanning the front of the house. "Daniel's here, so go around the side."

"Got it."

I look at James. "Do you need a minute?" If I take him in that office where Kenny Spittle is within reach, he'll be dead before I can even think of the questions we need to ask.

"For what?" James gets out, and I sigh, following him.

"To calm down."

"I'm calm."

I laugh under my breath, having to hold back from punching him in the face to snap him out of his bad mood. "Take a minute," I order, leaving no room for an argument. "Or have a drink. I'll meet you in the office." I follow my feet through the main house, meeting Tank in the foyer. "Where is she?"

"She went straight to your room," he answers, gesturing up the stairs. "The kid's in the kitchen with your mom."

"Is she okay?" My instinct takes me to the stairs, not waiting for Tank's reply. I could understand a retreat to our room if she'd pulled a stunt like Beau. But she didn't.

"Quiet," he says, making my pace increase.

"Has she been down since the kid arrived?"

"No."

Why didn't she go straight to Daniel? "Tell the men I'll be there in a minute."

I reach the top and find Beau's aunt gently knocking on the door to James's and Beau's room. "Beau, darling, want to talk about it?" Zinnea hears me and gives me a worried shrug. "What happened?"

"Don't ask," I reply, passing her, but I come to a slow stop when something comes to me. I turn to face her. "How was your shopping trip?"

She recoils, surprised. "Well, eventful."

"Before the eventful part."

Her head tilts. "Is there something specific you would like to ask?"

I smile. "Am I that transparent?"

"Forgive me, but in the short time I've known you, I've learned you're a straight shooter. No dancing around the point. Am I right?"

"You're right?"

"So ask me."

"Beau called me from the store."

"That would be when we lost Rose."

"What?"

"Only for a few minutes. She forgot something and neglected to mention she was going back."

Only for a few minutes? A few minutes is all it takes. Rose knows that. "What did she forget?"

"Shaving cream."

I can't hide my recoil. My wife hasn't shaved in three years. It's waxing or nothing. "Right," I say quietly, backing up, just as Beau swings the door open, her eyes batting back and forth between us. I know immediately she's heard our conversation. She's heard her aunt share something that shouldn't have been shared. What the fuck is going on and, more to the point, why the fuck don't I know about it? I tilt my head. "If Rose doesn't talk, I'm coming to you," I warn, knowing she knows whatever there is to know. Her lips straighten, and she inhales, but she nods, accepting, and that just puts me even more on edge. Because Beau obviously thinks I *should* know. What the fuck has happened? We've not argued, so why is my wife avoiding me? Plus, Daniel is in the kitchen with Mum. Why didn't she rush straight there to see him? To show him all the soccer kit she just bought?

I turn away and walk with conviction, my stomach doing cartwheels. I don't do nervous. Never have. Trust my fucking wife to fix that. I push my way into our room and scan the space. No wife. The bathroom door is closed. I approach it, listening. Nothing. Abandoning my need to shoulder barge my way in and demand answers, I force my instinct into a calmer approach. What the hell did Doc miss? What's wrong with her? Is it treatable? Will she be okay? "Fucking hell," I breathe, everything—

my head, my stomach, my heart—is in chaos. I tap the door lightly. "Rose, baby?" I call through the wood. "You in there?" What the fuck am I doing? This isn't me. I drop my forehead to the door. "Can I come in?"

"Yeah," she says, quiet and unsure, only compounding the anxiety swirling in my gut. I take the handle and push the door open, but I remain on the threshold, hesitant and as nervous as a man could be. She's sitting on the edge of the tub, hands in her lap, fingers twiddling. She looks up at me, tears pouring. *Oh fuck.* My fears multiply, but I find it in myself to pull my head out of my arse, disregard my own uncertainties, and go to her. My fierce warrior doesn't cry. She gets angry, upset, frustrated, but hardly ever cries. I fall to my knees and take her wrists, automatically scanning her arms for damage. The floor for blood. Nothing. It's a mild consolation.

She joins me on the bathroom floor, on her knees, and slips her arms around my neck, cuddling my clueless form. I want to ask. I don't want to ask. The unknown is driving me crazy.

And this moment, this scene on the floor in our bathroom, her crying, me comforting her, brings back a whole load of memories that I really don't want to remember. If she tells me anything like what she told me that day, if any man has touched her, violated her, assumed she's fair game, I will lose my fucking head. Those thoughts run circles in my mind, along with every serious illness that Doc could have missed, until I'm shaking in her fierce hold.

"Rose, you need to talk before I blow my stack," I warn, struggling to breathe, let alone talk. I feel her nod, pulling back, sniveling. I take her hair and push it over her shoulders. Take her chin and direct her face to mine. Take her hand, holding it firmly. "What's going on?"

She shakes her head. "I don't know how this has happened."

"What?" For the love of God, what's happened?

She roughly wipes at her face and stands, and I look up at her, blank, lost.

Worried.

She tugs me to my feet, leads me to the vanity, and points.

On a frown bigger than Miami, I look.

And step back.

Away from the pregnancy test.

The pregnancy test with two lines in the window. I'm no expert, but something tells me those two lines are significant, because why the fuck else would she show me a pregnancy test? "Rose, help me out," I murmur, dazed, my eyes unmoving, my hand flexing in hers. Another step back. My heart begins to thud relentlessly. My breathing is getting too fast to be safe. I peel my eyes away and look at her. My beautiful wife. My fierce, loyal, warrior. And my eyes fall to her stomach. "Are you . . ." I point a limp finger, taking another step back. Her tears seem to have vanished, and in their place, amusement. She finds this funny. She finds *me* funny. "Please talk." She needs to confirm what I'm seeing because I think I might be going around the bend. *Rose can't get pregnant.*

"I'm pregnant," she all but whispers.

I gulp. I swallow. I blink my hazy vision clear. The relief I feel is untold. She's not ill. No one's touched her. But . . . "How?" I murmur like an idiot.

"Well, you see, your dick—"

"But you couldn't . . . it was . . . I thought . . ." I can't even string a fucking sentence together. "What the ever-loving fuck?" I murmur, going to the sink and picking up the test, staring at the lines.

"Danny?"

"I just need . . ." I blow out my cheeks. "Air. I need some air." I leave the bathroom, my legs far from stable, and take myself to the terrace, flopping down in one of the chairs and lighting up, drawing on my cigarette urgently and exhaling, my foot tapping the ground, my knee jumping fast, my eyes still on the two little lines. This. I never in a million years thought about *this*. Why would I? She couldn't carry. Being a father never featured in my plans before I met Rose, and it certainly didn't after. When she told me every detail of her wretched past, how she lost Daniel, how she was treated, I was too consumed with anger and a need for revenge to consider the possibility that she was wrong. That she *could* get pregnant again. I took her word for it, put it to bed —after I'd killed the fucker who was the root of Rose's pain— and got on with a life loving Rose. Just us. Us and Daniel. And after three years of fucking like rabbits with no protection, the thoughts disappeared altogether.

Now? Now I'm staring fatherhood in the face?

I puff my way through my cigarette, savoring every hit of nicotine while willing my mind to untangle and give me some clarity. Some clear thoughts. I have only one.

This changes *everything*.

It also makes me love her more. Admire her more. Need her more. I'm sitting out here on my own, shellshocked. How does Rose feel about this?

I rise abruptly and turn. She's standing in the doorway, arms folded, her shoulder resting on the jamb, watching me. A small, amused smile gracing her face. And suddenly, my mind unravels. My thoughts clear. All I can see is her smile. Her happiness. A second chance that I never once dared dream I could give her. A pregnancy without fear. A birth without dread. A life without apprehension.

A baby that no one can take away from her.

"Fucking hell," I whisper, overcome with every emotion imaginable. And the biggest, most prolific one?

Determination.

Only I can ensure her stability. Her calm. And I will.

I go to her, slipping the stick in my back pocket, and take her face in my palms. Take in every inch of her. Her hair. Her eyes. Her flawless skin. The glow. And I kiss her. It tells her more than I could ever put into words.

"Finish it, Danny," she says round my mouth, taking my wrists and gripping me hard. She breaks my kiss. The resolve in her eyes matches the intensity of how I feel. "I'm not raising our baby in Miami."

I nod. Received loud and clear. Whatever she wants. Shit, what the hell is happening? Overwhelmed, I drop to my knees, kneeling before her, worshipping her like the goddess she is, and hug her stomach, feeling her hands stroking through my hair, softly massaging at my scalp. And I stay there for a long, long time, my face pressed into her tummy, my purpose renewed.

I eventually rise, kissing my way to her face. "I have to go."

She nods, tracing a line down my scar. "I know," she whispers. "We'll be here."

We. *We'll* be here. I grin and smother her with my mouth, making her giggle and writhe in my clutches. "Go," she orders, forcing me away, eager for me to see to business and come back to them. "I need to wash my face before I go downstairs and face everyone."

I nod and head for the door.

"Danny?"

I look back. She has her index finger held against her lips. Quiet. Keep it quiet. I mirror her and leave, shutting the door quietly behind me. And I stand there, momentarily bewildered again. And suddenly worried. I pull out my phone, dial Doc, and get walking.

He answers quickly as I check my surroundings. I see Tank in the foyer, Fury at the top of the stairs, Beau's aunt coming out of her room. Too many fucking people in my house. "I'll call you back," I say quietly, hanging up just as Beau appears, her hair wet, her signature ripped jeans and baggy shirt ensemble gracing her fit body. She falters, gathering her hair into a ponytail when she sees me, her expression unsure. It would be highly inappropriate, given what she's been through, to show even an ounce of happiness. Besides, I'm still raging mad with her. "Don't ever pull a stunt like that again."

She rolls her eyes. It's condescending. It's rude. It's fucking brave. "Don't start, Danny. I have my own stone-cold killer to handle, thanks." Her head tilts, and the slow formation of a smile appears. "She is, isn't she?"

"Don't know what you're talking about." I turn and get on my way, only letting my smile loose when my face is out of her view.

"It's great news," she says softly.

I stop, my heart sinking. She's happy for us. Her words were quiet, but there could be no doubting her sincerity. *Jesus.* I walk back to her and Beau, alarmed, slowly backs away. I don't know what's gotten into me, but I need to do this. I haul her into my chest. The poor thing has no idea what to do with me, her arms hanging limp by her sides. "I'm sorry," I say, squeezing my eyes closed.

"Don't make this about me, Danny," she breathes. "This is about you two, and it's happy."

"You need to go fix things with James."

"He's not talking to me."

"Are you surprised?" I pull out, holding her firmly by the tops of her arms. "If Rose had of pulled a stunt like that, I would—"

"What?" she asks, head tilted. "You would *what*?"

Good fucking question. "I'd put her in a cage." It's the first thing that comes to me, and Beau laughs, shrugging me off.

"Okay," she says, shaking her head. "Go take care of business, Danny. I need to go check on my friend." She backs away, eyebrows high. "My *pregnant* friend."

Fuck, that sounds good. "You do that." And I need to call Doc back. I walk on but something comes to me. "Wait, Beau," I call, looking back. "You've not talked to James at all?"

"No, I need to cool off."

I laugh under my breath. *She* does? James looked like he was one spark away from exploding. So he's not grilled her? Got any details? "What was Kenny Spittle doing in Walmart?"

"He was at the Minute Key Kiosk."

I nod, thoughtful. "And when you had him at gunpoint, what did you ask and what did he tell you?"

"He said he was being blackmailed with his father's life. Get the box or his dad dies."

Well, that's a shitter. "So he got the box for . . ."

"Someone."

"Contact?"

"Text."

"And that's it?"

"Yes, that's it. My interrogation was interrupted." She smiles sweetly as she lets herself into Rose's and my room, and I laugh under my breath as I go to the top of the stairs, signaling for Fury and Tank to take up their positions. They're quick to respond, Fury looking plain terrified. He should. I can't promise him James isn't going to shoot him for losing Beau.

"She's fucking fast, Danny," he says over an exhale, like he's been holding his breath since Beau escaped him.

"I'll try to calm him down," I say, passing them, receiving a curious, interested eye from Tank. It takes everything in me to maintain a straight face. But he'll soon need to know that my precious wife just became even more precious. I dial Doc, taking the stairs slowly. "She's pregnant," I say quietly, lowering to the bottom step.

"Well, congratulations, Mr. Black. I did suspect, but Rose insisted it wasn't possible."

"That's why I'm calling." I look left and right, watchful. "She had a really rough birth with Daniel. Hemorrhaged. Transfusions. She was told she couldn't carry again."

"An examination would be wise. Perhaps a scan to check her womb. A healthy, plump, juicy womb is a good womb."

Juicy? I grimace. "And if it's not?"

"One step at a time. No need to worry over something that might require no worry at all. Now, I'm going to need an ultrasound machine."

"Let me know how much." I hang up and stand. And sit straight back down when I get a head rush. "Fuck me," I breathe, rubbing at my forehead. Overcome. I'm overcome.

"Danny?"

I glance up and find Mum looking worried. "I'm fine." I take the rail and try again, breathing slowly and discreetly. "Where's Daniel?"

"Here," he says, his face in his phone as he comes from the TV room.

"All right?" I ask.

"Yeah, good."

My shoulders drop and I go to him, plucking his mobile out of his grasp. "Look at me when I'm talking to you."

He shrugs. "Sorry, Mister."

I narrow an eye on him. "Did Esther show you your room?"

"Yeah. How long am I staying?"

I bite my bottom lip. "How long do you want to stay?" I ask, testing the water. This whole situation will be a fuck-load harder if Daniel protests being here.

Another shrug. "I don't mind. Mom and Dad said it's up to me."

They did? Sounds like Derek has had to spew some confessions. "Then let's play it by ear." I ruffle his hair, return his phone, and head to my office. "Wanna go out on the water soon?"

He's suddenly chasing my heels, his phone forgotten. "Damn straight I do. When?"

"Maybe after the weekend."

"Will Mom come?"

I slow to a stop, thoughtful. "Yeah, but she won't be going out on the water."

"Why?"

Because she's carrying precious cargo. "She's fed up of losing to us." I flip him a wink and pick up my feet, making it to my office with Daniel still flanking me. So, of course, I hold back letting myself in, eyeing him. "Scram."

"What's in there?" he asks, his curiosity getting the better of him.

"Business."

"Jet skis?"

"The paperwork required to run a jet ski business, yes."

"Oh."

"Come on, Daniel," Esther calls from the end of the corridor, saving me. "You've still got some unpacking to do and Mom's got a surprise for you."

He trudges off, and I push my way into my office, bracing myself for what I might find. Surprisingly, no blood. Not surprisingly, James with a face like a slapped arse. I close the door quietly and join him by my desk, perching on the edge and casting my eyes around the room. Kenny Spittle is silent and sweating in the chair before us, Otto is hammering away at the keys of his laptop, and Ringo and Goldie are keeping a thoughtful silence by the drinks cabinet. Everyone, mute.

I fold my arms over my chest, purse my lips, wondering if

anyone is going to talk anytime soon. I have somewhere I want to be.

Two minutes later, still nothing, and I get bored of waiting. "Why isn't he dead yet?" I ask but keep my eyes on Kenny Spittle.

"I'm just trying to decide how," James replies quietly, blindly reaching behind him for my letter opener and inspecting it carefully.

"Do you mind if I ask him a few questions first?"

"Be my guest." James gets up and starts circling the room, and Kenny Spittle's wary eyes follow him.

"You were blackmailed into getting a safety deposit box or your father would be killed," I say, feeling James's eyes land on me. *Yes, try talking to your girlfriend, you stubborn fuck.* Kenny Spittle nods jerkily. "Where did you deliver it?"

"The beach," he murmurs, and I frown. "I was asked to put it in a sports bag by a towel and leave."

"There are thousands of towels on any beach in Miami. How did you know which towel?"

"It was a flag."

"What flag?"

He swallows. "It was decorated with a bear."

My shock isn't containable, and neither is James's. "What kind of bear?"

"The kind that will maul you if it gets its paws on you."

I laugh lightly, going to the cabinet and pouring myself a drink. Not because I need one, but because I'm celebrating. I smile at the amber liquid and knock it back. "And what were you doing at Walmart?"

"Shopping."

"For what?" I slam the glass down and face him, eyebrows high in expectation. His hesitance is a sign that he is unsure whether to lie. I can answer that for him. I look at James, who immediately circles behind our prisoner and slips his hand under his chin, yanking it back to expose his throat, "For what?" I ask again, calm and collected.

"Keys," he breathes.

Another look at James, and I just know he's thinking what I'm thinking. And I'm thinking: Why would the manager of a vault where safety deposit boxes are kept be having keys cut? "Tell me, Kenny. Did you take a peek at the contents of the box before you delivered it to the beach?"

"No. Of course not."

I look at James, who quickly places the blade on his throat. "You sure?"

"I didn't, I swear! I don't hold keys for the boxes." His entire body stiffens, his arms ramrod straight against the arms of the chair, his body pressed into the back.

"I believe you." That's why he's having keys cut now. I take my place back on the desk. "And after you kindly supplied the safety deposit box, were any further demands made?" I see his Adam's apple push into the blade from his swallow.

"Yes."

"And let me guess, it's for storage, am I right?"

A nod.

"And you decided you didn't want to be at the mercy of the unknown, so you decided to sneakily change company policy and hold two keys for every box. One to give to your customer, and one for you to keep. You know, as security. A backup policy in case you needed an out. But, of course," I go on, standing and wandering the room, hands in my pockets, "the money's good, isn't it, Kenny? Hard to say no to." He's just another greedy fucker with no morals. This town is full of them. "Lots of cash for little work." I purse my lips. "But don't tell me the Minute Key Kiosk cut the kind of keys you need," I say, regarding him carefully.

"I know the guy who runs it." He all but sighs. "He takes them away to his workshop to cut."

"So tell me about the arrangements you have with these criminals."

"I work late. I turn off the security cameras. They come, they go. That's it. That's all I know."

I nod. I think we've just found where they're storing their drugs and guns. James scowls, obviously reaching the same conclusion as me, as does everyone else in the room. At least, everyone who's here of their own free will. Speaking of which . . . "How is your father, by the way?"

"He's left town. I . . . it's—"

"Too much to handle?" I ask. "Dog eat dog? A man's world?" I bend and rest my palms on his knees, getting so close he tries to retreat as best he can with his head restrained. "You're playing a big boy's game, Kenny. And I'm about to tell you the rules." I give his knees a squeeze. "Listen carefully." I push off and sit on the desk. "Your father's dead."

"What?" he blurts, horrified. "How do you know that?"

"Because I killed him."

He jerks, his mouth open. "No."

"Afraid so. I'm sorry, I know there were"—I flap a hand in the air casually—"plans to move out of state and live his retirement with pot loads of blood money and no remorse for betraying endless people."

"Why'd you kill him?" he whispers.

"Your father was a bad man, Kenny. He betrayed me and, as a consequence, he's dead." I crouch. "He made the mistake of thinking another criminal's bed was comfier than mine. Safer than mine." I tilt my head. "Like father like son?"

"No," he breathes, shaking his head. "I'm nothing like my father."

That's fucking debatable, but for the sake of our end

game . . . "That's great to hear," I say, getting one more celebratory Scotch and finding the photo of Spittle and his family, waving it under Kenny's nose. "Your mum and wife are still alive. I assume you want to keep it that way."

Another nod.

"How's your new bed, Kenny?"

"Really comfortable."

I smile.

I stand on the steps of the house with James, watching Ringo and Otto bundle Kenny Spittle into the back of one of the Mercs. The sky is dark, overcast, the air heavy. Typical Miami. "Do you feel like enlightenment has hit hard?" James asks quietly, still holding the letter opener. The barbaric fucker is probably hanging on to hope that I might change my mind on letting Kenny live.

"Very hard." We've learned quite a few things, thanks to Spittle's equally greedy son. First, Beau's dead, bent cop uncle is the only way The Bear could have known Beau's mother was keeping a safety deposit box at Mid Bank. Second, The Bear has got himself an unrivaled storage facility for what he's bringing into the country. Third, he no longer has any pawns to use against Kenny Spittle, since his father is dead and we've sent his wife and mother away on an all-expenses-paid holiday. Fourth, the end is near. "I need to talk to you about something," I say to James, facing him.

He backs up, wary. "What?"

Fuck, this is harder than it should be. But Beau knows, and as soon as they're on speaking terms, which I anticipate to be in one thrust and a bellow of her name, she'll make sure James knows too. He needs to be prepared. I take a quick look around us, ensuring we're alone. "Rose is pregnant."

Silence.

Awkwardness.

His face is blank, and it's an expression I'm not used to. He eventually clears his throat, blinking and looking away. I know what he's thinking, so I put him out of his misery quickly. "Beau knows."

He shoots me a shocked stare, and I raise my eyebrows. "Women talk, mate," I quip, and he laughs under his breath. "I just . . ." Fuck, how do I put this? "Beau's fine. Well, she seemed fine to me." What the fuck do I know? Seeming fine and being fine are two entirely different things. "I know it's not the best time, what with—"

"I'm happy for you," he says, his hand coming up and resting on my shoulder, squeezing. "But confused as fuck. I thought kids were out of the question?"

I exhale loudly, raking a hand through my hair. "Me too. I've got Doc lined up to check her over. Something about a juicy womb." I frown to myself, and James releases a bark of laughter that startles me. He should laugh more often. I'd feel safer in his company. "I know." I shudder. "Anyway, I've got somewhere I need to be." I take the steps down to my car.

"Alone?" he calls, the suspicion in his tone palpable.

"Yes, alone." I need to talk, and there's no one around here who'll understand. "Keep the Rose thing under your hat." I don't know when or where will be the right time to share the news, but I do know it'll cause some serious worry, because everyone who knows me knows how fiercely I'll protect my wife. Now that she's pregnant? I'm a man more on a mission than I've ever been.

As I pull away from the house, the heavens open and the windscreen gets pelted with fat, relentless raindrops. The freeway is clear. It's probably a good thing, since my mind is elsewhere. It's one of those journeys you make that when you get to your destination, you stop for a moment and try to recall any part of the time it's taken you to get there. And can't.

Through the sunroof, I see the sky swirling, moving fast, carrying away the last of the gray clouds. The rain comes to an abrupt stop.

I get out and remove my jacket, slinging it on the driver's seat before taking a slow walk into the graveyard. His grave has settled, grass now covering the mound of dirt that was made three years ago. A few daffodils scattered. A headstone that reads simply "Mister." It was a sensible choice. There are many things I wanted to have engraved, but knowing the world I'm in, once they'd discovered where the notorious Carlo Black, my father, was buried, he'd be dug up. His grave vandalized. I wanted to ensure he really did rest in peace for all time.

"Well, what a turn up for the books, eh, Mister?" I say, settling on the grass and lighting up. He always wanted a kid and not a woman. So he took me. What would he think if he was here to see me wanting a kid *and* a woman? He'd tell me I'm stupid. He'd be right. But stupid feels good on me, and what I'm going to do because of a woman is definitely stupid. Plain, cold dumb. Dumber than faking my own death ever was.

My mobile rings. Brad. "Worried about me?" I ask when I answer, knowing he's probably shown up at the house and found me missing with no explanation from anyone of where I am. *Alone.*

"How many times do we need to go over it? Never, not ever, should you venture out on your fucking own, Danny."

"That's a yes, then," I say, smiling as I pull another drag. "I'm fine. Just visiting Pops. I've got a lot to fill you in on."

"James told me."

Oh, good. Saves me a job. But . . . "What exactly?"

"About our new friend Spittle Junior," he replies, and I breathe out. Brad is going to shit bricks what he finds out about

Rose. "But he hasn't told me your plan because you've kept your mouth shut on that little detail."

"Do you trust me?"

"No."

I smile. "I'll meet you at the club later." I hang up before he can browbeat me into spilling. Now's not the time.

And what the hell is that I see on Pops's headstone?

I slip my cigarette between my lips and push myself up, my forehead heavy as I move in closer. There's a piece of folded paper resting on top, held down by a metal paperweight.

With a bear engraved into it.

"What the fuck?" I breathe, turning on the spot, searching the graveyard high and low. The silence is suddenly eerie as I reach behind me and pull my gun, flicking my cigarette aside. I pocket the paperweight and take the note. Only the bottom of the paper is wet. The top is dry.

Splitting my attention between unfolding it and keeping an eye on my surroundings, I open it to reveal a phone number. Nothing else, just a number. The problem isn't only where the hell that paperweight and note came from, but how the fuck they knew where to put it. I don't need to ask myself *when*. I glance around me again, calming my breathing to a point I may as well be holding my breath, and with my jaw tight, I head back to my car, pulling my jacket out and throwing it onto the back seat before getting behind the wheel. I sit, staring at the graveyard that's now basked in sunshine. No more rain. I start the engine, pull away, and I keep my eye on the lane ahead. I take a left at the junction, heading back toward the city. Then an immediate right. A three-point turn. I pull over and leave the engine running, and I wait, sunk into my seat, eyes peeled, a constant sneer on my lips.

Five minutes pass.

Ten minutes.

Twenty.

Patience.

Half an hour later, a Lexus appears from the lane that leads to the churchyard, and I breathe in calmly, shifting in my seat, squinting to see better, but the glare of the sun on the windscreen is hampering my view. The car turns toward the city, and I pull out slowly, turning right at the junction. I keep my distance and dial Otto. "Take this license plate number and see what you can find."

"Got it."

I reel off the digits. "Gray Lexus," I add before hanging up and dialing the number left on my father's grave. He answers with silence, and I relax in my seat, my eyes rooted on the car up ahead being driven by . . . who? "What can I do for you?" I ask calmly.

"I have a proposition for you." A voice distorter. *Fucking coward.*

"What might that be?" An offer to crawl into his corrupt fold? A request for clemency?

The silence drags again, the tension in my car building. His inhale crackles down the line. "I'll give you peace in my city," he says calmly. There's a certain emphasis on *my* that I ignore—the deluded fuck—and I wait, patient, because I know there's a catch coming. "If you give me The Enigma."

My surprise is very real, but I still smile. His move is a huge red flag. An indicator of his frame of mind. He's losing, and he knows it. Men like this don't offer peace. "It's *my* city. So, it's a no from me."

"What is it, Black? You don't make deals with the Devil?"

I smile at the road ahead, my skin prickling with irritation. "*I* am the Devil," I say quietly. "And I'm about to take you to the lowest level of Hell." I hang up and realign my focus on the Lexus, following it back into town. It pulls into a gated underground carpark, and I curse under my breath, being forced to park across the street. I glance up at the apartment block. Ten floors high. At least ten apartments wide. "Fuck," I curse, getting out and wandering across to the intercom by the main entrance. Eight buttons across. Ten down. Only numbers, no names.

I call Brad and go back to my car. "He left a note on my father's grave," I say when he answers. "A phone number."

"Did you call it?"

"Yes. He offered me a deal."

"Then take it and let's get back to business. What does he want?"

"James." I get into my car, not surprised that Brad's next words are delayed.

"Fuck."

Indeed. "The note was wet. Only on the bottom where it was resting on the headstone. The top was dry."

"Meaning?"

"It only stopped raining when I pulled up."

A brief silence as I stare at the carpark entrance. "Where are you, Danny?"

"I followed the Lexus to an apartment block in town."

"For fuck's sake. Where? I'm coming." There's a collection of sounds in the background, and all I can think in this moment is . . . What would James do if the boot was on the other foot? I could hand over The Enigma on a silver platter and walk away. Go back to St. Lucia. Give Rose what she wants. Raise our baby in peace and safety. I rake a stressed hand through my hair, my mind in chaos.

"Danny!"

I startle and look at my dashboard. I'd forgotten about Brad. I return my eyes to the garage entrance. "I'm at—" The gates shift, and I sit up straight. The Lexus appears, the shadow created from the low ceiling of the garage hiding the driver. I quickly start my car.

"Will you fucking speak?" Brad barks.

I hang up, avoiding the inevitable shitstorm I'm about to create, and start to follow the car, my phone ringing persistently. All Brad. And then Rose flashes up on the screen, and I curse Brad's traitorous arse to hell and back, torn between answering and not. My sensible side somehow gets past the reckless side ruling me as I weave in and out of the traffic, struggling to keep the Lexus in my sights. I answer.

"Hi, ba—"

"Get your fucking ass home now."

I exhale my exasperation. If Brad wasn't so sure I would never kill him, this wouldn't be happening. "I can't do that," I reply calmly, hoping some of that calm might filter down the line and pacify my wife.

"You can," she yells. "We're getting married this weekend, and I swear, Black, if you die before then, I'll kill you."

I laugh. It's the worst thing I could do. "It all feels a bit shotgun now, baby."

"Danny!"

"Listen to me, R—"

"No, you listen to me. Get your murdering ass back here or I'm leaving, and I'm taking your baby with me."

My cheeks blow out, my pulse beginning to boom danger-ously. My wife sure does know how to push my buttons. "Do not threaten m—" The line goes dead, and I stare at the road disbe-lievingly. "She hung up on me?" Raging, I put my foot down, poking at the dial button on my steering wheel. I shouldn't go into this with anything other than a level head. "Fucking woman," I mutter as her phone goes to voicemail. I leave her a loving message. "Never, ever, ever, threaten to leave me again or it'll be *me* killing *you*. We'll discuss this when I get home. Start warming up those palms, baby, because mine are ready." I cut the call. "Fuck," I smack the wheel and wind down the window, welcoming the cool breeze that gushes into my car. *Cool down, Black.*

The engine of my car screams its protest. I'm getting too close to the Lexus, so I ease off the gas, my clawed fingers loosening around the wheel. It takes a left up ahead into the parking garage of a derelict building, and I'm forced to make a quick decision. I pull up across the road, get out, and turn my phone to silent, going to the trunk. I rummage through, looking for anything lingering that I can use. The best I come up with is a baseball cap. I slip it on, check the magazine of my gun, then jog across the road, keeping close to the face of the building when I make it there. I breathe in and slowly peek around the edge. The car's stationary, the driver's door open.

What I see next momentarily knocks me for six. *What the actual fuck?* A long, bare, willowy leg appears, the foot graced in skyscraper heels, and a woman slides out and flicks her hair over her shoulder. Fuck me, has he scoured the city for every single person who has a reason to hold a grudge against me?

My dead father's lover looks as self-important as she always did. I should have known Shannon would find some kind of warped protection elsewhere after I threw her out the day Pops died. The day she confessed what we all knew in an attempt to maintain her place in our world.

You must know it's always been about you, Danny.

But who is she meeting?

She walks with an air of cockiness across the parking lot and enters a metal door, glancing around her as she does. As soon as the door closes, I round the corner and jog after her. I pull the door open, my teeth clenched, hissing back air. I hear her heels hitting the concrete steps of the stairwell and look up to see a manicured hand sliding up the handrail. I keep to the outside and follow her up to the third floor, just catching the back of her cream jacket as she passes through an arch. I slow to a stop, gun poised.

"Hey." Her purr echoes around the shell of a building. "I'm here. Where are you?"

I freeze, my heart beats increasing to an uncomfortable pace.

"I did it," she says proudly. "I knew he'd visit his father's grave. God, how he still worships that old bastard." She laughs, and my finger starts to squeeze down on the trigger of my gun, my blood an inferno, my muscles tensing in an attempt to hold me back. She needs to die. Deserves to die. It's fucking tempting but . . .

I throw myself back against the wall. Breathe.

Breathe, breathe, breathe.

Don't kill her. Do not *kill her.* There will be no roots left this time. I need the entire web and she's going to lead me to the spider.

"Okay. Call me later." I hear her heels again. *Fuck.* "I love you," she adds.

I push my back off the wall and take the stairs fast but silently, breaking out into the daylight and breathing heavily. Instinct is trying to stop me, trying to send me back in that building to end the bitch's life. Sensibility won't allow it. I call Otto.

"The car's registered to—"

"Shannon Pike. Get me her address. Get me everything."

I make it to my car and throw my baseball cap on the seat. Brace my arms against the wheel. Breathe deeply. I'm about to make the biggest mess in Miami.

18

ROSE

By eight o'clock, he still wasn't home, and I was exhausted from worrying. I couldn't listen to Esther tell me that her son knows what he's doing anymore. She's as crazy as her boy. Daniel was occupied in his room playing on his PlayStation, and Beau seemed dead set on working out until she could no longer breathe, and then had dinner plans with her aunt so I took myself to bed and carried on being exhausted there.

I heard him come into our room at two a.m. I kept quiet and still when he crawled into bed. What I wanted to do was get up and go sleep elsewhere, if only to demonstrate how pissed off with him I am. But I didn't. He would have only put me back in our bed.

I eventually dozed off around four after endless hours of wondering what the hell is going on that meant he ventured into the city on his own, and then kept him up until the early hours. A debrief with the men, no doubt. But what about? I get the feeling that to make it to paradise again, I need to go through hell. I have little confidence in myself to make the journey. Especially now when I'm feeling so drained. Mentally. Physically. I'm plain wiped out.

I wake up at noon. Danny's side of the bed is empty, cold, telling me he's been up for a while. And I hate it. For three years, if the bedsheets were cool, it didn't mean that Danny could be in danger. It didn't mean that he was plotting someone's death, trying to ensure our questionable safety, or fighting for equilibrium. This daily aching pressure and emptiness didn't exist, and I miss that . . . peace. That ease. His presence. *Mentally and physically.*

I shuffle to the edge and stretch, exhaling heavily, my arms slumping down to the mattress with a thud. Tomorrow, we get married. Right now, I feel about as enthusiastic about that as I know Danny is.

Unable to shake my despondency, my mind weighed down with troubling thoughts, my body heavy, I flop back to the bed on a sigh.

"Mom?" The sound of Daniel calling me soon gets my ass into gear, and I sit up quickly, pulling my hair into a ponytail. "Mom, you awake yet?"

"I've been awake for ages," I call, standing as he pushes his way in. "Oh my." My hands go to my mouth, a lump jumping into my throat. "Look at you!" His suit is sublime, his sporty body carrying it well, his hair all floppy and his face cheeky.

He grins and pulls his jacket in. "Esther told me to get your approval before the seam . . . seams . . . se—"

"Seamstress."

"That's it. Before she leaves." He pivots slowly. "So? Do you approve?"

How could I not? Just look at him. My baby. He looks so handsome. So grown up. Emotion comes over me, and I fight my hand from my stomach. What will Daniel make of a new baby?

Will he be happy? Resentful? "I approve," I confirm, going to him and brushing at his shoulders, generally pulling and straightening his perfect suit, my need to be close overtaking. He won't be up for cuddles. It sucks, frankly.

"Great." He spins and dashes out. "I'm playing tennis with Goldie."

"What?" I call, going to the door and watching him rush down the corridor to the stairs.

"She used to play for her school back in England. She's challenged me."

"Take the suit off first." I jog after him. "Daniel!"

"Yeah, I heard you."

"Then answer me," I say quietly, leaning over the gold balustrade. Esther comes out of the kitchen, looking up at me. "Where is he?" I ask, not needing to state who *he* is.

She shakes her head mildly. "I don't know. He left with Brad, James, and the men a few hours ago."

I swallow. It's lumpy. "Okay." I look over my shoulder when I hear my cell ringing in the distance from the bedroom.

"I'll make a pot of tea," Esther says, and I nod, going back to our room.

I find my phone on the bed and my heart misses a beat when I see who's calling. I can't ignore her. "Hilary," I say in answer, lowering to the bed. "How are you?" I cringe. What a dumb question to ask. This woman didn't do things right, her desperation to be a mom getting the better of her, but I know she loves Daniel with everything she has.

"Getting by," she says, her voice undeniably shaky. "How is he?"

Oblivious. "Good. He's good." Inflating that would be insensitive.

"I just wanted to say thank you."

My back naturally straightens, my forehead naturally frowning, as I rack my mind for what I could have done that she could be thanking me for. There's nothing. "What for, Hilary?"

"For the invite."

"The invite?" A horrible feeling comes over me.

"You're renewing your vows."

I stare at the French doors that lead onto the terrace. "We are," I murmur. *What is he thinking?*

"It's lovely of you to think of us. To make us feel . . . included."

My heart is quickly aching for her. I don't know what her husband is up to, how on earth he's managed to get himself caught up in the underworld, but I do know Hilary is a good woman. She doesn't deserve this, no matter what she took from me. I wasn't a woman to her. Hardly even a human being. I was a nonentity, a likely drug addict, a hooker, a no-hoper. At least, that's what she told herself. That's what helped her come to terms with what she did. I have to remind myself constantly that she raised him well. Loved him. Gave him everything—respect, manners, and a heap of other qualities. "You're welcome." I feel like we're dancing around a massive, illuminous pink elephant. "Hilary, Daniel's safer here," I say, getting up and walking around our room, struggling to find the right words to ease her. I'm not sure what Derek has told her. How much she knows.

"Who are these people, Rose?" Her voice begins to break.

"They're dangerous." I won't beat around the bush. She must have figured out that much.

"And your husband? Who is he?"

My head in my hand, I drop to the bed again. I can't tell her that he's one of the good guys. My husband is no saint. He has more murders under his belt than I dare to admit. But he loves me. He loves Daniel. Even if he's being a selfish, reckless idiot. "He's one of the only men who can stop them," I say, because it's nothing but the truth. Him. James. Both have personal vendettas against the illusive Bear. They won't rest until they find out who he is and kill him. And I just have to sit around and wait for that to happen while going out of my mind with worry.

I hear a faint snivel down the line. "Promise me you won't cut me off completely," she begs. "I know I did wrong by you. I know you owe me nothing, but please, I beg you, please don't take him away completely."

"I do owe you, Hilary. I owe you for taking care of my son for so many years. And I would never cut you out of his life. We'll figure something out when the dust settles, I promise. But for now, his safety is my priority."

"Of course," she croaks.

"And I need you to know, Hilary, that Danny dealt with the men who were at the beginning of this mess. The men who you bought Daniel from, the men who abducted me, they are all gone. These people now . . . I don't know who they are."

"I wondered where the money was coming from," she says. "Derek's business was good, he'd said. He was finally earning the name he always wanted. New offices. New cars. The mortgage was paid off. I feel so stupid."

"Derek is a string in their bow. A tool they'll use or blackmail. Nothing will ever be for his benefit, only theirs. They dig and find skeletons in closets, Hilary. And they found a big one in yours."

"Daniel," she says quietly.

"Daniel," I confirm going to the bathroom and slipping on my robe. "And if they ever find out there's a connection with Danny Black's wife—me—it'll be game over."

"I understand." Another snivel. "You should know I'm filing for divorce."

"What?"

"I'm staying with my sister at the moment. Out of town.

Apparently, your husband advised Derek that it would be prudent. It's given me a lot of time to think."

"Oh, Hilary."

"I don't want your sympathy, Rose. I just want you to make sure Daniel is safe. The moment Derek took money from them, he put us at risk. I can't forgive him for that. I should go, I've kept you long enough. You must be so busy."

I look around our room. "Lots to do."

"You understand why I can't be there, I'm sure."

"Sure," I murmur. "Bye, Hilary." I slip my cell into my robe pocket and rub at my aching head, pulling the bedroom door open. "Morning," I say to Tank as I pass, hurrying downstairs. I fall into the kitchen, and Beau and Esther look up at me, both running eyes up and down my robe. "He invited Daniel's"—I make quote signs with my fingers—"'parents,'" I blurt. "Where's the guest list?"

Esther pushes the laptop across the island, looking wary, and I take a seat next to Beau, scanning the limited names in the spreadsheet. There's all of the obvious ones, all of the men, Goldie, Doc, us. Then I see Derek and Hilary. "Who's Turner and *guest*?" I ask, looking at them for an answer. Both shrug. I go back to the list. "Jerry?"

"Oh, that's the lad Leon hired to help run the boatyard," Beau pipes up.

Talk about scraping the barrel. "Kenny Spittle?" I frown.

Beau yanks the paper toward her. "What the hell?" she says, her lip virtually curling at the sight and sound of his name.

"Why did they have a picture of him?" I ask. I can only assume it's because they want him dead, and I'm pretty sure he can't be if he's down to attend our wedding.

"He manages a bank. The one where my mom kept a safety deposit box. He gave the information inside to The Bear, which is how he knows who James really is. That box is why my mother was killed."

"Oh, Beau," Esther says on a sigh, shaking her head in dismay.

I get it. I hear her. But . . . "You can't go off on manhunts like that, Beau." Good lord, these people are dangerous. "Not on your own." Not at all, actually.

She drops her bagel and dusts her hands off, exasperated. "Why does everyone keep forgetting that I used to be a cop?"

Okay, fair enough, she did. I won't remind her she no longer is, and I won't remind her she's still not completely physically healed. I'm not stupid. "Still, it's dangerous."

She rolls her eyes, and I reluctantly go back to the list, knowing I'm fighting a losing battle. This isn't only Danny and James's war. "Who the hell is Detective Higham? What is this, a police gala? This is ridiculous." I throw my hands up in the air, looking at Esther. "I hardly know these people."

"Um . . . you know this one."

I look at Beau. Her blue eyes are alarmed. "Who?" I ask, going back to the list. "What?" My eyes land on Perry Adams's name, as well as his wife below. "He's got to be joking." I drop my head. "Why would he do that?" And something comes to me. I look at Esther. "He's planning something." I throw my stare to Beau. "They're planning something. Have you spoken to James?"

Beau laughs. "No, I told you, we're not talking."

"This is supposed to be a happy time, for goodness sake," Esther cries, pouring tea. "And at the risk of annoying you"—she slams the pot down and divides her attention between Beau and me—"you both know the men you're in bed with very well, do you not?"

"Too well." Beau takes a piece of her bagel and pops it in her mouth, chewing slowly and thoughtfully. "I know what he's capable of, his moods, his drive, and I still haven't figured out if knowing is a good thing or not." She blinks a few times, falling silent momentarily. "I need to burn off some steam." She snaps to life, hops off the stool, and kisses my cheek. "It's going to be a lovely day," she says. "And tonight is going to be great too."

"What's happening tonight?"

"Your bachelorette party," she sings, backing out of the room. "Last night as a single woman."

I laugh out loud, as does Esther. I'm far from single. And far from being in the mood, constantly worrying and wondering when I'll get my husband back.

And if he'll be in one piece when I do.

Hiatus is pumping when we arrive. We're escorted to the front of the queue by Fury before being let past the red velvet rope by Nolan. No one calls out an objection. No one kicks up a stink. I feel like I have a sign on my back telling the world who I am.

We're shown to an area near the back, away from the rest of the club, with a personal waiter and more ropes holding the public back. I glance up at the blacked-out window spanning the back wall as I tail Beau. I know he's up there. Watching me. Not only because I can feel his arctic stare pinned on me, but because Tank is back at the house babysitting Daniel with a few other men, and there's no way I'd be allowed to leave the mansion without Tank. Also, the atmosphere in the club is tense, people looking and whispering. So yes, he's here. My husband. The Brit.

How I wish he wasn't The Brit, and yet my reasonable side accepts that without his name and reputation, we wouldn't have met. And we wouldn't be surviving now.

I lower to the plush velvet seat and follow a waitress's journey to our table, a bottle of champagne in one hand, glasses dangling from the other by the stems held between her fingers.

She lowers the bucket and smiles brightly as she sets a glass in front of Beau, Esther, and Zinnea. She must feel my eyes drilling into her, because she glances at me nervously, giving me an apologetic smile.

"He told you not to give me a glass, didn't he?" I ask, making the poor girl shift uncomfortably on her heels. I can't blame her for following his orders. I would. If I wasn't married to him. "A glass, please."

"Rose," Esther says warningly. "Please don't."

The mere fact she's backing up her son only spurs on my reckless intention. Esther doesn't even know why Danny's thrown out death threats to any staff who dares gives me alcohol. She doesn't know I'm pregnant.

"Yeah, come on, Rose." Beau shifts along the seat, getting close, and puts an arm around my shoulder. "You don't want to feel ill on your big day."

I look up at the window, and something inside ignites, starting to burn me from the inside out. I've not even seen him today. He was so happy and then so . . . distant. Absent. I don't know what he's up to, but I don't like it. He's being secretive. The last time he was secretive, I walked a path of utter ruin. It doesn't matter that my medicine was at the end of that path. I never want to relive those feelings of grief and loss. "A glass," I say tightly, my eyes unmoving from the window. I blindly swipe up the bottle and pour as soon as the flute is placed down by a shaky hand. I lift the glass to my lips, and my tongue barely skims the liquid before it's swiped from my grasp.

"No," Beau snaps, slamming it down. "You'll regret it. Perhaps we should go home."

I snort, my eyes landing on a pole across the club. *Kick him in the gut. Make him be present. Make it so he can't keep his distance.* The need is consuming me to the point I'm clearly not thinking straight.

I get up and saunter over to the stage, looking up at the girl hanging off the pole. "May I?" I ask politely. Her face, poor thing, falls like a rock, her eyes dashing around the club. "He doesn't kill women," I assure, her, smiling when she returns her eyes to mine. "Me, though?"

She's off the stage like lightning, and I sit on the edge, pulling myself up. Beau is hurrying over, Esther hot on her heels, and poor Zinnea looks rather perplexed. "For God's sake, Rose, do you have a death wish?" Beau tries to pull me down, but I dodge her hand, moving to the pole and taking it in my grasp, circling it slowly, my strides long, my gaze lifting to the window.

"Rose!" Esther hisses. "Get the hell down from there before you bring mayhem here."

I want to bring mayhem here. I want a reaction. I want Danny Black, The Brit, The Angel-faced Assassin, to come down here and put me in my place, because if he's going to force us into this world again, this is the only way I know how to survive it. With fire. With fight. With danger. I've found the woman I was. *Finally.* "Come on, you murdering asshole," I say quietly, casting my eyes across the club, seeing all attention aimed this way, some men looking downright alarmed, others, who don't know who I am, looking a little excited. I smile and thrust up against the pole, slowly and seductively crouching until my thighs are spread, the pole nestled between them, my dress around my waist.

"Rose!" Esther yells.

"Fury, get her down," Beau shouts as I arch my back and rise, the crotch of my panties sliding across the metal. There are a few whoops from the crowd, a few leery cheers, a few claps.

I smile sickly on the inside, looking up when I see the door leading to the office open.

He appears, as expected, but I'm caught off guard when he

doesn't charge at me and haul me down. He just stands there, hands in his pockets, his face poker straight, his eyes blazing, as I slowly grind against the pole with him watching me. And it doesn't escape my notice that suddenly no one else is. All men have turned away. Beau and Esther have returned to their seats. The bar staff is busying themselves.

I stare him down, hating the reaction his presence has spiked. Terror. Pure, raw terror in everyone. Except me.

I push my front to the metal until the pole is between my breasts and hook a leg around it. His head tilts. I slowly lower. He starts a casual stroll toward the stage as I bring my other leg up and slide down the pole until my ass meets the floor, my legs spread. His eyes fall to my exposed panties. His scar glimmers. He's mad but trying not to show it.

And when a man, a stupid, foolish, greedy man, lifts his eyes from his drink at a nearby table, Danny wanders over, cool and calm, places a hand on the back of his head, and slams it down.

Right onto the tumble of whiskey before him. It shatters, and the man shrieks.

"Take another peek," Danny says lowly, bending to get close to the guy's bloodied face. "I dare you."

His hand comes up in surrender, his head shaking, his apologies broken. And guilt explodes within me. Turning to look at me, Danny jerks his head mildly. "Get down, baby, before I kill someone."

My swallow lumpy, my throat thick, I find the steps and take them down to the club floor, pulling my dress into place. I chance a glance at Esther and Beau. The disappointment on their faces amplifies the guilt. The shame.

The anger.

I start to move past Danny, set on going home, getting out of here, but he moves into my path, blocking me. My eyes on his chest, I work hard on stabilizing my breathing. "You want to behave like a whore?" he asks calmly.

I look up at him in surprise and take no pleasure from the fury behind his eyes. A leopard never changes its spots. Isn't that what they say? Danny has fallen back into the underworld seamlessly. Fearless. Bold. Violent.

Me?

It's taking every effort to be all the things that once kept me alive. Loving Danny Black has changed me. And now I hate him more than ever for that alone. "Enjoy your bachelor party," I say, sidestepping him and walking toward the exit.

His palm is on my nape in seconds, his fingers clawing into my flesh. I don't bother fighting him.

"You told me once you wanted to be mine," he says quietly, his mouth near my ear.

"Maybe I'm regretting that."

His fingers squeeze more, and I wince. "Maybe I'm regretting *taking* you as mine," he hisses, and I inhale, unreasonably hurt. He could squeeze harder. Shake me. Push me up against a wall or fist my hair. But none of it would hurt more than those words. And he knows it.

Fighting vehemently to get my quivering lip under control, I let him push me through the club. We're quickly flanked by men on all sides, and I'm gently but firmly guided into the back of a Merc. He slides in beside me, Ringo gets behind the wheel, and I'm soon being driven away from my very brief, very spiky bachelorette party.

Danny pulls his cell from his inside pocket and takes it to his ear. "Be ready in half an hour," he says, and then hangs up, wedging his elbow into the door and staring out of the window.

"Who needs to be ready and for what?"

"I don't discuss business with the latest whore I'm fucking," he murmurs quietly.

I recoil, injured, as he slowly turns his eyes onto me. Cold eyes. Eyes without one hint of love in them. He looks me up and down in a way only he could. With hatred. Detachment. "You called it, Rose. Don't fucking push me when I'm already hanging off the edge of sanity." He goes back to gazing out of the window, and I shrink into my seat.

Makes two of us.

Back at the house, I'm marched up to our bedroom like an unruly child, Danny tailing me, not touching me, but as close as he could be behind. I'm not a woman who knows what's good for her. I'm a woman who's so tired of fighting. His patience has worn to nothing. My energy has been zapped. There's tension in the air, naturally, but I sense I'm not the one and only cause. Something has shifted in him, his mood dark, his persona edgy. It's the Danny I met, and I'm less than happy to see him.

He closes the door behind us and checks the time on his watch. *Be ready in half an hour.* It's been twenty-five minutes since I was escorted from Hiatus in disgrace. He's got five minutes to say what he wants to say. Or shout what he wants to shout. Perhaps even rip my dress off and exert his point with sex. I can see his restraint is ready to snap, but which way is he going to go?

His eyes land on mine with a bang. I can see what he wants to do. What he *needs* to do. And I need it too. Reconnection. Closeness. I need passion and pleasure and unadulterated Danny Black. Three years ago, when he took me as his prisoner, I knew he wanted me. I knew he was fighting his want. He's fighting now. I broke him back then. I will break him again.

I reach back to the zip of my dress and draw it down, letting the material fall away from my body. His eyes follow it to the floor, and he inhales quietly. Then he approaches slowly, his hands in his pockets. Coming to a stop only a foot away, he unhurriedly lets his eyes climb up my body, coming to a halt on my tummy. I expect to be seized. Ravaged. Instead, he rips his stare away and passes me, going to the bathroom and closing the door. I hear him talking as I stand in the middle of our room in my underwear, perplexed, and he appears a few minutes later, his phone still at his ear, making a call as he goes, my robe in his grasp. "It helps relax me," he says, holding it open behind me. I remain unmoving. "You should try it sometime." He waits for me to drag myself out of my motionless, confused state, and I slip my arms through the sleeves as he rounds me, holding his cell to his ear with his shoulder as he takes the ties and fastens my robe, his attention set on his task and his call. "Indeed. Every Saturday without fail at noon." He looks up at me, almost accusingly. "Good talking." He hangs up. "Bed," he orders, moving back, out of my space, not looking at me.

Reaching for him, I beat back the pang of hurt. "Danny, I—"

"Bed, Rose," he grates, stepping away, his jaw tight as he considers me. My hand drops heavily. "Get on the fucking bed before I put you there myself."

Desperate for contact, no matter how that comes, I goad him. "Fuck off, you bastard."

I don't get what I expect. A slap. *Bastard.* It's a trigger word for my husband, a guarantee to break his impassiveness. Not today, though, and I'm thrown. I get a dark smile. "I'm not touching you," he whispers.

"Why?" He's punishing me, and it hurts like hell.

"Get on the bed."

"No."

He moves so fast, I don't have a moment to back up. His hand clenching my jaw, he pushes his face close to mine, his nostrils flaring dangerously. "It's bad enough you expose *yourself* to your fucked-up need to prove some kind of fucked-up point. But my child?"

Finally, he's snapped, and it's a fucking relief.

"Bed," he hisses.

Yes, it's a relief, but I won't push him. I wrench my face from his hold, backing up to the bed, and I lie down as the door knocks.

"Mr. Black?" Doc calls.

"Come in," Danny all but grunts, ignoring my inquisitive face.

Venturing inside, Doc motions to someone behind him. "Bring it in."

On a frown, I push myself up to my elbows, waiting to see who appears. "Tank?" I say, as he backs his way in, pulling some kind of cart. He won't look at me, and that speaks so very loudly.

"Over by the bed," Doc orders, dropping his medical bag on the chair in the corner of our room as I sit like a mute fool. "Thank you."

"What's going on?" I ask. "And what is that?"

"An ultrasound machine," Danny says. His face. It's a mirror image of the expression he wore the night I met him. Unmoving. Emotionless. Determined. It's a look to suggest that any challenges will be met with fatal force. Unlucky for him, I'm immune to his deadliness.

"Don't you think this is something we should be discussing and arranging together?" I stand, needing a presence, and Doc falters in his motions, looking between us. He didn't know that I didn't know.

"There are many things we should be discussing, and we will when you're being reasonable," Danny replies, his stance wide. One eye falls into a slit. "Lie down."

Probably surprising him, I do as I'm told, but not because he's demanded it. I'm pregnant. I'm fucking pregnant. *Pregnant.*

Reality and reasonability has suddenly found me, and so has more shame. What was I doing? What was I thinking? I need to know it's going to be okay, and now not even my disdain for my jerk of a husband or my deep ache to defy him out of spite will make me put up a fight.

I open my robe and inhale when Doc squeezes some gel onto my stomach. "Ready?" he asks, arming himself with the probe and looking over his glasses at me. I nod and rest my head back, closing my eyes. Whooshes and beeps fill the room, drowning out the lingering screaming of Danny's foul mood, as Doc glides across my stomach, pushing in here and there. The stretched time of him not speaking, not telling me the baby is fine, begins to panic me. I open my eyes and turn my face toward the monitor just as the sound of a consistent, loud thrumming begins. I swallow, my stare rooted to the blob dominating the screen.

"Your baby," Doc says quietly, tapping at buttons and rolling a dial.

I remain mute and still, transfixed, my teeth sunken into my bottom lip. And the shame that found me multiplies one thousand percent. Because now it's real. Now it's not an idea, a notion, but something growing inside of me that I can see as clearly as I've ever seen anything.

"How many periods have you missed, Rose?" Doc asks, looking at me.

I'm quickly tense. "Why? Is there something wrong?"

Danny comes to life and makes his way to the bed, but his attention remains on the screen. On our baby.

"Everything is fine," he answers quickly, putting my mind at rest, smiling mildly. "I would estimate you're around twelve weeks, which is why I asked."

My mouth falls open. "Twelve?"

"Possibly nearer thirteen."

I blink rapidly, going back through the past few months, trying to recall my last period. I can't. They've always been quite erratic, and I always put that down to the brutality I was subjected to when I was just a girl.

I suddenly feel the heat of Danny's skin on mine, and I look down to see he's holding my hand. "And everything's okay?" he asks quietly, as transfixed as I was on the screen. I'm mesmerized by his face. It's softened, his lush lips slightly parted, his blue eyes shining with life rather than death. *There's the man I fell in love with.*

"The wall of the uterus looks okay."

"Just okay?" Danny asks.

"Okay is better than poor," Doc says, hitting a few buttons. "It's not plump or juicy, but it's okay. There doesn't appear to be any paper in the machine so I can't print a photograph."

Danny releases my hand and rounds the bed to the other side, pulling out his phone. He aims it at the screen and captures a picture. The first photograph of our baby. And he stares down at it for an age, his eyes taking in every tiny piece. Emotion creeps up on me, my eyes clouding.

"I'll give you some privacy." Doc wipes the probe and slips it into the holder on the machine before claiming his medical bag. Then he leaves, closing the door quietly behind him. The sound seems to knock Danny from his paralyzed state, and he looks up at me, staring for what feels like years, the hollows of his cheeks pulsing.

"I'm going to be a daddy, Rose."

Everything expands—my chest from my exhale, the welling of my eyes, the lump in my throat. I can't speak, can't find my voice or the words, so I shake my head and close my eyes, allowing the tears to roll down my cheeks.

His body is blanketing mine in a second, every hard, hot inch of him coating me, his face nestled deep in my neck. My sobs are quiet but so fucking loud, as I cling to him, holding him to me, beating myself up over and over, apologizing non-stop in my head.

On a long, heavy sigh, he eventually shifts, settling next to me. He wipes my eyes. Traces the contours of my face. Then he settles his hand on my tummy. "Feel that?" he whispers, never taking his eyes from mine. "That's everything you've ever wanted but never dared imagine could be. That's everything good about you mixed with what goodness there is in me." He strokes across my stomach, and I find his hand, holding it to me. "Don't be careless with your body, don't be careless with our baby, and don't be careless with my emotions." He dips and kisses the edge of my mouth. "I won't hold back, Rose. With the exception of my wife and her boy, there is nothing in this world that I'll guard more violently. Nothing I'll kill harder for. Nothing that could turn me psycho quicker than the risk of it being hurt. You're carrying my flesh and blood. You're bringing more hope into my world. I don't want to hate, baby. I want to love and be loved. Treasure and be treasured. I want life, I want you, I want Daniel, and I want our baby."

That's it. Any attempts to keep my emotions in check are doomed, and a barrage of tears fall as I reach for his shoulders and pull him onto me.

"I've been offered a way out," he murmurs quietly, almost unsure.

What? A way out. No more death and blood? We can go back to St. Lucia and be peaceful and happy again? I can be pregnant and not stressed. Have a labor without fear. "Then you must take it," I say resolutely.

I feel him nod against me, but it feels reluctant.

I don't question it. Whatever it takes, he must do it. I won't be interfering in business anymore. I won't be adding to his stress. I want to be out of Miami, and that'll happen quicker if I step back and let Danny deal with it.

You're bringing more hope into my world. I don't want to hate, baby. I want to love and be loved. Treasure and be treasured. I want life, I want you, I want Daniel, and I want our baby.

Because when I give this to Danny, he wins. *We* win. There is nothing that would stop me from making this easier for him now. Nothing.

19

JAMES

The mood in the camp is low. Everyone is tense, the women are out of control, and it's the eve of Danny and Rose's wedding. I'd tell Danny to cancel if I knew his livelihood didn't depend on it. And now Rose is pregnant. It's the worst timing, not only personally for Beau and me, but for business. Keeping Black to heel is a big enough task without the delicate condition of his wife. Now? Everything is suddenly amplified.

I finish the last mouthful of my drink, my eyes set on the club down below, where Beau is with Esther and Zinnea, her mood subdued, not only after the swift evacuation of Rose by Danny. Like I said, it's the worst time for Rose and Danny to be pregnant.

"Want another?" Otto asks.

I look over my shoulder and find him on the couch, hunched over his laptop. Goldie makes to get up before I've answered, ready to top me up. "I'm good," I say, making her falter, half up, half down. "I have some shit to deal with." I cast my eyes back

down to the club. The silence between Beau and me is screaming. The atmosphere tense. Danny and Rose's recent news is
only adding to it. Except she doesn't know I know, and it fucking
pains me to think she's suffering this alone. "Anything on the IP
address from the café?" I ask.

"Not a jiffy," Otto replies, sounding frustrated by that.

"Let me know if anything comes through." I stride out of the
office and make my way down to the club. Zinnea is drinking a
cocktail as elaborate and embellished as she is, while Beau is
sipping a bottle of water. Esther, wine in hand, spots me and
reaches for Zinnea, gaining her attention. They both stand and
leave, quiet and pensive.

Placing her bottle down, Beau relaxes and fixes me with an
expectant stare as I slowly lower opposite her, too far away. My
eyes fall to the flame of the candle in the center of the table, my
hand twitching to reach out. To feel the burn. I yank my eyes
away and look up. She's staring at the flame too. This distance
between us, both physically and emotionally, is wrong. She is
now the reason I am here. I am the reason she is here. We need
to fix this.

I lean forward and blow out the candle, holding my position
over the table, glancing up at her. "No more torture, Beau," I say
quietly. "This ends now."

"Will it ever end?"

"Yes," I answer assertively, because it will. Loose ends are
slowly being tied. The finish line is coming into view. Men are
talking, things are shifting.

"Do you know who he is?" she asks.

"We're close."

"And where is the bank manager?"

"Being held in a container at the boatyard."

"Did he talk?"

I inhale, backing up in my seat. Always so hungry for information. But I'm not spilling. Not after her last performance. If this plan is going to work out, I need no obstacles, no unexpected glitches, and my beautiful girl is a sure way to a huge fucking glitch. "Why can't you just trust me?" I ask.

Her inhale is to gather patience, her exhale to find calm. "I *do* trust you."

"Then trust me to end this."

I look up when I see Otto approaching, his laptop laid over his arms. His face tells me all I need to know. My shoulders straighten, and I locate Fury a few feet away, giving him the nod as I stand. He moves in promptly, and Beau's head swings between us as she rises to her feet. "What's going on?" she asks, her entire being ready to fight. And she will fight. I know she'll fight.

I circle the table and take the tops of her arms, forcing her attention to me and me alone. "Let me handle this," I say firmly but with obvious pleading. "I can't be out there worrying about you, Beau."

"You don't need to worry about me," she says. "I survived just fine before—"

"I restrained and distracted you?" God, how I wish I could tie her up now to keep her controlled. Gag her so she can't defy me constantly. Blindfold her so she won't see the carnage I'm about to create.

She draws back, shrugging me off.

"You barely survived, Beau." My jaw twitches. "You weren't living."

"And I'm living now?" she yells, shoving me away. "You call this living?"

"No, this is hell, but I'm fucking trying, Beau. I want a life with you, and it'll happen a lot fucking sooner if you just let me fix this." I yank her forward and grab her cheeks. "I fucking love you, I understand you, but I need you to stand down, Beau."

Her chin trembles. Her eyes well. She doesn't answer, and I don't wait for her to. I slam a hard kiss on her lips and turn, stalking out of the club.

"Derek Green just forwarded me an email," Otto says, flanking me. "I traced the IP address to the café Downtown."

"What did the email say?"

"It was congratulating him on a job well done."

I stop at the door and give Otto my attention. I don't need to ask.

"Roake walked free earlier today."

I breathe in deeply, my back tingling. "Not guilty," I murmur, and Otto nods, standing back, as if to get out of the line of fire. I stare at the street outside the club, my veins throbbing, my blood pumping. He's walking.

So now I can kill him.

A few guys brush past me, one jolting my shoulder, and Goldie's hand goes straight for her back, ready to draw, preparing for the unleashing of my temper. "It's fine," I say, taking deep breaths. There are more pressing matters.

"I'm not drinking with freaks," one guy mutters. "Since when did this place become a circus?"

I look back into the club, seeing Zinnea at the bar, drenched, her face the picture of shock as Esther tries to dab her down with some napkins. Beau catches my eye. Violence is distorting her features as she watches the men leave, the men who have just barged me at the door. She turns her gaze onto me, and I read her like I always read her. "Hold him," I growl, prompting Goldie to seize the guy before he makes it outside.

She drags him back, his protests loud, and his mates, eyes wide, flee without looking back. "Get the fuck off me, you dyke."

I pull my gun, claim him from Goldie, and slam him into the wall, so hard the building shakes, my snarling face up in his. Unfortunately for this piece of shit, he's caught me in a bloodthirsty mood, and getting rid of some of the pressure is exactly what I need before I go on a manhunt.

"What the fuck, man?" he garbles, stupidly trying to wrestle me off. My knee comes up swiftly, smashing into his groin. His squeal is high-pitched as he goes limp, and I release him and let him crumple to the floor, his hands cupping his balls. His eyes water, his groans long and painful.

"Arms," I order, and Goldie moves in, her smile dirty, as she pries his hands from his balls and pins them down.

"Wait, no!" he yells, "Please, no."

"Hope you didn't want kids," Goldie says, holding him in place with ease.

I stand over him, and he stills, his eyes wide, his legs flailing. I raise my boot, holding it in midair for a few moments, dragging out his wait for the agony about to consume him. "Has something offended you?" I ask, lowering my boot slowly and pressing it into his groin.

"No, nothing, please."

A few of Nolan's security join us, watching, silent. They know not to intervene.

I raise my boot and slam it down onto his balls, and he screams, his body trying to curl into a protective ball. Goldie ensures it doesn't, holding his arms, and I look to one of Nolan's security who quickly moves in and holds his legs down.

"Please," he mumbles, as I look to Beau, who's staring at the helpless piece of shit pinned to the floor. I raise my boot again and bring it down, over and over, snarling my way through it as he chokes and coughs, his eyes watering. I don't stop. Not until he's lost consciousness.

"Get rid of him," I order. "And find out where Roake is." I exit the club and go to my car, pausing when I hear a door slam. "Are you joking?" I whisper to myself, as Beau's ex heads my way. "What do you want?" I ask as two cop cars screech into the street, sirens blaring. They skid to a stop, four officers jumping out and jogging toward me. "What the fuck's going on?"

Burrows sniffs, saying nothing, his badge being flashed to anyone who'll look. I'm grabbed and manhandled to the hood of my car and slammed front forward onto the metal.

"James Kelly, I'm arresting you on suspicion of assault."

"Assault? That's a bit below your pay grade, isn't it?" I growl as my arms are shoved carelessly up my back. "Careful. Those hands give my girlfriend endless pleasure."

He jolts me brutally, sending bolts of pain into my shoulder. My jaw rolls, my teeth clench. "You do not have to say—"

"Ollie!" Beau yells, running out of the club, her face panicked. "What the hell are you doing?"

"What does it look like?" he snaps coldly, hauling me up and pushing me toward one of the police cars.

"Stand down, Beau," I say, reminding her of our conversation just five minutes ago. I cast a look to her ex. His smile of satisfaction is feebly masked. My lip curls, a million promises being made as I stare him down. I do not need this. "For fuck's sake," I yell, revealing my frustration and prompting Burrows to yank at the cuffs. "Is this the best you can do? Assault?"

"Oh, we have murder too," he says. "The evidence is sketchy at the moment, but I'm sure we'll straighten it out while you're in custody."

Translated: Remand. *Fuck.* "And who have I murdered?"

"Detective Spittle."

What the fuck?

"Your DNA was all over him." Burrows leads me to his unmarked car.

"You don't have my DNA."

He thrusts me in the back and pulls out a Q-tip, shoving it in my mouth. "Again, minor problem." He winks, holding it up. "All over him." The door slams, and I drop my head back, cursing my arse off as he wanders over to Beau, who's being held back by Goldie and Fury.

"You fucking snake!" she yells. "You stupid, idiotic snake! Do you actually want to die?"

"Is that a death threat?" Burrows asks, looking back at the police officers, eyebrows high.

"No, it's fucking promise," I say to myself, watching as he moves in, any arrogance wiped away, his face suddenly worried. He tries to pacify Beau. It doesn't work. I cast my eyes to Otto, nodding, telling him to get on with things. Locked up or not, this is still ending.

What a fucking inconvenience.

My arse is numb, my wrists are sore, my arms are aching. Three hours of questioning, hundreds of "No comments," and imagining a thousand ways I'm going to kill Oliver Burrows. It's nearly eleven. He's getting more and more worked up, his patience thin, constantly checking his mobile. He's waiting for the evidence he needs to throw me in a cell. Time isn't on my side.

"I will ask you again, did you kill Detective Spittle?"

"No comment," I say flatly, my eyes burning from staring at him so hard. "Let me ask *you* something."

"What?"

"What sound did you love the most from Beau when you fucked her?"

His fist comes down on the desk hard, his face turning a fetching shade of red. "Shut the fuck up."

"Did she scream?"

"I said shut up!"

"Moan?" I smile wickedly, not relishing the thought of anyone touching her, but loving his reaction. Because he will never have her again. "Her breathy gasps when she's about to come?"

He dives across the table and fists my shirt, shaking me. "I'll fucking kill you."

"Or are those sounds just for me?" I say calmly, never breaking my stare, his face up close to mine. "When I'm inside her," I whisper. "Moving. Watching her eyes glaze. Feeling her heart pound."

He roars, shoving me away before he starts pacing the room. "How did you meet?"

And here we have the crux. His jealousy. His hurt. He wanted to fix her and failed. I won't fail. "Back to your questioning, Detective Burrows," I say quietly.

"You're never going to see her again."

I smile. "Bet I do."

The door swings open, and a man appears, a man I recognize. I withdraw, watching him closely as he takes in the scene. Me, calm. Burrows, far from it. Harold Higham. "Uncuff him," he says, not only surprising Burrows, but surprising me too.

"What?" Burrows says, looking at Higham with a mixture of disbelief and disgust.

"I said, uncuff him."

"Are you mad? He's a murderer."

"Uncuff. Him." Higham states each word calmly, as I flick my interested attention between each man, wondering what the fuck is going on. Burrows curses and storms out, leaving Higham to do the honors himself. "You're free to go." He throws a bag on the table that contains my possessions—minus a gun—before rounding me and releasing my hands.

I flex my wrists and roll my shoulders, standing. "No charges?"

"No charges." He tosses the cuffs on the table and perches on the edge. "I got a call from the mayor."

"Adams?"

"I expect he got a call from The Brit."

I nod mildly, rubbing at my sore flesh. "Thanks for your hospitality," I quip, going to the door.

"I have one question."

I still, my hand on the knob. "What's that?"

"Who are you and Black hunting?"

"You know the answer to that, Higham," I reply, picking up my feet and making my way through the scores of officers at their desks, all eyeing me, all with faces screaming for me to punch. How many of the fuckers are bent? How many in the pocket of The Bear? My eyes fall onto Burrows, my pace never faltering, and I hold his hate-filled stare as I pass. "Dead," I whisper, making sure he can read my lips. *So fucking dead.*

I make it outside and stand for a moment, closing my eyes and breathing in the freedom.

"Still want me to stand down?"

My shoulders drop, my eyes remaining closed. "Not now, Beau." I'm working against a ticking time bomb, and my minor brush with the police has seriously delayed my plans. I open my eyes and find her in the passenger seat of my car, Fury at the wheel. The window is down, her arms folded and resting on the edge, her chin sitting pretty on her forearms. "You shouldn't be here." Fuck knows Burrows is gunning for me, and I wouldn't put it past him getting Beau in those cuffs. He has more on her than me.

I stride to the car and flick my head for Fury to get in the back. He looks ready to quit life. Slipping behind the wheel, I start the engine and go to my phone when it rings. "What's up."

"You're out?" Otto asks.

"No, the police let me take your call." I sigh, pulling into the traffic, checking my mirrors, watchful, because any decent cop would follow me. "What's going on?"

"Roake is celebrating his release in a bar on South Beach."

"How lovely for him. What bar?"

"Ventacini."

I look across to Beau, weighing up my options. I have two. Take her home and miss this opportunity or take her with me and knock one more man off my list of men to kill. *Fuck's sake.* "On my way," I mutter, hanging up and putting my foot down. "What do we have in the trunk?" I ask Fury in the rearview mirror, taking a sharp right, throwing him around in the back as Beau grips the handle above her.

"Full stock."

Beau faces me as I skid into another road. "How does Otto know he's at Ventacini?"

And so the questions begin. "We're tracking him."

"How?"

"His lawyer."

"You mean Derek Green?"

I don't need to know how she knows. Women talk. "Yes, Derek Green." He came good. He didn't really have much choice, mind you, but the moment Roake was found not guilty, the tracker was activated as planned. Roake was never going to prison. Only to hell.

"We're being followed," Fury says, looking out of the back window.

"Cop?" I ask, checking myself.

"No. Black Escalade. Three cars back."

I look up at my rearview mirror, seeing the nose of the Escalade nudging out. A smart cop would follow me. So why the fuck hasn't he, and who the fuck *is* tailing me? "I don't have time for this." I turn the wheel sharply, skidding across the road until the car is facing the other way. "Get down, Beau," I order, pulling off sharply. "You armed, Fury?"

"Armed."

I keep my eye on the Escalade coming toward us, although now it's slowed down. I take my foot off the gas, matching its speed, and we slowly get closer until we're cruising past. The driver's window is down, his arm casually resting on the ledge. Bold. So fucking bold. I see the tattoo first, coating the side of his face, a pretty scrolling of words in another language. Polish.

The Hound.

His eyes meet mine.

"Shooter in the back," Fury says calmly.

"Kill him."

He fires immediately and blood splatters the back window, the Escalade swerving. "Stand down," I order before Fury can take out The Hound, putting my foot down and burning off down the road.

"What are you doing?" Beau asks. "He had a clear shot."

"And so did the other shooter in the back."

She swings around, looking out the back window.

"Sorry, boss," Fury says. "Missed that one."

"Don't worry." I pull into a side street and slow to a stop by the curb halfway down. "Stay exactly where you are," I say to Beau. "I mean it."

She nods, and I glance up at the mirror to Fury. "Get behind the wheel. Leave the engine running. You'll know if you need to move." I pop the trunk and jump out, striding to the back and grabbing a grenade.

I walk into the middle of the road, and as soon as I hear the sound of tires, I pull the pin out with my teeth and release it like a bowling ball, sending it rolling up the concrete, just as the Escalade skids into the street. I watch as the vehicle slows to a stop, as expected, the driver obviously surprised to find my car stationary and me a sitting duck, unarmed, in the middle of the road. He's reassessing his plan.

I smile as my little bowling ball disappears under the car and

The Hound appears, hanging out of the window, a machine gun aimed my way. "Tell me," I call, mentally counting in my head. "What does it say?"

He smiles, his finger reaching for his face and stroking over his tattoo. "It says," he rumbles, his English broken, "today you die."

"You've been ripped off," I reply, shaking my head. "It actually says, today *you* die."

I detect his frown from here, and then the realization. It's golden. The moment of panic I see, the shouts I hear, before the Escalade blows up. It's fucking golden. Shrapnel flies, flames roar, body parts scatter. I would stand here and watch the fire blaze all night if I had time. Sadly, I don't. And one run-in with the cops is enough for one day.

I head to the car, pull a machine gun from the trunk, and get in the back. "Drive," I order, loading and tossing the belt over my shoulder. I feel eyes on me and glance up to find Beau studying me. I hate the interest coating her face. The unspoken praise. The satisfaction knowing another man is dead by my hands. "That'll be the last man you see me kill," I say quietly.

She doesn't reply, turning in her seat and facing the road.

Because she knows I'm talking shit.

With Otto on the line, I watch the entrance of the private bar from across the road. "Just wait until you can see Green," he says.

"How many in there?"

"Roake and five others."

"All his men?"

"Yes. Take them all out, that's the end of the drugs side of The Bear's business."

I take the handle of the door, ready. "You can cross The Hound off our list too."

"What?" Otto blurts.

"I ran into him on my way here. I expect someone advised him of where I was. So I gave him a little fireworks display."

"Burrows?" Otto asks, and I hum, noncommittally. "Fuck . . . me."

"It was beautiful."

Otto laughs, and I straighten in my seat when I see Derek Green appear at the entrance of the bar, lighting a cigarette. The lawyer having a celebratory drink with his client. "Gotta go," I say, hanging up and getting out.

"James," Beau calls, stalling me. I look back, and she closes her eyes, swallowing.

"I'll see you in a minute," I say, draping a coat over my arm to conceal my gun. "Promise." I make my way over to Derek Green, as he nervously puffs his way through his smoke.

"I haven't had one since high school," he says as the doormen eye me warily. "He's with me," Derek thumbs off a few notes and hands them over. "Joining the celebrations."

They nod and let us pass, and we walk into the foyer side by side. "Have you been told yet why a gun was being delivered to your office?"

"No. Not a word."

"Details," I order.

"Far back. Six of them, all armed, all having a whale of a time." He wipes his brow. "I'm a dead man walking, aren't I?"

"We're all dead men walking, Derek." I push my way through the door and scan the space, spotting Roake at the far back, distracted by a bit of arse being thrust in his face. *Can't Hold Us* Feat. Ray Dalton booms as I watch him slap the stripper's round backside, sending her on her way, before swiping up a bottle of tequila and swigging. "God, I'm such a party pooper," I whisper, dropping the coat and aiming.

I whistle.

All the men look up.

All reach for their backs on curses.

"Celebrations are over." I open fire, moving my gun from side to side slowly, taking them all out in seconds. Glasses smash, the stuffing from the plush chairs explodes into the air, screams sound, strippers run for cover, staff duck behind the bar.

I release the trigger and take in the carnage as the music still booms. Blood decorates the wall, the tables, the carpet. It's a mess. A beautiful mess of dead men.

I wander over and crouch, casting my eyes over the bodies. Not one sign of life.

But . . .

I rise and shower the bodies with more bullets before turning and walking out, pulling my Glock out of my trousers. The doormen back up into the nearest walls, hands up. "What did you see?" I ask, splitting my aim between them.

"Nothing," one murmurs, shaking like a leaf. "Nothing at all."

"You were on a break, yes?"

Both nod like demented puppets, and I look at Green. "You better hope they keep their word, Derek," I say, aiming and shooting out his kneecap.

He screams, dropping like a sack of shit. "Why?" He dribbles and rolls around, clenching his splattered knee.

"It would look odd if you came out of this unscathed, don't you think?" I turn to the doormen again. "CCTV?" I look up and around, seeing a camera in the corner.

"I'll get it." One of the doormen motions to a nearby door. "It's in there."

"Be quick now. I expect we'll have company shortly."

He hurries away, and I wait patiently, blocking out the irritating sounds of Derek Green squealing in agony. A few minutes later, I'm being handed a hard drive. "That's all of it?" I ask, looking up through my lashes. "No copies for security or anything like that?"

"No."

I nod, pushing the door to the security room open with the tip of my gun, and I use the last of my bullets to blow the system to smithereens. Then I walk away, tucking the evidence that'll ensure Derek's compliance into my back pocket. I cross the road and slip into the back of the car. Beau doesn't express her relief, but I see her whole being relax.

And fuck is that good because I need her. I need inside her now. My whole body is alive with adrenalin, and I see the moment she realizes what I need. Her pupils dilate, her breath quickens. I imagine she's counting in her head how many minutes it will take to get back to the mansion. I'll fuck her—hard, relentlessly—and then I'll take her to our room and have her again. She'll come. I'll come. And once we're both sated, once we're both sweating, broken messes, then I'll fix us.

20

BEAU

Fury pulls to a stop and looks to the mirror for instruction. The car ride has been deathly quiet, tense, but not with the same grim anger between us. It's been a tension I've missed. Craved. My insanely stunning boyfriend has one thing on his mind. Fucking. And after what's happened tonight, I'm completely on board. "I've got it," James says. "And thanks for today."

"No problem." Fury swiftly ejects himself, and then it's me awaiting instruction.

"Come here," he says flatly.

I look over my shoulder, noting his blood-splattered clothes before I notice the tightness of his expression. His eyes turn onto me slowly as he reaches for the bottom of his shirt, peeling it up his body and tossing it on the seat next to him.

"I want you, Beau. I want you now." He goes to his trousers and unbuttons the fly, lifting his ass off the seat and pushing them down with his boxers. He seizes his arousal, and my mouth dries at the sight of him stroking slowly down his shaft. I know the rear windows are blacked out. I also know it probably wouldn't have mattered if they weren't a few months ago. But now? He would never let anyone see me.

I glance toward the house.

"I can't wait." He reaches between the seats and takes my wrist, pulling me into the back. I land on his lap, my dress is shoved up, my panties pushed aside. My back snaps straight when I feel the swelling head of his cock skim me. "Lower."

I do as I'm bid, releasing the muscles in my thighs, and sink onto his lap, inhaling with every inch I take as his face tightens to the point it's distorted. "Shit," he hisses, his body softening, melding into the leather. I hold the back of the seat, my chin dropping to my chest as I subtly roll my hips. The doubt is immediately doused. The fire inside reignited. Sweat, blood, death, and sex saturate the air.

James takes my jaw and directs my face to his, slowly thrusting up as he does. My exhale is jagged, my torso rolling. The heat of our combined breaths is beginning to steam the windows, the air damp. "I love you." He strains the words, and it's all that really needs to be said. Because why else would I be here if he didn't?

I fall forward and take his mouth, starting to rock on his lap, soaking up every bit of the pleasure and our closeness. His hot tongue slips against mine, circling lazily, my hands in his hair hold him. And every reason why we agreed to just fuck when we first met comes flooding back. My mind is washed clean, and my heart no longer hurts. Only James can achieve this state of oblivion in me. And now, it's needed. No cruelty, no death, no injustice. Only pleasure.

If anything should be the death of me, it is this. But I won't die, I refuse to die. Not when I now have something wonderful and consuming to live for. It's something more than revenge. Ironically, James can give me it all.

He gulps, his fingers clawing harder into my hips. I pull back from his lips quickly, my pace speeding up, and I watch him coming undone, the mere sight taking me down the same path of ecstasy. His cheeks hollow from his bite. His eyes fix on mine. "More," he grates, slipping a hand onto my nape and fisting my hair. I rock faster, whimpering, my head dropping back, my mouth opening, my gaze unmoving from his.

It comes at me like a bulldozer, no avoiding it, crashing through my body ruthlessly. My hands shoot to the seat behind his head, bracing against the leather, my body jacking as my climax takes me out. I choke on nothing, trembling, hissing, clenching my eyes shut, doing anything to deal with the sensitivity. I hear his yell through my distorted hearing, feel the hard pound of his hips upward. I ride the wave, everything out of control, my body, my mind, my breathing.

I fall forward, my forehead resting on his throat, my palms sliding down to his bare chest, feeling him. Stroking him. My hands ball, my face turning, my eyes opening. The window is a perfect film of mist. Hazy. Glass but not clear. His heavy breathing is loud, and his arms round my back, holding me tightly.

"I'm going to ask you a question, Beau," he says, his voice hoarse. "And your answer is final."

I try hard not to tense and fail miserably. "What?"

"Do you want to leave?"

"What?"

"Tonight. We pack, we go. The game ends now."

I naturally withdraw, scanning his face for any signs of him taking those words back. There're no signs at all, his expression fixed. He's serious. "What are you talking about?" What's changed? Where's his grit gone?

"I'm asking you if you want to leave, because if you tell me yes, we'll go. Now." His fingertip meets the bridge of my nose and draws a perfect line down the length.

"I don't understand," I admit, caught off guard. Is The Bear dead and no one's told me? Is it over?

"That's not a yes." His smile is faint, my confusion amusing him.

"It's also not a no."

"So is that a yes?"

"Yes. No." I growl to myself, clenching at my hair. "I need to understand what's happening here." I wrestled with the notion of staying in St. Lucia. I loved the brief normality we'd found, but I didn't truly let myself settle on it, because I knew there were forces far greater than my need for peace at work. Ironically, it was James's and my combined need for revenge. But what if that need kills us? What good is finding what you're looking for if you don't get to actually have it? And on the other hand, what if this follows us forever, no matter where we go, no matter who we try to be? It could always find us. The only true, *safe* way out is to kill everything that poses a risk to our future. And yet none of those options are guaranteed. Each carries risk. Leave and we may only delay the inevitable. Stay and deal with it, we might never leave Miami at all. Not alive. "Oh God," I breathe, so torn. It's not just James and me now either. There's Danny and Rose. If we go, Danny will be left to deal with Miami alone, and that would mean while I might find peace, Rose could lose hers. I could never sacrifice someone else's happiness, a friend's happiness, for my own. My conscience would never allow it.

"We stay," I say assertively. God knows, there can't be many more men to kill. Between James, Danny, and the others, Miami has become the capital of murder. It's an all-out war.

"We stay," he says. It's not a question, not a way of asking if he heard me right because he's surprised I don't want to run away from the carnage. He's simply confirming because he knew what my answer would be. This is just his way of making it clear that if I wanted it, he would walk away, even if he *didn't* want it. Things are definitely changing, but I have to ask myself again where this has come from. Surely he's closer than when we arrived in Miami. Why would he walk away now? Why would I?

James starts to lift me from his lap. "Where's this come from?" I ask, wriggling to get my dress down as he lifts his ass and pulls his trousers up.

"I don't want you to feel trapped."

I laugh, forcing a scowl from James. "I was trapped before I met you, James." His reason is horseshit, and now I'm suspicious. "What's going on?"

"Nothing is going on." He fastens his fly.

I study his profile, not liking the sense of uncertainty radiating from him. "Do you have a bad feeling?"

His working hands still, and he takes a few moments to collect his thoughts, which only makes me more concerned. "We owe no one anything," he says quietly, looking up at me. "Please remember that. This whole fucked-up business is about you and me."

He's confusing me so much. And then I lean back, away from him, suddenly realizing his angle. "You mean Danny and Rose?"

"And your ex." He finds his shirt and slips it on. "And your father."

"I love Danny Black more than my father," I say, laughing. "Isn't that a fuck-up of impressive proportions?"

He's still for a moment, watching me as my amusement subsides, his expression almost pained. "I forgot how much I love your laugh." Reaching for me, James drags me onto his lap again. He forgot. So much has been forgotten in the past few weeks. "Your ex has got a real issue with me, as does your father. What can we do about that?"

I'm not laughing now, only smiling, but I'm frowning through it. My head hurts. "You either kill them, or you become a law-abiding citizen. Neither are options."

His eyebrows are quickly high.

"Neither are options," I repeat, my head tilted, my lip pursed. "Are they?" It's no secret that I'm not my father's biggest fan but, for the sake of clarity, I need to be sure my assassin boyfriend understands that killing him *really* isn't an option. The man who played a part in bringing me into this world is a necessary evil. And Ollie? He'll calm down eventually. I hope. "Answer me."

"Neither are options," he says, but it's halfhearted. "Come on." He opens the car door and gets out, holding his hand to me, and I accept, still eyeing him. My mind's filled with questions that I'm incapable of holding back, especially in light of James's offer to get up and go. "Is this nearly over?" I ask as he walks us to the house. Part of me prays it is, but the reasonable side of me knows that James would never suggest us leaving if he was close to finding The Bear.

"Yes," he answers simply, with no elaboration. It only heightens my suspicions. I pull him to a stop, looking past his big frame toward the kitchen, laughter and chatter emanating from the room. The eve of the wedding. Tomorrow—or today— just for one day, everything—blood, death, revenge—will be paused to make way for nothing but love and happiness. It feels like it could be the calm before a fatal storm.

I look up at James, who's waiting patiently for me to speak. "Tell me what's going on," I order, standing firm. Shit's always going down, but the past few days it feels like the tension has heightened. I feel like the end is in sight, but it's hazy. Uncertain.

He shakes his head slowly, his expression warning, and I take a step back, my mind racing. He's refusing because he knows I'll object. He knows I won't like what I'm told. And that means it's even more risky than what I'm used to from this man, and I'm used to some pretty risky shit. Jesus, how many men has he wiped out today alone?

"Have you ever once considered the fact that I was a cop? That I might be able to help figure this out?"

"Yes," he all but laughs. "All the fucking time."

"Then why won't you let me?"

"Because I made a promise to myself that you will not be in the firing line, no matter what. Haven't you suffered enough? Hurt enough?"

"I—"

"There you are."

Danny emerges from his office with Ringo and Brad, all with some form of alcohol in their hands. He looks between us, interested. "Everything okay?"

"Great." I force a smile, returning my attention to James, giving him a look to suggest we're not done. And he gives me one to suggest we are. We'll see. Tomorrow, or today, might be the wedding day, I'll give him that grace, but after that I want to know what's going on. "I'll leave you men to business," I say, reaching up and pressing my lips to James's cheek, keeping them there for a few seconds before heading to the kitchen. When I'm out of sight, I pause just shy of the door, listening.

"So I call in a favor from Adams to get you out of jail," Danny says, almost amused, "and the first thing you do is blow up the Poles and go on a shooting spree in a bar."

"News travels fast."

"What the fuck are you thinking?"

"I saw an opportunity. I took it."

I hear Danny huff. "We're supposed to talk about this shit."

"Are we?" James asks darkly. I find myself holding my breath, the atmosphere frosty. "So what were you three doing in there without me?"

"Just making some calls," Danny replies, equally as dark.

"Hey, come on," Brad pipes in. "We're supposed to be celebrating."

I quickly get my feet moving and enter the kitchen to find everyone congregated around the impressive island, drinks and snacks scattered across the space. I eye Goldie who, unusually, has a glass of wine in her hand. She rolls her eyes when she catches me staring. "Want one?" she asks, reaching for a clean glass and the bottle.

"Sure." I hop on a stool beside her and hold the base of the glass while she pours, casting my gaze around the crowd as James, Danny, Brad, and Ringo enter, joining the masses. Danny's and James's expressions match. Moody.

Esther busies herself topping up the bowls of chips, checking everyone's glasses are full, and then wiping down the countertops.

"Will you relax, Mum?" Danny sighs, plucking the cloth from her grip and tossing it in the sink. He takes her elbow and leads her to a stool, ignoring her protests. "Sit down and do as you're told." He pulls a wine glass across the island and places it in her hand. "Drink."

She pouts through a smile as I catch Rose's eye across the table. "Okay?" she mouths, and I nod.

"You?" I mouth back, getting a return nod. Then she jerks her head, looking toward the foyer. Naturally, my interest is piqued. Does she know something? I glance around the island, seeing everyone engrossed in conversation but, more importantly, James, Danny, and Brad are on the far side, talking quietly, engaged. *Plotting.*

I slip down from my stool, drink in hand, and round the island, stopping to check on Zinnea. She looks together, yet her sparkly outfits are a massive contributing factor to that. A disguise. But at least now she's dry. "My goodness," she breathes, squeezing my hand. "I know James was defending my honor, but I feel terrible for the upset it caused."

"You mustn't," I say. "Ollie was there to arrest James *before* he was defending your honor." Or venting his anger. Whichever, the loose-lipped idiot who insulted Zinnea was asking for it.

"Whatever for?" She pulls up, frowning. "Don't answer that. I'm learning very quickly that the less I know, the better."

"How are *you*?" I ask. Doc's mentioned an improvement, but I'm still worried. I know better than anyone how to feign being okay.

Just the question makes her pull in air, and she looks around the room, almost in awe. "It's like being a part of a family, isn't it?'

I should laugh, but I don't. She's talking about acceptance, and Zinnea has never had that from her own family. But what happens when this is over? When James and I leave? Zinnea will have no one. Lawrence will have no one. I can't allow that. "Just like family," I muse, giving her a kiss on her cheek. "Don't upstage the bride tomorrow, will you?"

She laughs, and it's gruff, making her stop immediately and check to see if anyone caught her accidental slip from Zinnea to Lawrence. Clearing her throat, she tops up her glass and sips all very ladylike as Esther moves in and compliments her on her flamingo-pink nail polish.

I peek across to James and Danny, seeing their attention is on Brad, who's talking with his hands. I find Rose and indicate toward the door, making my way there, Rose following.

"Hey," I say when we're out of the kitchen. She's glowing. Smiling. Happy. She looks amazing. "I assume you and Danny have gotten over your quarrel."

She laughs quietly. "For now, yes. What do you know?" she asks, coming in closer, keen for me to spill.

My shoulders drop. "Nothing. I thought you knew something."

Her face twists. "I don't know anything. What happened tonight? Why'd you call Danny?"

"My ex arrested James. Danny called in a favor from the mayor."

"Perry Adams?" Rose balks and then her eyes narrow. "There's definitely trouble afoot, Beau," she says, and it's fucking hilarious. "What's so funny?"

"There's always trouble afoot, you nut."

"It's something more. Danny said there's a way out, but he's being cagey. The last time he was cagey, I went through hell."

I hum, thinking. A way out. How? And does James know about it? Surely not if he asked me if I wanted to leave tonight. What the hell is going on, and why are Danny and James suddenly so hostile toward each other? My thoughts are disturbed when my cell rings, and I stare at the screen, my heart picking up pace. It's past midnight. I see Dad rubbing at his chest. I see his pale face.

"Dad," I say, answering. "Are you okay?"

"Is this some kind of joke?" he asks, sounding outraged. I'm stumped, my mouth still hanging open to speak. "An invite to their wedding next week?"

I swing my stare to Rose, who backs up. "What?"

"An invite," I murmur, waiting for her to catch on. "To the wedding." Does Danny fucking hate me?

"What?" Rose blurts.

"It's a damn insult," Dad bellows. "I'm a respectable businessman and he's a criminal!"

My whole being deflates. I am so done having this conversation. I was actually worried about him. "I'll graciously accept your decline, Dad. Your absence is expected." I stab at the screen with my thumb. "Why the hell would he invite my fath—" I pull up, thinking. And it clicks. "Distraction."

"Huh?" Rose frowns.

"They're trying to distract me."

"Well, what about me? You're not the only one smelling something iffy. I told you they were planning something."

"You're the bride," I point out. "They don't need to distract you because everyone else will." Her attention will be demanded left and right.

"So my wedding really is going to be a decoy?" Her indignance is palpable.

"Looks like it." I face the kitchen where the men are all inside, my senses tingling.

"The asshole," Rose breathes. "What do we do?"

"What *can* we do?"

"God damn it, tomorrow is supposed to be a vacation from the shit." She huffs and puffs, and then she's looking at me with a sorrowful expression that I one hundred percent don't like. "I need to talk to you about something else."

"What?" I ask, as she takes my hand and leads me to the staircase.

"If it's too much," she says, lowering to the step and taking me with her. "I can talk to him."

"What's too much? And who's him?"

"Danny wants to announce about the baby." Her lips twist. "Now."

My stomach turns painfully, and I try with everything I have not to let the stab of pain show on my face.

"Doc scanned me earlier," she goes on quietly, unsure, and I hate that, yet I'm incapable of fixing it. "I'm over twelve weeks."

Past the most likely period of miscarrying. *Unless you get shot.* "Of course." I scramble for the right words, scramble harder for the smile I need to give Rose. The one she needs too. But I'm feeling so mixed, struggling with my emotions, fighting to show my elation for her while hiding my devastation for me. My head and my body are at war, my mind screaming to speak, my body wanting to curl into a hopeless ball. "You absolutely must." I grab her hand and squeeze. This is her time. Full of hope. Full of positivity. Unlawful men aside. "And enjoy every second of it." I smile and pull her in for a hug. I never want her to feel bad for being happy. Like always, I'm fighting it hard not to project my desolation on others, especially not on Rose. This is a miracle for her. And still, I fight to hold back my tears. And I fight hard. "Do you think he can wait until I'm back?"

"Why? Where are you going?" She pulls away, her face worried and questioning.

"I need to take my meds." I shamelessly circle my stomach. "I think I've overdone it today, what with bachelorette parties, arrests, and trying to pull my pregnant best friend off a strip pole."

Rose laughs, laying a palm over her forehead. "Obviously, I want to die."

I lean in quickly and kiss her cheek. "Obviously. Tell Danny to wait for me before he breaks the news." I jump up quickly and take the stairs fast. "I want to be there." I'm holding back the dam as I hurry down the corridor, and as soon as I'm in our room alone, I fill the silent space with my sobs, clenching my face with my palms and sliding down the wood to my ass, sounding as hopeless as I'm sure I look. And the pain in my stomach just won't relent. Won't go away. For just a moment, I had what Rose has. That awe. That fear. That uncertain joy. That was mine. And even though fucking James in the car centered us again, I feel this aching, devastating tear inside my soul. Every other pain is forgotten with this fresh agony.

It's finally hit.

It's finally sinking in, and it hurts so fucking bad.

The door jars behind me. "Beau?" James calls. I jolt with his constant pushing of the door, not bothering to wipe at my face. Not bothering to fix myself. I'm *really* not okay, and I can't pretend I am anymore. At least, not with James.

I shuffle forward on my ass, giving him room to open the door, and when he muscles past and finds me on the floor, all I can do is smile lamely, my lip wobbling, my face drenched.

His big body seems to shrink before my eyes. I hate that too. I sense things are coming to a head and, as much as I don't want to be an added problem, I can't find it in myself to fight the onslaught of emotions. I'm done. Exhausted. The adrenalin has gone. *Empty.*

Silently, he takes my hand and gently pulls me up from the floor, engulfing me in his arms and lifting me from my feet. His move gives my sadness another hit of sorrow, and I bury my face in his neck, my body jumping, my cries ruling me. I haven't lost control like this since Mom died. Back then, I was blinded by my grief, unable to see what lay ahead. Now? Now I know what lies ahead, and it scares me. I know what needs to happen, what we both need to find closure for the murders of the people we love the most. But this new grief feels somehow unstoppable. It feels like there will never be a cure, and it's terrifying. James taking me to those places that always released me from my torment doesn't feel like it could work now, which leaves me dangling off the cliff, ready to plummet into the darkness with no lifeline to bring me back.

He walks across the room and eases me down to the bed, reaching behind him to detach my arms from around his shoulders. I can't look at him, my eyes low. I don't want him to see the utter hopelessness in me. I don't want him to feel like I do, because if he doesn't believe he can fix me, I don't know where that leaves us. Our anguish has always been shared, whether silently and unknown, or with the truth. It lightened the weight on our shoulders. Offered respite. And on top of my shredded emotions, I feel guilt, because it wasn't only me who lost the unexpected glimmer of light beyond our purpose.

"Beau," he breathes, trying to encourage my chin up, trying to find my eyes. I resist, fighting against the pressure of his finger. "Beau, look at me."

I shake my head, swallowing, trying desperately to rid my throat of the overwhelming lump, jolting with every inhale I attempt to make. I can't breathe. Can't feel anything except the overpowering emptiness that crushed me when I woke from my coma. Can't see anything but James's face when he told me.

I know what's coming, I know the feeling, the uncontrollable panic hijacking me. "No." I will it away, standing from the bed, pushing James back. I frantically search the room for Dexter. Where is he? I look for the drawers that Dexter always kept the paper bags in. Where are they? I search for Uncle Lawrence, for his peaceful balcony that he always took me to. They're not here. I gasp, reaching for something to cling to, defying the pull. I grapple at the material in my hands, feeling something grab me, hearing the bellow of a man.

"I can't breathe," I gasp, heaving, searching for air. "I can't breathe!" My heart thunders in my chest, my pulse booming in my ears, my vision hazy from the blackness creeping in from the sides.

And then it's there, over my mouth, and I grab it, urgently pulling in oxygen as my strung body gives and I sink into something soft. The black begins to clear, and I blink, staring at a gold chandelier, disorientated.

"Fuck . . . me," someone whispers, as a hand strokes through my hair.

"What happened?"

I swallow, my breathing regulating, and drop my eyes. "Aunt Zinnea?" I mumble into the bag, willing my mind to straighten out. The bag continues to crumple, the sound deafening. My face feels taut, my throat hoarse, my chest tight. I remove the bag and try to sit up, but I'm met with force, two spade-like hands pushing into my shoulders and forcing me back to the bed.

"Take it easy." He appears above me, his handsome face cut with worry. "Please don't tell me you're okay or I'll lose my head."

"I'm not okay," I whisper jaggedly, taking the bag back to my mouth, as James virtually exhales his relief and Zinnea whimpers her sorrow, reaching for James's arm and resting her hand there.

"I'll give you a moment," she says, coming to the bed and dipping, feeling at my hair as she kisses me. "My darling."

I swallow, as a new batch of tears comes, and I surrender to the heartache. Zinnea will be missing Dexter in this moment more than any other, her husband always there, calm and controlled, to get us through these times. It's so hard to comprehend the level of his betrayal when I think about him during those episodes. Compassionate, light. He had all the time in the world to remain by my side, as well as keeping Zinnea calm, while I fought through my attack. But it was all lies. Deceit. How did I not see that? His darkness.

Zinnea's struggling to keep her own emotions in check as she backs out of the room, the vivacious woman wilting with every step she takes.

"She shouldn't be alone," I say, trying to get up again, worried about her state of mind. I hate that she's seen me like this when she's swimming against the tide herself.

"I'll message Esther," James says, stopping me, at the same time going to his cell and typing out a message. Within a few seconds of clicking send, he gets a reply and tucks it away. "Come here." He takes the bag and helps me to the top of the bed, settling beside me and hugging me into his side. I relax in his hold, feeling my muscles yield and my heart quieten. I store this closeness and feeling in my mind to call upon when I need it. I must remember this. James can soothe me. Not like he has so often in the past with sex, but how he is now simply with his arms. Holding me. It's another form of communication without words. But we need words now. If we're going to make it through this loss, we need words.

"When I lost our baby," I whisper quietly, building the courage I need to speak clearly and confidently, "I felt the same intense pain and hollowness that I felt when I lost . . ." I close my eyes and curl further into his side, fighting that pain back again. "It hurt," I whisper. "Still hurts, and it's getting harder to control it." It's backward. It's angering. After the shock of my pregnancy, I allowed myself to consider an existence beyond struggling. Beyond the bitterness and hate that ruled me. James and who he is, what he stands for, was easier to wrap my mind around. Because we are the same in a sense. Polluted. Tarnished. We could fix each other, move forward, but our pasts would never change. A baby? It felt like redemption. Bright hope. An opportunity to channel all my energy into loving rather than hating. And what I hate in this world is the very thing that stole that opportunity from me, and despite having James to love, there was suddenly more to loathe. More to resent. More pain to feel.

James remains silent against me. I don't need his words, because I know better than I know my pain that he feels the same. He has more reasons to kill now. More men to hunt. It's his outlet. He's mine. And the distance between us lately, our loss, isn't relieving that.

St. Lucia helped, but it was short-lived. I'm a master at concealing my grief as well as my scars, and these past few days I've made a conscious effort *not* to cover my scars. It was a pathetic attempt to convince everyone I'm okay. Even more pathetic that I thought I could convince James. "I'm not okay," I admit, feeling his mouth fall to my hair, breathing me into him, his arms constricting. "I'm not okay, and a desperately want to be okay." A baby won't fix it. That's not what I'm saying I need. It was an unexpected opportunity, something to deal with, and we did. Now, my priority is getting both of us out of Miami alive. Alive and with no risk of being taken back to hell again, but until we can leave, I just have to deal with this constant, dull, consuming pain. I feel like I'm in limbo, my sadness and hope colliding and exploding constantly. Rose's news has only amplified the odd sense of longing inside of me. But it will happen again, and it will happen when we don't have death tailing us. When we have nothing to focus on but each other. "Rose is pregnant," I murmur, and immediately feel his chest sink under my hand with a big inhale. "I'm okay." I smile to myself. I can't be anything but happy for her. It's a gift. Perhaps not at the right time, but it's such a beautiful gift. It's also hope for us, because we know Danny, and now, more than before, he will move heaven and earth to get Rose out of Miami as soon as he can, which means we can leave too. We can leave and start to properly deal with the mess that is us.

"I know." James encourages me from the warmth and safety of his body and takes my chin, looking down at me. "Danny," he says in answer to my questioning face.

I'm worried this will trigger James too, bring on a fresh bout of anger and resentment. He needs his head on straight and his mind to think clearly. Is this the reason why Danny and James seem a bit off with each other? "I want you to be happy for them."

"I *am* happy for them. But I can be sad for us too." He gently rolls me to my back and lies lightly over me, framing my face with his big palms. "I've been waiting for you to open up. Hoping. I can't see you like this, Beau. Tell me what I can do."

"You know what needs to be done."

He nods, brushing at my cheeks with the pad of his thumb. "I want you to pack your things," he orders. "Be ready to leave."

"When?"

"I don't know yet. Just be ready."

I nod, and curl my arm around his neck, pulling him down and pushing our lips together. It takes only a second for us both to open up, to introduce our tongues, to swirl and roll them through each other's mouths. This isn't advancing into more. This is just loving.

With everything I have, Beau, I fucking love you. Broken, fixed, happy, sad, I love you. If you do anything, just remember that.

I let our closeness, our love, pull me in and hold me in a place far brighter than the real world, absorbed by his mouth and his devotion, and we kiss, softly and slowly for an eternity. It's the medicine I need right now, and I'm prepared to overdose on it.

James is the one to end our bliss, and he breathes in deeply, wiping my mouth with his thumb, smiling tenderly as he flicks his eyes up to mine. "Can you make me a promise?" he asks, and I nod, because that is what he needs now, just as much as I need his gentleness.

I already know what he's going to ask me for. "I will stand down," I say, my eyes searching his. I see no darkness at all. Only love. He needs his darkness to get through this.

On an understanding nod, he eases off me, pulling me up from the bed. "Come with me." He leads me to the bathroom and stands me by the sink, running the faucet and wetting a washcloth. He proceeds to pat at my skin, dabbing down the blotchiness, no doubt.

"How bad?" I ask.

"Beautiful," he replies simply, combing his fingers through my hair and pressing his lips to my forehead. "Are you ready?"

A few deep, stabilizing breaths and a nod, as he discards the cloth and takes my hand, assessing me, before taking the lead, guiding me back toward the celebrations.

The first thing I do when I enter is search for Zinnea, and to my relief, she's here, smiling, though I detect the worry behind it. She spots me, and I'm quick to signal that I'm okay before she moves her gaze to James, looking at him in a way I've never seen before. Appreciation. Trust. She can see his love for me. That will give her some peace. He nods and sits me on a stool, putting a glass of wine in my hand and twisting the cap off a bottle of beer for himself. The chatter hasn't died, neither has the laughter, and I take it all in as I lose myself in my wine.

"Are you okay?" Rose moves into my side, her worried eyes checking every inch of me. "You've been gone so long." She follows James's path across the kitchen to Danny and Brad.

"I'm absolutely fine," I tell her.

"He didn't seem happy."

I look across to James, just as he looks across to me. Checking on me. "We talked." I smile at him before giving it to Rose. "It was needed."

She exhales, evidently relieved. She was worried. She doesn't need to know that it wasn't wasted. "I'm glad."

"Yeah, me too. But enough of that," I say, chinking my wine with her water. "I didn't miss it, did I?"

"No, I told Danny to wait for you." Rose suddenly looks a little awkward. "Can you act surprised? I don't want Esther or Daniel to know you knew before them."

"Of course. How does this work?" I gasp, my mouth falling open, and Rose laughs.

"Let's hope they're not looking at you when they find out."

"That bad?"

"Terrible." She searches the kitchen, and I watch as Danny gets her attention, showing the ceiling his palms. She shrugs in return, prompting him to make his way over. "He's still on the

PlayStation with Tank." Her nose scrunches. "It's important, apparently."

Danny rolls his eyes and traipses to the kitchen door. "Hey, kid," he yells, and I hear Daniel call back from the TV room. "Not in a minute," Danny yells. "Now, or your jet ski will be sold to the lowest bidder."

Shaking her head, Rose turns her attention back to me. "Sounds scary, doesn't he?" She laughs under her breath. "If only Daniel knew." Watching with an eagle eye as I sip more wine, she pouts. "I bet that tastes amazing."

"Delicious," I confirm, making her nose wrinkle. "Don't worry. Only another six months before you can enjoy a glass again." I swig more back as she throws me a playful, dirty look before being collected by Danny and taken to the other side of the kitchen.

He doesn't tap a glass. He smashes his fist down on the counter, making everyone in the room jump and look his way. "I need you all to shut the fuck up for a second," he declares, as Daniel races into the kitchen, Tank jogging along behind him. "It's too late, kid. I sold it."

Rose nudges him in the side and Daniel snorts his disgust, swiveling and making a sharp exit. "Then I'm going."

"Get on a chair before I put you on one," Danny says, his tone deadly. "Now."

Wisely, Daniel backtracks and slumps moodily onto a chair, his bottom lip pushed out as Esther pacifies him with a can of soda and a ruffle of his hair that he tries and fails to shrug off.

"I have something to share," Danny says, earning another nudge from Rose. "We. *We* have something to share."

"I don't like the sound of this," Brad says, his eyes narrowing on Danny. "What the fuck's going on?"

Esther gasps, stands, and puts her hands over her mouth. "Don't tell me you're . . ." But she can't finish, and I feel James move in behind me, pushing his front into my back and slipping his arm around me, clenching my hand. I lean back into him and link our fingers, squeezing.

"You're what?" Brad asks, stepping forward, his eyes jumping between Danny and Rose, his suited form tensing. "What's going on?"

"Having a baby," Danny declares, a dirty smirk on his face, deepening his scar. He's enjoying this, and not only because it's happy news. Brad looks like he's turned to ice, still and unmoving. Frozen.

"What?" he whispers.

"Mom's pregnant," Daniel declares, looking at Brad like he's stupid. "Do you need me to explain how?"

"Oh my God!" Esther screeches, diving across the kitchen and seizing Rose.

I bite my lip, feeling eyes on me, and when I check, I find Zinnea, Otto, and Goldie all looking this way, pensive. I smile at them, and it's real, before I get up, leaving James behind, and go to my friend, hugging the shit out of her while Esther moves her excitement onto her son. "Oh my God," I gasp in her ear, smiling when she laughs.

I kiss her hair, give her that little bit more of a squeeze, and break away, letting everyone else in the room at her.

I catch Danny's eye over his mom's shoulder, and I smile before I go back to James, who's taken my stool, settling between his thighs and resting back against him, taking in the scene. The happiness. And truly, I feel it for them too.

Amused, I watch as Daniel worms his way through the crowd and finds his mom. He jumps up and kisses her. "Can I go back to the TV room now?"

"No, you can go to bed. It's late."

"Ah, man!" he whines. "Just one more game. I need to beat him."

"Fine, one more." She looks at Tank, who nods, following Daniel's fleeing form from the kitchen.

"Pregnant?" Brad murmurs, still frozen in position, his beer held in his limp hand. "How the fuck did that happen?"

"Let's draw Brad a diagram," Goldie declares, making Ringo chuckle. "Get me some paper."

"Do you need me?" Fury asks, appearing next to us.

My glass pauses at my lips. The big giant Viking wants to join his brother and Daniel.

"It's a twin thing." He shrugs his massive shoulders, looking awkward.

"Go," James says from behind me.

"I feel like singing," Zinnea declares. "Yes." She's up fast, climbing up the stool onto the island, her platform heels looking less that supportive, her glass of wine splashing everywhere as she juggles holding it *and* herself up.

"Be careful," I call, wincing when she slips a little on a wet patch. "Oh Jesus." How much wine has she had?

"Everyone," she declares, throwing her arms up in the air, commanding the room's attention. My smile is very real. Here she is, the illustrious Zinnea Dolly Daydream. "I'm going to sing a little song for you." Esther whoops, and Goldie, oh my days, starts cheering. "For the special couple," she adds, holding an invisible microphone to her mouth. "On the eve of their special day. May there be happiness, love and—"

"No murder," Rose yells, pinning Danny in his place when he looks at her with a dark smile.

The whole room falls apart, including me. It's madness. Complete madness.

"And definitely no murder," Zinnea says on a disbelieving shake of her head before coughing her throat clear and taking another sip of her wine. Courage. There's courage in that glass. I'm willing her to take all the wine she needs, because it's been a long time since she's done this, and her audience is very new.

She bursts into a unique rendition of *I Gotta Feeling* by The Black Eyed Peas and cheers and whoops ring out. She's made my evening. Seeing her like this, performing, in her element, is another form of medicine to me. I watch her, fascinated and content, as she sings her way across the island and back again, stepping over glasses and dishes.

James turns me around to face him. "You need to pack."

"Now?"

"You won't have time tomorrow. The wedding will be all stress and speed."

"Does Danny know about this?" I ask. "I know something is going on, and I know I promised to let you do your thing, but Rose will blow her top if her wedding is ruined."

"The wedding will be beautiful," he says, too confidently.

"You didn't answer my question. Does Danny know about whatever it is you're planning?"

James looks across the kitchen, and I follow his stare until I find Danny. He's looking this way, not immersed in the attention or celebrations.

Thoughtful.

Jesus, what the hell is about to go down?

21

DANNY

I didn't sleep a fucking wink, and not because I'm getting married.

Again.

To the same woman.

It's all just an extravagant smokescreen. The end is near. The best wedding gift I could give Rose is freedom, no matter the cost, no matter the sacrifice. She's had a taste of it. We both have. For three years, we've been lost in a blissful bubble of relaxed island life and coupledom.

James changed that. Actually, technically, Spittle did.

I roll over in bed and bury my face in the pillow, hearing the shower running. It's five thirty. She didn't sleep either, tossing and turning all night, but for very different reasons. She's stressing. I'm not. As far as I'm concerned, she is my wife, my soul, my life, even if a non-inaugurated *someone* "married" us the first time on the beach in St. Lucia three years ago. But Rose demanded it, and what Rose wants, she gets.

Sometimes.

On a groan, I push into the mattress with my fists and get up, stretching as I walk to the bathroom. I open the door and stand on the threshold watching her rinsing her hair of suds, her eyes closed, her head tilted back. There are a million temptations before me—her throat, her boobs, her wet, slippery body, to name just a few. I pout, pinning down my dick as it swells and starts to throb.

"Don't even think about it," she says to the ceiling, carrying on her happy way washing her hair.

My face falls into a frown. "What?"

"I have too much to do." She turns away from me, facing the spray, and scrubs at her face. "I don't have time."

What the fuck? "You don't have time," I say to myself, walking slowly toward the stall, my eyes narrowed, every glorious inch of her calling for me. I step in and seize her, slamming her wet body against the wet tile. "Today is all about us," I whisper, taking a nipple and rolling it between my finger and thumb, amused at the sight of her trying to ignore the rush of desire. "And doing this,' I say, taking my other hand to her pussy and stroking softly, at the same time kissing her neck, "is a massive part of us."

"You shouldn't have even slept in here. It's tradition."

"We're not traditional." My finger slips across her hot flesh.

"Shit, Danny."

"Hmmmm," I hum, sucking and biting at her.

"Stop."

"No."

"Please."

"No."

"But your mo—"

"No." I thrust my fingers into her and watch in satisfaction as her head slams against the wall and her lungs expel endless air. "Enjoying that, baby?"

"Ye—"

"Rose?" My mother's voice infiltrates our moment, and I pull out and back away quickly, alarmed.

"What the hell is my mum doing in here at five thirty?" I ask, reaching for a towel and stepping out, covering myself.

Rose, smiling like a sly cat, saunters out too and pulls on a robe. "I told you. We have lots to do."

"Hello?"

I scowl and fling the door open, finding Mum in workout gear. "You going in the gym?" I ask, looking her up and down.

"I'm dressed for comfort and speed." She tugs at the bottom of her sports tank, looking past me. "Where's Rose?"

Nearly on my cock. "Five thirty, Mum?"

"The ice sculpture is being delivered in half an hour."

"We have an ice sculpture?"

Her hand slaps over her mouth. "No. No ice sculpture." Smiling, she edges past me into the bathroom, claiming Rose and pulling her out. "I've made breakfast."

"Of course you have," I mutter, watching as my mother hauls my wife from the room. "I guess I'll go in the gym." My shoulders drop, my cheeks puff out, and I mutter my way to the chair in the corner of our room, grabbing my shorts and a black t-shirt, pulling them on. After I've shoved my feet into my trainers, I text Brad.

Workout?

Fuck off. I'm not talking to you, DADDY.

See you there.

I head to the gym, the house quiet, obviously—it's five fucking thirty—and stop off in the kitchen to grab a bottle of water. The island is no longer cluttered with used glasses and empty snack bowls, but now decorated with every pastry imaginable. Coffee pots are evenly placed and, of course, a few teapots too. Did Mum actually sleep last night?

Neither my wife nor my mother looks up from the laptop when I enter. "I'm just getting some water," I say, passing them and opening the fridge. No response. "In case I die of thirst," I add, unscrewing the top. Still, nothing, from either of them. "Just popping out to murder someone," I mutter, passing them again on my way out.

"Danny," Mum moans, sounding wholly disapproving. "Not today, please."

I drop my head back, laughing my way out of the kitchen. "Not today, Mother," I call, taking a swig of water as I pass back through the foyer. I look up the stairs when I hear the clicking of . . . heels?

Coming to a slow stop, I watch as Zin . . . Lawrence hurries down, fastening the belt of a silk robe that's embellished with flamingos, his actual real hair suffering a serious case of bedhead, his face free from makeup, but his lashes still unfathomably long and curled. "Morning," I say, making him look up from the careful placement to his kitten-heeled slippers on the marble steps. I smile at his hairy leg poking out of the robe.

"Oh, morning," he says, starting to faff with his short hair, as if he's got someone to impress. "What did I miss?"

"Nothing so urgent you couldn't have taken the time to get your stockings on." I smirk when he rolls his eyes.

"You'll go to hell, Danny Black."

"If I'm lucky," I reply, leaving Lawrence rearranging his robe around his legs. "They're in the kitchen. Brace yourself."

When I near the gym, I hear a constant, loud thumping sound. I push the door open a fraction, looking through the small gap. I catch Beau in the middle of a roundhouse kick. "Jesus," I whisper as the leather punch bag swings, so hard it nearly puts a hole in the ceiling. And she doesn't stop there, proceeding to knock ten tons of shit out of the swinging target, punching, kicking, generally looking like she wants to kill the cow all over again. She eventually lays off, hugging the bag, panting.

I make a point of closing the door loudly but, clearly beat, she only manages to turn her head to find out who's joined her. "I work out alone," I say, wandering over to the bench press.

"Me too," she replies, pushing away from the bag and removing her gloves. "So are you leaving?"

I smile, setting my water on the rubber mat. "What did the bag do to you?" I ask, reaching for a fifty and loading it on one end of the bar. She shouldn't be over-exerting herself like that. She's not my responsibility—I wouldn't ordinarily give two shits —but she and Rose have grown close. And . . . well, that's it.

Beau, out of breath, looks at the punch bag and jabs it lightly with her bare fist. But she ignores my question. "I never got to congratulate you." She doesn't look at me, going to the unit on the far side of the gym and dumping her gloves. "Congratulations."

I study her back as I collect another fifty, splitting my attention between her and the bar. That's not strictly true. She told me she was happy for us. Same thing. "Thanks," I say quietly as she remains facing the wall, unwilling and unable to look at me. I take no pleasure from her pain. None at all. I'm elated, Rose is elated. It's a tricky balance to find a happy medium between that and compassion for Beau and James.

I settle on the bench, pretty fucking stumped. What the fuck do I say to her? "Are you okay, Beau?" I ask, and immediately kick myself. What a stupid fucking question. I saw her when she joined us in the kitchen last night. I watched her embrace Rose and fight with everything she had to show nothing but happiness while on the inside I know she's dying. And I watched James collect her and make their excuses to leave, seeing his girlfriend grow closer and closer to revealing her true emotions. And I ask if she's okay? *Shit.*

"All good," she says, still facing away from me. I see her reach for her face, trying to be discreet with her quiet sniff. My eyes fall briefly to the punch bag. That bag was a number of men. Dexter. The Bear. Her ex. Maybe even her father. She swings around with an air of confidence that I'm so not buying. "Nervous?" she asks, and immediately frowns to herself.

I hitch an interested eyebrow. "Should I be?"

"It's your wedding day." She busies herself with the gloves she just discarded.

Is my wedding what she's actually talking about? Or something else? "What do you know, Beau?" I ask outright.

She eyes me. "Nothing. What do you know?"

"Nothing."

"Then we both know nothing." She smiles, totally fake, and walks away hastily. "Rose needs me."

I lace my fingers, stretching my arms out, my eyes lasers on her back. "See you later," I say quietly, but she hears me, her steps faltering a fraction before she finds her pace again.

Nervous? Can't say I was. Now? *What does she know?*

She meets Brad at the door. "Morning," he says, stopping and following her path as she rushes past.

"Morning," she calls, not looking back.

Brad pouts. "Someone's in a hurry," he muses, pulling the towel from around his neck as he finds me on the bench. He dazzles me with a stupid smile. That's fake too. He's as delighted about today as a pig booked in at a slaughtering house. "Nervous?"

I roll my eyes and fall back to the bench, taking a grip of the bar. "No. You?"

"Depends which part you're talking about." His face appears above me. "Best man duties, or murdering duties?"

"Who are we murdering?" I ask.

"We? No, not *we*. Me. I'm seriously considering murdering *you*."

"No blood at the wedding," I warn, flexing my hold before lifting it out of the anchors. "Rose will go ape."

"Oh, so we should be wary of your wife, but not the megalomaniac with an army of murderers following him through Miami like the Pied-fucking Piper."

I bring the bar down to my chest slowly and ease it back up, repeating twenty times. "Those murderers are dwindling." We've killed half the fuckers at the top and fed them to the sharks. "It's all coming together."

"Right," Brad says, taking the bar and resting it in the holder. "It's all coming together."

I stare up at him, wiping my brow. "Where's James?"

"Why?"

"Can you just answer a fucking question without interrogating me?"

"You don't trust him."

Trust no one. It's what Pops always said. Do I trust James? Did I *ever* trust James? Does he trust me? I'm not sure of anything. "You know I don't trust anyone." I take the bar again. "So where is he?"

"I don't know. I've not seen him this morning."

Good. I pump out another four sets of twenty, have a few jabs at the punchbag, distracted, and row for fifteen minutes. My workout has done nothing to relax me. I collect my water from the mat. "I'm going out on my jet ski."

"Why?" Brad calls, smacking the button on the treadmill to slow down.

For fuck's sake, he's like a woman. "Because it relaxes me."

"So you *are* nervous." The laughter in his voice makes me want to shove the punch bag up his arse sideways.

"Fuck off," I call back, swinging open the door. "Don't forget to decrease the weight on the bar."

"Fuck you," he yells, and I laugh, heading to our room. I'm intercepted on the stairs by Rose, and I take a moment to drink in the sheer stunning beauty of her looking all flustered in a white robe, her hair piled high.

"I need you," she says.

Oh, she can see me? "I need you too, baby," I practically growl, bending and lifting her onto my shoulder.

"Danny!"

I take the stairs urgently before we're interrupted by someone again. I need to let off some steam before I go—

"Rose?" Mum calls.

"Are you fucking kidding me?" I mutter, swinging around to find my mother, who has apparently turned into the sex police, hands on her hips at the bottom of the stairs looking unimpressed.

"Put her down," she warns. "You're not supposed to see her this morning, let alone maul her."

Anyone else in the world who demanded such a thing would be dead in a heartbeat. But my mother? I growl and lower Rose to the step below, showing my mother my displeasure. "She started it," I say childishly.

"I need you to help with something." Rose takes my hand and leads me back down the stairs. God help me, why ever did I agree to this? I rub at my face with the back of my hand. "The tent firm have sent the wrong bulbs."

I'm stumped. "What?" I ask, being dragged into the garden and into the tent, which is now adorned in white. Everything white—the balloons, the flowers, the tablecloths, chairs, even the floor. White. Pure, unblemished, bright white. It's a conscious move on Rose's part.

"The bulbs," she says, pointing up at the twinkle lights draping from the ceiling, going all the way up into the eaves. I smile, being reminded of our favorite restaurant in St. Lucia. "They're the wrong color."

"There is no color." They're standard bulbs giving off a standard light that you'd find in any room in any house.

"Yes, it's apricot light. I asked for white."

My head could explode. "And why do you need me?"

"Well, do you like them?"

"They're lights."

"They're apricot lights."

"Not white lights," I say tiredly, getting a punch in my bicep for my trouble. "Rose, baby, I could not give two fucks what color the lights are." All of this is going over my head. Lights, ice sculptures— "What the fuck is that?" I ask, pointing to a table in the corner.

She pouts. "That's our cake."

"That's a fucking skyscraper," I say, going over to it, my gaze lifting the closer I get to keep the top in my sights. "Jesus," I breathe. It'll take us ten years to get through this thing. "You do realize Barbie and Cindy will swallow it whole if they sniff it out."

"Yes, I realize that, hence they're in their kennels. The company could only deliver at the crack of dawn because it was a short-notice order. They have other cakes to deliver."

I reach forward and drag my finger through the sugar cream.

"Danny!"

"What?" I ask, my finger hanging out of my mouth. Fuck, it's good. I lick my lips as Rose looks at me in exasperation. She needs to chill the fuck out. It's my cake. "Baby, stop stressing." I agreed to this because she deserves an elaborate party where the attention is all on her. My queen. She deserves something normal. If I'd known it would turn her into an anxious mess, I would have denied her. She can't seriously be having fun.

"I'm not stressing." Her shoulders drop, and her gaze goes from worried to warning. "Promise me you've got nothing shady planned today."

"Promise," I say quickly, slamming a kiss on her lips and beating a hasty retreat. "I'm going out on the water," I call, pulling my phone out to check the time. It's not even six fucking thirty and I'm already knackered.

"What?" she yells, coming after me. "Why? What if I need you?"

"You just proved categorically that you don't," I say on a laugh, taking the stairs. "Besides, I could do with some R&R."

"Why, are you nervous?"

I smile too myself as I reach the top of the stairs. "Around you, baby. Always." Who the fuck knows when that pearler of a right hook will be launched? And if she knew what I was going to do now, that fist of hers would fire like a machine gun in my face repeatedly.

After I threw on some gray sweatpants, a white T-shirt, and my trainers, I stopped by my office to collect some cash before I went to my car and found Brad in the passenger seat, still in his gym kit, sweating. I didn't say a word. Neither did he. We drove to the boatyard with Kings of Leon's *Closer* on low, both of us silent. Thoughtful.

When we arrive, Leon's got my ski on the water as instructed.

"Getting nervous about next week?" he asks, grinning as he wedges my Sea-Doo into the sand bed before wading out.

Brad chuckles, earning a dark look. Then he clicks, and my look becomes darker. *Yes, next week.* His head tilts in question. "Where's my wetsuit?" I ask, heading for the cabin, lighting up as I go.

"Hanging on your locker."

"Get mine out," Brad says, following me.

"Yes, B-Boss."

"And my ski."

"Leave it, Leon," I call over my shoulder. "He's not going out on the water today." I make it to the men's changing room and grab my wetsuit, dragging it back outside with me. I meet Brad, who's coming up the steps after me.

"What do you mean, I'm not going out? I want to go out."

"Shut up, you bitch." I head for the yellow container, Brad flanking me, Leon chasing our heels. "You're not going out," I reiterate, taking a key from my back pocket and unlocking the padlock. "And neither am I." I haul the door open, the sound of creaking metal piercing the early morning quiet. "*He* is."

Both Brad and Leon crane their necks to see inside the container. "Who the fuck is that?" Brad asks, taking in the pitiful form of a man tied to a wooden chair with extra strong cable ties.

"I don't know," I admit, pulling a knife from my back pocket. "He won't talk."

"Well, where did you find him?"

"I didn't."

"I did," Leon chirps up, his chest practically swelling with pride. "Trying to break into the ski storeroom."

"With a bag full of explosives," I add, passing Leon my wetsuit and crouching in front of the unknown man. "Still not up for telling me who sent you to plant a bomb on my ski?" It's like déjà-fucking-vu.

"Fucking hell," Brad breathes, raking a hand through his hair and starting to pace outside the container. "What now?"

"Now our little friend here is going for a race on the water." I cut the cable ties and throw him to the floor, pinning him down while Leon and Brad wrestle him into my wetsuit.

"No, please," he yells, squirming.

"Oh, it speaks," I muse. And it's Irish. "Keep the fuck still," I bark, delivering a nose-breaking right hook.

"Ouch." Leon winces, standing back when we're done. "Are you going to do what I think you're going to do?"

"Depends what you think I'm going to do." I nod to Brad to take his other side, and we hoist him to his feet. "There." I give the dribbling, bloodied piece of shit a dazzling smile. "All ready for a morning cruise across the beautiful sparkling water." We start walking him out of the container toward my ski on the water. "Something tells me today is going to be a scorcher."

"No, please. I can't tell you who sent me because I don't know!"

"That's a crying shame."

He goes weightless between Brad and me, lifting his feet from the ground in an attempt to hinder us. Of course, it doesn't. "Please, I beg you."

"So the bomb's on the ski," Brad says as we load him onto my Sea-Doo, his protests coming thick and fast.

I pull more cable ties from my pocket and strap his wrists there, while Leon—God love that kid's initiative—takes care of his legs, weaving rope around his feet and feeding it around the ski. When I'm done, I smile and tap the side of my machine. "Loaded," I chirp. Poor shit's crying now, mumbling nonsensical words to the handlebars. "Did you take care of the steering?" I ask Leon.

"Sure did." He smiles, too fucking proud of himself, pulling out his phone and showing me the screen. "All controlled from here."

"Jesus," Brad says on a light, disbelieving laugh, shaking his head at Leon. "You fix the bomb up too?"

He shrugs, looking unimpressed. "A few wires and a timer. All standard stuff."

"And where's the detonator?"

I slip the key cord into place and start the motor. "I expect someone out there has it." I step back and nod for Leon to gag him, which he does quickly and efficiently. "Bon Voyage."

Leon takes control of the ski, and it chugs slowly out on the water as all three of us stand on the shore, watching. "Take it out as far as you can," I order, glancing around the cove before checking the time.

"Now what?" Brad asks.

"Now Leon gets to have a bit of fun before someone out there presses the button on the detonator." I give the hobo a slap on the back and pull out the twenty-grand wedge from my back pocket, pushing it into his chest. "Good work, kid."

"No problem, D-boss. What about the dude in the other container?"

"Just keep feeding him and watering him." I walk away, Brad on my heels.

"Still nothing on Spittle's son's phone?"

"Not yet." I slip into my Merc, keen to get home and get on with giving my wife the day of her dreams.

I take the stairs slowly, fastening my tie as I do, the sound of my dress shoes hitting the marble echoing around the foyer. The house is quiet. It's a fucking miracle. The women are all upstairs getting ready, the men too, and the garden is packed with people putting the finishing touches in place.

When I make it to my office, I close the door and pour myself a drink, settling in the big chair behind the big desk. My throne. I sink into the leather, close my eyes, and see Pops. He looks proud. He fucking should be.

You got any family, kid?

No, Mister.

Get in the car.

I smile into my darkness and swig back my drink as there's a knock on the wood.

"What?" I call, and a moment later, Daniel's head is poking around the door. He grins, glancing around, hovering on the threshold. "You can come in, kid." With my blessing, he ventures into a room I'm well aware has been a source of fascination to him since he arrived. He quickly looks unimpressed. I don't know what he was expecting to find. A rug drenched in blood? Thank fuck for Goldie, who apparently is always on top of the minor things others forget.

I take him in as he wanders to the chair on the other side of my desk, his suit looking like it was made for him. It was. But the kid needs to learn how to dress. I rise and round the desk. "Stand up," I order, motioning impatiently with my hands. He lifts, looking down as I unfasten his tie and pull at the lengths. "You start here," I say, holding up the ends. "The narrow side shorter than the fat side."

He shrugs. "Beau's unc... aunt tied it."

I smile as I cross one end over the other. "How's your mum?"

"Panicking."

"Why?"

"She's worried the ice sculpture will melt." He jerks, slapping a palm onto his forehead.

"We have an ice sculpture?"

"No. No ice sculpture."

I laugh lightly and push the knot up, wriggling it. "See? That's how you fasten a tie." I brush off his shoulders and fix the lapels of his jacket. "Better."

"Why are you getting married, anyway? You already are." He slumps back down to the chair as I return to mine.

"We're renewing our vows."

"Why?"

"Do you want to ask me something I can answer?"

"Okay." He points to the glass of Scotch before me. "Can I try some?" He smiles cheekily, and I take the tumbler, turning it in slow circles as I regard him. Then I push it across the desk and sit back, watching as he takes it coolly, all Billy Big Bollocks. He takes a healthy mouthful.

And chokes.

"Man, that's disgusting." He gives the glass a filthy look and pushes it back across the desk to me. "Does all alcohol taste like that?"

"Yes."

"I'm never drinking it again." He sticks his tongue out and wipes at it with his palm. "Gross."

"Only real men can drink Scotch, kid. You're not a man. But you will be one day."

"Am I staying with you and Mom until then?" he asks, fiddling with his knot, trying to loosen it.

"What do you want to do?" I ask, hoping for the answer I want and actually need, not only because he's not safe with Hilary and Derek. Daniel's "father" is minus one kneecap and his marriage is on the verge of collapse.

"I like it here," he says, but it's reluctant. "I miss Mom . . . Hilary . . . my other mom and dad, but"—he shrugs—"I dunno."

The kid's not even fourteen yet, so it's no surprise he's struggling to express his emotions. "You feel bad," I say, taking my drink. Guilt. It's written all over his face. He feels guilty for wanting to be here. Take away the crime, of course, and what you have is a mansion with all the trimmings—gym, tennis courts, a pool, cinema room, and a whole lot more. But it's all irrelevant. No kid can survive with only material things. In addition, he has Esther, who faffs and feeds him, two Vikings to take on, who are, apparently, shit hot at Call of Duty, and an army of other father figures around him. This isn't a regular life, but when it's stable, it's a good one, and it's obvious Daniel likes being here. Plus, and what may top it all, it's the safest place for him to be.

"But if I go back, I'd feel bad for Mom. My real mom."

"Your real mum is a warrior," I say, winking, unwilling to tell him that it would break Rose if he chose Hilary and Derek over her. Rose would accept it. But it would kill her. Having Daniel here was never going to be ideal, but I'm working on it.

He smiles. "What happened to your dad?"

"He died."

"I heard he knew Al Capone."

I laugh, and I can't deny it's slightly nervous. Who the fuck told him that? "Al Capone was before my dad's day," I say reaching for the drawer and pulling it open. "My dad would have wiped the floor with Capone." I place the photo of Pops on the desk, smiling at the sight of him—his cream suit, shades, his customary brandy and cigar, his full head of hair, albeit silver.

"That's him?" Daniel asks, claiming the picture and studying it, looking a little awe-struck. "He looks like a movie star."

It's exactly what I thought the day I first saw him getting out of a flashy Merc in a dirty old alley in London. "That's him. The infamous Carlo Black. I called him Mister."

Daniel's eyes shoot up. "And you're kid," he says, his lips stretching into a grin.

"I'm kid." Fuck me, I have a lump growing in my throat. I

clear it and throw back more Scotch, my glass pausing at my mouth when I hear the dogs in the background going ballistic.

"Granny Esther let them out to feed them," he says, and I smile at his fond reference to my mother. Fuck, I hope she's keeping them away from the cake.

"Why are they barking?"

"They don't like the priest," Daniel says.

"Father McMahon's here?"

"Granny Esther's feeding him too."

I laugh under my breath. Everyone around here will be as big as a house if Mum has her way. I reach into my inside pocket and pull out my phone when it rings. "Go throw the ball for Cindy and Barbie for a while," I order him quietly as I stare down at the number, ready to take the call. Ready to end this. "Don't get your suit dirty."

"Sure." Daniel jumps up and speeds out of my office like a whippet, slamming the door behind him.

I flinch and answer my phone. "Leon."

"Your gorgeous jet ski just exploded into a million pieces," he says, sounding mesmerized. "Fuck me, D-Boss."

I'm not surprised. There was enough C-4 to take out a cruise liner. "The time? Exactly."

"Exactly twelve twenty-one."

"Good." I neck the rest of my Scotch and slam my glass on the desk. "Lock up and get your arse over here."

"Why?"

"Because you're invited to my wedding."

"Your wedding's next wee—" He pauses, his brain catching up. "It's not next week."

"You got a suit?"

"No."

Of course he doesn't. Leon's one on those people who

showers daily but always manages to look grubby. "Anything at all?"

"No."

"You'll do as you are." I hang up and fall into thought, my mind running in circles, and when my phone rings, I look down and see a London number. "Hello."

"Black?"

"Depends who's asking."

The guy chuckles. "Eugene Conner," he says. "And I've found your man."

"Where?"

"Panama."

"You're shitting me?"

"I shit you not. He's closer to you than me, mate. I've got men there. We're holding him in a warehouse by the city airport. So what am I doing with him? Killing him? Torturing him?"

"Hold your horses," I say on a laugh. "Can you get him to Miami by tomorrow morning?"

"You owe me," Eugene says, hanging up, just as an email from Brad lands, giving me everything I need to know on the building I followed Shannon to. It confirms what I've learned.

"The fucker," I whisper.

"Who's a fucker?"

I look up and find James in the doorway, my mind so distracted, absorbed, I didn't hear him come in. I shake my head and motion for him to sit, getting up and collecting a bottle and another tumbler. "Nice suit," I say, pouring him a drink and topping myself up. "You rent that?"

"Fuck off," he retorts, making me chuckle. "You nervous?"

Fuck me, anyone would think I had something to be nervous about. "There's only one thing in this world that makes me nervous," I admit, not quite believing I'm divulging this.

James's eyebrows slowly rise, his eyes on me over the rim of his glass. "Rose."

"Rose," I confirm, not surprised he's concluded correctly. I have a feeling James is in the same boat. I lower back to my seat. "Whether she loves me, whether she always will, whether she's safe." The corner of my mouth lifts. "Whether she's angry." I toast the air. "To the women who make us nervous."

"Cheers." He necks his drink.

"What's it like out there?" I ask, nodding to the door.

"Busy. It's a fucking big affair for a wedding with very few guests."

Our private ceremony on the beach in St. Lucia was hardly legit. And really, the only thing that makes today any different is Father McMahon taking the service. "And how's that front looking for you and Beau?"

James falters as he lowers his glass to the desk. "It's not been mentioned."

"And you need it? Marriage, I mean."

His smile is ironic. "It just feels more final."

"More end than don't."

"So why did you succumb to the institution of holy matrimony?" he asks, sitting back, getting comfortable.

It's a good question, one I've thought about endlessly over the past few years. I didn't need it to know Rose is mine. She was mine before I got a ring on her finger. Since she was a girl, Rose was alone. No family, nothing, and her baby was stolen from her. "I think subconsciously I was trying to offer her stability. Promise her something that could never be taken away, whether stolen or killed." I plan on keeping that promise.

"That sounds reasonable." He rests his elbow on the arm of the chair, skimming his chin with the side of his finger. He's digging deep for his reasoning. Not that it matters. They won't be getting married.

I lean across my desk and fill his glass back up, the chink of the bottle on the side rousing him from his daydream.

"I'm taking Rose to St. Lucia tomorrow night." And hopefully we won't be coming back.

James's eyes narrow a fraction. "You're talking like the job's done."

"It will be," I assure him. "Let's go skiing tomorrow morning."

"Why?"

"I want to show you something."

His jaw starts to roll, his impatience thick. "Talk, Danny."

"We found Brunelli."

His impatience transforms into something far more deadly. "Where?"

I hold a finger up. "We agreed. No business today, or it's *your* funeral." No one needs to know about my little dabble with some C-4.

We both look at the door when it opens and Brad enters, all suited and booted. He immediately finds me, his eyes questioning. I give him a nod that he reads well, his inhale subtle, but his eyes? They're loaded with fury.

"I need a few minutes on my own," I say, reaching for the Scotch again, turning it one way, then the other, studying the still liquid. Neither of them speak, both leaving quietly. But James is definitely on edge, and he has every right to be.

I find the picture of Pops and look straight into his eyes. "Don't trust anyone," I whisper, pulling up a number and glancing at the clock, dialing, and taking my phone to my ear, getting up and pacing slowly back and forth.

I wait a few seconds for him to speak. He doesn't. Of course he doesn't. He's currently on the other end of the line wondering, fearing, if Danny Black has returned from the dead once again. "Surprise," I say lowly, my lip naturally curling. "Sorry, I couldn't die today. I'm getting married next week, I'm sure you've heard." Still, nothing. It's a standoff, a stupid fucking play for power. He can have the power, just for now. I've got a wedding to get to *today*. "So this is how it's going to be played, huh?" I ask. "Are you going to carry on blowing up things in Miami until you hit your target?" Still, he doesn't speak, and I fucking hate that it's getting under my skin. Not even the shock of me still breathing got him talking. Let's get this fucking done with. "I want some guarantees."

"What?"

"Peace and freedom for me and my family. I leave Miami, you will never hear from me again, and I don't ever want to hear from you."

"Done."

"And I want to know who you are," I add. "If I'm giving you The Enigma, you give me your identity. That's my only way of guaranteeing my freedom." I cannot leave Miami not knowing who this bastard is. "That's my only way of ensuring my family's safety."

He inhales, the distorter muffling. "Okay."

He's weighed up his options, and it didn't take long. My offer is the best he'll get. He knows that, and I can't keep dodging death, because there will come a time when it won't be dodged. "There's a green container at my boatyard. I'm sure you know where it is. He'll be in there at seven tomorrow morning. I'll make sure of it."

"Why the change of heart?"

I look at the door where my family is beyond. I see Daniel. See my wife sleeping peacefully in our bed in St. Lucia. She hasn't slept like that since we got here. Uninterrupted. All through the night. And I see the image in my mind of my baby on the monitor. But I don't need my enemies knowing I have another Achilles heel on the way.

I don't answer, hanging up and staring at the painting hanging over my safe. I walk across and pull it down, turning the dial until it clicks open. I reach in and pull out a VP9, checking the magazine before replacing it, getting the painting back on the wall just as Daniel bursts into my office. "It's time, Mister."

"On my way, kid."

22

ROSE

The dress is my taste, and it's what I like. Just enough flesh revealed and off the shoulder. My tall body feels comfortable in the floor-sweeping, figure-hugging silk gown, and the shade of red is not *whore* red. It's classy red. It's not tarty.

Because I'm not a tart anymore.

I love it. Danny will love it, and, more than that, he will love what me in this dress symbolizes.

Freedom.

It represents control, but not *being* controlled. Ironic, really, since my love for Danny absolutely rules me. But not him. He will never control me. And to pay homage to the fact that no man will ever control me again, I'm standing outside the tent alone, just as Danny said I would. In my long red gown. That I chose all by myself.

I smile, brushing my bare hands down the silk. No flowers. Empty hands because I don't need to cling to anything anymore. Clinging suggests a fear of it being taken away. Nothing will be taken from me. Not this day. Not my beautiful son, who I saw walking back down the aisle once he'd seen me and blown me a kiss. *God, I love that kid.*

Not my beloved, death-dealing groom, who texted me a picture of the queen of hearts half hour ago.

I approach the pergola arching the entrance on steady legs. The smell of honeysuckle is potent. The entire inside space comes into my sights, but I see nothing except him, his back to me, his tall, dangerous body adorned in the finest black suit, his dark hair still on the longer side, small locks flicking out here and there. My masterpiece. Deadly in every sense of the word.

Only when Nina Simone's *I put a Spell on You* starts does he look over his shoulder, a wry smile on his insanely handsome face. A small laugh escapes me as everyone else turns to see me.

"I'll ask this only once," Danny calls, his face full of expectancy as his whole body turns leisurely to face me. "Do you want to be mine?"

My heart constricts but feels like it bursts all at the same time. Could I love him more? "I want to be yours."

"Then what the fuck are you doing just standing there, woman?" he asks, making Father McMahon balk a little and everyone else laugh. And so he sets the tone for our wedding, lifting his hand for me to go to him, which I do. There's no lazy, lengthened wander down the aisle. No taking my time for people to take me in. If I wasn't in heels, I'd probably sprint to him, but I am, so I take a safer walk, reaching him in no time, with still virtually the whole track to play. He takes my hand and tugs me into his body, putting his mouth to my ear. "You. Are. Exquisite," he whispers, starting to sway us, turning us in circles, pulling back to get me in his sights. And so is he. Trimmed, even stubble, his scar prominent, his eyes bright with happiness rather than coldness. I'm one of only three people in this world who gets this side of Danny Black. Soon, it will be four people.

He is oblivious to Father McMahon and the congregation watching and waiting. "Tell me you love me," he says.

"I love you."

"Tell me you trust me."

"I trust you."

"Tell me you're happy."

I laugh, and he nudges me for an answer, his smirk matching mine. "I'm so, so, *so* happy." I link my arms over his shoulders, lacing my fingers together on his nape.

"I think you're crazy," he murmurs.

"I think you're mine," I reply.

"I think you're beautiful."

"I think you're mine."

"I think I hate you more than I've ever hated you before."

I circle his nose. "I think you're mine," I whisper back.

"Do I have a choice?"

I take his hand and lay it over my stomach. "What do you think?"

His smile is one of those smiles that doesn't fit his deadly persona, as he looks at my stomach. "I think you want a crazy, murdering, depraved arse to be your baby daddy."

I laugh, and it's unstoppable. "Whose name is Danny Black."

"Whose name is Danny Black," he confirms. "You ready?"

I nod, looking past him, seeing Beau sitting close to James, her palm resting on his thigh, his hand covering hers. Her smile is small but there. Her damaged arm covered. My happiness suddenly feels so incredibly wrong, and my heart breaks for my friend, especially when she mildly shakes her head at me, silently willing me not to feel sorry for her. Impossible. I feel like I'm standing here with everything I *never* dared dream of, while Beau continues her battle to comes to terms with what she has lost.

23

JAMES

I have never in my life been to a wedding, but I'm pretty sure this is not how they're done. Then again, I've not been living in a normal world for some time, least of all now. Regardless, it was a beautiful service. It was personal, almost private, and as I sat there with Beau close to my side watching Danny and Rose doing their thing, oblivious to the small congregation of family and friends, all I could think about was how hopeless I feel. I've experienced pain of unthinkable levels, but knowing Beau is hurting for reasons other than her mother's death and her uncle's betrayal is raw agony. The former I can and plan on fixing. The latter I have no clue how to right. And the helplessness only emphasizes the rage inside. I need to channel that energy before it consumes me.

There's one grand round table in the room. One table seating everyone. This isn't a big wedding in the sense of guests, but colossal in the sense of lavishness and expense. It's like an elaborate dinner party with friends. The food—all eight courses

Goldie?

"What do you think?" James asks sardonically. "If she knew the root of her trauma had been found, she wouldn't be out there relaxed, drinking, and wearing a fucking dress, would she? She'd be kitted out in everything she needed to torture a man to death." James looks at me, clearly stressed out, and I can't help but wonder if it's because he'd like to make a mess of him too. What the fuck did this guy do to Goldie to warrant such stress and fury? "I strongly advise you to get Brunelli the fuck out of here," James continues, helping himself to a drink. "Unless you want your wedding to be a bloodbath, because that's exactly what it'll be if Goldie sniffs him out."

Something tells me it could be a bloodbath if I let James at him too.

"What did he do to her?" Brad asks, looking between both James and Otto for an answer. The tension levels are through the roof.

Yes, what did . . .

It hits me, and I inhale, standing back, an unstoppable shudder coursing through me. "He raped her," I say quietly.

James's jaw has gone into spasm, his hand shaking as he carries the glass to his mouth, his eyes glazing. "I found her in an alleyway beaten black and blue. I intervened, gave him a few digs, but he got away."

A few digs? I bet. My jaw starts twitching wildly too. I need to contain James *and* myself. "Fuck," I hiss, discarding my glass and going to the door, swinging it open. I don't know much, but I do know time isn't on our side right now. I can't sit and wait for him to be brought to my office. "No one touches him," I warn, making my way to the entrance of my house, swinging the door open. Len is just coming up the steps, two rough-looking fuckers tailing him, and between them, a pitiful looking bloke with scraggy hair and a scrawny body. Inappropriately, I imagine the fucker trying to get handy with Goldie now. She'd crush him. And, God help me, I want to see that. "Get him back in the car," I order curtly, making the two guys stop in their tracks.

"What?" one asks, looking mighty inconvenienced. He has nothing on me. "We were told to bring him here."

Jesus, Conner is one efficient man, I'll give him that, but I gave him explicit instructions for a fucking reason. "It's my wedding day, and I made a promise to my wife I'd be conducting no *business*. If you two fuckers make me break that promise, I won't think twice about setting her on you."

"Who are you?" Brunelli demands, his bony face twisting. "Why the fuck am I here?" He bucks and wriggles, yelling his protest, and I feel my nostrils flare, anger rising.

"Get him in the fucking car," I hiss, looking back at the house, checking the coast is clear.

They start to back up, and I see James in my side vision moving in. I throw my arm out to stop him passing, facing him, forcing him to look at me. "He's Goldie's," I remind him, hoping the words cut through the red mist. "Tomorrow, he's Goldie's."

Otto lends a hand, taking James's arm and easing him back. "Come on, Kel," he says.

"Get Leon," I say to Brad, and he goes straight to his phone as Len ushers the men back into their car with Brunelli. "Anyone got eyes on Rose?"

"I'll go," James says, backing away, being sensible, leaving me to deal with this.

"Leon's on his way," Brad calls, just as the kid himself darts around the corner, Jerry plodding along as fast as he can behind him.

"Rose and Beau are suspicious," he says, slightly out of breath. "What's going on?"

"Len's gonna drive you to the boatyard." I put my hand out,

and a gun lands in my palm courtesy of Ringo. I pick up Leon's hand and put it in his grasp. "The guy in the car, the skinny fucker, I want you to put him in a container, you got that?"

He stares down at the gun, mesmerized. "Got it, D-boss."

"Only shoot him if it's you or him, okay? We need him alive."

Leon nods, and I gently push him toward the car, giving Len a nod. He knows what to do. "Now, can I get back to my wedding?"

"Yes, please do," Rose says, making every hair on the back of my neck rise. *Shit.* I throw Conner's men a dark look, and they speed up their departure, looking past me full of caution.

"I need the restroom," Brad says, making a hasty getaway.

"Yeah, me too," Ringo grunts, following.

"Wait for me," Otto calls, leaving me alone with Rose.

I look up to the heavens for some backup, before pulling a smile from nowhere and facing her. She's a fucking vision, a blazing, beautiful vision in red, and everything about her gown sets my insides alight. "Baby," I purr, arms out, beckoning her to me.

She doesn't entertain me. "You're in trouble, Black."

I pout. "It wasn't my fault." I start to plead my innocence, daring to get closer. "I swear, it was unexpected. I've sent them away. I'll deal with it another time."

She looks past me to the cars driving away. "Who was it?"

I decide to tell the truth, even if, selfishly, it's tactical. "It was the man who raped Goldie."

As expected, she looks at me in horror. "What?"

I shrug. "James asked me to find him. I asked an associate in London to look into it. Turns out the guy was in Panama." I thumb over my shoulder. "I only found out this morning. I didn't think they'd turn up with him today."

"What are you going to do?"

I have no idea why she's asking. Given my history, she knows full well what happens to a rapist if they're unfortunate enough to cross my path. Admittedly, I would have taken the greatest of pleasure in ending him, might have even risked the wrath of my wife on our special day to do it. But Brunelli is Goldie's demon to end. Not mine. Not James's. "What am I going to do?" I ask, swooping in and claiming her, feeling her soften in my arms. "Nothing."

Her suspicion is warranted as she leans back, letting me kiss her front, from her throat to her belly. "I don't believe you."

"He's not my demon, baby." I look up at her. "She doesn't know we've found him yet. Let's keep it that way." Goldie, the uptight she-warrior, is as carefree as I've ever seen her. She needs that. Uninterrupted time to let her hair down, wear a dress, and drink without fear of attack.

Rose smiles, her compassion and understanding shining through. It's just another reason why I'm infatuated with her. "She's like another woman." She takes my arms, squeezing my biceps as I haul her back up. "I need to give you your gift."

"Anything to do with the big crate out back that's covered in sheeting?"

"You saw it?"

"You can't miss it." I throw an arm over her shoulder and lead her to where I know it to be. "I bet it's not an ice sculpture," I quip, my face straight, earning an elbow in my side. I have to admit, though, I'm dead curious about what this illusive ice sculpture actually is.

"Are you ready?" she asks, breaking free from me and taking the edge of the cover.

I slip my hands into my pockets, relaxed, smiling on the inside at her excitement. "Ready," I confirm, and she whips off the cover revealing a live-sized imitation of my jet ski. I let out a puff of laughter, as I wander around it, taking in the incredible detail. It's all accounted for, the art, the streamline curves, even the controls on the handlebars. I smile, reaching the back and dropping to my haunches, finding what I knew I would.

Danny.

Just *Danny*.

Because that is who I am to Rose. Not The Brit. Not The Angel-faced Assassin. Not Mister, Kid, a monster, or a murderer.

Just . . . Danny.

Ironic that my actual ski is probably still smoking as I stare at a frozen version of my machine. I rise again, doing another lap, taking in the detail, how it sparkles, my hand running over the ice. It's beautiful, mesmerizing. Like a massive fucking diamond.

I would admire it all day if . . .

I peek at Rose, and the subtle concave of her chest tells me she's read my mind. I jerk my head in order, and she drops the cover, sauntering over, slipping the top half of her dress off and pushing it to her waist, and as soon as she's within reach, I seize her. "Consummation?" I whisper, making her bite her lip through a small grin.

She pushes her naked breasts into my chest, and I reach out and place a hand on the beautiful ice sculpture, holding it there for a few moments before cupping her boob. "Ready?"

She inhales sharply. "Yes." Her desire-drenched voice sends more blood to my dick. I need to get us out of sight quickly. I grab her hand and haul her through the doors, pacing to my office urgently, aware that Rose is half naked.

I lock the door and fall to the couch, lifting my arse to push my trousers down, settling back down on a gulp. I offer my hand and her lips press together as she takes it, lifting the bottom of her dress and climbing up onto my lap, settling. I blow out my cheeks and grit my teeth as she rises to give me room. I circle my cock, move her knickers aside, and nod for her to lower, which she does with exquisite precision, my erection sinking into the mind-blowing heat of her pussy. I groan, my shakes instant. "Jesus, Rose," I mumble, taking her hips, my gaze hooded and low. The contrast of fire and ice is intoxicating. Invigorating. I push my face into her chest and take a few deep breaths, bracing myself, the veins in my dick throbbing. And then I lift her and pull her down hard on a gruff bawl, and the pace is set. Lift, drop, over and over, the sensations sending me into orbit.

She cries out, her fingers hooking into my shoulders, bunching the material.

"Hold on, baby," I order roughly, lifting and banging her down constantly and consistently, every pound spiking a yell from me and a whimper from Rose. I look up at her through my drowsy eyes, hypnotized, her expression of raw ecstasy the best gift of all. Her eyes are wide, revealing endless sparks of light. Of love. I feel like my heart could explode.

And my dick.

I start grinding on each thrust, knowing I'm close, and she grabs the hair at my temples, her jaw tight. She nods, air bursts out of me, and as soon as she stiffens, I let it happen, jerking as I reach the pinnacle of pleasure, my head exploding along with my cock. "Ohhhh, fuck," I wheeze, blinking back the stars in my vision, desperate to see her face as she tips the edge. Her eyes are squeezed shut, her arms braced against my shoulders, her fists clenched, holding on for dear life. "Rose," I garble.

"Yes!"

Fucking hell, she's still riding high. I grit my teeth, starting to spasm, fighting through the unthinkable pleasure and sensitivity. "Rose," I bark.

She starts to yank and tug at my jacket, her chest pumping,

and she peels her eyes open, finding my eyes. "Oh God," she says on an exhale falling forward into me.

"Yes," I confirm, resting my head back, getting my breathing under control. She circles her nose with mine. "I love you," she whispers, and then she licks the length of my scar.

It's tingling madly. And not because my wife's tongue is there.

ROSE

He carries me draped across his arms into the tent, and everyone cheers our return, getting up from their seats.

"Time for our first dance," he says, setting me on my feet and pulling me into his chest. He looks at me gently as *Let Me Touch Your Fire* by A R I Z O N A begins, and I smile at him, falling into the gentle sway of his body. And it's perfect. The track, our closeness, the way he's looking at me. It's not the first time I've thought how crazy it is that I'm the safest woman alive in the arms of one of the most dangerous men alive. Totally crazy. And yet here I am, safe, and head over heels, madly in love with the man who took me as collateral not so long ago. The man who slapped my face. The man who held a gun to my head and threatened to pull the trigger. It didn't take me long to figure out that an element of his uncontainable rage and temper was because of his mixed emotions toward me. His prisoner. Or *guest*, as he so eloquently put it. But he ended up saving my life instead of ending it. I did the same for him.

His icy eyes shine down at me, his face expressionless, a lock of his dark hair falling across his forehead, still damp from sweat. His scar glows. His stubble looks rough.

And he's perfect.

Overcome with so much fucking love for him, I drape my arms over his shoulders and bring our faces closer. "I love you," I whisper, kissing his scar. He's fire. Bright, beautiful, and dangerous. But more than that, he is irrefutably mine.

He shifts his hands to my ass, getting a possessive hold, hunkering down a fraction. "I fucking hate you too." Moving in, he kisses me like there is no audience, consuming me whole in typical Danny style as we sway, hardly moving at all.

I come out of my stupor when he breaks away, and I sigh, nestling my face into his shoulder. Something catches my eye, and my contented smile falls. "Oh God." I only mean to think the despairing thought, but by the feeling of Danny's body stiffening against me, I've spoken it. He makes to pull away, but I hold on to him tighter. "Let's stay like this," I suggest, way too enthusiastically, trying to get him swaying again.

"What the fuck's wrong, Rose?" he asks, demanding, his voice one I know never to mess with. *Shit, he's going to kill.*

I take in air, pressing my lips together, pulling out and facing his straight face that's a whisper from transforming into anger. "Um," I peek past him again briefly, cringing. "Do not react," I demand, taking his jaw and directing his face to mine when he tries to look over his shoulder.

"You're beginning to piss me off."

"Your mom's dancing with Otto."

The widening of his eyes tells me all I need to know, and I quickly scan the vicinity for backup, holding on to him. "No, she fucking isn't," he growls, gently prizing me away.

"Hey," I snap, yanking him back into me aggressively, forcing him to look at me. "Leave it," I warn, trying my hardest to meet his fierce expression.

"Or else?" he asks, somewhere between interested and caution.

"Or else you'll be sleeping with the dogs."

He recoils, stunned, but I stand firm. "Pardon me?"

"You heard, Black." I settle back into his shoulder. "She's not just your mother, she's a woman." A very attractive woman, still in her prime. I find them again on the dance floor, smiling as Otto whisks her gently around. She's laughing, her face alive, her smile so bright. And in that oyster gown, she looks incredible. She has a banging body for a woman her age. It was only a matter of time before a man plucked up the courage to make a move. Hats off to Otto. "You will leave it."

"Okay," Danny agrees quietly. "But just keep me facing this way."

I relax, my worry stowed for now, because there's not a chance in hell Danny's thoughts on it will go unsaid. I spy Beau guiding a reluctant James to the floor, the man looking as uncomfortable as a man could be. But he'll dance with her. He'd do anything for her. And her world revolves around him. *God, she needs some joy though.* She tucks herself into his front, her cheek under his neck, his hand stroking up and down the material of her scarred arm. She looks peaceful. I hate that it's a veil.

I watch them, feeling their despair as well as I've ever felt my own. James pulls back, his chin hitting his chest to look down at her. Did she just stagger? I frown, and it happens again. Mild, but a definite totter on her heels. "I think Beau's drunk," I say, linking my arm around Danny's neck, unable to get close enough to him, remembering the one and only time I've seen him absolutely inebriated. It was heartbreaking. It was relieving. It was the moment I unequivocally knew I was soul crushingly in love with the monster. But it was only soul crushing because I didn't think I could have him and every devastating piece of him.

Yet here I am. I have the monster. I have my lost boy. I have our baby growing in my tummy.

All in a red dress that I love.

I don't know whether it's because it's the first time today that I've had to think, but I wonder with reluctance whether this is the calm before the storm. "Thank you for an amazing day," I whisper. He doesn't answer, just holds me closer. But what happens tomorrow? I can't forget Danny's words. He has a way out. When might that happen? Do I want to know? Do I *need* to know? Damn my curiosity. "What's the way out, Danny?" I ask, mentally scorning myself and my need.

"Shhhh," he says, all soothing, rubbing his face into the crook of my neck. It doesn't ease me at all. The fear is deep, and it's rising. He can hardly blame me after what I went through the last time he found a way out.

"Danny, I want to know." I need to prepare.

"No, you don't."

"I do," I grate, getting fired up. "I *need* to know."

He shakes his head. "No, Rose."

"Danny, tell me." The more he evades me, refusing me information, the more I'll worry. The more the fear is stoked. I wrench myself away and look at him. His expression is cut. Frustration. Annoyance. I stand firm. "Tell me."

"No."

"Damn it, Danny," I hiss, trying to keep my anger and volume contained. "Tell me."

"Fine," he snaps, moving in and yanking me to his body violently. "For our peace, for you, me, Daniel, and our baby to walk away from this fucking shitstorm," he says quietly, everything about his persona and words hiking up my dread. "He wants James."

My heart slows in my chest, my eyes darting to Beau and James on the dance floor. "What?" I murmur, my body refusing to move now, our swaying bodies static.

"That's our way out." Danny holds me with one arm, and the next thing I know, Daniel's with us, and Danny has his arms around all of us. All *three* of us. I kiss his head and then look at my husband. *Adoration. Reverence.* That's what I see in his expression. Love for his wife and children.

I swallow my despair that dwells alongside my joy. The possessiveness and protection he's exuding is potent.

Determination.

He'll do anything to keep us safe.

JAMES

I need her on form tomorrow. I need her head clear and her mind straight. A hangover is not the way forward, but I can't deny her that sense of freedom, even if it's temporary. It started with a stagger. A few sways. Now, I'm virtually holding her up. "I think it's time for bed," I say diplomatically.

"I'm not drunk," she slurs, slumped against my body.

"Sure you're not," I say on a sigh, taking her chin and directing her heavy head up. Her eyes are rolling. She's not just drunk, she's plastered. Drink her way through it. It was the only way. "Come on." I turn her and scoop her up.

"I want to dance," she protests, her limp arm shooting out and pointing to the cake.

She can hardly stand, let alone dance. "You can dance in your dreams."

She pouts as Rose slips away from Danny, joining us. "Bedtime?" she asks, eyeing Beau.

"Probably about an hour ago," I confirm. "Goodnight."

"Night," Rose says softly, smiling sadly at her friend. "Love you, Beau," she adds, and I frown, looking back as I carry Beau out of the tent. Danny moves in and takes Rose's arm, pulling her gently back onto the dance floor.

"Balloons," Beau sings, coming to life, scrambling in my arms. "Shoe."

"What?"

"My shoe. I need a shoe."

I drop her, confused, and hold her while she removes one of her strappy heels. "Freeze, motherfucker," she yells, swaying, swiping out her arm.

"What are you doing?"

"Freeze!" She lunges forward and swings at the balloons, popping one. She jumps out of her skin. "Don't move." She swipes again, the move making her spin, and I grab her quickly before she face-plants. "Stay exactly where you are," she yells, fighting her way toward the arch and lashing out. Balloons pop left and right, and she laughs.

What the fuck?

"Okay, it's definitely time for bed." Sweeping her up and confiscating her shoe, I head inside and take the stairs, Beau bobbing in my arms. I make it to the bedroom without her throwing up, which is a fucking achievement. I sit her on the bed and start to strip her down. "Water?" I ask.

"No. Take me back to the party," she demands, trying to get up. I don't even need to try and stop her, her uncooperative body doing that for me.

"Painkillers?"

"No, they don't work." She squints, trying to see me. "I want to marry you."

I smile as I peel her dress up over her head, tossing it aside. "Then ask me."

"Will you marry me?"

"In a heartbeat," I reply, reaching back for her bra and unclasping it as she sways.

"Good. I want a baby."

I swallow, nodding as I draw the lace down her arms. "Then ask me."

"Can we have a baby?" she slurs, her uncoordinated arm reaching for my face. I drop her bra and let her feel me. "Can we?"

"As many as you want," I whisper, gazing into her drunken eyes. "Anything else?"

"I want to live where the sun always shines. I want to see you every day, love you, look after you, grow old with you."

God, I love this woman. If only she was always so honest. There's no mention of revenge. No mention of death. And as I look at her now, totally inebriated, I see no darkness in her. Only life and hope.

She wants that life? She can have it. All of it.

Just as soon as I've dealt with tomorrow.

I've never seen Beau drunk. It was oddly calming, even if her happiness, her dancing, her laughs, were a temporary mask. But seeing her like that last night made me see the woman underneath all the pain. The woman she wants to be and, God, the woman *I* want her to be.

Smiling. Happy. Content. Honest.

I prop myself up on my elbow, seizing the opportunity to study her closely, stroking through her hair, taking in every inch of her serene face. She's dead to the world, and no doubt will be for a while. It's a blessing.

I lower my mouth to her cheek and breathe her into me. "I love you," I whisper, mentally promising to be back before she wakes up. She'll need painkillers. A hand to hold while she walks to the bathroom. Help brushing her teeth. Water. A hug. Sunshine on her face. I'll give her it all.

After I pull the sheet up her back, tucking her in, I rip myself away, getting up and going to the bathroom. I don't bother showering, as I'll shower after we've been out on the water. Fuck knows, I need it to clear my head. I slip into some sweatpants, a zip-up hoodie, and get some trainers on, pulling a baseball cap on as I leave our room, forcing myself not to look back. *Do. Not. Look. Back.*

Closing the door quietly, I glance at my watch as I walk through the house, reaching the top of the stairs to find Danny emerging from the corridor that leads to his office, his hands in the back of his jeans where he's inevitably just tucked his gun. And to demonstrate that I'm on the same page, I pull mine out and check the magazine.

"Ready?" he asks on a knowing smile, going to the door and pulling it open.

"Are you?" I counter, passing him, not bothering to tuck my gun away. I'll feel better with it in my hand.

"I'm ready," he confirms, falling into stride beside me, looking at me out of the corner of his eye. "It's a blinding morning to go out on the water."

"I agree." We arrive at the Merc. "I assume you're driving."

"Would you rather?" he asks, all civil and nice, letting a small smile loose as he holds up the keys.

"No, I'd rather admire the view." I swing the door open, falling into the seat, and rest my gun on my thigh. Nothing would make me relinquish my hold. "Lovely day yesterday," I muse, seeing the tent still up, the balloons framing the entrance now looking droopy and sad, some gone completely. I allow a secret smile, remembering Beau stabbing at them with the heel of her shoe, slurring cop talk. *Freeze, motherfucker. Don't move. Stay exactly where you are. Bang. Bang. Bang.*

And banging is going to be her head when she wakes up. "Put your foot down," I say quietly, as Danny crawls along the drive to the gates.

"You in a hurry?"

"Yeah. As it happens, I am."

"She was pretty wasted last night."

I feel him looking across the car at me, but I keep my eyes forward, seeing one of his men come out of the gatehouse and hold a hand up. Beau was more than wasted. She was fucking obliterated. "A lot on her mind." I'm not telling him anything he doesn't already know.

"Haven't we all," he replies quietly, returning his attention to the road and accelerating once we're out of the mansion's grounds.

The drive is silent, uncomfortably so, both of us clearly distracted. That's not a good thing. Being distracted is never a good thing.

As we rumble down the dirt track toward the boatyard, I instinctively scope the overgrowth, on my guard.

"What's up?" Danny asks, obviously sensing my cautiousness.

"Something doesn't feel right." My hand flexes around the handle of my gun, my eyes high and low.

He chuckles, and it's fucking irritating. "In our world, James, we should always be on our guard."

I exhale, turning a cold look his way. "And isn't that the fucking point?" I ask, taming my twitching trigger finger. "I don't want to be on my guard anymore." I don't want to be full of worry every time I leave Beau's side. I don't want to be looking over my shoulder constantly. Doubting everyone. Suspicious of everything. It's fucking exhausting, and I resent having to waste my energy on it when I could be using that energy elsewhere. Like on Beau. On life, not fucking death all the time.

"It's a settling notion, isn't it?" he says as we roll to a stop by the cabin. "Imagining a life without danger." Looking across at me, he turns in his seat slightly. "I had it for three years. I highly recommend it. And I would do *anything* to get it back."

I nod, understanding him, and take the handle of the door, getting out and breathing in the fresh morning air, as Danny gets out and lights up. "Which one is Brunelli in?" I ask, scanning the containers.

"Don't do it," he warns, blowing out the smoke, the heat hitting the cool air creating a dense cloud above his head. "He's Goldie's. We agreed."

"Which one," I ask again, my words tight.

He points with his cigarette, his head shaking mildly as he takes an extra-long drag of his smoke. "The green one."

I stalk toward the green container, my pace even, my heart rate surprisingly steady. "I'll leave him breathing," I call back, noting the padlock on the door. A padlock that's unlocked. I look back at Danny. He's leaning against the bonnet of his Merc, puffing his way through his cigarette.

"Hurry up," he shouts over. "I want to get out on the water."

I take the handle, slowly pull open the door, and scan the inside. No Brunelli. I'm not surprised. But the Heckler pressed into my forehead?

Now that's another story.

BEAU

Oh, good God. I squint my eyes open, feeling like I've got a mouthful of sand and someone stamping on my head. My face is squished into the pillow, my hands buried beneath. I shift. It hurts, my tiny movement creating a tremor that seems to sail through me and finish in my head with a bang.

Closing my eyes, I give up trying to move, and relax. That hurts too. I'm never, ever drinking again. Teeny tiny snippets of last night start to filter into my banging brain. The dancing. The shots. My own personal shoot-out with a load of harmless balloons. *Oh God.* James carrying me to bed. Stripping my uncooperative body down while I protested and demanded he take me back to the party. I was having such an amazing time. I was happy, content, free. I would swear up and down I want those feelings of uninhibitedness back, but if this is the aftermath?

"Ouch," I murmur, gingerly negotiating my body up. I place my bare feet on the soft carpet. *Bang.* I lift my ass off the bed.

Bang. I rise to standing. *Bang.* I take a couple of steps toward the bathroom.

Bang, bang, bang.

"Oh, God help me," I mumble, folding to the floor, the effort to walk too much for my delicate body. I get to my hands and knees and crawl butt naked to the bathroom, the bangs more bearable. Just.

I make it to the shower, pull myself up the glass panel and flip it on, then feel my way around the room until I'm in front of the mirror that hangs over the sink. "Good lord." I look haggard. Absolutely shocking. I snatch my toothbrush from the holder and slather it in paste, shoving it in my mouth and scrubbing the taste of stale alcohol away. Two long swigs of mouthwash, a splash of cold water on my face. I brace my hands on the edge of the sink, my breathing shallow. And I pull up, carefully treading my way back to the bathroom door. The bed is empty. He probably couldn't stand the smell of me anymore or my snoring. Oh, God, was I snoring?

I cringe my way to the shower—a combination of embarrassment and pain—and step inside. I'm a statue under the spray, without the energy to even wash myself down. I'll stay here all day. Just stand here and be rained on.

"Beau!"

I jump, startled, and swing around too fast, having to grab the glass panel to hold myself up. I wipe the water away and find Rose snatching a towel down from the rail, thrusting it toward me. "What's going on?" I ask.

"We have to go," she blurts, flapping out the towel and holding it up. "Come on. Hurry up."

"Go where?" I step into the white cotton and wrap myself up.

"The boatyard."

"Why?"

"We just have to!" She races out of the bathroom, leaving me to follow, confused.

"Rose, what's wrong?" I ask, making her stall at the door. She turns, her eyes welling, her lip wobbling. I retreat a few steps, not liking that look on her.

"Danny and James are gone."

I frown, but it soon hits me, a memory muscling past the fog. "They've gone out on the jet skis." Is this a case of pregnancy emotions? She's acting crazy. Completely unreasonable.

She shakes her head, her eyes dropping like rocks to her feet. "We need to go."

A horrible, awful feeling comes over me, and I step forward. "Rose?"

"Please, Beau, can we just go?"

"Tell me what's going on," I order calmly, feeling anything but.

I see her visibly swallow, building up the courage to spill whatever it is she knows. "I think Danny's going to do something stupid." She moves back, putting herself in the corridor.

Stupid. My brain feels like it has an electric shock, more memories coming to me. My eyes dart across the carpet at my bare feet, things slowly clicking together. "He said he's taking you to St. Lucia today," I tell her, looking up, not at all bothered if I've ruined a surprise. What the fuck is going on that Rose is clearly struggling to tell me? "James told me to pack." I move forward, not meaning to appear threatening, but I'm struggling in the face of worry. Why would Danny and James go skiing the morning after the wedding? Of all the times, why this morning? And why am I only considering this now?

Nervous?

Should I be?

I inhale. I was referring to the wedding when I asked Danny if he was anxious. Making idol chitchat. But remembering his face now, the questioning, I think he thought there was more to my question. Did he misinterpret it as a red flag? A twisted warning?

It crashes into me like a tidal wave. He doesn't trust James. I exhale, my heart clattering. "Has Danny set James up?" I ask, not giving her a chance to answer, my brain going into overdrive.

"Are you saying James was planning for you two to leave too?"

"He said it was nearly over."

"So James could be setting Danny up?"

"Fuck!" I yell, running to the closet and grabbing some yoga pants and a sweater, attempting to rein in my temper as I fight my way into my clothes. I can't blame Danny any more than Rose can blame James. They're both determined men. He's got a wife and two kids to protect. What do James and I have? And who is setting who up?

I race past Rose, still pulling my sweater down my body, my wet hair getting caught up in the neck. "Beau, wait," she whisper-hisses behind me, but my sprinting legs don't slow, carrying me down the stairs fast.

"Keys," I say, scanning the foyer. "Where do they keep the keys?"

"What about your car?"

"I have no idea what James has done with the keys." And Dolly would wake the whole of Miami up. Plus, I can't guarantee she'd even start after so long sitting unused. I turn and see Rose nearly at the bottom of the stairs. "Don't run," I yell, watching her feet moving fast. Too fast. "Rose, don't—"

"Shit!" she yelps, tripping over her own feet in her urgency. All I see is the solid marble floor. And for the first time, the signs of a small bump.

"Rose!"

She makes a grab for the handrail on a startled cry, and I

shoot forward, my heart in my throat, catching her before she hits the deck. "Oh my God," she gasps, grappling at my shoulders as she finds her feet again.

"What are you thinking?" I snap, helping her get steady.

"I—"

A door closes upstairs, and I dart my eyes past her, hearing the light pad of footsteps, someone coming to investigate the noise. "This way," I whisper, pulling her along to the corridor that leads to Danny's office, getting us out of sight. I position her by the wall, ensuring she's stable before I release her and hold my finger to my lips in order for her to quiet, peeking around the wall to the top of the stairs. I find Uncle Lawrence—his natural hair a wild mess, his makeup still on, and his Flamingo kimono open and exposing his slender chest—sleepily looking around for the source of the noise. He looks as rough as I feel. "Go back to bed," I whisper, willing him to return to his room so we can get out of here.

It's only a few seconds before he wanders back to bed, although it feels like centuries. "Keys," I whisper, turning to Rose. She looks a little pasty as she holds her stomach, and I know alcohol isn't the cause. I take her hand and squeeze. "Rose, we need some car keys."

She swallows and looks toward Danny's office. I hurry down the corridor and push my way in, coming to an abrupt halt when I find Brad and Ringo on one of the couches, still suited, a couple of bottles of Scotch on the floor. I bite my lip and creep farther in, scanning Danny's desk, rooting through his drawers. No keys anywhere. *Damn it.*

"Brad," Rose whispers.

I look up and find her in the doorway, pointing to Brad's comatose state on the couch. My eyes fall to the pocket of his pants, where a key fob is poking out. I pad over quietly, bending, reaching, my eyes jumping from his face to my target repeatedly.

One little flick has the fob hitting the floor with a quiet thud. I swipe it up and hurry away, taking Rose's hand as I pass and pulling her along. More noises emanate from upstairs when we reach the front door, the gruff, sleepy voices of the Vikings making my feet move quicker. I pull the door open, get Rose outside, and quietly close it behind us. The sun hits me like a brick to the face, and black spots hamper my vision as I rush to Brad's car, which seems to be as far away as it could be.

I fling the door open, get one foot inside, and freeze, the sounds of groans coming from not too far away. "What's that?" Rose asks, looking over the roof of the car at me.

"I don't know, but we don't have time to find—"

"Goldie?" she says, looking past me. I turn and find the bushes rustling, mixing with the groans, a flash of blonde hair breaking up the greenery. And then Goldie's head appears, one hand clenching it. Any other time, the sight would be comical. Not now.

"Get in," I order Rose, falling behind the wheel and starting the engine. "Quick, Rose!"

She drops into the passenger seat, craning her head to see out of my window as Goldie rises from the bushes, still in her lovely dress, sticks and leaves poking out everywhere. She clocks us, frowns, steps out, and I put my foot down, wheels spinning, no doubt waking up the rest of the house too. I smack the steering wheel in frustration, the gates coming into view. The *closed* gates. I take my foot of the gas, trying to slow to a more reasonable speed within the grounds of the house before the guy manning the gate hears us.

"There's no way Bud will let us out." Rose says what I'm thinking, just as he appears, putting his hand up in gesture as we approach in Brad's car.

We'll be fine if he opens the gates before he realizes it's not Brad in the car. So I flash the headlights and sink into the seat, watching as he reaches inside the gatehouse. "Come on," I say quietly, as daylight begins to seep through the two wooden panels of the gates.

"They're opening," Rose says, pulling the visor down.

My foot is itching to slam down on the gas, but I remain patient, the gatehouse and Bud getting closer, and as soon as I make eye contact with him, I slam on the gas, seeing him darting back to the gatehouse.

"The gates aren't open enough," Rose says as the car jars, the wing clipping the left-hand panel. "Shit!"

I yank the steering wheel to the right, and the car judders, skidding onto the road outside. Rose reaches up to the roof as I get the car under control, and we're soon speeding away from the mansion.

I settle, focused on the road. "What time did they leave?" I ask.

"I don't know. I woke up and he was gone."

I gulp and nod, hoping and praying my fears aren't warranted. Hoping Rose has it all wrong. That Danny isn't about to sacrifice James for himself. Or James for him.

"Beau," Rose says quietly, turning in her seat and looking back at the road behind.

I peek up at the rearview mirror, seeing a car gaining on us. "Shit." A Range Rover pulls up on the driver's side, flanking us, and I look out to find Otto looking murderous behind the wheel.

"And here," Rose says, almost sighing, staring out the passenger window where Ringo is on the other side in another Mercedes, looking equally as furious. Another glance at the rearview mirror shows Brad in yet another Mercedes, racing up behind us. And to complete the entourage, a Range Rover pulls into the lane in front of us. *Goldie.* They all begin to brake tactically, forcing me to slow down too. It's a move we used so many times in the police force, and now it's being used against me. I'm cornered.

I look across at Rose, feeling defeated and angry by my concern for her. I can't smash my way out of this. I can't risk injuring Rose. I've a lost a baby. I wouldn't wish it on anyone, least of all my friend.

I smack the steering wheel with the ball of my hand as we gradually come to a standstill in the middle of the road, my eyes closing, my head dropping back, defeated.

Otto swings the door open and pins me in place with his infuriated stare. "What the fuck are you playing at?"

"Danny and James are at the boatyard," I say calmly. "Did you know that?"

His immediate wrinkled forehead tells me he didn't.

"Know what?" Brad asks as he joins us, obviously catching the tail end.

Otto keeps his eyes on me. "Danny and James are at the boatyard," he says. "Did *you* know that?"

"I didn't know that."

"So he kept the drink flowing until the early hours," Otto practically growls, "hardly touched a drop himself, because he needed us to oversleep, nursing hangovers, while he has a clear head to do . . . what, Brad? What the fuck is he up to?"

Brad looks like a deer caught in the headlights briefly, but that soon converts into anger. "I'll kill him," he seethes, punching the side of his car. "I'll fucking kill him." He marches to the back of his car and pops the trunk, appearing again armed with a machine gun. "What else have we got?" he asks, prompting everyone to start efficiently rummaging through the trunks of all vehicles.

"You," Brad says, pointing an accusing finger at Rose, who's silent beside me. "You . . . you . . . you . . ." He growls and gives his attention to everyone else, while Rose and I sit, mute, watching them assessing the weaponry situation. I don't know if I should be relieved that Brad didn't know. Could he be acting? I assess Goldie and Otto. They're wondering the exact same thing, both of them quiet and wary as Brad curses and swears his ass off.

What the fucking hell is going on?

———

29

DANNY

My stomach turned as James disappeared through the door, throwing back a questioning look as he did. Fuck, if this doesn't pan out, I'm dead. I flick my cigarette away and immediately light another, not allowing my eyes to leave the container, my ears listening carefully.

The sound of my mobile ringing makes me jump. "For fuck's sake," I mumble, looking down at the unknown number. I have a quick look around the boatyard, feeling eyes on me from any place they can hide. It was a given. I knew he wouldn't expect me to keep my word. I hope seeing me actually riding solo will make this run smoothly so I can get back to the house, pick up my wife, kid, and mother, and get the fuck out of this city.

I take the call, answering with silence. A few crackles down the line, the sound of an engine in the background. "Black," someone says, and my spine straightens, wary. This isn't a voice I want to hear right now.

"Higham," I say quietly, aware of listening ears, wherever

they are. And for that reason, I force myself to relax, working my way through my second smoke. "And what do I owe the pleasure?"

"Do you happen to be missing a jet ski?" he asks.

"No, why?" That machine will be in a million pieces at the bottom of the ocean, along with the body parts of the little fucker sent to rig it, if the sharks haven't had him. If Higham's calling me, it's because some debris has been found. Undoubtedly unidentifiable.

"Some parts washed up on a private beach."

"There are thousands of jet ski owners in this city. Why'd you assume it's mine?"

"Might have something to do with the serial number registered in your wife's name."

Oh. Well, that's a shitter. Of all the pieces that could have found their way onto a fucking beach? "Stolen," I say, and he laughs.

"Black, I think you're in the wrong business."

I smile, but it falls when I feel something press into my temple, something cold and hard. I look out the corner of my eye, finding a meaty-looking fucker, arms braced, a face like a slapped arse. "I think you're right," I reply to Higham, prompting the fat fuck currently holding me at gunpoint to wedge the barrel in a little farther. I bite down on my teeth and close my eyes, digging deep for some restraint before I murder him slowly. This was expected. It doesn't make me like it, but it was inevitable. "Anything else?" I ask Higham. "I'm kind of busy right now."

"Yes, actually. The invite to your wedding next week."

"What about it?"

"Well, it's very nice of you and all that, but an FBI agent at the wedding of a known criminal wouldn't look good, if you know what I mean."

"I understand," I say quickly, hanging up to deal with the small matter of a gun pressed into my temple. "I made a deal," I say quietly, my body tingling with the need to lash out.

"I'll ease off as soon as we have confirmation."

No accent. Not Irish, not Russian, not Polish. So he's just an ape who's been handed some power? "I'm telling you now, ease off on the pressure and I might think twice about fucking bludgeoning you when you get word The Enigma is dead."

Only because he knows who I am does he listen, and it's a wise move. The pressure eases, and I breathe back the red mist threatening to fuck this all up. Rose. Think of Rose. Think of Daniel. Of my baby. Containing myself is paramount if I'm going to walk away.

I look out the corner of my eye again, turning my head a fraction to get him in my sight. "So what do they call you?" I ask, taking another drag of my cigarette. "The Whale? The Elephant?" I smirk, and it's filthy. "Or haven't you reached animal status yet?"

"Shut up," he barks, making my smile widen.

"We'll go with The Hippo." I drop my eyes to his round gut bulging over his belted trousers. Fucking hell, I could put a bullet in him and it wouldn't stand a chance of breaking through the blubber and reaching his internal organs.

So I'll aim for his head.

Just as soon as The Bear walks out of that container, this prick is dead.

30

ROSE

I accept Brad's wrath. I'm too worried to argue, my thoughts circling, going over the same thing again and again. Danny's smart. But James is smart too. Danny is deadly. I never thought I'd meet a man to match him . . . until James. Danny loves me fiercely. Would die for me. I swallow, looking across to Beau sitting silently beside me in the back of Brad's car as we race toward the boatyard. I know James feels the same way about my friend. So who will come out on top? And which one of us will be without?

Desolate, I reach for Beau's hand and squeeze, wondering if she's thinking what I'm thinking. I know she is when she constricts, but she doesn't look at me.

Brad pulls off the main road, glancing to his mirror to check the others are close behind. "You will stay in the car," he says curtly. "Do you hear me, Rose?"

"I hear you," I say, closing my eyes, knowing what's good for me. Myself, I would risk all day long. But our baby? Never. And Danny will expect that. Demand that. Kill me with his bare hands if I don't get myself killed first.

It's in this moment I begin to understand the level of James's hatred. How helpless he must feel and the scale of his need to end this. Because it's the reason Beau miscarried, and it's the reason Beau nearly lost her life. I can appreciate the mayhem that Danny would create if he were in James's shoes. And now I can appreciate James's.

I drag my tired eyes open and squint when I see where we are. "We're going straight in?" I ask, sitting forward in my seat. "Brad, are you mad?"

"Don't you think they'll have every bush, tree, and inch of coastline covered, Rose?" he asks, rolling down the dirt track toward the boatyard, putting his hazard lights on as he does. Like a "we come in peace" sign. What the hell? He looks at Beau in the rearview mirror. "What I said to Rose goes for you too," he warns.

Beau looks away insolently. I know it's going to happen before Brad has a chance to engage the child safety locks on the rear doors, and even before she moves. That look on her, it's pure and utter recklessness. "Beau," I say quietly, reaching for her, but she's gone, jumping out of the car. "Brad!" I yell, and he slams on the brakes, kicking up endless dust and dirt. "Oh my God," I gasp, instinct making me jump out of the car too. "Beau!" I yell, watching her run like a gazelle.

"Fuck!" Otto bellows as he sprints past, yelling after her, followed by Goldie, who's barefoot and still in her dress.

"Oh God, no," I murmur, watching as Brad and Ringo hold their machine guns up, both cursing.

"For fuck's sake," Ringo grunts, looking at Brad for guidance. Brad's jaw goes into spasm, his eyes flicking from me to the car, trying to decide what to do with me.

I shake my head. It's not a *no*, it's a *I don't know*. They won't leave me on my own. They don't want to take me. My head is utterly fucking scrambled, along with theirs. But Beau has dashed off, and Danny is here somewhere. Alive?

That thought alone has me picking up my feet, déjà vu kicking in, the same feelings of dread and panic gripping me as it did three years ago when Danny made some deals. "Shit, shit, shit," Brad curses, seizing me and walking me to the back of the car, popping the trunk and pulling out a bulletproof vest. "There's only one," he says. "Take your sweater off." He lays his gun down as I do as I'm told, pulling it up over my head quickly and letting Brad get the vest on me. It's way too big, but at least it comes down to my thighs. I get my sweater back on and let Brad claim my hand, walking us the final few yards to the boatyard at a surprisingly steady pace. The cabin comes into view, and my heart drops when I see Danny with a gun aimed at his head.

My whimper is quiet, but Brad hears it. "Be calm," he says quietly, holding up his weapon when the guy behind Danny pulls another gun from his pants. And more men appear, all armed. "I'm putting it down," Brad says, placing it gently on the ground, Ringo following suit.

"What the fuck is she doing here, Brad?" Danny yells, his eyes burning holes into his friend.

"She'd be here without me if I didn't fucking catch them on the freeway." He rises, squeezing my hand.

"Where's Beau?" I ask, looking around, "And James?"

"God damn it, Rose," Danny yells, just as Beau comes running out of the cabin, looking frantic.

"Where is he?" she yells, her face red with rage, her attention on Danny and Danny alone. "Where the fuck is James?"

I cast a worried look over to my husband. "In the green container," he says, getting a jab of the end of the gun for his trouble.

Beau swings her eyes to the green container. I can see her heart pumping from here. "Who with?" she asks as Goldie moves in slowly, ready to catch her when she runs.

I hate the grave look on Danny's face. Positively hate it.

31

JAMES

So it's straight to business, then? I actually can't believe who I'm looking at. The man can act, and he can act well. I inhale and raise my hands as another man pats me down, being too rough for my liking. "What the fuck's going on?" I ask, being wrestled to a chair in the corner as the suited, smart fucker sneers at me, silent and imposing. At least, he's trying to be. I've thought of a million ways to kill this fucker. All slowly. All painfully. Now, as I stare at him, I just want to end him quickly.

"James Kelly," he finally says, and I cock my head, interested. No voice distorter. He doesn't sound half as deadly without it. "Or should I call you The Enigma?" He cocks a leg and perches on the edge of the table that's positioned in the center of the container. "Or Kellan James. Which do you go by these days, because I'm pretty sure all those men are dead?" His smile isn't dark. It isn't dangerous. It's plain smug.

"What has Black promised you?" I ask, peeking out the corner of my eye to the tip of the gun.

He says nothing, but he smiles wider, and it's all I can do to stop myself cutting it off his face.

"Tell me," I order, turning my death stare from the gun to his comfortable, relaxed body on the table. He shouldn't look so chilled. "What have you promised him?"

"Something he won't get." He rises and starts to pace the room, casually. Stupid fuck.

"Maybe I have something *you* will want to keep," I reply coolly, my face remaining impassive when he looks at me. I hold my hands up and slowly reach for my hoodie, pulling the hem up to reveal the waistband of my joggers. Naturally, my move makes his goon stiffen, thrusting his gun forward in threat. "Easy," I say quietly, slowly pulling something out and holding it up.

He looks at the picture, his lip twitching, ready to curl. "Shannon's safe," he says, dismissing me.

"You sure?" I look across the container to an old cupboard in the corner, prompting both men to look too. It's the opportunity I've been waiting for. Time to strike.

I swing my leg, taking out the guy that's holding me in place with his gun, his body crashing to the floor with the lack of his legs holding him up. I rise, grab the chair, and launch it across the container at The Bear, before giving the man on the floor a swift kick in the gut and a stamp on his head, knocking him out. I swing around, catching the fucker gaining his balance, his arm lifting with the gun. *Fuck.* I wedge my palms into the edge of the table and run, sliding it across the floor and slamming it into him.

"Fuck," he yelps, losing his grip of the gun, his torso folding over the table. I dive across the metal top and grab the gun, aiming it at him as I get off and back up.

"Oh, how the tables have turned," I whisper, smirking at his leering face. "You should have brought a lot more men."

"Fuck you," he breathes, shoving the table away from his thighs.

I hear a few noises from outside the container. "Oh, you did bring more men," I say, reaching for the cupboard door. He clearly thought Black was more of a danger than I am. I don't know whether to be insulted or relieved.

Wait, I do.

I'm insulted. Plain insulted.

I pull the cupboard door open, revealing the blonde who Danny followed back into town from his father's grave, bound and gagged. "Now let's talk business." I yank her out and get her in front of me, relishing the disbelief on The Bear's face. "Your phone," I say, nodding to the table.

He keeps his eyes on me as he reaches into his pocket. But he doesn't pull out a phone. He pulls out a tidy little handgun and aims our way. Not gonna lie, I'm astounded. And when he pulls the trigger and her body jerks, my surprise turns into shock. *Fuck.*

She crumples to the ground, leaving me without a shield, the gun now aimed at me. Well, this is a twist I didn't anticipate. "She was a money-grabbing whore," he says, stepping forward. "And now I believe the tables really have turned." He pulls the trigger, and my body jerks, sending me slamming into the wall behind me on a hiss. My shoulder immediately aches. "Take a seat, Jam . . . Eni . . . now." He laughs. "Really, I just don't know what to call you."

"I know what to call you," I grate.

"What's that?"

"Dead." I lunge at him.

Bang!

And fly back on a grunt, the bullet hitting me square in my chest.

32

DANNY

Bang!

I flinch, watching as Beau fights and struggles in Goldie's arms, swearing, cursing, screaming, calling me every name under the sun. "I'll fucking kill you!"

She only stills and quietens down when the sound of a metal sliding lock sounds. I hold my breath, as everyone's attention moves to the green container. It's not James who emerges.

I swallow as the twisted fuck who's played us all strides across the gravel with confidence, but I notice he has a small limp. "I'll let you do the honors." He smiles, tossing me the trigger button carelessly. If I would have placed my bets, and I did, I would never have expected James to lose this fight.

"Perry?" Rose gasps.

"No!" Beau shouts, starting to fight again, prompting Otto to move in to help Goldie restrain her. "What are you doing?"

"What the fuck is going on, Danny?" Otto asks.

I look at my wife. Her hands are over her mouth, her eyes

welling. I look at Brad. He looks as grave as I feel. But my options are limited. I swallow, casting my eyes over Beau's flailing, screaming form, holding up the trigger. "We walk away," I say to Perry calmly, and he nods.

"What the fuck?" Goldie yells.

"Blow it," Perry says evenly, relishing the drama, his hands in his pockets.

"No!" Beau screams.

I breathe in, giving her regretful eyes. "I'm sorry," I whisper, pushing down on the button.

"Danny," Rose screams.

"Noooooooo!" Beau breaks free from Goldie, and I yell as she starts running toward the container. "Beau, for fuck's sake!" I bellow. "Get a—"

Bang!

A ball of fire bursts into the sky, halting Beau in her tracks, and everyone shields their eyes from the blinding glare. She falls to her knees, broken, staring at the raging fire, and I rip my eyes away from her collapsed, crying form, unable to handle it.

I find Rose. Her devastation is equally unbearable, her head mildly shaking, as if she can't believe what I've done. The disappointment. I can't say I like it, and in complete shame, I look away from her too, finding Perry Adams. He's always been a snake. But I never, not once, considered he could be The Bear. And now, watching him delight in the carnage, I have no faith that he'll keep his word. And that's more of a problem with Rose and Beau here. God damn those women. I loathe their loyalty.

I can feel the gun still pressed into my skull. "Time to ease off," I say, pulling away, only to have the gun rammed back into my head. I still, pushing back the monster before he erupts and gets us all killed.

"I'll ease off when I'm told to."

"Your death just got messier," I say darkly, turning my eyes onto Perry. "Tell him to back the fuck off."

The sick smile he gives me says more than his traitorous mouth could speak. "I don't think so," he muses, nodding to his men. They all start moving in, herding us like sheep toward the cabin as the fire rages not too far away. I watch Brad claim Rose, bringing her to me, and Otto pulls Beau to her feet, walking her along. Her eyes meet mine. I know of the levels of hatred reflecting back at me. I take Rose's hand and walk up the steps to the cabin, turning when I reach the top.

I scan the yard, mentally willing him to hurry the fuck up. "You're out of your depth, Perry."

He laughs. "You know, three years ago when you asked me to dig up everything I could find on the Greens, I assumed you were using the skeletons in their closet to blackmail them." He looks at Rose. "Of course your whore would need an attorney."

I inhale discreetly. "Call her a whore again, I will kill you, Adams."

"Danny," Rose whispers, squeezing my hand, telling me without telling me not to poke the fucking bear.

"I never imagined the kid they bought was Rose's," he goes on.

I glance across to Brad and give him a moment of my eyes. He shifts, uncomfortable. Then I look at Ringo. When my eyes catch Otto and Goldie, I see understandable utter contempt. *Fuck.* I turn my stare onto the green container, seeing the flames beginning to subside, and I smile, the extinguishers dowsing it from beyond disguised by the roar of the flames. Another flick of my eyes to Brad and the others, who all discreetly look toward the container too. Then I look at Beau, willing her to see me. *Look at me, Beau.*

"Tell me, Adams," I say, holding out four fingers on the hand hanging by my side. "How do you want to die?" Rose's body tensing tells me she's reading the signs. I just hope everyone else is. I drop to three fingers, squeezing her hand.

"I'm not dying, Black. You, your whore, and your pathetic army are the ones dying."

I drop to two fingers. *Hurry up, hurry up.* My eyes scan the dying flames. "We made a deal." One finger.

"I've changed my mind."

I make a fist. No fingers left. "More fool you," I breathe as the hatch that leads to the bunker flies open and James steps out, a machine gun in each hand. Fuck me, it's like the rising of the Phoenix. "What took you so fucking long?" I call.

I hear the collective inhales of everyone behind me as Perry and his men turn, confused.

"Drop," I yell, dragging Rose to the floor, hearing everyone hitting the deck behind us. But I have to see this, so I look up as James starts showering bullets across them, walking through the embers, sweating, smeared in muck, his body vibrating. It's a mixture of the guns and his fury, and yet I can see by the satisfied sneer on his face that he's enjoying himself. The men drop like flies, the noise is deafening, and I watch the show with a smile until no man is standing. The yard is littered with bodies, the dusty air dense, the echoes of gunfire ringing in my ears.

"What the actual fuck?" Ringo murmurs from beside me, his jaw lax. "Should we call him Rambo now?"

I chuckle, watching the dust floating down to the ground, revealing James standing at the front of the mass grave, casting his eyes across his victims. He lets the machine guns fall from his hands, and they hit the ground with a thud.

I slowly push myself to my feet, helping Rose up too, before guiding her to a chair and sitting her down, giving her a thorough checking over. I pull up her sweater. Check every arm and leg. Her face. Stunned. I smile and kiss her. "It's over," I say roughly.

"You . . . you . . . you both planned this?" she asks, looking completely spaced out.

"Of course."

"But . . . I . . ." She shakes her head. "What the fuck, Danny? How did you know it was Perry?"

"I told four people I'd be skiing yesterday at various times. My jet ski blew up at precisely twelve twenty-one. I told Perry I was out on the water at noon every Saturday. He had my father's lover working for him, so I followed her to a building he worked from when he was running for mayor."

She can only stare at me in shocked silence. I feel the same. I'm so fucking stupid for not seeing it. I didn't trust him, not at all, but . . . The Bear? It's almost laughable.

I look past her to the others. All look as blindsided as I feel. "Everyone good?" I ask, getting silence in return. No doubt I will be copping the wrath of each of them. But the job's done. Or nearly done.

I turn and face James, finding him holding his shoulder, where his hoodie is bloody. "Feel better?" I ask, lighting up a cigarette. He wipes his brow roughly and looks for Beau. She's in shock, her body a statue, her face a picture of disbelief. "Good to know you trust me," I quip, getting her attention. I accept what's coming, bracing myself as she walks slowly toward me and lands a stinger of a slap across my face.

I grit my teeth and slowly take a drag of my cigarette, exhaling. "You're welcome," I murmur, recoiling when she lands me with another. That one, I definitely didn't see coming. "I'm in a tolerant mood, Beau, given the circumstances," I say quietly.

The nostrils of her small nose flare, her eyes blazing, as she swings around and marches toward James. Like me, he braces himself, widening his stance and anchoring down. She belts him so hard, I flinch harder than when she cracked me one. Just let her have her moment. Let her be rid of the anger.

Eyes closed, his head to the side, James visibly cracks his jaw back into place. "Is that all you've got?" he asks seriously, and I laugh under my breath as she reaches forward and rips his zip-up open, revealing his vest. Then she launches herself at him, wrapping every limb around his frame and clinging on. "More like it," he says around a hiss of pain, holding her as he walks to a rock and perches on the edge, having a moment with her.

A stirring on the ground gets my attention, and I wander over to the only body showing signs of life. He's on his front, so I wedge a boot into his side and push him to his back, growling down at him, taking in the bullet wounds just north of his knees. "I did say I'd kill you if you called my wife a whore again." I drop to my haunches as I take a long drag, blowing it into his face before stubbing out my smoke on his cheek, snarling as he yelps and weakly fights me away. "Nothing to say?"

His dribbling and moaning is pitiful, and really fucking annoying.

"I want to kill him," James says from behind me.

I look back, finding he still has Beau stuck to his front. "No, *I* want to kill him." I stand, joining him. "We agreed. You play Rambo, I kill Adams."

"I've changed my mind," he says firmly. "Me."

"No, me," I retort.

"No, Danny. I get to do the hon—"

Beau releases James's shoulders, turns, takes my gun, aims, and blows out Adams's brain before dropping the weapon and resuming her position, hiding in James's neck. We stare down at Adams in disbelief, James with his mouth open, me with my smoke hanging limply out of my mouth.

"Well, that's solved that little conundrum," Brad says, helping himself to my pack of Marlboros and lighting up.

James smiles, and it looks good on his murderous face.

"I think I need a vacation," I say as Rose joins me, moving into my side and hugging me close.

"I wouldn't mind a holiday too." James tries to put Beau on her feet and fails. "A bit of sun on my face." She looks up at him and smiles. It's the first smile I've seen on her that's true. Real. Happiness.

"I'll take one too," Brad pipes in.

"And me," Ringo grunts.

"Count me in." Goldie shrugs. "I've never had a holiday."

"St. Lucia it is, then," I declare, reaching into my pocket and pulling out some keys, tossing them to James.

He catches them and lets them dangle from his finger, pointed toward Goldie. "You have a job before we can go on holiday," he says, prompting her to frown and reach for the keys tentatively. "In that container."

She looks across to where James is nodding, then to everyone else, her eyes passing across each and every one of us. "What is it?"

"A surprise," I say, watching as she walks across the stones in her dress and opens the door, looking inside. I see the lift of her shoulders, and I look across to James, seeing he's watching closely in fascination.

"Did you load it?" he asks without looking at me.

I can only smile. "Fully loaded." I had Leon lay out every tool, knife, and weapon known to man on a table inside that container. We won't be seeing Goldie for a while. "And what are we doing with Kenny Spittle?" I ask.

"Let me think about it," James grunts, rolling his shoulder.

"Get your arse to Doc." I start to walk Rose back to the car, and the first wail of pain sounds from the container when I open the back door for her. I flick my cigarette away, glancing back, seeing Brad and Ringo following us. But James, Otto, and Beau?

They're still sitting there, and they'll wait outside that container until Goldie decides she's had enough.

"Flight leaves tonight," I call.

James holds his hand up in acknowledgment. They'll be there. Of course they'll be there.

Don't trust anyone.

I understood why Pops lived and died by that mantra, but I also knew that putting my trust in James Kelly would finally allow all threats to die. And by gaining my freedom, it seems I've also gained a family.

I smile and slip into the driver's seat, looking across to my wife. She's gazing at me, taking in my light, relaxed self. I put my hand on her thigh and she seizes it. "You remind me of someone I used to know," she says quietly. I smile and pull away, looking up at the sun as Otis Redding comes on the radio and *The Dock of the Bay* joins us.

EPILOGUE

St. Lucia – Two Weeks Later

JAMES

Slumped back in the white rattan chair on the terrace, I watch Beau on the beach, returning after her walk with Rose, Esther, and Zinnea. I can't see her face clearly. Can't see her expression. Her smile. But it'll be there. Peace looks good on my girl. And it feels fucking great on me.

Her pale blue sundress is flapping in the breeze, along with her hair, and her arm is bare. Except for the thick layer of sunscreen I rubbed in this morning, which I know will have been topped up throughout the day by one of the girls. I've missed her today. I've been busy, spent hours on the water with the guys, but she was on my mind every second. Every moment of my headspace dedicated to her. No plotting. No blood. No revenge.

Just Beau.

I smile as she approaches, her straw sunhat dangling from her hand, her feet bare and sandy. She clocks me in the chair and the corner of her mouth lifts as she walks the path, eyes on me. She drops her hat and climbs onto my lap, falling onto my chest and exhaling. No words. But we're certainly getting better at speaking them. I let her be, quiet and still in my arms, as I look out at the ocean.

"Remember Rose and Danny's wedding?" she asks, keeping herself hidden in the crook of my neck.

"No," I reply, getting a nudge. "Which bit?"

"The bit when I was stupid drunk."

"Oh, that bit," I say, smiling. "When you blew out the brains of many dangerous balloons?" I feel her lips stretching across my skin, her hands pressing into my pecs gently.

"No, the bit when I told you I want a baby."

God damn my heart for skipping a few beats, and I know she felt it. I'm really fucking surprised, not only because she remembers, but because she's brought it up. I've not mentioned her drunk ramblings or the demands she made because . . . well, she was drunk. I've thought about them, though. Non-stop.

"Why are you tense?" she asks.

"Why are you hiding?" I throw back, and she stills against me. "I'm not tense."

"I'm not hiding."

"Then let me see you, Beau Hayley," I whisper, turning my face into her hair and kissing her. "Let. Me. See. You."

She slowly eases away from my body, her hands pushing into my chest, and she looks at me with too much uncertainty in her eyes. And it's all because of who I am and what I do. She shouldn't love me. She shouldn't understand me. She shouldn't want babies and marriage and a happily ever after with me.

"Hi, it's me," I say, staring into her eyes.

"Who's me?" she asks, her head tilting, a small, unsure smile on her lips.

"James Kelly."

"What do you do, James?"

"Love you," I whisper. "That's all I want to do."

"And when our kids ask us how we met?"

I sigh, taking the tops of her arms and stroking my way to her wrists. "Let's cross that bridge when we come to it."

"Is the bridge far away?" She looks tentative, and I smile, unsure as she nibbles her bottom lip.

"It's close, but we need to make sure it's safe to cross."

"I think it's safe."

"Are you an expert ex-bridge builder, as well as an ex-cop?" I seize her hips, edging forward. So the bridge is Beau's body, and while it's stronger, I'm not sure it's ready for the strain of a pregnancy. "We should talk to Doc."

"I feel okay."

This is all good and well, but . . . "What about the marriage part? Are we skipping that bit?"

"I can't marry you," she says, her fingertip tracing the edges of the bandage on my shoulder. "Because you killed Dexter."

Sledgehammer, meet my face. I stare at her, mute, as she watches me closely for my reaction. I know I'm giving her what she wants. Guilt. "I killed him before you asked me not to." *What the fuck am I saying?* "How did you know?"

"Ollie called me."

I am in no position to be agitated or pissed off. And yet here I am, really fucking agitated, and massively pissed off. "Where'd he find the body?" Or more to the point, how? Because Danny assured me it could never be found.

"He didn't."

"Then . . ." I pause, as Beau's eyebrows slowly rise. "There's no body, is there?" Of course there's no fucking body. It's undoubtedly been ripped to shreds by sharks.

"Only yours if you don't tell me what happened."

"Burrows didn't call you?"

"Yeah, he called me. But not about that."

What the fuck kind of conversation is this? "Beau, why are you saying things to intentionally stoke my temper? What did Burrows want?"

"You know what he wants. Me alive and you dead. Now tell me how you killed Dexter."

"You really don't want to know," I assure her, and she withdraws, looking like she doesn't know if she wants to know. "Really," I reiterate.

"What did you do?"

"I killed him. That's it. An eye for an eye, Beau. The end."

"Did Danny know?"

Fuck. "No." *Fuck, fuck, fuck.* "We need to get ready for dinner." And I need to put an emergency call in to Danny. "Come on." I ease her off my lap and put her on her feet.

"That's it?" she asks as I turn, making me halt halfway. "End of conversation?"

I close my eyes and gather myself. "I don't know what you want from me, Beau. I can't turn back time. I can't change that, same as I can't change him shooting you."

"An apology, maybe?"

I face her? "For killing him?"

"No, James, for lying to me."

"I'm sorry," I say on an exhale. "All day long, I'm sorry." For lying, yes. But for killing him? Certainly not.

Pushing past me, she enters the bedroom, saying nothing, leaving me full of doubt on the terrace. So now what? "I want you to block Burrows's number." So I say that? *You fucking dumb-arse, James.*

She looks back at me, amused but insulted all at once. "I need to get ready for dinner." Going into the bathroom, she closes the door. Translated: don't join me. It's probably safe for both of us.

But neither Beau nor I have ever been all too keen on playing things safe.

I push my way into the bathroom, finding her pulling her knickers off. She slowly unfolds her body. Watches me, waiting for what I'm going to say or do. "Let's make a baby," I say, holding out my hand. "Now. Here."

"I don't know if you're ready to be a father," she replies, leaving my hands hanging. *Ouch*.

"I wasn't ready to be yours either, Beau. But I am, and I'm so here for it."

Her smirk is too fucking cute. "Don't lie to me again."

"Never."

Wandering forward, she reaches up on her tiptoes and breathes into my face. "Let's make a baby," she whispers, slipping her hand past my boxers. My torso folds, my back teeth biting down hard.

"Get on the bed," I order, and she drops me, sauntering past and crawling onto the mattress, raising her hands above her head. I pull my belt off the back of the chair and straddle her chest, strapping her to the wooden headboard. "Don't fight the bond," I say quietly. "You ready?"

"More," she whispers huskily, arching her back.

We could have taken the short route, but Beau wanted to feel the last of the sun on her face. So we took the beach, all the way along the shore to the small, winding path that leads to the restaurant. Hand in hand, both of us barefoot, both quiet. My white shirt is fastened by one button, my loose trousers damp at the hem, my hair, frankly, wild. I feel her head rest against my upper arm, her hands clinging on, and my eyes fall to her scarred arm.

Exposed.

"Can you hear that?" she asks, pulling us to a stop.

"What?"

"Listen." Her finger comes to her mouth, hushing me. And I hear it.

"Is that Zinnea?"

Beau laughs, pointing up the beach to a nearby bar. "It's her first performance. She got a weekly gig every Saturday night."

"God help St. Lucia," I mumble, Zinnea's voice getting louder until we're passing the bar. She's on stage, flaunting every color imaginable in some form or another—dress, makeup, wig.

"Darlings!" she calls over the mic in between verses of Tom Jones's *She's a Lady*, making me wince and Beau wave. "My niece, everyone. And her dangerously handsome fellow, James." Her grin is impish, my head shake weary. "I'll join you soon, my darlings," she croons, before launching into the chorus.

I see the entrance for the pathway up ahead and, thankfully, by the time we make it there, Zinnea's singing has faded out completely, being swallowed up by the sound of the ocean.

"Here they are," Esther says, getting up from the table when she spots us. "I was just going to call."

I release Beau's hand and let her go to the girls, all kissing her cheek and showing her where to sit.

"Okay?" Danny asks, clicking his fingers for a waiter, who soon arrives with a bottle of vodka.

"Good." I pull out Beau's chair for her and take the one next to it. "Where's Daniel?"

Rose points to the ocean, and there he is, zooming across the water on his jet ski, two others in fast pursuit. Tank and Fury, who have been reassigned. I'm not sure yet if they're happy about that. "Wine?" Rose asks Beau, the bottle hovering over her glass.

"Not tonight." She helps herself to some water, and I smile to myself.

"Something you're not telling us?" Danny asks, winning my attention.

"Oh for fuck's sake," Brad mutters. "Don't tell me you two are pregnant too or I'll quit mafia life."

"We all just quit mafia life." Ringo laughs, necking a bottle of beer like it could be a shot.

"What did I miss?" Otto asks, approaching the table, looking dapper. I cock an interested brow as he takes the chair beside Esther, feeling the instant chill from the man a few seats away. I glance at Danny. He looks like he's preparing for a kill. *Jesus, Otto, of all the women in this world, you choose The Brit's mother?*

Esther pours him a wine, and he thanks her with a knowing smile. He's also trimmed his beard. And I can smell his cologne from here.

"Who are you trying to impress?" Goldie asks, making Otto still, his glass at his lips. She's a fine one to talk, sitting there with . . . lipstick on? She walked out of that container two weeks ago with not one mark on her. She emerged a different woman.

"Yes, who?" Danny asks.

"Danny," Esther says lowly, and everyone bats their eyes from mother to son, waiting for what comes next. Knife? Fist? Gun? There have been many occasions since we all arrived a few weeks back when Esther has been missing at the same time as Otto. Many times. Everyone, bar Danny, has played ignorant. Danny, however, has called Otto's phone persistently each time he's been missing. "Leave it, please." Esther gives her son a warning look, and his nostrils flare as Rose reaches for his hand, squeezing.

"Drink up," she orders, pushing his Scotch toward him as the waiter slides some dishes of olives onto the table. "So who popped in to see Zinnea?" Rose chirps, trying to divert her husband's foul mood away from Esther and Otto.

"We just walked past," Beau says, plucking an olive from the bowl. "She's got quite an audience."

"We'll have to go in and see her after dinner," Esther says, passing the menus around the table. "Let's order, I'm starving."

"That's because you missed breakfast," Danny mutters, shoving his face in his menu. "And lunch."

"Danny," Rose breathes, and I smile, watching the stone-cold killer sulk like a child, flicking his eyes *and* a curled lip at his wife.

"Should we have a little chat?" Otto speaks up, and the whole table falls silent, all eyes jumping between them.

"Oh fuck," Brad whispers, as Danny casually turns the knife at his setting. "Otto, I can answer that for you."

"Yes," Danny says, standing abruptly, sending his chair shooting back. "Let's have a chat."

"Danny," Esther gasps, jumping up. "No. No chatting."

"It's okay," Otto says, calm as can be, reaching for her arm and gently urging her back to the seat, his eyes never moving from Danny. Rose is suddenly up too, her face up close to Danny's, words being spoken urgently.

"We're good," Danny says, placating her, encouraging her to sit. "Aren't we, Otto?"

"Good," he agrees, standing. "Walk and talk?"

Danny's smile is the smile of a killer, and I shake my head. But I know Otto too. Not as callous or fucked up, but a killer nevertheless.

"I'll ref," Brad declares, swiping up the bottle and pointing it toward the beach as they wander off toward the path. Esther is edgy, Rose is now looking furious, as Beau pours her some wine and holds it up. Rose, distracted, grabs the glass and takes it to her lips.

Pauses.

"Stop!" Beau yells. "Shit, what the hell am I doing?" She confiscates the glass and takes it to her own mouth.

Pauses.

Pouts.

"Well, if you two won't . . ." Goldie sings, claiming the wine. "Anyone got any popcorn?"

"Do you think you should go?" Beau asks me, looking as nervous as her friend and Esther.

"Nope," I say over a laugh. "Let them hash it out."

"Oh God," Esther cries, making grabby hands for the bottle in the middle. Otto and Danny disappear through the opening in the wall that leads to the beach, and Esther is quickly up from her chair. "I can't just let them kill each other." She flies off across the restaurant, and Rose is soon following quickly.

Me? I take my time getting up and put my hand out to Beau. "Some comedy with your evening meal, madam?" I ask as she laughs her way to her feet.

We leave Goldie and Ringo at the table and head for the wall, and when the beach down below comes into view, I see Danny and Otto walking a slow circle, their sleeves now rolled up. "Who's odds-on favorite?" Beau asks, sitting on the wall and swinging her legs around to dangle.

"Depends if they play fair." I move in behind her and drape my hands over her shoulders, smiling when she holds them. Danny's the first to swing, and boy does he swing, delivering an ear-splitting crack to Otto's jaw, sending him flying back to his arse. Then he dives on him, and they start to roll and wrestle around on the sand, grunting, punching, yelling. They're going to be here awhile. "Come on." I pull Beau up, seeing Brad leading Esther and Rose back to the table, obviously reaching the same conclusion as I did. Leave them. They won't kill each other.

We all sit down, order food, and everyone falls into conversation.

I smile, relax back, and enjoy the company, but I take the most pleasure from watching Beau talk happily with the girls, every now and then looking at me, as if checking I'm still here. Always. I hold her hand on my lap, smiling as I take a sip of vodka, and cast my eyes around the table. I ordered an army, and I got one.

And as fucked up and unexpected as it is, I've also got myself a family.

By the time starters arrive, Danny and Otto are back from their brawl on the beach, each of them disheveled, Danny wiping blood from his lip, Otto from his nose. Everyone remains silent as they sit, take a drink, and start tucking into their seafood. Not a word spoken.

I think it's out of Danny's system, at least for tonight.

Once the table's cleared, we all decide to take our after-dinner drinks at the bar down the beach so we catch the end of Zinnea's performance. We make it in time for her last song, and while the men order drinks, the women file onto the dance floor and cheer her on. And of course, they demand an encore when she's done.

My mouth falls open when she breaks into *Gangster's Paradise*, and Danny starts chuckling, Brad spits his drink out, and Ringo and Goldie, for the first time ever, laugh their heads off. We settle at a nearby table, the men alone, and it's weird. Usually, with no women, we'd be strategizing. Plotting. Figuring shit out. Lining up the next kill. Instead, we're all just sitting here, mute, but I guarantee we're all enjoying the silence.

Until Danny's phone rings. I don't like his frown, and I don't like the lift of his eyes to find me. "Who?" Brad asks, as Danny clicks answer and sets it on the table, prompting us all to lean in.

"I'm truly injured you thought that piece of power-tripping shit Adams was me." He laughs, and my cheeks blow out, my body moving back in the chair. "He was useful for a time."

What. The. Fuck.

I look at Danny and see shock. I've never seen shock on him. His fists are balling, and as I look at my hands, I see two white rocks, the blood gone from my fists.

"So the games continue, yes?" he says, sounding all too happy about that. "James. Danny. I look forward to the next round." The line goes dead, and Danny's fist crashes down on the table, making everyone's glasses jump.

"Fuck," he barks, swiping his hand out and smacking the cocktail menu off the table. "How?"

I look across the bar to Beau, who's twirling, laughing, singing on the dance floor.

Happy. Calm. At peace.

It's an illusion.

"Well, it was a nice holiday while it lasted," I say quietly, raising my drink to my lips, my eyes falling to Beau's tummy. Hoping. Praying. "What time does our flight leave?"

The story continues in Book 4 of The Unlawful Men Series, coming in January 2023.

ABOUT JODI ELLEN MALPAS

Jodi Ellen Malpas was born and raised in England, where she lives with her husband, boys and Theo the Doberman. She is a self-professed daydreamer, and has a terrible weak spot for alpha males. Writing powerful love stories with addictive characters has become her passion—a passion she now shares with her devoted readers. She's a proud #1 *New York Times* Bestselling Author, a *Sunday Times* Bestseller, and her work is published in over twenty-five languages across the world. You can learn more about Jodi & her words at: JEM.Website

Find Jodi on

ALSO BY JODI ELLEN MALPAS

The This Man Series

This Man

Beneath This Man

This Man Confessed

All I Am – Drew's Story (A This Man Novella)

With This Man

The One Night Series

One Night - Promised

One Night - Denied

One Night - Unveiled

Standalone Novels

The Protector

The Forbidden

Gentleman Sinner

Perfect Chaos

Leave Me Breathless

The Smoke & Mirrors Duology

The Controversial Princess

His True Queen

The Hunt Legacy Duology

Artful Lies

Wicked Truths

The Unlawful Men Series

The Brit

The Enigma

The Resurrection

Book 4 in The Unlawful Man series - Coming January 2023

Check out Jodi's brand new Regency Romance Series, coming in 2022

—was, as expected, exceptional. Oysters to start. I know that was personal too, especially when Danny made a public display of feeding them to Rose and begged her not to chew. The silver service staff has cleared the tables and pretty much all of us are resting back in our chairs, full to the brim with good food and wine.

I feel Beau's palm stroking circles across my back, like she's getting comfort from my scars, and my eyes fall to her arm. I don't know if it's a negative or positive thing that it's covered again. I reach for her hand and peel her fingers from the wine glass, bringing it to my mouth and kissing the back for no other reason other than wanting to show her some love. Show her that my need to be close hasn't waned. That I love her with every fucked-up, murdering fiber of my being. Always will. And yet I might have to accept that she will never marry me, because I can't keep the fact that I murdered Dexter a secret forever. I know that.

She looks up at me and smiles mildly, working her hand up to my neck and rubbing soothing circles there, twisting the hair at my nape in between.

"So Goldie's in a dress," she muses, peeking out the corner of her eye across the table, where my fearless female sidekick is necking wine like it could be water. In a dress. It's unheard of, as is drunk Goldie, but with each day that's passed, I've seen her struggling to hold up her fierce front. Maybe it's the women she's suddenly surrounded by. Maybe it's the sense of relaxation. Who the fuck knows, but I'm happy for her. "I hope you didn't mock her," she adds.

"I'm brave, Beau, but not that brave." And neither are any of the men. "Danny's invited me out on the water in the morning," I say, trying to hide the shudder her touch on my neck is spiking. "He's planning on taking Rose to St. Lucia tomorrow evening."

Her playing fingers pause, her face somewhere between

worry and wariness. "They're leaving?" She looks across to Rose. "But she's not mentioned it."

"I don't think she knows. And have you mentioned *we're* leaving?"

"No," she says slowly, returning her attention to me, her expression sarcastic. "Because I don't know *when* we're leaving."

I say nothing, pulling her in close and kissing her temple.

Soon. Very soon.

24

BEAU

Everything so far has been smooth and without drama, but I can't help but feel like I'm bracing myself for an explosion. James has told me to pack, which I have. I've learned Danny is planning on taking Rose to St. Lucia. Both suggest the end is in sight, so why the hell can't I see it? I try to quieten my erratic heart and fail. It isn't because I'm fearful of what may be going down. Today has been so much harder than I imagined. Things seem to be slowly knitting together for Danny and Rose, but I can't help but feel like for us they're slowly unraveling.

I look up at James when he slowly rises from his chair, my face questioning. "Where are you going?" I ask, trying to keep the panic from my voice. He's the only thing anchoring me right now, the only thing keeping me here and relatively stable. "I'll be back in a second." He kisses my head, but his eyes are on Danny, who's rising from his chair too. Naturally, Rose looks at her husband in both warning and worry. He catches it, smiling, but he still leaves, taking his drink with him, and James follows, along with Brad, Otto, and Ringo. Nolan remains at the table, and I soon figure out that there's a good reason for that when he shuffles across a few seats and starts keeping a tipsy Goldie busy, topping up her wine glass.

I move my eyes across to Rose, feeling her staring at me. Her head tilts, her jaw tight. I discreetly show the ceiling my palms. I have no idea what's going on, but my stomach is twisting anxiously. I'm even more suspicious when Esther joins Rose. That woman would do anything for her son, including distracting his wife while he murders someone on their wedding day. The Bear? Is he immune from the murdering hands of James and Danny today? I bite my lip, unsure.

"Darling girl," Zinnea coos, dropping to a chair beside me, relieving a consistently wary-looking Father McMahon from her bold presence for the first time since we all sat down hours ago. The fairy lights are now twinkling above, the music playing a little louder, cocktails now being handed out. "What a beautiful day. Small, intimate, but so extravagant too." Her eyes widen when a waiter offers her a tray loaded with various elaborate glasses, all as colorful as Zinnea. She pulls two pink cocktails from the tray and hands one over, pushing her blonde wig over her shoulder. Her fake lashes flutter, her cheeks glowing with some sort of shimmery powder. She looks remarkably together, and I know part of that is because of me projecting calmness. "How are you feeling, darling?"

Don't ask. "I'm fine," I say, reaching for her hand and squeezing, faking a smile to within an inch of my life. "It's been a lovely day."

She sighs, nodding, casting her eyes around the table to the remaining guests. "Odd, isn't it?"

"What is?"

"Acceptance."

I look around, seeing the Vikings with Daniel between them,

Rose's son showing them something on his cell, and then across to Goldie and Nolan, who have been joined by the guys who run the boatyard. The priest is talking to Doc, still looking quite bewildered.

"All of these people were strangers to me weeks ago," she says, sighing, "and now they're so much more."

I wrap my lips around the straw and suck, wincing at the strength. And wincing at the thought of leaving. Not Miami, but this house. These people. There's no doubt that without them, without this support network, no matter how bizarre it is, I'd be far worse off. James needed an army. He found one. But he also found a fucked-up family, and walking away from the safety blanket of Rose and the others is going to be a challenge I never anticipated.

James has said we're leaving. When, I don't know, but I also don't know *where* he's taking me. Something tells me it's not St. Lucia. And something horrible and unsettling is telling me I might not see Rose again.

25

DANNY

I know it won't be long before Rose is hunting me down. No business today, it's what I said explicitly, and yet here I am stalking to my office, Brad, James, Otto, and Ringo in tow. I read the look Ringo flashed me after he took a call from Bud on the gate. Who the fuck is here and, more significantly, why?

I swing the door open and make a beeline for the bottle. "Who?" I ask shortly, trying to contain my anger.

"Two of Conner's men," Ringo replies as I swing around in surprise. "And a guest. Len's escorting them here."

"Conner?" James looks at me in question. "British Conner? Is that who found Brunelli?"

"Yeah." I knock back my drink, glancing down at my watch. We've been gone three minutes. I give it ten until the search party arrives, and no man will want to be in the vicinity of my wife when that happens, least of all me.

"Fucking hell," Otto breathes, dropping to the couch. "Does Goldie know?"